FLOATING HOLIDAYS

FLOATING HOLIDAYS

a novel

CHRISTOPHER TOROCKIO

Black Lawrence Press
New York

Black Lawrence Press
New York
www.blacklawrencepress.com

Cover photo: © 2007 Debra Baida / www.debrabaida.com
Design: Sarah Crevelling and Colleen Ryor

ISBN 978-0-9768993-8-9

Many, many thanks to Stuart Dybek, Chuck Kinder, and Fred Leebron for their endless support and encouragement. Thanks also to Diane Goettel for her kind insight and dedication, as well as Sarah Crevelling and Colleen Ryor at Black Lawrence Press; to Dan Donaghy, Troy Fornof, Jim Ritchie, Susan Mazzei, and Dan Torockio for their friendship and generosity; and to Anne Greene and everyone at the Wesleyan Writers Conference.

For support during the writing of this book, I am grateful to Western Michigan University, Eastern Connecticut State University, and the Vermont Studio Center.

Special thanks and love to Halle and to Giovanni.

For my mother and father

FLOATING HOLIDAYS

ELEVATOR GOING DOWN

Directly across Seventh Avenue from the twenty-six-floor glass and steel structure occupied by the offices of Electro-Lite Corporation is B&D's Coffee Shop. When Toby Avellino steps down off the curb, carrying his usual large French roast in a white paper bag, he sees Francis coming toward him, hobbling authentically if not a little theatrically across the brick-lined street. Francis's Steelers cap is pulled below his eyebrows to guard against the November chill and his facial expressions are indistinguishable in the pre-dawn glow of the yellow street lamps. Toby is prepared. It is Monday morning and he knows that, most likely, Francis has not eaten anything substantive since Friday. Toby removes a warm bagel from his paper bag and, holding it in his free hand, heads across Seventh, not bothering with the crosswalk since at ten to six downtown traffic is not yet a murmur—mostly delivery trucks and an occasional road crew, people in no particular hurry to get where they're going. Francis, apparently, is in no hurry either. He stops and waits, several steps into the street, swaying casually, only one button (the very top one) of his ratty overcoat actually buttoned, his muted reflection splashed across Electro-Lite's glass front wall. When Toby reaches him he holds out the bagel. Francis stares down at it as though bewildered for several seconds and Toby waits. A taxicab approaches them from the intersection at Wood Street and, after pausing a moment, the driver pulls out into the left lane and passes the two men. In ninety minutes, Toby thinks, this would not happen. Horns would be blaring, motorists screaming and cursing. Now, though, no harm is done by their standing several steps into Seventh Avenue. So he waits for Francis to finish his charade—a charade that Toby realizes helps Francis to somehow feel better about accepting the bagel, which, finally, Francis does accept.

Still, they continue to stand ten feet into Seventh Avenue.

"You all right?" Toby asks.

"Yeah," Francis says, turning the bagel in his hand, examining it as if it contained a clue of some sort. "A-okay."

"That's good," Toby says. "How about we get out of the street."

Francis turns and looks back over one shoulder, then shifts and looks over the other. His beard rubs against the collar of his wool overcoat and makes a scratching sound, like sandpaper. He nods and they move onto the sidewalk.

"Look, I have to get into work," Toby says. "Did you call your wife this weekend?"

"Weekend," Francis says.

"Yeah, weekend. Whatever."

Francis lowers the bagel to his side, then lowers his eyes to Toby's shoes.

"You said you were going to do that. I gave you the money for the phone. Remember?"

Francis shrugs.

"All right," Toby says quickly, realizing that he's begun to unintentionally scold this man, something he does not want to do. "I have to go now. Take care of yourself. It's supposed to get pretty cold today."

"Yeah," Francis says. He's holding the bagel out at his side now, awkwardly, like a trophy he's embarrassed to have won.

"And think some more about making that call."

"I will," Francis says and Toby, not completely satisfied but not altogether disturbed either, turns and, white paper bag in hand, heads for the doors of Electro-Lite Corporation. Pre-dawn conversations like this one, he thinks as he revolves into the lobby, have a tendency to assume a dreamlike quality by lunchtime.

After dismissing Charles, the security guard who had the misfortune of drawing the previous night's shift, Toby settles himself behind the big, shiny, black Formica desk in the front lobby. He sets down his bag, stows his coat in the compartment underneath. Everything he does makes a sound that echoes throughout the high-ceilinged, marble-lined lobby. Toby removes his coffee

CHRISTOPHER TOROCKIO

from the bag, sits, and tears open three packets of sugar. On the desk, behind the high credenza in front, are three telephones, a couple of phone directories, a schedule of the day's visitors to the building, and a computer, the screen of which displays the face of the employee who has most recently inserted his or her company ID card into one of the two slots located on either side of the desk. Two years ago, Electro-Lite got high-tech with regard to security. Now, no one can pass beyond the outer lobby without first inserting an employee ID card. The computer records the date and time the employee arrives and illuminates a green light next to the slot signifying that it is okay for the employee to pass through the waist-level chute and beyond the lobby. If the computer detects a body passing through this chute and a card has not been verified, an alarm sounds.

As manager of security, Toby was an integral part of the process that changed the building over to this system, and now he is in charge of its operation. It was a lot to comprehend at first, and provides Toby with a lot more responsibility, something he appreciates. One downside, though, is that Toby now receives a considerable amount of ribbing from the other employees, whose jokes are flat insinuation that Toby thoroughly enjoys maintaining the security system, enjoys hassling people when they forget their ID badges. Barney Fife Syndrome. Toby is aware of these jokes, but they do not bother him much. Not much. The perks of the job definitely outweigh the drawbacks. As manager of security he does not have to wear a blue polyester uniform like the other guards. He gets to wear a jacket and tie like everyone else. He is friendly with many senior level executives and occasionally attends to their needs; he's met a few famous politicians when they've visited the company, and he has several times met and spoken with Thomas P. Corbett, Sr., Electro-Lite Chairman and CEO several times. And, despite the jokes, most fellow employees are friendly to him, even respect him in that way that people respect those who are understood to be subordinate.

Toby sprinkles the sugar into his coffee and then checks the schedule to see if any foreign representatives will be visiting the building this day. He finds that executives from Korean and Belgian utilities are scheduled to meet with Lou Tepper, General Manager of International Projects, which means Toby has one additional task to perform this morning—a task he developed himself and is in fact quite proud of. It was decided, upon his suggestion, that the company should purchase flags of every country with which Electro-Lite does business, so that when representatives of a particular country visit the building, that particular flag can be displayed in the lobby, alongside Old Glory and the Electro-Lite logo.

The suggestion was approved, but with far more difficulty than Toby anticipated. This was the previous year, 1995, and money, as it is today, was tight. Despite the fact that Electro-Lite brought in nearly three billion dollars in annual revenue, and top management did not blink at casting away nearly a million bucks to flit foot the bill for a week-long customer meeting held every February in Boca Raton, these crummy flags actually became a major issue. Toby was instructed to solicit bids from flag manufacturers. He had to justify every penny that would be spent. He found that a decent quality replica flag would run from two to five hundred dollars, with varying discounts depending on the quantity of flags purchased. What it all meant was that, with customers representing thirty-six countries, this little flag idea of Toby's could cost the company as much as fifteen thousand dollars, including mounting attachments and storage boxes. A pittance in the old days, in the seventies and early eighties, back when every day Electro-Lite was awarded another contract to design or build a new power plant. But not now.

Toby did finally get approval for the flags, and for him the whole experience served as a first-hand indicator of the times. Everything is more complicated than had been expected going in, and nothing is a sure thing. Including one's job. Layoffs of significant size were coming at a clip of two or three a year now. Toby is becoming accustomed to watching people whom he couldn't remember not being around, carrying boxes of belongings out through the revolving doors. He finds himself becoming, like many people around here, he suspects, immune. In the past few years there have been no fewer than five major layoffs, as opposed to the one layoff in the previous twenty-seven years of Toby's career at Electro-Lite.

And then there's the morale issue. Nobody knows when the next layoff is coming. People dedicate more and more of their time to covering themselves, looking busy, justifying their existence. Toby's job, with the exception of the high-tech security system, has not changed much, and he understands that he is one person who (probably) cannot be let go. The idea of a corporation the size of Electro-Lite not employing a head of security in one of its most important and visible offices is unheard of. But not impossible; not today. He sees what's going on around him, the sullen expressions on the faces of people as they slide their ID cards through the sensor in the morning. And it makes him sad. It makes him realize how quickly thirty years of good memories can be wiped away, like they never existed.

Toby decides to wait for Ben, the guard with whom Toby will work today, and let him put up the flags. Ben is young—he's twenty-two—and gets bored easily, so putting up the flags will be a nice, albeit brief, diversion for him. Besides, Toby doesn't feel like it. He can't stop thinking about Francis. Perhaps, he thinks, he should just call Francis's wife himself. Someone has to. Regardless of the events that led to their falling out and his subsequent state of homelessness (the details of which Toby does not know nor wish to know) Toby is certain that Francis's wife would be interested (not to mention entitled) to know that her husband has managed to contract lung cancer. Even if she does not care about Francis's well being, at least she'll know. Since Francis does not smoke (at least Toby has never seen him smoke) the cancer very well might be of a genetic nature. Or something to do with where they once lived, something in the air or water. If either is the case, Francis's children are at risk and his wife's knowledge of his situation could go a long way in shielding them from a similar fate. Maybe he'll try this argument with Francis, Toby thinks. Surely he hasn't lost the ability to be reasoned with. In the five years of sporadic interaction Toby has had with Francis, Toby can recall several occasions, early on mostly, when Francis participated equally in some conversation or another before shuffling off down Seventh Avenue with the danish or five-dollar bill Toby had forked over. Specifically, there was the time Francis told Toby about his wife and kids; the time he told Toby *never* to help him; the time he told Toby that he had at one time studied to be a mechanical engineer, and that was why he felt comfortable in front of the Electro-Lite building; and the time, most recently, when he admitted to having been diagnosed with lung cancer by the physician at the free clinic.

Of course Toby has always understood himself to be somewhat of a skeptic (not a cynic, though, there is a difference) and realizes that Francis might very well be crazy and have made everything up. But Toby doesn't think that's the case. He can't exactly say why he doesn't think it's the case, but he doesn't. And that's enough.

He just about has himself talked into calling Francis's wife himself (though he doesn't know her phone number, where she lives, or even her name; plus, she could be his *ex*-wife by now) when he looks up and sees the main door begin to revolve and then spit Ben into the lobby. Ben is tall and bone-thin and his blue uniform looks excessively heavy on him, like it's weighing him down, drawing his narrow shoulders in. His cheeks and nose are pink from the cold. The sound of his shoes clicking on the tile floor echoes across the huge expanse of empty lobby. He's carrying a folded up newspaper. When he gets to the desk behind which Toby is sitting, Ben stops. His straight, black hair is still wet from his morning shower and is frozen at the ends.

"I hate when it starts getting light later," he announces. "I hate driving to work when it's still nighttime. And, damn, it's cold out."

Toby leans back in his chair. "Why didn't you just wear a coat?"

Ben waves away this suggestion. "I just wasn't expecting it. I'm not ready for it to be so cold yet." He heads around behind the desk.

"It's November. This is Pittsburgh," Toby says. "Are you new here or something?"

But Ben has forgotten this conversation. He opens the newspaper to the sports page and begins skimming the top story about the previous day's Steelers game.

"Korea and Belgium today," Toby says.

Ben nods. "Uh-huh," he says, and keeps reading.

Toby knows he should say something to Ben. Tell him to put away the paper until his lunch break, get those damn flags hung, look alert. Doesn't he know that people who need jobs far more than he does are losing them every day? People with families. People with twenty, thirty years of service. As recently as a year ago, in fact, Toby *would* have said something to this effect. Because that's the way he felt. But now, the whole situation at the company has become so preposterous. Everything seems so arbitrary.: hundreds of people let go on any given day, within any given department, for any (or no) given reason. Working your ass off provides no shelter, creates no diversion. The long and short of it is: if Toby is told he has to let someone go, it's going to be Ben. So, as long as the kid's work gets done, why worry him to death? Why pile on the guilt? Why play a game that can't be won?

"Just make sure they're up before seven," Toby says.

Ben opens the paper to page two and folds it back at the crease. "Will-do, cap'n."

Outside, orange light leaks in between the taller buildings to the east, spilling across the roof of B&D's Coffee Shop, and sending a familiar glare through the glass front of Electro-Lite Corporation. This is Toby's favorite part of the day. The lobby—the building itself—is all but empty, quiet. And he has perhaps the only indoor seat in all of downtown Pittsburgh that affords the luxury of watching the sun rise between two perfectly positioned skyscrapers. Behind him, Ben rustles more pages, and Toby watches the sun seep outward, spreading. But the glare becomes too much, and he turns away.

Michael Dunne will have forgotten his ID badge, again. It is Monday, and a certainty. From the start, after he was transferred to Pittsburgh from Electro-Lite's corporate headquarters in New York a year or so ago, he and Toby began treating his forgetfulness as a running joke. Michael would approach the front desk with a grin on his face and Toby would return the smile while shaking his head in mock disbelief, and then assign a temporary ID badge to Michael. It's something Toby looks forward to, is looking forward to now.

As quiet and unassuming as Toby's morning has been up until seven o'clock, when Ben descended the ladder after hanging the Korean and Belgian flags, he never could have predicted the agitated commotion that would ensue. People begin arriving to the office much earlier than usual, and pause to talk much more (though there is always, these days, a heightened need to congregate and to gossip). Toby watches as they enter through one of the three revolving doors and wait for the person behind them. They look away when they speak. A lot of people are early today, but few are actually at their workstations. A buzz of activity is in the air, but also a strange reluctance. Toby's guess as to the increase in Monday morning activity is simply that there are only three work days remaining until the Thanksgiving holiday, so people are trying to cram as much into those days, meet as many deadlines, post as many sales, as they can. Not to mention that after Thanksgiving the big numbers game will begin—everybody trying to figure out how in the world they are going to meet their annual financial objectives by December 31. Nerves.

But that is only part of it.

Toby signs in a visitor from the Sewickley office; he assigns a visitors' badge and gives the man directions to conference room

120A, where a meeting of Eastern Region marketing personnel is to begin at eight. This person is early but Toby sees that he is carrying a slide projector and flip-chart, so he figures the guy, who is sweating heavily beneath a brown tweed jacket and whose shoulders are flecked with dandruff, needs time to set up. When Toby turns back around and sees Michael, black gym bag slung over his shoulder, next in line to be assigned a temporary badge, he smiles and shakes his head in that mock-disappointed way he knows Michael has come to expect.

"Not already," Toby says. "It's only Monday, for crying out loud."

"Thought I'd get a jump on things," Michael says. He tries to smile but when it doesn't work he abandons it.

"When are you gonna let me fix you up with one of these?" Toby holds up a long necklace made of white plastic links, like a toy, with a big metal clip fastened to it.

"How many times do I have to tell you," he says. "I'm not going to wear my ID badge around my neck. It's just not going to happen."

"Fine," Toby says and tosses the necklace back into a box filled with them. He kicks the box aside. "Have it your way." Toby understands Michael's position but enjoys giving him a hard time about it anyway. It's not difficult to spot those people who wear their ID badges around their necks. They're the same people who also are wearing suits from 1973, have five extra-long strands of hair swept lengthwise across a fleshy white scalp, and ink stains on their breast pockets despite the heavy-duty plastic pocket protectors inserted there, presumably to guard against such accidents. None of this bothers Toby but, with regard to Michael, it gives him a target at which to aim. He takes out a temporary ID badge form. "Social Security number?"

"You know my Social Security number by now, Toby."

"Yeah, I do," Toby says, reaching for a pen. "What is it?"

Michael rattles off the numbers. "That sound about right?" he asks.

"It'll do." Toby transfers the information to the form, then punches it into the computer so that when Michael slides this temporary badge through the slot the computer will register the same information as his regular ID badge. Michael stands and watches distractedly. He's glancing, Toby senses, back at the artwork on the far wall: splotchy blue and yellow paintings— originals—in metallic modern-looking frames that Electro-Lite purchased by the pound. Toby tosses the badge across the desk to Michael. "Same time tomorrow?" he says.

Michael lets out a long breath. "Hopefully," he says.

Toby chuckles (such statements are usual Electro-Lite cynicism) but then stops when Michael does not join in. "What's that supposed to mean?"

"Nothing," Michael says, taking his temporary badge in his hand. He flips his gym bag higher up onto his shoulder. "There's just a lot of... stuff going on today. Possibly some changes. I don't know." He shakes his head, hard, as if ridding it of a troublesome thought. "I'm sorry," he says. "Never mind." He clears his throat and straightens.

Michael came to Pittsburgh as a result of his first big promotion. A public relations specialist, he was given significant responsibility at Electro-Lite's Power Generation Division at a relatively young age. Toby guesses he is thirty-one, thirty-two. He doesn't know much else about him other than that he has demonstrated a reluctance to stand among those groups of younger professionals before and after work, at lunch, in the smoking lounges, to speculate. And that he frequently forgets his ID badge.

"So is there going to be some kind of announcement?" Toby asks.

Michael clips his new badge onto the metal loop of his gym bag and takes a step back. "I don't know. Probably not. Thanks, Toby." Then he heads off and follows a group of people through the security stalls and back toward the elevators.

On the elevator, nobody speaks. Anything worth commenting on has been done down in the lobby. Michael Dunne steps out onto the tenth floor and weaves through the rows of gray, felt-lined cubicles to his office. He hangs his coat behind the door, stands for a moment, glances around. In the year and a half he's been here his office has not changed much. It has the appearance of containing someone who is either not completely moved in or in the process of moving out. The tan cork walls are bare, with a few exceptions: a cardboard poster printed with the 1996 Miami University of Ohio football schedule, the Electro Lite vacation schedule (major holidays, two days at Thanksgiving, two at Christmas, plus a floating holiday usually added a day before or after July 4), the headline and clipping of a story he ghost-wrote for *Inc.* magazine ("Electro Lite Chairman Flexes his Muscles"), and a map of the United States. The silver-framed two-by-three-foot picture that had been nailed to the white office wall—a snow-capped mountain peak at sunrise superimposed with the typically corporate, right-thinking message, "Determination..."—now sits on the floor, squeezed into the narrow space between the wall and Michael's desk, which is equally bare. On top of it are several manila folders of current projects, and little else. Michael believes himself to be suffering from some sort of office design deficiency. He has no eye for knickknacks, no sense of what types of personal items are appropriate to display. So, with one exception, he displays none. The exception is a tiny, metal backboard and rim atop a 12-inch pole and affixed to a wood base. A cherry-sized basketball is around somewhere, although Michael couldn't even hazard a guess as to where it might be at this moment. The thing, when completely assembled and operational, is called The Executive Basketball Set and was given to Michael by his wife, as a joke. This, he displays proudly.

This morning Michael Dunne has two items to which he must attend. First, he has to complete his expense report. He hasn't filled one out in three months now and American Express wants to be paid. The other thing he needs to do, which probably should be done immediately but no doubt will wait, is to devise a press release that adequately explains Electro-Lite's reasoning for the announcement that will come at two o'clock this afternoon: approximately eleven thousand employees—a large percentage of whom are from the Pittsburgh office—will be laid off, effective December 31.

Michael drops his duffel bag, sits heavily into his chair. In the office next door, Drew Barnhill is laughing, talking loudly with someone on the phone. No doubt his feet are up on his desk, Michael thinks, right next to his steaming "I'd rather be fishing" coffee mug and cheese danish. Drew, a manager in the area of Quality Assurance, knows how to decorate an office. Pictures of his family, usually on a boat somewhere, dominate his desk, along with an enlarged photo of Drew, an odd smile on his face, shaking hands with Jack Klugman. There also are framed Electro-Lite award certificates and QA guidelines strategically tacked across the walls, an elaborate QA diagram of some sort drawn in several different colors on the marker board, a hat rack in the corner behind the door, and a gold, wok-shaped ashtray on the side credenza.

The QA force will be cut by nearly two-thirds. Michael cannot help thinking this as he listens to Drew's heavy, stuttering *heh-heh-hehs* through the wall.

Michael rifles through a drawer until he finds an expense report form. Coming up with all the necessary receipts will be a test, he knows, and in the end he'll probably have to kick out some of his own money. How does he get himself into these situations? Nobody else he knows ever has to use his own money for business expenses. People go out of their way to make sure such things never happen. Drew, still laughing away, is one of them. Michael wouldn't be surprised if Drew's *made* money on business trips, QA inspections or whatever the hell they are. Well, more power to him. If you can pull it off, Michael figures, have at it. He understands all too well that the company is not going out of its way to make sure you get what's yours. But Michael is incapable of pulling off such capers. In the four years they've been married he and his wife, Natalie, have managed to build up nearly thirty thousand dollars in debt. With nothing to show for it. They live in an east side apartment (more than they can comfortably afford, but not crippling in and of itself). They each drive cars just slightly out of their price range. They have a nice stereo system, a laptop computer, a pseudo-leather sofa. None of their possessions would give away their financial state. It's the little things. Like last year when they decided they wanted a dog. They got one—a purebred Shetland sheepdog—at the mall pet store for eight hundred dollars, on their Visa. Things like that. And things like Michael losing track of his receipts and having to pay with his—their—own money.

Next door, Drew hangs up the phone. Outside his office, Michael can hear hushed voices coming from a row of cubicles. They're breaking down the plausibility of various rumors, careful, for some reason Michael cannot fathom, not to let the PR guy hear. But Michael's heard the rumors—everything from a fifty percent across-the-board layoff to Electro-Lite looking to sell the entire Power Generation Division outright to the Japanese to the elimination of the beloved floating holiday. But Michael knows the truth and is inclined to believe he would come clean with it right now if someone would just ask.

He knows he's putting off the announcement material. Ever since Friday, when Dennis, Vice President of PR and Michael's boss, told Michael what was going to happen Monday and what they needed to do to prepare, Michael has had pains in his stomach. Not that the news came as a surprise—there'd been talk, discussions—but the officiality of it, the confirmation, was jarring. This is not what he had in mind when he received his first promotion: writing press releases and talking points for executives and answering the indignant and rightfully perplexed questions of the media and (former) employees every six months when the Electro-Lite gods decide a massive "restructuring" is needed. A while back, he found that he was becoming immune to it all, even beginning to understand the philosophy behind the measures. But, somehow, this one is different. All-encompassing. This will hit too close to home, affect people within earshot. Natalie tells him that worrying about it will only make things worse, affect his job performance, and that won't do anyone any good. It'd just get *him* laid off, and then who would be there to act as the voice of reason in the PR department? But Michael knows Natalie gives him too much credit. And besides, he suspects the notion of him losing his job in some strange way terrifies her a little more than he wishes it did.

Michael doesn't wear a watch—an idiosyncrasy that, contrary to the insistence of others, has led to no problems whatsoever—but he guesses he's wasted about an hour messing around with this expense report. He gathers the still-uncompleted forms and the receipts he does have, and sets them aside. He takes a breath, slips two fingers down his collar and tugs outward.

"Busy?"

The head and neck of Alex Quinby extend into the doorway, the rest of his long body hidden from Michael's view.

"In what sense?" Michael says, leaning back in his chair, so grateful for friendly company he's afraid he might cry.

Alex slides his whole body inside the doorframe. He smiles. "Any sense. Your choice." He's carrying a plastic water bottle filled with some greenish-yellow liquid. Gatorade probably.

"Then yes," Michael says. "I'm busy."

"Good. That's the trick these days, you know. Look busy."

"Nope," Michael says. "That phase has passed. Looking busy doesn't do any good anymore."

Alex steps all the way into the office, closes the door behind him. Then he sits in the chair across from Michael and sets down his bottle. "Okay, so what've you got?" He is tall and lanky and has trouble crossing his legs in such close proximity to the desk. Michael's always thought Alex looks like one of those guys who can fold himself up into a small, square box. He was the placekicker for the Pitt football team for two years in the mid-eight-ies. He once made a fifty-eight-yard field goal but consistently struggled his entire career from close range. Now he's a financial analyst and wears bright, absurd ties that look as though they were finger-painted by a one-year-old. Today's is especially re-pulsive, Michael notes: silver and black streaky background with dark red splotches, like a car crash.

Alex repositions his legs, settles in. "Spill it."

"Big one coming," Michael says, surprising himself. Alex is a good friend, probably the only true friend he has within the com-pany. They lived together in New York for a year while Michael and Natalie were engaged, and were promoted within a month of each other to the Power Generation office in Pittsburgh. Alex, who is originally from Pittsburgh, was a tremendous help with the transition. What else is there to say? "This afternoon. It's huge."

"Jesus," Alex says. "How many this time?"

"A bundle. Eleven thousand. Don't say anything."

"Yeah." Alex lifts his tie and lets it fall back down to his chest. "Well, I mean, Jesus. Where are they going to come from?"

"Here, mostly, and from the subsidiaries. Sewickley, Monro-eville, Greentree. It's a bloody mess. I don't have any more detail than that. Officially the statement is that Electro-Lite is laying off approximately eleven thousand employees, many from middle management, most of whom will be taken out of Power Gen of-fices in and around Pittsburgh. Effective December thirty-first."

"Happy holidays," Alex says, a little too theatrically for Michael's liking.

"Yeah. Hey, seriously, don't say anything. Seriously."

"I seriously won't. Christ, why so many?"

"You've seen the numbers. Taiwan suspended construction. We totally miscalculated the revenue from the job we did in Spain. And we fucked up the repairs we were doing for Georgia Power this spring so badly they told us to leave and not come back. GE finished the job."

"I thought that was a mutual decision. That's the statement you released."

"That's called public relations, jackass."

Alex sighs heavily. He's worried about his own job, of course, and he'd like to be reassured, but Michael knows only numbers, not names. They sit there for a moment, each looking down at a different spot on Michael's desk. Then Alex begins to laugh.

He laughs and shakes his head and unfolds his long, spiny legs. Michael pictures Drew next door, perking up his ears, wondering what's going on in the next office. "What the hell," Alex says. He pats his knees as if to get up, but then he just stays where he is. "This sucks," he says. "I guess I saw it coming, though. We all did. But then everyone talks and talks about something like this and nothing happens and before long you start to believe it's not going to happen. You know what I'm saying? The talk doesn't seem attached to anything real."

"Yeah."

"This division is going to miss its objective by fifty million dollars this year. Did you know that?"

"I had a feeling. People around here don't want to know bad news like that is coming. Everyone's optimistic until the truth hits, and then it's like, 'Oh, my God. What happened?' Well, what happened is nobody wants to step up and say, 'Hey, we better fix this now, before it's too late.' But that's like admitting you were wrong in the first place."

"Then the response is to lay people off. We have no other choice. We're going down, baby. Lighten the load."

"Right. And Wall Street gets a kick out of it, so...."

Michael knows he and Alex are taking a simplistic view of the matter. Of course many more factors go into such a decision. It's just that lately he's finding it difficult to be impartial. Views such as those he and Alex are currently are putting forth just *feel* better. Somehow, that's the point he's come to.

But Alex is still going. "I told Myers. I told him in July. I said, 'Look, these objectives are crazy. There's no way in hell we can make this. No way.' And I wasn't the only one either. But he just kept it buried. Didn't want to be the bearer of bad news. We sit back and hope we get his humongous last-minute job that will save the day. When are we gonna learn?"

December thirty-first, maybe, Michael thinks, but he doesn't say it. He just nods. He doesn't want to talk about it anymore and he realizes now that he never really did.

"I'm thinking of trying to transfer over to the real estate division," Alex says.

"I'm thinking of quitting," Michael says.

Alex blinks, stares across the desk while Michael assesses the words he's just heard himself speak.

"What?" Alex says finally.

"I don't have the stomach for this. I thought I did, but I don't."

"The stomach for what?"

"I don't know."

Alex shrugs. "Well, then maybe you should quit."

"I can't," Michael says. "We owe too much money. Nat's trying to start her own business—that interior designing stuff I was telling you about—and, well, you know she's having a lot of trouble. We can't afford the transition time, even I found something else right away. We'll be talking bankruptcy." Suddenly Michael realizes he's been—consciously or unconsciously, he's not sure—considering this scenario for some time. "And she wants to have a baby," he adds then, for good measure.

Alex reaches out and fingers the twine on the tiny basketball hoop. "Yeah," he says. "Well."

"Sorry," Michael says. "This is just starting to get to me a little. Like I said."

"It's cool," Alex says and with apparent effort, stands. "I better get back before Myers comes looking for me." He picks up his bottle and sucks some of the toxic-looking liquid through the tube.

"Keep your head down."

Alex swallows loudly. "You bet. Lunch?" He turns the knob and pushes open the door.

"Not today. The announcement is set for two and I don't know what-all shit's gonna be going on up until then."

Alex nods, slides his fingers along the inside of the door jam, like a carpenter examining his own work. "All right," he says, and turns.

"Hey, Alex—"

"Yeah?"

"Stop by a little later. Maybe before you head out to lunch."

"Can-do. You gonna be all right with this?"

Michael shrugs. "Sure. It's just the way things are now. The way of the world."

"Atta-boy."

"Don't ever let me hear you say that again."

Alex laughs, looks away, laughs some more. "I'll see ya," he says then and lopes away to his office on the fourteenth.

With the door now open, the smell of coffee wanders in. Michael sits perfectly still for several seconds, breathing. Then he makes a fist with his right hand and presses it, hard, into his eye socket.

The press release is easier to write than Michael anticipated. Lately, they just seem to flow, a natural process.

"In its continuing effort to provide the finest, most cost-effective products and services to its power generation customers, Electro-Lite Corp. today announced today that it will reorganize several of its core businesses. It is the corporation's hope that these changes will make Electro-Lite a stronger, more focused, financially progressive organization, and provide higher returns for its shareholders.

"As a result, Electro-Lite will be forced to eliminate the positions of approximately eleven thousand of its employees. Corporate management regrets this aspect of the necessary restructuring effort, but is confident that those employees who are not affected by the layoff will be part of a far more efficient, forward-moving organization...."

Michael stands suddenly. He realizes he is sweating; he can smell himself, a smell he identifies as sorrow, or something close to that. He puts on his jacket, then his overcoat; he shoulders his duffel bag and heads for the door. On his way out of the office he picks up The Executive Basketball Set from his desk and puts it under his arm.

The sweat comes easier on the elevator. He can feel his shirt beginning to stick to his back, a dampness between his toes.

At six the elevator stops and a young woman steps on. She smiles. Her hair is brown and her dress is red and pretty and unbusinesslike. Michael wonders if she'll still be here come January, or if her life will undergo one of those unaccounted-for detours, one of those moments that claims the possibility of a sound, restful night's sleep as its price and makes a person stop—actually stop—and say, "What am I going to do now?"

Michael watches the numbers above the elevator door as they descend. He hopes he looks all right, hopes his breathing isn't audible. Above the doors the 3 lights and stays lit and the doors open. The woman steps off, flicking another pleasant smile in Michael's direction as she leaves. Again the downward motion grabs at his chest.

When the elevator jerks to a stop at the first floor Michael waits as three people—all men, all white, all in blue suits, two with red ties, one with yellow—get on. They're talking about mortgage rates. One man is thinking of refinancing, one of the others has already done so and is sharing his experience. Michael stays put, against the back wall. The doors close, a button is pressed, and they start up again. The next time the elevator stops is at sixteen so that's where Michael gets off, with the three men. They proceed down a corridor of offices (all empty) past a window looking out over the Monongahela River, to a T, where Michael separates from the three men (he's lost track of their conversation), heads for the stairwell and walks down six flights to his own office. He drops the Executive Basketball Set in the trash can, sits down at his computer, and finishes the press release. He adds a couple of sentences regarding money that will be saved as a result of the layoffs and applied toward Electro-Lite's increasing debt, a quote by Newton Sarver, President of the Power Generation Division, and the fact that affected employees will be notified by December 12. He checks it for spelling, grammar and empathy, prints it out, takes it to Dennis' office, leaves it on his desk. It is on his way back to his own office that Michael notices he is still wearing his overcoat.

By noon—working non-stop, not thinking—Michael has written a summary of the layoff situation for Newton Sarver, just for his information. He also has written a separate letter for Sarver's signature, to be distributed to all employees tomorrow that more or less explains the reasoning behind the layoffs. Actually, this is Stringer's job, but Michael is on a roll and doesn't, for some reason, want to stop. It's standard stuff anyway. All Michael did was update the letter from last March, when forty-five hundred employees went out. Different numbers, different dates, same results.

Dennis has not been around. Most likely, Michael figures, he has been in meetings all morning and will come by early this afternoon to fill Michael in and assign him to some sort of post-press conference damage control project or another. An easy way to find out would simply be to call Gloria, Dennis' secretary, and ask, but not only does Michael not care what's going on at this particular moment, he doesn't want know.

He figures he might as well take the letter and summary up to Sarver's office. If he gets back before Alex stops by, maybe he can go to lunch after all.

✳ ✳ ✳

The last thing Newton Sarver needs today is a luncheon engagement with the six winners of Electro-Lite Power Generation's Quality Performance Award. The awards are given every quarter and the winners—in addition to a certificate and a hundred stock options—receive the privilege of having lunch, on the company, at the Common Plea with the division president. There really couldn't be a more inappropriate time for such a thing, Sarver thinks as he slides his card through the security sensor, but there isn't enough time to cancel. Actually, if someone—Stringer or Tussy or Dunne or his secretary or even himself—had remembered this luncheon last month, when the decisions were being made, or even last week, then maybe there would've been time. But things are so hectic, and canceling a Quality Award luncheon at the last minute sends a bad message; it presents a certain irony that makes Sarver uneasy.

A car and driver are waiting outside on the street. Sarver steps across the sidewalk feeling a quick, jolting chill on his face, and climbs into the back seat, carefully. He looks at his watch, shifts the bottom half of his overcoat beneath him, making sure nothing is bunched up or awkward. Such technicalities have a tendency to kick-start the pressure and ache in what feels like his stomach but what he fears, for no good reason, is his prostate.

"I'm a little late," he tells the driver.

"Have you there in three minutes, sir," the driver says, pulling out into traffic.

"No hurry."

They hit all three red lights heading up Seventh. Sarver knows he should be using this time to think about his remarks for the luncheon. But what can he say? Nice job, this is what you work for, but, unfortunately, two and a half out of the six of you won't be with us next month? And they'll want to know the status of the business. It's an opportunity for them to get the inside scoop directly from their leader. What can he possibly say?

"Take your time," he tells the driver.

But the driver is right. It doesn't take much longer that than three minutes before they're making the turn onto Grant Street, heading past the courthouse, and then pulling right up to the front door of the Common Plea.

Inside, Sarver is directed to a large, round table in the back of the darkened, oak-trimmed restaurant. Around the table are the six award winners along with Marlene Stringer, the employee communications manager. They all stop talking as he

CHRISTOPHER TOROCKIO

approaches. Marlene looks down at her watch, then accusingly up at Sarver.

"Hello, folks," Sarver says, settling cautiously into the empty chair to Marlene's left. "Sorry I'm late. Marlene's kept you entertained, though, I trust." A few strained laughs. Sarver takes his napkin from his water glass and lays it across his lap, then suddenly realizes he should have gone around the table and shaken everyone's hand. But that is now impossible.

"I'll get a waiter," Marlene says, standing. "And we can order as we go along. How about if we start by going around the table and introducing ourselves." She turns to the man sitting at her right. "Why don't you start, Bill," and then she heads off.

Sarver is not paying much attention. He looks over the right shoulder of each person as he or she provides a name and a department. Sarver nods, smiles. At one point he says, "I started out in fluid systems, too." As the sixth person finishes her introduction, Marlene returns with a waiter in tow.

"Let's just order," Sarver says. "Relax a little."

So that's what they do, though Marlene is not pleased. Sarver can tell this is not the way she wanted things to run. Her plan was for him to be speaking while they ordered—congratulating them, providing his views on the future of the business and how dedication like theirs is the cornerstone of any and all success in that future, mixing in a little humor, etc., etc. That's the way these things work. She is aware of the two o'clock announcement as well and wants to move this little affair along as quickly as possible so Sarver can be back in his office by one, latest. But Sarver, for some reason, finds himself fighting her expectations. The lower regions of his stomach have cramped up so badly now he can feel a tingling in his fingertips.

They talk for a while about an island off the coast of North Carolina Sarver has never heard of where two of the award winners vacationed this past summer. Both claim that it is the best-kept secret on the East Coast. Then they talk for a while about the unusually wet autumn they've been having, until suddenly the man who works in fluid systems—Sarver forgets his name but is impressed by the sheer whiteness of his hair in contrast to the many colored pens held in his shirt pocket—says, "Mr. Sarver, I appreciate this award. But, in my opinion, I think it's important that employees know that if they put forth the effort for this company that they'll be rewarded not with a certificate and a free lunch, but with a job."

All breathing stops. Faces turn away. "I mean no disrespect," the man adds, apparently sensing the discomfort he's caused his co-workers. "It's just that, well, I think it's an issue—at least it's something that I frequently hear discussed—and I wanted to hear what you had to say about it."

Sarver straightens; the pain beneath him melts away. He takes a sip from his water glass, sets it back down, clears his throat. "If you're looking for some sort of guarantee," he says, "then you are severely deluded."

"I'm not looking for any guarantee," the man says.

"Yes, you are."

The man from fluid systems lowers his eyes. Sarver just stares at the pen caps in the man's pocket: red, blue, black, green, red, purple, red. Someone, off to the left, picks up a roll and butters it.

"Anyone here who is looking for a guarantee would be better served—" Sarver pauses, not sure what he's going to say next—"getting their undertaker's license. This company is moving forward, and you people are here, at this table, because you are doing what we believe is necessary for us to move forward." Sarver folds his arms across his chest. Actually he has no idea how these matters are decided (he signed a paper put in front of him some time back that approved them for the award, and that's about as much as he knows on the issue). And, it occurs to him, he must look like King Arthur, addressing the Knights of his Round Table. They're all waiting for him to say more, reassure them. Well, who's going to reassure him? He takes a breath, lets it out regally. "None of you, I can see, are new here. You see the trends. You know the way things are now, see the condition of our market. You have to deal with it just as I have to deal with it. Whether you believe it or not, my job is no more secure than any of yours. Maybe less. I don't know why, but for some reason that fact seems to make people feel better." He shouldn't be saying these things, he knows; it's all true enough, but if Corbett and the Electro-Lite board decided to go in another direction and get a new Power Gen president, Sarver knows he'd be in a lot better position to recover than some engineer from fluid systems. He places the palm of his hand on top of his head where he finds that beads of warm sweat have formed, a tiny pool inside the confines of his bald spot, like a bay. "I could draw you diagrams and charts as to why this is," he continues, "but, quite frankly, I think it's a lot easier to understand that that's just the way things are now. So—"

he turns and addresses the fluid systems man directly again—"if you want to know how I feel about it, what my take is, I'd say enjoy your lunch, invest your stock options. Those are really the only guarantees I can give right now. Excuse me, please."

Sarver pushes out his chair and stands. The pain that had settled in his stomach shoots down into his thighs; there is a hard dullness behind his eyes, although he finds it hard to believe that this is from the prostate. He turns and heads for the front of the restaurant, and the door. Behind him, there is only silence, until he hears Marlene, voice shaking, say, "He's been under a lot of stress."

"Take me to the hospital."

The driver turns around in his seat, right arm up on the passenger headrest. "Sir?"

"Mercy…Hospital," Sarver says, unable to breathe. "Please hurry."

"What's the matter, Mr. Sarver?" The driver is now turned completely around. "Can I help?"

"Yes. Drive me…to the fucking hospital."

"All right. Sure."

The driver turns back around and in seconds they are pulling away from the Common Plea and on their way up Forbes Avenue toward Mercy Hospital. Sarver bites down. His entire body hurts now: his stomach, shoulders, knees, hips, chest, eyeballs—a crown of pain revolving around the hot, molten core at the base of his torso.

"It's not my fault," he says.

The driver checks the rearview mirror. "What's that, sir?"

Sarver believes he can taste blood now. They travel past the Palumbo Center and at the next red light, the driver stops.

"No!" Sarver says.

The driver hits the gas. Sarver has to hold onto the door handle and close his eyes. This pain is not natural. A knife, many knives, have got to be sticking out of him.

"Please," he says.

The driver does not answer.

"Try to understand."

Finally the car is stationary and the driver helps Sarver out of the back seat and into a wheelchair.

∗ ∗ ∗

Marlene Stringer hands a dollar to the valet and climbs into her new Acura. She is livid. She has never believed that Newton Sarver is the man to lead this division and nothing has more adequately served to prove this suspicion than his behavior at lunch today. A man in his position has to exude an air of self-confidence, of sternness and purpose and character. But this guy is nothing more than a glorified engineer (he said it himself, in fact: "I started out in fluid systems, too"), a geek with a contractor, a couple of extra degrees and friends in the right places. What this business needs, Marlene understands, is someone with a set of balls, someone who knows the business. But if Sarver knew the business, or had any balls, for that matter, the eleven thousand getting whacked next month would have been gone a long time ago.

Before pulling away from the Common Plea Marlene checks herself in the rearview mirror. She adds a layer of lipstick and notices for the first time that Claire, that idiot at Headliners, has completely screwed up her highlights and now her hair is the color of low-fat margarine.

"Moron," she says, and hits the gas.

It's five to one. After Sarver retreated from the restaurant, Marlene and the six Quality Award winners silently picked at their salads for a while, and then Marlene went ahead and told them the way things really were. Yeah, she told them. Maybe she shouldn't have, she thinks now, looking out her window at the storefronts gliding slowly past, but she was startlingly angry, even for her, and a little embarrassed, and she went ahead and told them about the layoffs. So, fine, she'd be the bad guy if Sarver couldn't handle it. She doesn't mind. One thing she believes she's learned in her eleven years with the company is that sometimes things need to be said, and with each passing year she finds she has a little less trouble saying them. She's also found that she's developed the opinion that this company really could use a good cleaning out—just get rid of all the excess baggage and start from scratch. When she walks through the building anymore, there's a dolt at every turn. What do these people do anyway? she wonders. It's just that she's come too far for this current batch of spineless weasels at the top to go messing with her success. She's privy to all of the decisions made at the division level and even has access to the chairman on occasion. For a woman, in this Men's Club haven, that's pretty damn good. Of course, having no children to hold her back helps, as does having a husband in Electro-Lite's marketing department who is as committed to his work as she is hers and doesn't mind the hours or opinions she keeps.

Then, waiting at the light at the corner of Seventh and Smithfield, she suddenly considers making the turn, heading across the bridge to Station Square and taking a room at the Sheraton. She could call Jack and, she has no doubt, he would be there within fifteen minutes, his tie off. He'd dump an appointment, skip a meeting with the chief of staff if he had to, but, yeah, he'd be there.

But the thought actually provides Marlene with the motivation to return to the office. She has some items prepared for the press conference that she wants to get to Sarver. She'll fax copies to the corporate office as well, just so they know she's the one who prepared them. If nothing else, she'll get some exposure out of today's fiasco, a little face time. Most likely Dunne's been sitting on this responsibility anyway, so if he feels like she's stepping on his toes she can always defend herself by saying, Well, it needed to be done and, since we're all in this together, just one big happy family all working toward the same goals, what difference does it really make?

Traffic is slow. Lunch traffic. Marlene slips into the left lane for a block or so, then over into the lane for busses only. When she reaches the Electro-Lite building she swings around to the back and enters the underground parking area through the shipping and receiving entrance just as the sky opens up and the rain begins. She waves to the guard who is positioned on a stool, hat pushed back on his head. He has one of those adult crushes on her, she knows, that is annoying and useful at the same time, though every day it seems to be becoming a little more annoying and a little less useful.

She finds a spot between two support beams—perfect, no doors can ding her from either side—and swings her legs out. She straightens her skirt across her thighs, slings her briefcase over her shoulder, and hits the button on her key ring to activate the Acura's alarm system. The two-tone *bleep-blip* echoes through the vast, cavernous garage. Once that sound has subsided the only sounds are from Marlene's heels clicking over the cement and, somewhere beneath that, the steady pulse of the rain on the street beyond the open shipping and receiving doors. She establishes a comfortable pattern as she heads for the elevator. Then, when she's about fifty feet from the doors, she hears something else; heavier, unsynchronized sounds, more shuffling than clicking, and she picks up her pace.

When she gets to the elevator she hits the button, pulls the belt of her overcoat tighter around her waist, and turns. Coming toward her are Dunne and that financial guy, Quigley, or something like that.

"Gentlemen," she says when they're close enough. "Have a nice lunch?"

Dunne does something with his face—a smile or a wince. "Wonderful," he says. "You?"

"Oh," Marlene says, tapping one foot impatiently. "It was interesting, if nothing else."

Neither man responds, so Marlene adds, "We had the QA Awards luncheon today," and presses the already-lit elevator button.

"Perfect timing," Dunne says. "Do you know Alex? Alex, this is Marlene."

"I think we've met," Marlene says.

"How's it going?" Alex says,. though, for some reason that sends a sudden jolt of full-blown anger through Marlene, he is looking down at the combination trash can-ashtray next to the elevator doors. A second later the doors pull apart and the weird rage washes away as the three step on in. It is warm inside, and humid, and the smell reminds Marlene of a damp, overused dishrag.

Halfway to the lobby, Dunne takes a deep breath—a sigh— and lets it out. From across the elevator Marlene can actually feel his breath brush by her neck. She says, "Everything ready for two?"

Dunne glances over at his friend, then lowers his eyes. "Everything," he says, with a touch of sarcasm that is strengthened by the pause. "Everything. Yeah, everything's ready."

"Good," Marlene says. "Because Sarver's got his head in his ass today. Farther up than usual. You guys are going to have to hold his hand the whole way I'm afraid." She lets that sit for a moment. Then, when the garage elevator opens into the lobby, she smiles and heads off, heels clicking across the marble.

She doesn't want to ride up to ten with Dunne and what's-his-name. The fact is she's still appalled at Sarver's behavior at lunch and as a result has no tolerance for what she's come to identify as a subtle but very real element of immaturity in Michael Dunne.

Feeling, oddly, like the target of some sort of pursuit, she walks around the back of the front desk to the other side of the lobby, slides her ID card through the slot, and heads for the adjacent set of elevators where she rides up with three people she's never seen before—three men, all in short-sleeve dress shirts. In November! Marlene unzips the briefcase hanging at her hip and fumbles around inside for some imaginary item. She doesn't want to talk about the weather with these people or about the fact that a long weekend is coming up or how miserable everyone is. She doesn't want to hear that. One man reaches into his pocket casually and jingles what sounds to Marlene like about ten bucks in nickels. She keeps digging in her bag.

"Boy, someone's busy, huh?" the nickels guy says, and laughs, a short, wet snort.

Marlene looks up. The guy's glasses are about three inches thick. "You could say that," she says, thinking: If it were up to me, you'd be number one on the list of eleven thousand. No doubt.

In her office she gathers the material she's prepared and asks Florence, her cataractic secretary, to deliver them to the appropriate people. Then she sits, flips through her pink message slips, and puts a call in to Newton Sarver.

Nobody answers. Not even his secretary. The phone—the phone of the division president!—rolls over twice, three times, until it's finally picked up by the kid (Ben?) at the front desk who not only doesn't know where Sarver is, he doesn't even know whose line it is that's rolled all the way over to the main switchboard phone. This Ben has a crush on her, too, although, because of his age, this particular crush seems more understandable to Marlene.

"Newton Sarver," Marlene says. "Maybe you've heard of the guy? He runs the place. So to speak."

"Yes, ma'am," the kid says. "Yes, I've heard of him. Only I don't know where he is or when he'll be back." He pauses before adding, "Or anything."

Marlene hangs up the phone, stands, checks the afternoon schedule and sees that the press conference is set for Auditorium C on the first floor. Then, in a rush of familiar, welcome adrenaline, she heads off to Sarver's office, on twenty-six.

The auditorium is awash in chaos—the only suitable word that comes to Michael's mind—and Michael stands back against the big white marker board and watches everything. At one end, men in suits, along with Marlene Stringer, form frantic, makeshift huddles. A few words and phrases are blurted out, often by more than one person at a time, then that huddle breaks apart and forms two more. Michael tries to remember the scientific term for this process—or at least what this process reminds him of—but all he can come up with is osmosis, which he knows is wrong. At the other end of the modest, neutrally carpeted auditorium are about two dozen men and women in jeans, a tie or pants-suit here and there, behind cameras on tripods.

This is Michael's first press conference. Sure, there've been a couple other layoffs since the time he took his current job. But they were minor by comparison. In the past they simply sent out a statement: Electro-Lite will lay off approximately three thousand employees, we regret... etc., etc. But eleven thousand is a lot of people—people—and Newton Sarver (surprisingly to some, though Michael is not sure himself) was receptive to PR's suggestion that the action be addressed directly in a press conference. That kind of mass layoff, Michael's department put forth, can't be buried in paragraph three of some press release. You'll end up having to answer even more questions—antagonistic ones—that way.

But Newton Sarver is nowhere to be found and the suits are nervous. In some way that Michael cannot quite comprehend, people seem to be doing something, moving about frantically, as if everyone, except Michael, has been given an assignment to complete immediately. But what could they be doing? All there is to do is wait. He looks out at the members of the press. Most are at least in their forties—seasoned, serious business reporters—except for the camera operators who got stuck with this dry assignment. Most likely each is wishing he or she were out covering a shooting or a coked-up prostitute threatening to jump off of the Sixth Street Bridge. Yeah, that's what these cameramen are thinking. And who could blame them? That's the way it is with ambition.

Michael watches the flurry without focusing on any particular aspect of it. Bodies float in and out of his vision, like moths across the outside of a window. He stays up against the marker board and allows his mind to separate from the activity around him, to establish in himself the comforting sensation of distance, of being inherently apart from what's going on around him. Every now and then he hears voices speaking in gruff whispers, the words themselves inaudible except for an occasional few. Occasionally emerging from the white noise, he hears: Postpone... I'm just saying... well, then... under my arm... crazy... I'm not the man... embarrassing as hell... and then, in a voice that is certainly feminine, yet intrinsically brusque and severe and unmistakably Marlene Stringer's, Gone and done it this time, the fool.

Then something occurs to Michael, grabs him firmly by the midsection, pulls, and instantly destroys that elusive element of distance: What's happened to my ambition?

He looks around the room now, thinking, I have to help. But how? He walks toward the center of the auditorium, in the area about halfway between the podium and the row of reporters' cameras, and joins a huddle already in progress. But as soon as he's noticed by the group, the voices stop. Michael glances at the circle of faces as they simultaneously turn away. Finally, Morton, the stocky, thick-lipped division controller, says, "Marlene won't like it. She'll raise a stink."

Just then Michael notices that Dennis, his boss, is standing across from him. He says, "Fuck her. She'll get over it. It's not her job anyway."

Morton shrugs. "Your call."

Dennis takes a breath, checks his watch. He scratches his cheek and takes another breath. Dennis, in Michael's opinion, is the sharpest dresser in the company. His suits are silk and fashionable—never navy, seldom pinstripes—with a flawlessly matching silk hankie in the lapel. The patterns on his shirts (like today's, simple, muted charcoal stripes that blend naturally into the pine green suit) are equally meticulous. Michael believes that the reasoning behind Dennis' attention to his wardrobe springs from two causes: as director of PR, he views himself as outside the day-to-day stereotypes of the number-crunching business suit crowd; and, secondly, it helps to take the focus off of his bizarrely large, round belly. Dennis is not fat, except for his stomach. His arms, legs, neck, everything, are thin, normal. But he looks, well, Michael has always thought the guy looks pregnant. His belly is round and smooth, not flabby or hanging, like he's hiding a basketball under his shirt. And never has this been more apparent to Michael than the two times he saw Dennis outside the office, when his boss was wearing a t-shirt, untucked, and jeans. Hence, Michael reasons, the suits.

But now Dennis looks down at his shoes and rubs the back of his neck. On top of his head there is a bald spot the size of a silver dollar of which Michael has, until now, been unaware.

"Maybe we should check with New York," Morton says. "Corbett should know what we're doing here."

Dennis looks up. "No. There's no time. These people are waiting."

"No offense, Dennis," Morton says. "But so fucking what? Let them wait all goddamn day. We don't have to do this at all."

"Yes we do," Dennis says, hissing almost. "Can you imagine—canceling a press conference and then laying off eleven thousand people? Can you possibly comprehend the public relations nightmare that goes along with something like that?"

"As opposed to the nightmare that goes along with sending a lower level PR rep in front of the news media to announce eleven thousand layoffs? Is that our alternative?"

"What?" Michael says. "What's that?"

Morton and Dennis look across the huddle at each other; everyone else looks away. "You know the details well enough," Dennis says. "You put Sarver's talking points together for this. Hell, you probably know more than Sarver. And, more importantly, there are aspects you don't know. We have to make this announcement. We have to do it now. Nobody has any idea where Sarver is. And of the rest of us, you're the most prepared to deliver an appropriate statement. I'm not going to get all caught up in the political aspects of who is up there. One aspect of public relations procedure is knowing when to disregard it."

Michael cannot think; he can't swallow. Morton turns away, his back now to the huddle. "What about you?" Michael says. "You're my boss. A vice president. You're... I mean, that's your job, right?"

Someone else turns away, but Michael is looking hard and straight into Dennis' eyes. Dennis swallows, a move that makes Michael suddenly want to take his boss by the throat. "All right," Dennis says. "You're right. Of course you're right. But, Michael, I want you up there with me to field questions." He turns to Harold Diaz, the division's personnel director and backhands him lightly across the chest. "I want you to make yourself available, too."

"Fine," Diaz says. Michael does not know Diaz—a huge man with tight, curly hair and one enormous, furry eyebrow traversing his forehead—and has never thought one way or another about him. His chest is of some significance, though, wide and solid, and it occurs to Michael that he would not have chosen to strike him there the way Dennis has.

"All right then," Dennis says. "The hell with it. I'll make the announcement—just read it straight from your remarks, Mike—then take questions. Michael, I want you up at the podium with me. Harold, stay in sight."

"Um, what if someone asks where Sarver is?" Michael says.

Dennis' eyelids do a quick, fluttering thing, like he is trying like mad to hold them open under extreme conditions. Morton turns back around to face the huddle. Diaz's eyebrow forms a long, wide W.

"Just say he was called away on other business. Unavoidably," Michael says. "And he regrets not being here. If they ask where, just say you're not at liberty to disclose that—at a customer's request—and move on."

After a moment, Dennis nods. Out of the corner of his eye Michael sees a camera operator begin dismantling his equipment, preparing to leave.

"Cancel it. Get these people out of here." Marlene's head enters the huddle, all eyes, wide and green, surrounded by a crown of deep yellow hair. "Nobody can find him," she says. "You've got to cancel this thing now, Dennis."

"Just calm down, Marlene," Dennis says. "We'll be all right. We're not canceling." He turns away and walks over to a chair against the wall where he opens his brief case and extracts some papers—the one's, Michael notices, he dropped on his desk earlier that morning.

"What in God's name is he talking about?" Marlene asks Michael.

"He's going on with it. He's giving the statement."

"Don't tell me that," Marlene says.

"Okay."

"Has everyone lost his fucking mind here?"

Michael shrugs.

"Look, Marlene," Diaz says, stepping in. "It's going to happen. Momentarily. That much is certain, for better or worse. Now, with all due respect, if you're not going to be supportive, you probably should leave."

Marlene stares up at him. The sight engenders in Michael a sudden fondness for Harold Diaz. At the same time, though, he finds that he would prefer a scenario in which Marlene is set loose upon the room and stops this mess in its tracks so everyone can just leave. That, actually, is much more appealing to Michael.

But Marlene drops her eyes. "It's your funerals," she says, and heads off to find a chair. From the side, Dennis approaches the podium, calling Michael over with a flick of his head.

Michael can sense the voices around him diminish; he can sense the members of the media take notice, understands that they are focusing their cameras, hitting the record buttons on their tape machines. He follows Dennis to the podium and stands behind his left shoulder. He watches as Dennis carefully places the thin stack of pages onto the podium's slanted surface; the microphone, active and sensitive, picks up the papers' rustling and broadcasts it across the auditorium. Dennis reaches inside his jacket and takes out his reading glasses. With one hand he shakes them open and slides them onto his nose. Finally, he looks over the top of them at the audience. The cameras are poised, pointed.

"Thank you for coming," he says. "We apologize for the late start, but we had some last-minute details we wanted to work out so we'd be able to give you the most up-to-date informa-tion possible." He glances down at the papers in front of him, touches their upper right corner, looks back up. "Newton Sarver, the president of Power Generation Division, sends his regrets. He was called away by a customer this morning and is unable to be here. My name is Dennis Tussy. I'm Vice President of Public Re-lations, and the announcement I have today is a difficult one to have to deliver, but one that we at Electro-Lite believe will make us a much stronger organization and ultimately will enable us to continue operating as a significant performer in the Western Pennsylvania business economy. We also hope to maintain much of our Pittsburgh presence." Then he pauses, looks back down at the sheets of paper—the same ones that scrolled out of Michael's printer—takes a breath that travels through the wires and spills out of the speakers, and begins reading.

Michael isn't listening. He's watching one reporter—a woman, thirty-two, thirty-three maybe, with short brown hair and a young boy's face that is not at all masculine-looking but, in fact, quite sweet. She is scribbling in her notebook at a frantic rate, trying to keep up with Dennis. Every few seconds her eyes shift upward to the podium, then back to her pad. She flips a page overtop of the spirals, folds it back, keeps writing. She just wants to get the facts of this story and get out of here so she can write the thing up and move on to her next assignment. She does enough of these and maybe she'll get a better beat, one people are interested in. Michael does not fault her for this. She's not laying off eleven thousand people. It's merely her job to report that Electro-Lite is. If she does it poorly, or doesn't do it at all, then she's out of a job. Everyone's cutting back nowadays, after all; there's no secret about that. Her story will come as no surprise to anyone.

The woman stops writing and looks up. Now that Michael has a chance to get a good look at her face, he notices that she actually is very pretty in a tom-boyish but still delicate way. He also notices that the reason she has stopped writing is because Dennis has stopped talking.

"Are there any questions?" he says.

Michael isn't sure what he expects. An all-out assault maybe? Questions and accusations flying from every angle? What happens, though, is nothing. No hands go up; no voices jockey for position to be heard. Nothing. A couple of reporters look at each other. One leaves, slinking out the rear entrance of the auditorium as if trying to go unnoticed. Suddenly, Michael wonders if he could possibly be this far off, if the elimination of eleven thousand jobs is not even a significant event anymore. Are we that familiar with such things? Then, as Marlene, who has been sitting in the front row, stands to leave, too, the short-haired reporter Michael has been watching pipes up and says, "Could you provide us with any particular events that led to this action?"

Movement around the room slows. Marlene sits. Michael believes he can read everyone's mind: Well, we might as well hear the answer.

Dennis touches his tie, as if making sure it is still there. "What sort of events?" he says. "Could you be a little more specific?"

"Anything," the woman says, shrugging, notepad held in front of her in both hands. "Any event or occurrences that helped form your rationale for firing eleven thousand people. Were there any events that led to it?" She pauses, then adds, "Or just the usual?"

Dennis clears his throat. He takes the pages before him in his hands and taps the bottom edge of the stack as if evening it out, for some reason. "Um," he says, and stops.

"I'll take it, Dennis." Michael steps forward. "I think I know what she's getting at."

Dennis slides one step to his right.

Michael looks out over the auditorium. He sees Marlene, an

amazed expression on her face. The other faces in the room have the unmistakable appearance of having nothing better to do but see what happens. "Ma'am," he says. "I'm Michael Dunne."

She nods, and when Michael does not continue, says, "Patricia Cross. *Tribune-Review.*"

"Hi," Michael says. "What you're asking, I'm sure you realize, is more complicated than it might appear. You're aware of that, right?"

After a moment, the woman nods self-consciously, a single, flinching movement.

"I thought as much. Nonetheless, I think the kind of thing you're looking for is this: Our division—Power Generation—is in all probability going to miss its objective—I'm talking sales, revenue, the whole ball of wax here—by more than fifty million dollars."

"Jesus," someone says from behind Michael. The tone is not one of interest or even surprise; it is one of sudden horror.

"You see, Ms. Cross," Michael says, "the market is not exactly what you'd call ideal these days for building power plants and, unfortunately, we're making it even harder on ourselves. For example—" Michael's initial fear is gone now, he's just talking to this person—"the work our service people did at a plant for Georgia Power Company was so... inadequate, that the utility told us to leave in the middle of the job. GE finished it. We lost about five million on that job." Michael turns to the side and scans his co-workers. "Is that figure accurate, Mort?" he asks the controller. "Check me if I'm wrong on that."

Morton is stark white. He notices his mouth is open, closes it, nods and shrugs at the same time.

"It's close anyway," Michael says, turning his attention back to the reporter. "The long and short of it is, we miscalculated. There are many reasons for it, but the true disappointment is that we chose not to accept that fact until now, which of course is too late. Are there any other questions?"

"I'll take it from here, Mike," Dennis says, sliding back behind the podium. He actually puts his body between Michael and the microphone, instead of letting Michael step away first.

"Sure," Michael says, stepping back. He glances down at Marlene, who is anxiously picking the lipstick off of her lips. Off to the left, someone (Diaz?) stifles a laugh.

"Thank you for coming," Dennis tells the crowd. "Good afternoon."

"Mr. Dunne," someone calls out, a narrow-faced man in jeans and a blazer, standing next to a camera, "why wasn't this information included in today's press package?"

"Because it's not confirmed," Dennis says curtly. "It's unofficial information and not for publication."

"But," the man says, "it's on tape. It's on video. Confirmed or not."

"Well," Dennis says, "it's unofficial."

Soon the journalists begin filing out of the auditorium. Michael is back against the marker board again; he's staring across the room at Patricia Cross, whose back is to him; she's hunched over her notebook, jotting down some last-minute thoughts. If nothing else, Michael hopes she gets a good story out of this, something that'll help her.

More huddles form. This time, though, Michael is involved. He's involved to the extent that he's the topic of discussion.

Patricia Cross is the last of the reporters to leave. By the time she heads for the rear double doors Michael can hear the hum of the heating ducts above the hushed voices around him. Then he heads for the exit himself, falls in several paces behind Patricia Cross, who has not so much as looked in his direction since he left the podium. A second later she is gone, leaving this mess for good, except, Michael suspects, for the brief time it takes her to write the story. This story. The door eases closed behind her.

"Michael...Michael," a voice—it is Dennis's—calls from behind him. But Michael keeps going.

* * *

By four, word is out. Newton Sarver is in the hospital—that much is apparent—but why and how he got there is a question for debate throughout the Electro-Lite hallways. Rumored ailments range from a massive heart attack to kidney stones to a nervous breakdown. Also up for discussion is what to do about the situation. Two factions have developed, so far as Toby can tell from his post behind the front desk: those who believe the proper course of action is to stay put, affix a stoic expression, and carry on into the early evening or however long it takes to put forth the appearance of dedication in the face of adversity; and those who figure, to hell with it, what's done is done, let's go home.

Officially, none of this really matters to Toby. He's on the clock until four-thirty, regardless. Personally, though, if he had a choice, he would prefer to wait and see if another report on Sarver's condition comes in before he leaves for the day. Over the years Toby has developed a genuine fondness for Newton Sarver that goes beyond the requisite respect he's had for past division presidents. Perhaps it has something to do with Sarver's personal stamp of approval for Toby's flags, but Toby chooses to believe he would have recognized Sarver's work ethic, his compassion and interest in others, whether or not the man blessed the flags. Sarver worked his way up from a staff engineer to become the leader of a billion-dollar entity. His taking notice of a couple of flags is entirely beside the point.

Of course Toby knows there will be no call from the hospital, or from anyone for that matter, updating his boss' condition. Had it not been for the press conference, there would have been no phone call at all. The word Toby received at around two-thirty was from a nurse at Mercy who said Mr. Sarver had been brought in with a "medical condition" and he had insisted on someone calling in to say he was "indisposed" before he would permit anyone to treat him. How all these other people found out about it, Toby has no idea. The only person he told—appropriately, he thought and still believes—was Iris, Mr. Sarver's secretary.

Toby sits in his chair, watches as the people pass by outside on the sidewalk. It looks like rain again, but that could be just an illusion of the slightly tinted front glass.

He is not a fan of illusions. Perhaps that's why, as he stood in front of the auditorium's rear door, watching Michael Dunne deliver that statement of blatant, long-awaited actuality to the press, an undeniable sense of... satisfaction—or simple ease maybe—quietly but surely ignited somewhere in the depths of his blue and gold Electro-Lite soul. This company has been good to him, he knows, for thirty years, and he is grateful. He is paid well; he is trusted with significant responsibility. He's always been proud to tell people where he works. But in the past couple of years, things just haven't been the same. An atmosphere of what Toby can only describe as overwhelming self-centeredness has permeated the place that, to Toby's mind at least, is discouraging. Maybe it's always been here, he thinks, but was undetectable because the company was making money. Now, as Toby has suspected—though he had no idea it was this bad—it is not. Not enough anyway, and Michael Dunne's statement seemed to add a degree of perspective to that fact.

But it doesn't really help. Toby understood, even at the time, that he was the only person in that auditorium who was experiencing that surge of vague satisfaction. What remained after Michael Dunne walked past Toby, ignoring the calls for him to return, and continued on through the security gate, dutifully dropping his temporary ID badge into the return box, before getting on the parking garage elevator and disappearing, was hysteria. That's how Toby chooses to classify it now: hysteria. Marlene Stringer was the most adamant—not in putting forth a solution, Toby noted, but in continually restating the problem. She took her shoes off and for the five or so minutes Toby stood watching, stalked the front section of the room, approaching clusters of suited men, making sure each knew what was at stake, hands waving in ambiguous demonstration.

"Every customer'll be calling tomorrow," she said to Dennis Tussy. "You know that, don't you? There's no question there. I hope you have something brilliant planned to say to them. I hope everyone in the goddamn company has something brilliant planned, because the calls are going to be coming from everywhere and to everyone. Christ, this is going to cost us." Then, as if for good measure, she added, "And Sarver—God, he's an ass."

That's when Toby slipped out.

Now it's raining—something Toby is now sure of; he can hear it, spattering on the pavement and sizzling under the tires of passing cars. For a moment so brief it has no discernible beginning or end, Toby thinks of his daughter. She works in New York—a lawyer whose specialty seems to change every few months—and he sees her and his son-in-law maybe once or twice a year, at least each Christmas, an occasion that for eleven thousand people around here will be miserable. His daughter's job is secure, he knows that, but every so often a panicked thought of her passes through his mind; then he reassures himself, and it drifts away.

So Toby shifts his thoughts to Michael Dunne, tries to picture the young man behind the wheel of his car, cruising in the left lane of the Parkway toward Squirrel Hill or Shadyside or whatever trendy, yuppie neighborhood he lives in. What's going through his mind right now? Is anything going through his mind? Or is he just sort of dazed, taken over by the steady rhythm of the windshield wipers, jarred conscious only by the sudden darkness and morbid rushing hum when he enters the Squirrel Hill Tunnels? Toby can see Michael's face as he suddenly senses that change in atmosphere. There is recognition in his wide, brown, shadow-hidden eyes as he exits his rain- and travel-induced meditation and remembers with dread what has just happened, back at the office, in the auditorium. The words form in front of him, as if emerging from the yellow guide-lights along the tunnel's inner walls: What have I done?

Toby shudders. He smooths down the hair around his ears with his fingertips, clears his throat. Kevin Lennon, a wheelchair-bound mechanical engineer, scoots by behind the guard desk, lifting an eyebrow to Toby in greeting. Toby smiles, watches him glide past. For the first time, Toby views the man as broken. Beyond repair.

Underneath the rear credenza there is a camera, a Nikon 35-millimeter with manual focus that Toby bought for himself when he was promoted from head of security at Power Gen's Turtle Creek plant to the downtown headquarters office. He reaches down and takes the camera in his hands. He's always liked the way it felt: solid, a piece of equipment. It may not be a steam generator or reactor vessel or whatever else the people around here design and build, but it's something. It's his. And the pictures he takes with it are his own creation. He especially likes the clicking sound of the shutter and the calculated whine of the film advancing; and now, for some reason he's not quite sure of, he feels like he should document the events happening here today, happening now.

Ben is not around. Probably he's down in the fitness center, Toby figures, chatting it up with the two girls who run the place. That's okay, though. Ben's young. He lacks perspective. He's never known the good days. Just layoffs and net losses and lawsuits. He doesn't know the way things could be, and that's not his fault.

A group of four people—three men and a woman—approaches from the east wing, talking in loud but muted whispers. They stop at the ATM machine and the three men wait as the woman inserts her card and begins pressing buttons. They're still talking. Toby raises his camera. He focuses in on the woman at the money machine; the men are in the shot, too, in the foreground, though not in focus. At one point, while waiting for her cash to be dispensed, the woman, who Toby recognizes but does not know personally, turns and says something to the group. She rolls her eyes exaggeratedly behind tiny, round, very smart-looking glasses.

Then Toby hears someone say his name.

Dennis Tussy slides his ID badge through the sensor. Toby lowers his camera. "Sorry, Mr. Tussy. I didn't catch that."

Dennis smiles offhandedly, clips his badge onto his brief case. His coat is freshly dry cleaned, his mustache recently and precisely groomed. "That's all right, Toby," he says. "I just asked if you had any big plans for the holiday." He takes a couple of steps toward the garage elevators, then turns back, in case a reply is offered.

Toby takes a breath. "You bet," he says. "Going to my daughter's in New York."

Dennis nods, but his heart's obviously not in this, which makes Toby wonder why he asked the question in the first place, then repeated it. Camouflage, maybe; a facade. "New York at Thanksgiving," he says. "Should be beautiful. Lucky you."

"Yeah," Toby says. "Lucky me."

"All right," Dennis says, then, apparently coming up with nothing to follow that, turns and heads off. When Toby looks back over at the ATM machine, he finds that the people—his subjects—are gone.

A minute later, though, a man—not an employee—sporting what is very close to a traditional crewcut appears from the elevator corridor and approaches the guard station. He drops his visitor badge into the slot, signs out in the register, tucks his plaid scarf down into the front of his overcoat, and heads off across the marbled lobby, shoes clicking, echoing. When he reaches the revolving door and places his hand on the wide metal rail, the man pauses. He looks through the glass, considering the rain for a moment. Then, his hand still on the rail, he glances back inside. Toby snaps his picture.

The rain has taken the form of a mist that doesn't fall but hangs suspended in the air by the time Toby leaves for the day. Although his car is parked in the lower level garage he chooses to leave through the front door. He wants to stop at B&D's for a cup of coffee and a biscotti before he heads home, maybe read some of the paper he didn't have a chance to get to today. And he wants to check on Francis.

Traffic is a mess. It always is when the weather turns a little bad. Toby doesn't bother crossing Seventh Avenue at the crosswalk, as traffic is stopped in both directions and poses no danger. Even when the light at Stanwix changes to green, nothing moves. Toby tries to notice the faces of the people on the other side of the windshields, read something in them, as he passes by each front bumper, but there is nothing. One woman in a red blouse absently touches the corner of her mouth, adjusting her even redder lipstick, even though the day is over. A man sings along with his radio, face locked in an expression of legitimate anguish. When he reaches the other side of Seventh, Toby is confronted by a thick-browed man in a grey sweatshirt and sweat pants who wants to sell Toby a miniature reproduction of the Duquesne Incline made out of birdseed. The man has the odd creations set up on a folding card table outside of Woolworth's—along with other models representing the Civic Arena, the Cathedral of Learning, and, most absurd of all to Toby, Steelers coach Bill Cowher.

"They make a great Thanksgiving centerpiece," the man says.

Toby picks up the Cathedral of Learning.

"Whoa, dude!" the man says and, reaching across the table, removes it, gently, from Toby's gloved hand. "These ain't no toys. You don't just go scooping them up like there's nothing to it."

"Why not?" Toby has, completely unintentionally, become interested in how this guy, or whoever made these things, got each tiny kernel of birdseed glued together with such intricacy. And why? And wouldn't the misty rain have a more harmful effect on them than Toby simply touching them?

"Because," the man says, replacing the Cathedral on the card table. "These are delicate works of art, Jack. They'll break. And you don't just whip up another. That ain't the way it works."

"Why would I want something on my Thanksgiving table that could break so easily? And what about the rain?"

The man stares back at Toby. His heavy forehead twitches.

"How much?" Toby asks.

"Twelve," the man says. "Fifteen for the coach. That took some doing. Look at the jaw."

Toby nods. "Pick it up again," he says.

"What?"

"The Cathedral of Learning. Pick it up again. I want to see something."

The man squints at Toby for a moment, then does what he's told. He picks up his birdseed edifice and holds it up by his chest, a quizzical expression on his face.

Toby pulls his camera from the deep right pocket of his overcoat and, before the man can react, quickly focuses and takes his picture.

"Hey," the man says.

"You have a permit to sell your wares here, I assume," Toby says.

"Huh? Hey, what is this?" The man is still holding the Cathedral of Learning, eyes and forehead now a mass of confusion. "Who are you, dude?"

"Security," Toby says, dropping the camera back into his pocket. He knows this is what people dislike about him, what they snicker and laugh at behind his back, but sometimes he can't help himself. And besides, this time he has an objective. Francis once told him that he avoids areas where there are street vendors because they annoy people, irritate them, and make them even less likely to drop a couple of bucks on a homeless guy. That's why Francis isn't around, he figures. He's been forced a block or two over, off Seventh, to an area with less foot traffic and less awning coverage from the rain. These things are important to Francis. Francis is a terrible homeless person. He has trouble adjusting to his surroundings, a skill Toby believes is essential if you have no home. Then Toby wonders if Francis found a way to call his wife, like he told him to. Most likely not—again, the rain. It throws off Francis's whole equilibrium or something. He simply can't function in it. "I'm just making sure you're properly permitted to do business here," Toby adds.

Finally, the man sets the Cathedral back down on the table with the rest of the objects. His mind is racing, trying to come up with a response that will be accepted, yet impossible to confirm or deny. "All right," the man says. "Beat it now. You're scaring off my customers."

Toby reaches inside his coat and removes a tiny, spiral-bound notebook. He pulls his gloves off with his teeth, then stuffs them both into his pocket. "Could I have your name, please."

"Sure," the man says. "Butch. Butch Butchson." He pauses then adds, "Butch B. Butchson. The Third."

Now he's being played with, ridiculed, and Toby recognizes it at once. But what can he do? He chose to take things this far. It was his decision. He could have said no thank you to the birdseed Cathedral and left. But he didn't. How else could this end, really? Toby senses the man across from him smiling as he writes down the name he's been given. For good measure, he writes "birdseed" next to the name. "Mr. Butchson," he says. "I'm going to check this out. If you do not have a permit, I suggest you vacate the premises and refrain from this activity until such time as you do obtain one. Do you understand?"

"Ten-four," the man says. "Roger-Wilco."

Toby flips the notebook closed and replaces it inside his coat. "Good." He turns to go.

"Copy that," the man says. "Over and out."

Toby does not turn back around; he keeps going. B&D's is only two doors down, but it seems to take forever to get there. As he reaches for the handle (the hand poking out of his overcoat is white—shriveled from the cold rain—and it's shaking) he hears the sweat-suited man's voice calling out to whoever will listen: "Great Thanksgiving centerpiece idea!"

Inside B&D's it is warm, but it is a muggy warmth. Steam from the ovens hangs in the air and the smells of coffee and baking bread lend to it an added, potent element of saturation. But this is all right with Toby. The atmosphere is familiar. He gets in line behind a young woman carrying two paper shopping bags with handles. She is well-dressed, well-groomed, in a beige, thigh-length wool coat and pretty matching mittens. She stands up straight, perfect posture, with her feet together. Her thick, blond hair brushes the shoulders of her coat. She is about his daughter's age.

Toby checks the chalkboard menu above the white-aproned woman taking orders at the counter. He realizes he is not hungry, and he has drunk more than enough coffee for one day. Still, though, he stays in line. What he wants is not written up there. What he wants is what he once had, what he now—for the first time, though he's seen it coming for a while—understands no longer is obtainable. He wants the past. All of it. He wants his wife back, alive and well and free from pain. He wants his daughter back in Pittsburgh—not the way she is now, married and motivated and successful—but five years old, with her dirty face and rounded belly and frilly pink socks. He wants something to work toward, to hope for—something out there in his future, beckoning to him. His life within the confines of Electro-Lite's walls seems to him the only constant aspect he has known for some time. And now that's gone, what he knows of it anyway. Regardless of whether or not he is affected by these upcoming layoffs and changes, things will be wholly and tangibly different. Attitudes—what Toby remembers once being called "vibes"—will never be the same. He's not sure why that should matter—many will lose much more—but it does. It is everything, or very nearly everything, to him now.

He thinks: I am fifty-four years old.

When the young woman in front of him reaches the counter Toby figures he better go ahead and order something. No use getting out of line now; he's waited this long. He'll get a couple of muffins. If he should happen to see Francis before he gets to his car, he'll give them to him; if not, he'll just take them home.

The woman orders a cappuccino. She wants it in one of B&D's plastic travel mugs, which costs an additional four-ninety-nine. It's reusable, though, and handy, so Toby does not view the purchase to be as lavish as he might. As her cappuccino is being prepared, the young woman takes off her mittens. Toby spots an engagement ring on her left hand. It flashes every now and then as she digs into her purse, searching for something, shopping bags flapping all around her. There is no wedding ring, so far as Toby has seen, just the solitaire—a big one. She keeps digging and digging. Her hair has fallen down over her face and she is getting frustrated, expelling short bursts of moaning breath. When her cappuccino is placed in front of her, Toby takes a step forward. "Let me get that for you, miss," he says, and reaches into his pocket.

She freezes, looks up at him. Crazy strands of blond hair are pulled across her face and her hands are buried in her purse to mid-forearm. One shopping bag hangs from the point at which her wrist enters the purse, the other dangles from the crook in her elbow.

"I can..." she begins. "I mean, I know my wallet's in here somewhere."

"It's okay," Toby says. "I'll get it for you. I'm happy to. You hold on to your money." He smiles. "You never know when you might need it."

The young woman relaxes. "Thank you. That's very sweet." She shakes the stray hair away from her face and rearranges the packages in her hands. Just like that she has put herself back together again. Toby pays the aproned woman behind the counter and orders his muffins (two blueberry, two cornbread, two bran). The young woman, after a moment's hesitation, takes both packages in her left hand and picks the B&D's travel mug up in her right. "Thanks again," she says. "I'm a little embarrassed."

"Oh, don't be silly," Toby says. "It was nothing. And besides, it looks like you've had a busy day."

They both glance down at the packages in her hand.

"Yeah," she says. "Well..."

Toby's bag of muffins is placed in front of him. Again he reaches into his pocket.

"I really appreciate this," the young woman says, turning. "Really."

"Don't mention it," Toby says.

She wants to leave, Toby can tell, but she feels as though she should say something else, show just a little more gratitude. But Toby wishes she'd just go. He doesn't want to be the source of some sort of ethical dilemma to her.

"It's all right, sweetheart," he says, and winks—as fatherly a gesture as he can remember. She smiles at him—not a broad, teeth-baring, mechanical smile, just a little one that serves simply to convey the mutual understanding Toby was hoping for. She heads off quickly then, bags rustling, and as Toby hands more money across the counter he realizes—since the rain has picked up again and leaving B&D's now seems foolish—that he might in fact be hungry for a muffin or two after all.

SHOPPING DAYS TO XMAS: 28

At the bottom of Natalie Dunne's underwear drawer there is a book, *What to Expect When You're Expecting, Fourth Edition*, the simple existence of which embarrasses her. She takes it out now, as she often does, and, standing in the middle of their bedroom, empty suitcase lying open on the bed, flips through the pages with her thumb, like a child watching the pictures move, playing out some scene. Again, as always, she considers throwing the book away. It is contraband material, in their apartment under false pretenses. She is not expecting, after all, at least so far as she knows. That's one thing. Another is that she's been off the pill now for more than four months, nearly five, without Michael's knowledge. Every time this notion forms in her mind she feels like a thief. There is no reason, she knows, for her to be so deceitful, other than the way Michael's jaw clenches and bulges out at the point where it connects below his ears, and his eyes do that awful shifting thing, every time she raises the issue. It hurts her when she sees that. But it's nothing compared to what he'd feel if she—as she now suspects—has succeed in getting pregnant this way, as she originally intended.

Natalie puts the book back in the drawer, covers it with underwear and pantyhose. She should throw it away—she should. Reading it gives her no pleasure. She has to sneak small bits of it, like a drug addict, when Michael is out of the apartment. She often cries while reading it, though she doesn't know why.

But, no, she can't throw it away. Even knowing the risks, the consequences, she can't throw it away. And every day it becomes that much more difficult to bring the subject up to Michael, to confess, as she still plans to do. It is especially difficult now, given Michael's situation at work. She's never seen him so upset as Monday afternoon, when he came into the apartment, soaking wet, overcoat unbuttoned and hanging from his shoulders. At first she thought he'd been mugged. She remembers how she immediately wondered about his eyes. They were wide and crazy-looking, the eyes of panic. Yet, at the same time, he looked so sleepy. She's never seen that in him before. He sat on the sofa, still in his dripping overcoat, elbows on his knees, rocking forward and back. He was sure he was going to be fired, and this thought terrified him. But he also spoke of quitting. His job was beginning to cause him to hate himself, he said. He couldn't live like that. It wasn't worth it.

How could she possibly tell him now? What, exactly, would she say?

When they moved to Pittsburgh she thought it was the perfect time to start a family. Getting her own interior design company up and running would take time, she knew that, but Michael's promotion took the pressure off. They had a lot of bills, but they'd work all that out. People with bills have babies, too. They'd be fine. And her parents were in nearby Ligonier, which was important to her. She did not want to deny her parents easy access to their first grandchild. Everything seemed perfect to Natalie, except for her husband's poorly veiled reluctance. We owe too much money, he was fond of saying. Don't you want to get your own career going first? You know, if there's a kid, there's no more you and me. Ever. No more weekend jaunts to Atlantic City. And so on. But she'd considered all this and hoped that the simple fact that she felt ready to have a child would be enough for him. And, to be fair, he finally did agree. "If that's what you want," he said.

She didn't think she'd go through with it. One morning she didn't take her pill and all day long she kept expecting herself to take it, but then the day was over and she went to bed and she never took it. Even as she lay there, looking up at the gray, shadowed ceiling, listening to Michael breathe next to her, she expected herself to get out of bed, go to the bathroom and take her pill. That's all it would take. But then it was the next morning, and then a week later, and by that time it seemed pointless. She threw the pills in the trash.

What bothers her most is how this has become such a

struggle. Having a baby should be the next natural step, a sign of healthy progression in their marriage. Something they both want. She and Michael are not a couple in trouble, by any stretch. From their relationship—the way it is now—she could want nothing more. He is considerate and affectionate and he thinks of her, goes out of his way for her. They are friends. They never have arrangements where "private time" apart from the other is set aside, as is the case with other couples they know. Not because one can't function without the other—it's not puppy love, as it may once have been—but a simple acknowledgment that each feels comfortable in the other's company. Simple. If Michael wants to go out one night with Alex, he goes. And she does the same with her tiny circle of girlfriends. But neither searches for such opportunities; there is no pre-established "guy's night" or any such thing. When she goes out with the small group of women she knows from the building or the gym, each of whom are either newly married, like her, or ensconced in some level of a relationship, she always finds herself out of place in conversations where the others express a communal sense of exhilaration in spending time away from their respective partners. They look forward to these nights, consider them a necessary element of keeping their relationship intact. Without them, who knows? Natalie listens, even laughs along, but what she really appreciates—when she's dropped off in front of their apartment building at the end of the night—is looking up at their third floor window and seeing the lights on, knowing that he is home and still awake.

So why is this baby thing so difficult?

She's not sure she could explain it to someone if she were asked, but the simple truth is although she certainly feels comfortable with Michael, she is not content.

Michael is in the living room now, sleeping. Ever since Monday he's been sleeping a lot. Natalie moves away from the dresser and walks to the closet, distracted, head cocked slightly, trying to listen through the fuzzy television noise for any signs of life emanating from the living room. It's not as if there's anything to worry about, she knows; but, still, she doesn't like all this sleeping. She believes there's a sign buried in it somewhere, a piece of evidence she's supposed to recognize and address. Where the hell are her instincts?

The rain picks up again, slapping against the pavement three floors below in steady palpitations. Natalie takes two sweaters from the closet and carries them to the bed. She places them flat in the suitcase, folds the sleeves across the chest as if positioning a corpse in a coffin. She tries to remember the last time, if ever, the thought of Thanksgiving triggered in her a sense of dread, as it does now. It's always been her favorite holiday, hands down. This time of year the air around her parents' house in Ligonier takes on the crisp, dry smell of transition. Leaves that have spent the past two months dying and falling get picked up in the wind and kicked around, everything shifting, changing. She's never hated the onset of winter, as most Western Pennsylvanians do. The smell and feel of the year's first fire in the fireplace is something to behold.

She remembers her and Michael's first Thanksgiving together at her parents' house. It also happened to be the first one after her grandfather had died and she remembers how her grandmother, from the moment she walked in the door, looked lost, confused, unsure of where to stand or how to sit or where to put her purse for safe keeping, as if she'd never seen these people—her sons and daughters, grandchildren, nieces and nephews—before and had simply been dropped on the doorstep against her will and left to fend for herself.

Michael quickly fell in with her two brothers and uncles in the family room—watching football, pouring drinks for everyone, keeping the fire going. Natalie hardly saw him and she took that to be a good sign. In the kitchen, she continually asked if she could help but was told no, to relax, and so that's what she did. She pulled herself up onto the counter top and sat, feet dangling, with a glass of wine, watching her mother and aunts assemble the meal like a corps of well-trained engineers, exhibiting much more skill and dexterity than could possibly have been taking place in that football game down the hall. The sight of it all made her feel safe, cared for. Natalie herself was no cook, nor did she care to be. She and Michael ate pasta mostly, or sometimes one of them would stir-fry up some veggies. Or they ate out. She had no desire, then, to hone her domestic skills. She was going to be an interior designer, a businesswoman, an entrepreneur. Yet on that Thanksgiving day—that one in particular—she couldn't help but feel a certain sense of admiration for these women, an acknowledgment of...what? Their worth? Certainly not. What even gives her the right to think such a thing? she finds herself wondering now. After all, she isn't an interior designer, she isn't an entrepreneur. She's...What is she? Natalie sits on the bed, cranes her neck to see out the window that overlooks Belefonte Avenue. She can't see the street itself, though. She's too low. All she can see is the red and black brick of the building across the way, and fallen leaves from the maples growing of the sidewalk blowing upward against the force of rain.

She's gone and upset herself again. Lately she's finding that she needs no outside influences to bring her down. She's capable of accomplishing that task all on her own. She finds that, yes, she admires her mother and aunts for preparing Thanksgiving dinner. Is that wrong? Is there some degree of arrogance involved in her consciously feeling that she needs to decree her admiration for such a thing? What does that say about a woman who at the same time is trying to get pregnant behind her husband's back? She lies back on the bed and listens for Michael's breathing. She's gotten to the point, over these long, exasperating two and a half days, of being able to sift out the TV sounds, the hum of the refrigerator, the traffic from outside, the rain, and hear only Michael's strained, throaty, anxious breaths. That's it, she decides suddenly. This weekend she'll tell him. She'll tell him what she's been doing with the birth control pills.

The decision calms her. She closes her eyes and listens for ten, fifteen seconds, placing the show on television as a *Seinfeld* rerun, and soon, before she has a chance to filter through the murk and detect her husband's breathing, she drifts off to sleep herself as well.

Michael is dreaming. It's the same dream he's had every time he's fallen asleep for the past three days, with one minor variation. True to form, in this case, his teeth feel soft and awkward in his mouth. Annoying. Unnatural. He can't help running his tongue along them, especially the top incisors, can't help pushing against the sharp tips. They feel too big, too jagged for his mouth. The rest of his body has no physical bearing. There is no scene to this dream, no location, just big, awkward, annoying teeth—especially those jagged incisors—that he can't help touching with his tongue. In this dream, he becomes more and more agitated, pushing harder and harder at the incisors with his tongue. Soon he finds himself biting at them with his bottom teeth, orchestrating a weird underbite with his jaw and effectively ripping at those hellish top incisors until, inevitably, one works itself loose. And then, usually, he stops, waking up soon afterward to learn, thankfully, that his teeth, though experiencing a strange tingling near the roots, are all firmly planted and accounted for.

Today, though, he does not wake up. When one of the incisors snaps loose, he finds that his tongue continues to prod at it, pushing outward until the roots strain and weaken. Rotating the now-hanging tooth in tiny circles with his tongue, Michael is frustrated by the conscious, bone-on-bone sensation he feels as the loose tooth comes in contact with those around it. He pushes out his bottom jaw and bites upward, hard, and the incisor—expelling a horrific crunching sound—pops out completely. At this Michael feels a sudden burst of panic (Oh my God, I tore my tooth out!) but that is soon replaced by idle curiosity. He spends some time examining the vacated space with his tongue and finds that it does not take long for a wave of relief to wash over him. He likes not having that damned jagged incisor. It's comfortable. But the hole left there feels as though it extends all the way into his head. To attain true comfort, he'll have to get rid of all his teeth.

He's just about ready to get started on this project—beginning with the other top incisor, of course—when he feels a sudden pressure in his lower extremities. What startles him initially is the fact that he even has a lower extremity in this dream. Until now, he's only been aware of his head, and even that in a vague, assuming sort of way. The pressure keeps on—harder and more insistent now, coming in quick, pulsating bursts. Michael opens his eyes, seeing only white. The whiteness comes together in the form of his living room ceiling. Outside it is raining steadily, one of the incessant downpours to which Pittsburghers are becoming accustomed. Again the pressure. Michael looks down the length of his body to find Dewey, their eight-hundred-dollar Shetland sheepdog, with his front paws up on the sofa and his snout buried in Michael's crotch. This is one of Dewey's favorite activities—inserting his snout in an unsuspecting groin and pushing. Though harmless, it can come as quite a shock to first-time visitors to Michael's and Natalie's apartment.

Dewey pushes again, eyes closed, paws braced against the sofa's cushions. Having just awoke, Michael finds that his groin is less sensitive to Dewey's efforts than usual, which affords him the opportunity to pause and consider the intricacies of his dog's objective. "What are you doing?" he asks Dewey, whose ears perk up though his snout stays buried. He's still driving hard. "Hey, I'm talking to you." Finally, Dewey stops pushing and raises his head. "What?" he seems to say. Then he lowers his head again, getting back into position; but Michael sits up, swings his legs over Dewey and drops his feet to the floor. Dewey watches critically, trying to devise a plan that would enable him to maneuver back in between those same legs. For purposes of distraction, Michael reaches down and scratches underneath Dewey's chin, the only thing this expensive, store-bought dog enjoys more than crotch-driving, though that's a tough call.

Soon Michael, still sitting up, begins to feel himself drift off to sleep again. He has no idea what time it is. It's growing dark outside, dark shadows traverse the living room, but that might just be a result of the weather. Before he has a chance to fully drift off, though, the phone rings. Michael listens to one ring, then two, coming at him from the kitchen and bedroom, as if in stereo. He expects Natalie, who's actually in the bedroom, packing for their weekend at her parents', to pick up, but the phone rings a third and fourth time and then the answering machine clicks on. Michael hears his wife's detached voice float in from the kitchen, telling whomever that "we" are not in right now. Michael stays seated, tongue curiously probing his incisors, and picks up the pace on his scratching, causing Dewey to tilt his head so far back that the dog has to catch his balance to keep from toppling over backwards. At the tone, Alex's voice: "Dunne, pick up, man." A significant pause—more than enough time for Michael to get to the phone. "Dickhead, you there? Pick up." Another pause, shorter this time. "Listen, I'm at Doc's. Meet me. I'll be here till, fuck, I don't know, forever maybe."

When the machine clicks off, Michael listens hard for signs of life coming from the bedroom, but all he can make out is the rain, apparently coming down sideways now, vigorously rattling the Belafonte Street window.

Shadyside, Michael has heard people say, has become an oxymoron in and of itself, and Michael can see where this inference comes from. The stately urban neighborhood comes complete with oak- and maple-lined streets, severely overpriced Victorian homes, big-windowed Brownstones, trendy espresso bars and jazz clubs, designer clothing stores next door to strategically decrepit thrift shops, at least two aromatherapy salons, a half-dozen art galleries, and a doggie spa at which Dewey has twice vacationed.

And then there's Doc's Place, a bar, the unabashed subtlety

and unpretentiousness of which has made it an increasingly trendy spot as of late, as if its efforts to be decidedly un-hip have worked in reverse.

But what makes Shadyside such an oxymoron, Michael contemplates as he turns the corner onto Walnut Street, is that, despite its upscale designation making it nearly impossible to live in on less than two hundred grand a year (his and Natalie's first mistake), it's not the sort of place in which you want to be wandering after dark, which now is coming on. Sometimes Michael has noticed garbage piled high atop overflowing dumpsters in an alley between two turn-of-the-century homes beautifully landscaped with azaleas and dogwoods. There are as many stray cats wandering around town as BMWs. Last year the police began finding body parts (all of which turned out to belong to the same person) in some of those dumpsters. How do such things happen? Michael wonders. Who lets them happen?

Natalie, he knows, would just as soon move out to Monroeville or the North Hills, some suburb where the rent is cheap and the neighbors are old. She'd pack up tomorrow if he gave the word. But he likes it here. He likes the neighborhood, the central location, the fact that there are people on both sides of them as well as above and below. He likes returning home from work and having to search the street for a parking space. He likes that he can walk to Doc's.

He should have brought an umbrella, though. Now that he's on Walnut it's not so bad—he can duck periodically beneath shop awnings—but by the time he made the turn off of Belafonte, he was soaked through. But bringing an umbrella would have meant looking for one, and he didn't want to wake Natalie—who he found sleeping on top of the covers, next to their open, partially packed suitcase—with the opening and closing of many closet doors.

Doc's Place is nearly empty, as Michael could have predicted at six o'clock on a Wednesday. It will get crowded, though, soon—the night before Thanksgiving usually does. He stops in front of the big picture window that looks in at the front area of the bar. Two men are playing darts, no one is at the pinball machine. Two young women in jeans and sweaters (home from college for the long weekend, Michael assumes) mull over the selections on the new CD jukebox, holding draft beers in plastic cups. Evenly spaced around the bar—a big rectangle that takes up the center of the room, inside of which two bartenders talk casually—are a man who could easily be confused as homeless, two lawyerly looking women in dark business suits, and Alex, also in a suit.

Inside, Michael hangs his overcoat on a hook in the corner and runs a hand through his wet hair, matting it down. The two girls at the jukebox have decided on The Romantics' "What I Like About You." Pleased, they smile at each other for a moment before taking a couple of steps away and settling against the wall to nurse their beers and, Michael suspects, wait for the remainder of their group, most of whom they haven't seen since summer break, to arrive.

"So this is the beginning of forever, huh?" Michael says, sliding onto the stool next to Alex. "Looks a lot like Wednesday."

Alex turns, regards Michael as casually as if the two of them had been sitting there together for a good while. Michael recognizes Alex's tie: black and white lighthouses over a backdrop of solid sea-green. "What?" Alex says.

"On your message. You said you were going to be here forever."

Alex turns forward again, elbows on the bar, shoulders hunched; his tall, rangy body has taken on the shape of a question mark. He laughs sarcastically, mostly air. "My *message*. Fuck you. You were home."

"Yeah. But I was incapacitated. Dewey had his nose in my crotch."

"Whatever. What are you drinking?"

Michael looks down between Alex's elbows where there is a short glass of dark liquid. "What are you drinking?"

"I don't know. Jack, I think."

"Giving thanks early, are we?"

"I don't know what the hell that means." He turns toward Michael and, for the first time, examines him. "You swim here or something?"

Michael doesn't view this question as requiring an answer, so he leaves it alone. One of the bartenders, a stocky guy with an egg-shaped head who goes by the name Angel, makes his way over to them. Michael orders an IC Light and waits for the plastic cup to be set before him. Alex, who has turned forward again, doesn't move. He just keeps his gaze focused on the two square feet of bar between his elbows. Michael reaches into his pocket and drops a soggy ten next to the napkin dispenser, which Angel, heading back to where the other bartender is standing, ignores.

"Where were you this afternoon," Alex says, picking up his

glass and sloshing its contents around in little circles. He's still looking down at the bar.

"What do you mean? When?"

Alex shrugs. "Around three, I guess. I came by. No sign of you."

"Oh. I left early today. Around two or so. Doesn't everybody the day before a holiday?"

Alex nods, downs the remainder of his drink. What Alex doesn't know, but what Michael is sure his friend suspects, is that Michael showed up late and left early both Tuesday and Wednesday. There's not much for him to do at work anyway. Dennis has left him out of every meeting called over the last two days for the purpose of devising a PR strategy to combat the problem Michael created Monday afternoon. Michael knows only that Marlene Stringer, along with Dennis, was involved in those meetings and that Newton Sarver, still in the hospital following emergency surgery, was not.

Perhaps, Michael knows, he has only himself to blame for his not being invited to the meetings. After Monday's press conference, Michael drove home, got into bed, and slept until ten the next morning—nearly eighteen hours straight. By the time he made it into the office, everything was in motion. He has no idea what the status of the problem he's caused might be.

"I'm on it," Alex says suddenly. Michael figures he must have zoned out for quite some time because he notices now that Alex has a fresh glass of whiskey between his elbows.

"On it?" Michael says. "On what?"

"The list. I'm on it. I'm whacked."

For a second, Michael is confused. He honestly has no idea to what Alex could be referring. When it finally dawns on him, he is both privately embarrassed at having missed the reference and even more confused at his own ignorance, since this is what he was afraid Alex was going to tell him in the first place.

"How do you know?" Michael says.

Alex turns to him. "I saw it. Would you believe that son of a bitch Myers left it sitting out on his desk today. Right on top of everything. I go in there to see him about something—his ditzy secretary Alma's nowhere to be found, right?—so I go in to leave a note on his desk, and there it is."

Alex throws back the hefty remainder of his whiskey then cocks the glass behind his ear like he's going to throw it across the bar, but then he just sets it down and slides it away.

"Jesus," Michael says. "He wrote out a list?"

Alex doesn't answer, just motions across to Angel for another round.

"How many were on it?"

"Me and three others. Martinez, Asselstine and Cox. It was typed out. In alphabetical order." Another breathy laugh. "I'm out, man. Whacked. Fucking unemployed."

Angel refills Alex's glass, an extremely generous shot, then moves away again.

"Sounds seniority-driven," Michael says. "Pretty straightforward."

"Yeah," Alex says. "The fucker didn't even have the guts to whack the people who deserve it."

Michael doesn't know what to say. He saw this coming, had a sickening suspicion that this is what Alex wanted to talk to him about. Hell, Michael himself could be on some list somewhere, for all he knows. He doubts it, though, even after Monday's performance. Sarver has confided in the public relations staff, as recently as a week ago, that there is a strong chance that the Electro-Lite businesses will be realigned, with the Power Gen Division becoming a separate entity and run apart from the rest of the corporation. If that happens, Electro-Lite will need to kick its public relations efforts into overdrive (that's Sarver's word). Customers will have to be kept apprised of the division's game plan (another Sarver term), what to expect, what not to expect. As will shareholders, Wall Street and the public. Some PR reps may be sent off to other divisions that might be expanding. And in any case, Sarver has said he wants to work harder on the division's general perception, which isn't good. So yeah, if he chooses to believe what he's been told, Michael, most likely, will still have a job come December 31.

The problem is that now, as he sits watching Alex work on another shot of Jack Daniel's, such a scenario seems a bit, well, strange, even though Michael's seen the numbers. He already knew, for example, that four people were going to come out of the financial planning Pittsburgh office. He just didn't know who, nor did he allow himself to believe one of them could be Alex. He also knows that many more will be taken out of quality assurance and human resources and middle management across the board. The number identified for public relations is zero. Common sense, however, dictates that the first departments to take hits are those that do not contribute directly to a company's revenue, but do contribute to its overhead. And, given those parameters, public relations is just as prime a candidate as financial planning or human resources. More so, perhaps. But, then again, could a major division of a major corporation really lay off the guy who delivered the message to the press that there was going to be a layoff? What's the irony factor of such a thing?

"I can't believe he wrote out a list," Michael says again.

"Typed it out," Alex corrects. "And listen to this. I see the list sitting there, right? And, you know, I can't believe it. So I sit down in his chair for a few minutes, not really thinking anything. Then, since I'd come in there in the first place to leave him a note, I figure I'll leave him one. So I take a yellow sticky thing and write on it, 'Dave, stopped by to see you, call when you get in,' or some fucking thing like that. Then I sign it and stick it right on the list."

"You didn't."

"What do you think?"

"So then what? Did he call you? No way were you supposed to see that list. Myers must be going berserk."

"No. Haven't talked to him. I walked down to your office but you weren't there, you bastard."

"Sorry. I've found it prudent to keep a low profile these last couple of days."

"I don't blame you." Alex turns and Michael believes he sees the shadow of a smile playing across his friend's face, although it might just be the Jack making its presence known. "Listen," Alex says then, swiveling randomly back and forth on his stool now. "I've been thinking."

"Uh-oh."

"Seeing has how you're so miserable at work. And I no longer work, period. I was thinking maybe we should, you know, start up a little business of our own."

"Sure. Okay."

"I'm serious."

"You're a moron."

"But you said you were thinking of quitting. You said you didn't have the stomach for it anymore. Those were your words. Remember that?"

"I also said Natalie and I are heading straight for bankruptcy."

"All the more reason."

Michael turns away. At the jukebox he sees the two college girls again. They both have the same hairstyles—shoulder-length, sandy blond, fluffy and frayed like cotton—but one is considerably thinner than the other. It's this thin one who appears to be charged with the decision making. She inserts the dollar into the slot, presses the buttons, and it is this thinner one who takes the two empty cups to the bar for refills. The heavier one waits against the wall between the jukebox and pinball machine and a few seconds later a U2 song Michael remembers from his own college days spills from the speakers.

"What kind of business?" Michael asks. For the first time Michael looks down at his cup and finds it empty. He holds it out toward Angel, waves it around a little. "Have you even thought of that?"

"Yeah," Alex says. "I've thought of it."

"And?"

"And I haven't exactly come up with anything yet. But I'm just one person. We have to put our heads together."

"Jesus Christ, Alex. Do you—" Michael pauses to allow Angel to set another beer down on the bar and move safely out of earshot. "Do you know what goes into starting a business? *Any* kind of business? Do you know what kind of capital investment that takes? Do you have any idea how much money is required, up front, to get something like that off the ground?" He takes a drink. "Goddamn, man. You're the financial guy here. Didn't any of this occur to you?"

Immediately Michael regrets having said this. Alex has just found out he's lost his job. He's entitled to some unsubstantiated daydreaming, to reach a little, to consider all the options, even if those options aren't so realistic.

"I'm sorry, man," Michael says. He takes his hand and sets it on Alex's shoulder. Alex looks to Michael the way he must have looked in college, on the Pitt Stadium Astroturf, after pushing a potentially game-winning chip-shot field goal badly off to the right. It occurs to him that his friend is now another one of those people inside of whose head those terrible words will be constantly flashing: What am I going to do now?

Michael takes his hand away. "Look, what are you doing for the weekend?"

Alex shrugs. Michael remembers being told something about how Alex's mother was going on a cruise over Thanksgiving with her current boyfriend and, if Michael remembers correctly, Alex was in fact quite pleased with the situation, something about his not having to subject himself to the madhouse that is his revolving family's Thanksgiving.

"We're going to Nat's folks' in Ligonier. Why don't you come?"

Alex lets go a sudden monosyllabic laugh, almost as if he's choked on something. "I don't think so. It's not necessary."

"No one said it was necessary. It's just—four days. You know?"

Alex rolls his empty glass between his palms. When Michael looks up he finds that Doc's has become crowded. Someone is occupying the stool next to him and the people grouped around all four sides of the bar are two rows deep. Two steps above the sunken bar area, every table is in use. Those without seats stand off to the side watching a basketball game play silently on the big-screen.

"This isn't such a great time for me either, you know," Michael says. "We both could use a sympathetic ear."

Alex takes a breath. He's not convinced Michael's situation is as dire as his own, Michael can tell. "You sure Natalie won't mind?" he says. "Or her family?"

"I think they'll be able to deal with it."

Alex nods. "I want to drink tonight, though. You okay with that?"

Actually Michael is not okay with that. He's already sleepy again and he knows Natalie will want to leave early in the morning. Besides, it seems to Michael that Alex has been drinking, quite significantly, already tonight.

"Of course," Michael says.

Toby hasn't slept at all. As the plane begins its descent into La Guardia it occurs to him that starting this weekend off unrested could be a terrible mistake, although there's nothing much he can do about that now. He's already nervous. He only sees his daughter a couple of times a year and when you factor in the obstacle of her husband's family, who also will be there, the possibility of any significant conversation—something Toby believes is necessary though he doesn't know why—between he and Ellie becomes that much more difficult.

He never returns home from these visits feeling satisfied. This in spite of the fact that he doesn't even know what he means exactly by satisfied. All he knows is that he goes into these visits wanting to accomplish something, and when he boards the plane to return to Pittsburgh, he feels as though he's missed an opportunity, an opportunity to accomplish that something. It's a hollow feeling. His last visit, the previous Christmas, is a perfect example. They went to see Cats, which Toby thought was a bore and actually a little ridiculous, even though he understood that he was supposed to be impressed by the whole experience. Ellie, while they waited for the lights to go down, kept leaning over in her seat to say, in a confidential whisper, things like, "Broadway. Pretty nice, huh, Dad? Now you can say you've been on Broadway." But Toby didn't care one way or another about Broadway. Or the Empire State Building or Times Square. Even when Ellie and Todd brought him to Yankee Stadium two summers ago, an experience he always believed he wanted to have, something substantial was missing. Ellie wore a pretty sleeveless sundress and she and Todd kept gazing across Toby at each other, smiling, as if they'd succeeded in their top secret project and had done something wonderful, which of course, once Toby forced himself to consider it, they had. But still, it was strange. When you go to Yankee Stadium for the first time, you're supposed to remember every detail—not just the score, but the starting lineups, what every player did on each at-bat, the announcer's voice, every play made in the field, the contour of the grass, the color and texture of the dirt, the smell of the place. All Toby remembers is Ellie and Todd smiling at each other, and likening their gaze to two parents who had brought their child to Disney World.

And that's not what Toby has ever been after. Call him old-fashioned, but he'd much rather sit around Todd and Ellie's apartment all weekend, watching old movies (or even new ones), reading the newspaper, making cold cut sandwiches for lunch and eating them standing up at the kitchen counter, playing Trivial Pursuit if they felt particularly adventurous. Toby would prefer these activities not because he's getting older. Not because he's getting dull or lazy or tired. But because he wants to visit. The fact is he doesn't feel as though he knows his daughter anymore, and the whirlwind outings only further blur the lines. Ellie, Toby knows, feels like she has to prove something to her father, whatever that something might be. But the only consistent result is Toby getting back on the plane feeling as though he failed at something.

This is a Thanksgiving trip, though. Maybe it would be different.

A series of awkward, turbulence-driven bumps nearly knocks

over Toby's half-empty glass of Coke. Within seconds a flight attendant appears, removes the glass from Toby's tray, and instructs him to replace the tray and lock it into position. They're beginning their approach into New York.

Toby smiles, does as he's told. The flight attendant continues up the aisle and when she's out of earshot the man in the window seat next to Toby gives Toby him a soft elbow to the ribs and says, "I hate landings. Sometimes I freak out."

The man is mid-forties maybe, mustache, dressed in a navy blue suit and yellow paisley tie. He could be a fellow Electro-Lite employee for all Toby knows. These are the first words the man has spoken since the runway in Pittsburgh when he said, "Excuse me," while squeezing past Toby's knees to his seat.

"Freak out?" Toby says. "What do you mean?"

"I mean sometimes I lose it," the man says and gives a nervous, two-syllable laugh: heh-heh. Sweat has formed in his mustache and on his forehead and he has begun sliding his rings on and off his fingers. "I just thought I'd warn you beforehand. In case." He smiles, holds it, but his eyes are moving all around.

Toby scootches to his right, the whole inch or so he has available to him inside the armrest. "You lose it. Sir, I don't know what you're saying."

"Sometimes I vomit," the man says quickly. "Sometimes other stuff."

The plane drops jerkily for a second or two, then rights itself and continues its gradual descent. The "fasten seatbelt" sign flashes on.

"It isn't funny," the man says.

"Nobody said it was, sir." Toby removes the airsick bag from the pocket in front of his own seat. "Here. Hold onto this."

Toby wonders if he somehow asks for such inconveniences, invites them. There's no question in his mind that he's the only passenger on this sold-out flight who's seated next to someone about to suffer a nervous breakdown.

Suddenly, as if in response to Toby's consideration, the man jerks in his seat, then stiffens. "Oh, boy," he says. "Ohboyohboyo-hboy."

A cold, prickly sensation moves up the back of Toby's neck, immediately followed by pouring sweat. He looks around apologetically, hoping nobody's paying attention to what's going on in row 12, seats A and B, and, if someone is, to convey his innocence.

Again the man to Toby's left lets fly with a disturbing twitch, this time accompanied by a strange shoulder movement, almost a shimmy. "All right," the man says. "Okay, here we go. Yes, sir. Yessiree." He says these words loudly, as if about to make an announcement.

Another variation of the twitch: this time, immediately following the shudder, the man taps the side of his head against the oval window while driving his thumbs up into his armpits. "Oh, boy," he says. "Come on, now." He turns and looks directly at Toby, hugging himself. "Yes, sir," he says. "Yessiryessiryessiryessir," then knocks his head against the widow.

"Hey. Pal," Toby says. "Sir, calm down now." He takes the man by the shoulders but is unable to keep him from banging his head against the window. Trying to flip through possible solutions in his mind, Toby quickly does the only thing that presents itself: he reaches up and presses the button to call a flight attendant.

The man stops slamming and again turns to Toby. "Yessir," he says, this time looking directly into Toby's eyes as he does, as if he's trying to communicate with him in a foreign language. Then the man makes an odd sound, like, "Hungh." He's removed one thumb from an armpit and with his free hand he reaches up and tears the plastic window shade from its moorings.

This gets the attention of the people sitting in the row behind. "Hey," someone says. Soon people are standing, ignoring the seatbelt regulation, trying to see what's going on. A flight attendant, tall and blonde and pretty despite the scar on her chin and her big, man-sized hands, appears in the aisle then and—idiotically, it strikes Toby—asks if everything is all right here. The plane jerks, bounces, steadies.

"Get going!" the man says, clawing at the window now. "Yeah!" Toby waits for a second or two for something to happen, for someone responsible to do something, and it is when he inadvertently catches an elbow in the forehead from the man, who now is pressing his back and shoulders into the seat, legs braced and flexed in front of him, and seemingly trying to—roughly—hide his sweaty red face with his biceps, hands flailing at the wrists above his head, that Toby decides to end this ridiculous spectacle. Reverting back to his security training days, Toby quickly slides his forearm under the man's shoulder and applies a firm half-nelson while securing the other wrist behind the man's back.

The man is all breathing and grunting now. The sound reminds Toby of a cornered raccoon. Then he makes a noise that sounds like, "*Kaah.*"

Toby stands and drags the man, kicking, backwards into the aisle. The flight attendants, staring, back away to give him room.

"What do you want me to do with him?" Toby says. "Where should I take him?"

The attendants look at each other. "We'll be on the ground in ten minutes," the big blonde one says.

"You want me to release him?"

"Oh, boy," the man says, crying now. "Oh, please. Listen." Toby can't see his face and is glad of that. The man in his arms sobs for a moment, takes a deep breath and screams, "Fuck you! Fuck you! Ahh!" Then, just as suddenly, as if having expelled every ounce of energy at once, he slumps at the shoulders and says, quietly, "Fuckers. Yeah."

The big stewardess takes a step back. Her eyes, which Toby can see, are big and green and her scar more red and prominent now. "No," she says. "No. Please. Bring him up front. Maybe we can strap him into one of the attendants' seats."

"Cocksucker," the man says, casually. "*Kaah.*"

"How about a hand?" Toby says to the only male flight attendant.

After a moment of confusion, the male attendant—who is in his mid-twenties, athletic-looking and, Toby knows, far better equipped than himself to subdue this nut—bends down and takes the man, who has all but quit struggling now, by the legs. Together they carry his limp, occasionally twitching body to the front of the plane.

Having dumped the guy onto a fold-out seat that faces backwards, toward the other passengers, Toby stands off to the side and watches as the male attendant, the big blonde, along with a third—an older, hard-looking woman with short, dark red hair and piercings all the way around the cartilage of her ear—strap the hysterical man in. Such action is no longer necessary, however. The man is spent. The method of restraint is a simple shoulder harness against the front wall, behind which sit the oblivious first-class passengers. If he cared to, the man could simply unfasten the harness, as his hands and arms are largely free. But he's had it. The hysteria has run its course and now the man simply sits, head hanging awkwardly on his shoulder, chin

CHRISTOPHER TOROCKIO

resting on his collarbone, eyes open and still, small pockets of foam-white drool forming in the corners of his mouth.

Toby stands with the flight attendants a couple of steps from the man, watching him for sudden movements. How did this guy even get a ticket for a commercial airline, Toby wonders.

"They don't check those things," the blonde stewardess says, and Toby realizes he must have spoken out loud. "As long as they have a credit card..." and she lets her words trail off. Her eyes are still on the man, who appears to be asleep, only with his eyes open.

"But he told me this happens to him," Toby says. "He said, 'Sometimes I freak out during landings.' I asked him what he meant by that. I guess he showed me."

"I guess." The scar on the stewardess' face is a deep pinkish-red now, perhaps having drawn the color from the rest of her face. Toby notices, now that he is standing right next to her, that she is a least a couple of inches taller than he is, even without her modest heels. And probably, despite her scar and height and sturdy frame, a couple of years younger than Ellie.

"Isn't there a security procedure for these kinds of things?" Toby asks her now. "I mean, wouldn't that make a hell of a lot of sense? You can't—" He was going to say, You can't be too careful, but decides against it. Even airlines don't have time for security of sufficient quality. "Cutbacks everywhere," he says, and his words are immediately followed by the captain's voice over the loudspeaker notifying the flight attendants to prepare for arrival. None of them move, though. They just stand watching the slouching, drooling, mustached man who not five minutes ago had thrown a fit in the seat next to Toby's. He considers saying something like, Hey, this doesn't mean you don't carry on and do your job, but he figures the suggestion would lack authority, seeing as how he's still standing there, too, and not exactly following protocol. Within moments the plane touches down stiffly, causing everyone but the now-restrained crazy man to grasp at the air for balance.

Todd Sizemore heads back toward the chair-lined area around gate C-44 carrying a bag of popcorn. Ellie watches him toss a couple of kernels into his mouth as he walks, then turns her attention back out the window at the lit maze of runways. She's now beyond the point of simple exhaustion. She can't feel her legs, apart from the dull, lingering sense of heaviness that's settled there. And her head. She notices now, as she watches a USAir 737 taxi into view, wing lights blinking, that her head feels heavy, too. Especially the front, behind her eyes and down behind her cheekbones. And that's just how she feels. Imagine how she must look. But she doesn't want to think about that.

"Is that it?" Todd says, extending the bag to her.

She shrugs, ignoring his offer. "Must be."

"Right on time," he says.

She nods. Todd shifts the bag to his right hand and glances at his watch. Then he steps over to the big glass windows and looks intently out, as if trying to extract some hidden philosophical significance in his own reflection. He's a good-looking man, Ellie observes for what must be the millionth time, but somehow he carries this off in spite of himself. He's developed a slouch at the shoulders that comes across as more sloppy than natural. Lately he's taken to intentionally under dressing, wearing inappropriate clothes to formal functions, even when they're Ellie's functions. The most recent example of this, an example that frequently creeps into Ellie's thoughts, as it has now, was two weeks ago when Todd met her after work at a restaurant—a very nice restaurant—on West End Avenue where her law firm was celebrating the retirement of a longtime partner. Semiformal, she told him. For some reason, though, Todd found it necessary to show up, late, in jeans, work boots (which have never been used for work), a plaid, flannel shirt, unbuttoned and untucked, over a white t-shirt. Completing the outfit was a Hofstra ball cap. Backwards. And, really, there was no precedent for Ellie to be angry with him since, over the past several months he'd been establishing this very identity. Ever since he decided to scrap computer network administration and concentrate full-time on his "music career" (Ellie always inserts the quotation marks in her mind). But, she has to ask herself, constantly it seems: Is that so bad? Any of it? He makes less money now, practically none, in fact, and he dresses inappropriately—or, at least, what Ellie and her colleagues would consider inappropriate. But, Ellie considers as she watches him now, tossing back one kernel after another, like a machine, her husband is honest. She can trust him. And he likes her father, something that, this weekend especially, she very much appreciates.

He seems antsy, though. Wound up. The jetway hasn't even

been attached to the plane yet and already Todd is crumbling the empty popcorn bag in his hands. A moment later, three uniformed security guards along with a blue-suited USAir representative appear and hurry over to the big red metal door of gate C-44. One of the guards—a thin, flexible-looking man with a narrow, pointy chin and arms too long for his blue polyester shirt—jangles a ring of keys until he finds the one he's looking for. When the door to C-44 is open, the three guards disappear quickly into the long hallway. The USAir rep turns and looks around the terminal self-consciously. Using the heel of his hand, he pushes his glasses farther up the bridge of his nose.

"Man, they're slow," Todd says, turning away from the window. "Huh?"

Ellie doesn't answer. It's only been a minute or two since the plane taxied to the gate.

"Come here," Todd says, and extends his hand. Beyond him, Ellie can see movement behind the plane's tiny oval windows. When she steps over to Todd he puts his arm around her shoulder and they look out at the plane and runway as if at a sunset. Over to the side the door to the jetway swings open and a heavy woman in a wheelchair is wheeled into the terminal. Ellie turns and watches as three small children run over to the woman, bend down, and hug her. Todd sneezes.

"Bless you."

"Thanks. You know, maybe another Broadway show was a bit much. He didn't seem to particularly enjoy the last one."

"Well this is a fine time to mention it."

The first wave of passengers begin spilling out into the terminal. What her father does not yet know is that Todd's family recently had to cancel their visit—something about Todd's father, a psychiatrist, having to stay with a new patient who is on particularly shaky ground. So now it's up to the two of them, alone, to entertain her father.

"It's no big deal," Todd says. "It just occurred to me."

"It occurred to you because you don't want to go." She steps out from under his arm.

"Not true," he says with genuine good nature. Ellie looks at him. Leather-sleeved baseball jacket. Black t-shirt underneath.

"You like my dad, don't you."

Todd smiles. "Yeah. He's accepting. He makes me laugh."

A moment of familiar affection seizes her then, but quickly fizzles when she stops to consider the phrase, Makes me laugh.

"What do you mean, he makes you laugh?" she says. "My father is not a funny man."

Ellie waits.

"I think I just get him. You know what I mean?"

There is a pause in the exit of passengers for several minutes, then the three airport security guards who boarded the plane step off the jetway and into the terminal with a scrawny, tousle-haired man in tow. The man is obviously in their custody, though he is not handcuffed. Each of the three security guards have at least one tight-fisted hand on the man's suit jacket, and the USAir rep is following along behind. The man's legs do not want to keep pace and with every step Ellie expects his legs to just stop, for him to collapse and have to be dragged by the guards. This doesn't happen, though, and soon all five men are out of sight.

Again, passengers begin spilling out into the terminal.

"I thought maybe we could take him to my show Saturday," Todd says then. "I'd like for him to hear me play."

"You're playing Saturday?" Ellie says, turning to him. "When did this happen?"

"A couple weeks ago. I was afraid to tell you."

"Jesus Christ."

"Sorry," he says. "I just didn't want to pass it up. I, you know, I get so few."

She takes a breath. "Where?"

"Silvio's. Pays two-fifty."

The flow of deplaners has slowed. Silvio's isn't that bad a place—more of a coffeehouse than a bar or nightclub. But that's not what concerns Ellie. What concerns her is that she hasn't told her father that nearly six months ago her husband quit his job, forfeited his generous salary, his health benefits, his pension and 401K access, for the occasional two-hundred-dollar gig. The concept itself will be lost on him; the fiscal reality will not.

"Oh, hell," she breathes, to herself mostly.

Todd sneezes, makes a motion with his head. "There he is."

Ellie turns to find her father, garment bag slung over his shoulder, talking to one of the stewardesses, a big blond woman who is holding her shoes in her hand. The stewardess laughs, touches her father on the arm, then walks off in her stockinged feet down the terminal, suitcase wheeling along behind her.

"Hey, Toby," Todd calls out.

Ellie's father squints until he locates the source of his name. Then he hoists the garment bag higher onto his shoulder and heads toward them, expressionless. In his hand, Ellie notices, is a rolled-up copy of what must be the complementary in-flight magazine.

✳ ✳ ✳

It takes her a while to find an umbrella, but when she does Natalie locks the apartment door behind her and descends the two flights of stairs to the street. It is nine-forty and she wants to make it to Meg's Shadyside Drug Co., corner of Walnut and Aiken, before it closes at ten.

It's not a far walk, but Natalie lingers. She strolls. Halfway down Belefonte she stops to call to a cat, prowling in the shadows between two apartment buildings. Natalie crouches down, holding the umbrella above her with one hand while holding the fingers of the other out to the set of glowing yellow eyes and making tender clicking sounds. The eyes disappear. On Walnut she window shops. The clothes in Banana Republic are bland. She can't keep up with Victoria's Secret—new styles every week, it seems. Ann Taylor has gotten really old, The Gap really young. There is a muscular man in a short-sleeve shirt, checking driver's licenses out in front of Doc's. He's sitting on a stool beneath the overhang and, though there is no line to get in, there is a steady stream of people entering. Cars pull up front, stop, and let a couple of people jump out while the unlucky driver heads off in search of a rare streetside parking space. The rain is light, but steady. It will not let up. Natalie can see her breath now. She walks past Doc's big front window and stops. The place is pretty crowded; the night before Thanksgiving always is. There is much laughter in there and Natalie can feel the bass from the jukebox pounding in her chest. She feels like what she is: an outsider. A group of four men is playing darts. People lean over the bar waving money, trying to get the attention of one of the two bartenders. A waitress tries to squeeze through to the back room holding a pitcher of beer over her head. A man gets up from the bar and, in his vacated space, she can see Michael. He's leaning forward with one elbow on the bar, head propped with his hand, facing away from her, facing Alex, who is speaking, casually, factually, like a network anchorman delivering the evening news. She watches for a moment. Her feet, she realizes, are dry and comfortable in her tennis shoes. Why she should notice something like that, now, she has no idea. She continues down Walnut, stopping only once more, to glance briefly at the sleeping kittens in the pet store window.

The fluorescent lighting inside Meg's Shadyside Drug Co. is harsh and fuzzy. The place is small. It does not carry two-liter bottles of soda or greeting cards or pocket calculators or mailing supplies. It has drugs, like the sign says. The pharmacy in back, however, is closed.

Natalie shakes the wetness from her umbrella and closes it. Before her, racks of merchandise, four rows. The white-smocked, white-haired woman behind the cash register stares at her. This woman (Meg?) wants to go home. Natalie starts looking around. The pain relief aisle: Aspirin, Tylenol, Bufferin, Advil, generic brands. Cold and Flu: liquids, gelatin capsules, disks that dissolve in water. Next aisle—general hygiene stuff: toothpaste, deodorant, mouthwash, acne soap. She turns the corner; the fluorescent lights hum above her. Now, as she browses, she has taken to commentating in her head: Next we have the tummy medicines. Hmm. Pepto Bismol, Mylanta, Gaviscon, Phillips Milk-of-Magnesia. Ugh. Okay. Uh-oh—Ex-Lax, Correctol, Metamucil. So, what do we have here? Preparation-H. All right, there we go, we're scouring the depths now. And...*ta-da*! Feminine products. All our friends are here: Tampax, Carefree, O.B., Playtex. Sounds like a cheer. Vagisil. Now that just sounds gross. She folds her arms around herself, each hand holding the elbow of her opposite arm. Then she sees them, in big colorful boxes. She can't believe how many brands there are. Some have pictures on them: women smiling, red-cheeked, men and women embracing. Some have photographs of catalog-cute babies, also smiling, or being embraced. She looks over her shoulder. The white-haired woman lets her arms hang limply at her sides. She licks her lips, sucks them in. Natalie needs to make a decision. She'd like to read all the boxes, make an educated choice, but there is no time. She grabs one off the shelf (there is just a picture of a woman on it; no man, no baby) and she sees that simplicity is stressed with this product. All you have to do is pee on a stick. Well, she can do that. No mixing, no chemicals to add, and she figures, Okay. She takes the box to the white-haired woman at the register.

The woman looks down at the box. "Is this all?" she says.

Natalie can't help emitting a little laugh. "Isn't this enough?"

Back at the apartment she waits for Michael. It is the right thing to do. Dewey sits with her as she watches Lettermen. The box sits on the coffee table; every now and then Natalie looks at it, and the woman smiles back at her. When Lettermen is over she goes to the bedroom and finishes packing and when she's done with that she comes back out to the living room, puts a blanket over her and flips randomly through the television stations. Rain rattles the streetside window. At one-fifteen she hears Dewey snoring by her feet on the sofa. She's been watching an infomercial on getting rich through buying up all kinds of real estate. You have to send for a series of videos to find out how to do it. The people who are talking about how wonderful the program is sit by a pool at a Hawaiian resort. They wear golf shirts and pretty sundresses and their hair is well-moussed in the stiff island breeze. Behind them, palm trees bend at awkward angles. One woman, who, when she first ordered the videos was severely in debt, bought up (somehow) a dilapidated apartment building and resold it the same day for a twenty thousand-dollar profit. The videos told her how to do it. The videos cost just three easy payments of eighty-nine-ninety-five, plus shipping.

When the infomercial ends at one-thirty Natalie untangles herself from the blanket and stands. She picks up the box. Dewey lifts his head, regards her for a moment, lowers his head again. As if in some sort of cruel, preconceived spite, knowing Michael will be home any minute (Doc's will be closing soon), she takes the box into the bathroom. She switches on the light and exhaust fan. She locks the door.

BLESSINGS

They should have left last night—Michael knows that, but by the time he hobbled back from Doc's, drunk and wet and, for the first time in weeks, feeling pretty good, generally, and broke the news to Natalie that he'd invited Alex along to her parents' house for Thanksgiving, such a goal no longer seemed attainable. Besides, Natalie didn't look so hot, like she'd either just awoke or hadn't slept in days. At first, Michael thought maybe she was sick, seeing as how he found her in the bathroom, behind a locked door, on which he knocked for more than a minute before she finally came out, acting sheepish and disoriented, accepting Michael's condition and news regarding Alex with a level of nonchalance that, to Michael, was way too obvious, though he let it go.

They're late leaving Thursday morning, too. But this late departure isn't either of their faults. It is Alex's. Despite his pounding head and cotton-dry mouth, Michael managed to pull himself out of bed the moment he rolled over and heard the coffee maker gurgling in the kitchen. That was at eight-fifteen.

Now it's after eleven and Natalie isn't pleased. Michael sits on the sofa, pretending to watch the football pre-game show, tie-knot pulled all the way up, both shoes on, laces tied. He's ready. Natalie is wearing a sweater and corduroy skirt. As she paces the living room floor she grabs the bottom edges of the skirt and gives a hard tug. After four or five passes she stops, drops down onto the sofa to Michael and slaps the fronts of her thighs. "Well, I have to call them," she says. She's looking straight into the TV.

"Call them," Michael says.

"I have to. We wouldn't get there till after one if we left right now."

"Okay. I think you should call. Let them know what's up."

She looks at her watch, then back at the TV. She doesn't get up. "I can't believe you did this," she says.

"What?" Michael says. "I'm ready." He holds his arms out to show her.

"No. I mean inviting Alex."

He turns to her; he is ready for this, too. "He just found out he's going to lose his job," Michael says. "He's my friend and he's your friend, too, and it's Thanksgiving."

That was what he had planned to say, and he said it in just the right tone. But now, looking at her, it doesn't seem to have had much impact.

"Come on, Nat," he says. "Is it really that big a deal? I know your folks won't mind. I know that."

"That's not the point," she says, rising.

"Ah, there's a point. Now where getting somewhere."

"Oh, shut up," Natalie says. She says these words making only a half-hearted attempt to keep them under her breath. She moves off into the kitchen, tugging again at the hem of her skirt. After a few seconds, Michael hears dialing. The tones startle Dewey, apparently, who lurches to his feet, legs flailing in all directions on the hardwood until he can steady himself, and trots into the kitchen to check on things. Michael finds he is sleepy again. Dead tired. There's a soft, spongy sensation behind his eyes, and his extremities are numb. He makes a fist, squeezes. As he listens to the murmurs of Natalie's apologies to her mother, Michael thinks of his own parents, their Thanksgivings. He sees his father sitting at his place at the table—people all around, food all over, TV still on and loud in the next room so that any change in score can be easily heard—appearing to arbitrarily choose someone off the top of his head to say the blessing, when of course it is obvious he already knows who he will pick, in fact has probably known for days, weeks maybe, having applied some systematic rotation formula.

"Hmm... let's see," he says and his eyes search the table, eyebrows moving, lips sucked in. Michael remembers everyone sitting perfectly still, hands folded in laps—even the adults—until his father's eyes settle on that year's selection. "How about... Sarah. Would you mind saying the blessing this year, sweetheart?"

And, of course, you didn't have a choice in the matter, which wasn't necessarily bad. Michael remembers a combined sense of muted panic—like hoping to avoid getting called on in school when you haven't done your homework—and anticipation, a sense that, if the eyes were to land on you, you would have succeeded in something, you'd win a prize, you would be chosen. It is one skill his father has always had and, unlike the others—his ability to extract inappropriate confessions from family members as well as strangers, for instance—it never gets old.

He never called on Michael's mother, though, except for once. Usually she found an excuse to get up from the table, but even when she didn't she was in no danger of being chosen. Ever since Thanksgiving 1985, Michael's first post-college Thanksgiving, his father has known better. That day, as Michael remembers it now, was doomed from the start. The tradition of Michael's father giving the Great Grace Wheel a spin to see where it would land had been going on for, in Michael's terms, forever. The first time it landed on him was when he was seven years old, at which time Michael thanked the Lord for allowing the Lone Ranger to survive the previous week's shootout and for whoever cooked the stuffing because they'd forgotten to mix in the chopped walnuts, something Michael hated and could never understand. He was chosen three or four times after that as well, but still the wheel never seemed to land on his mother. At first Michael just thought she was unlucky, and he felt bad for her. But then, one year, 1985, a time when Michael had long since stopped considering his mother as a possible grace contributor, and was past the age of caring about such things —at least in the anticipatory or gamelike sense he once had—it happened. Even then, though, at twenty-two years old, Michael did not immediately consider the fact that his father was not spinning a wheel, but consciously placing it. His mother was not finally a benefactor of random chance, but the victim of a pre-conceived ambush.

Of course, just as Michael now knows the full and true account of the situation, he also knows that his father meant no real harm. He knows that his father simply wanted to involve his wife, finally, in the game he'd created—had been wanting to ever since the game's inception—and to appear clever in his springing it on her this of all years. He thought it'd be a kick.

But the plan backfired. Now, sitting on the sofa, listening to the erratic murmur of his own wife talking on the phone with her own mother, Michael remembers the look that seized his mother's face that day. He was sitting across from her, he remembers that, and before all of his father's words even had a chance to find the air and work their way across the table—those words being, "Hmm, how about for a special treat this year we hear from the lady of the house"—the features on his mother's face suddenly expanded, drawing outward from the center, making her face appear much wider than it actually was. Her hair was pulled back, providing good, straight-on views of her severely reddening neck and ears, and, though she made no sound one might associate with excessive breathing, her chest began to heave in quick, arrhythmic bursts.

People—aunts, uncles, cousins—stared at her, then looked around at each other. Most vividly, for some reason, Michael remembers how the pendant his mother was wearing—a heart, nothing fancy—lay nestled in the dimple below her throat and moved up and down with her exaggerated breathing. She tried to swallow then and nearly choked, causing someone—Michael can't remember who—to say, "Shirley, dear God, are you all right?"

She nodded, gave one good hard cough which seemed to chase the red from her face, nodded again. Michael looked over toward his father then who sat casually observing, reclined in his chair even. A couple of people got up to approach his mother, to check on her. One person patted her on the back. Michael's father, though, put a stop to this, got everyone back on track. "Okay, Shirl? My sweetheart honey blossom. You ready to proceed now? The bird you worked so hard on these last two days is getting cold." He pointed at it. "Look, goose bumps," he said, and laughed.

Michael was twenty-two years old, old enough to put a stop to this, but the severity of his mother's reaction made him take pause, and it occurred to him suddenly that, odd as it was, he understood it. Not the resulting action itself, certainly, but the force behind it, the whatever-it-is that makes one terrified to speak to God in the presence of family. That. So Michael stood, with every intention of putting a stop to the proceedings. But then his mother said, "Dear Lord," and everyone bowed their heads, except Michael, who remained standing. Then his mother said, "Thank you for the food we are about to enjoy. Thank you for our good fortunes, with the notable exception of our dear Aunt Ida's leg having to be amputated. That was a rude and terrible thing to do to her. You know how she loves to go on long walks. What was very nice, however, was your helping Michael to land that wonderful job, even if it will take him all the way to New York." Michael could feel the wide eyes of his family shift from his mother to himself. Still standing, he kept bowed his head down and stared with great interest at the bowl of sweet potatoes, the crispy top layer already beginning to turn a deep crimson, taking on the appearance and consistency of damp cardboard. "And, dear Lord, while we're on the subject," his mother went on, "I take severe exception to your apparent disinterest in Donald's colon." Here the stares shifted from Michael to his father at the other end of the table. To this day Michael has not been able to figure out how his new job was "on the subject" of his father's colon, but he understood that detail to be trivial and altogether beside the point. "I've been asking you for help in this matter, yet you allow the...the...infestation to continue. I think—"

"Shirley," Michael's father said.

"—you should take a long, hard look at the circumstances you've arranged here. There's no reason for it. No reason at all." Here, though Michael was still looking down at the congealing sweet potatoes, he could sense his mother shift in her chair and rearrange the napkin on her lap before continuing. "I'll be look-ing forward to a more encouraging diagnosis from Dr. Pressey next week. Now then, thank you for enabling all of us to be to-gether on this day, and for..."

Michael doesn't remember the rest. What he does remember is that Dr. Pressey did in fact provide his mother with a more encouraging diagnosis: the tumor, contrary to what was feared, was small and benign and could be taken care of with a rather simple procedure. That was good to know, especially seeing as how Michael, up until that Thanksgiving dinner, had no idea that anything at all might potentially be wrong with his father.

That was eleven years ago.

Michael slides his hips forward and lets his shoulders sink down into the cushions of the sofa. He hears Dewey let go with a restrained, high-pitched bark. Natalie tells him, politely, to knock it off, then says, "Sorry, Mom."

On the television a woman reporter is standing along the sidelines of the Silverdome in Detroit. She's providing an injury update for the early game between the Lions and the Minnesota

Vikings. Michael tries to concentrate on what the woman is saying. He does not want Natalie to hang up with her mother and come back into the living room to find him sleeping again. Of course he knows that all he has to do to avoid that scene is to get up. Just get up off the couch and walk around. That'd do the trick. But he also knows that he is in the process of making a conscious decision to stay right where he is. That knowledge bothers him, triggers in him something he can only relate to self-loathing, though he doesn't truly believe that's the case. He closes his eyes and listens.

Minnesota's top receiver, the woman is saying, may not play in this afternoon's game because of a lingering quadricep injury. "Coach Green told me just a few minutes ago that it's a game time decision," she says, adding that, if the receiver is unable to play, the Vikings' offense will be missing nearly eight million dollars worth of talent, once you add in the salary of their starting tailback, who is out for the season with a torn-up knee.

Eight million dollars. Michael tries to do the math, tries to tabulate how long it takes one of these players to earn Michael's own annual salary. He abandons this project quickly, though, on the grounds of there being little to be gained in it. The comparison is apples to oranges. And besides, Michael earns decent money. Nine out of ten Miami of Ohio public relations graduates would kill for his job, probably. So those facts, coupled with his and Natalie's situation of being thirty thousand dollars in debt, credit cards maxed, interest accruing, with nothing but a crummy, crotch-obsessed dog to show for it, only leads Michael to suspect that even if he made eight million dollars a year, he and Natalie would find a way to make it disappear.

He's always believed that he learns from his mistakes. After all, he's an intelligent man, with common sense and an eye for what he likes to call appropriateness: knowing instinctively what action befits what situation. But now, he's not so sure. Never before has he had so much trouble imagining things coming together, situations working out for the best. He's come to expect tragedy, to anticipate it without being able to avoid it, and he realizes that, if nothing else, his father and mother have each passed on at least one trait to him: from his father, his extraordinarily thin wrists and ankles; and from his mother, her fear. And her stark honesty in the face of it.

Alex shows up at a quarter to twelve. He's wearing the same clothes from the night before, except the shirt is untucked. And he's not wearing his suit jacket. Other than that, the first thing Michael notices upon opening the door is the tie. Somehow, it occurs to him, it looks even brighter now, more ridiculous, in the daytime.

"Well, lookie here," Michael says.

Alex, standing in the doorway, opens his mouth to speak. When nothing comes he closes it and lets his cheeks puff out with air. Then he just stands there for a second or two. He opens his mouth again—he has something he wants to say apparently—but before he gets anything out this time Dewey appears from the side, lifts his front paws up onto Alex's thighs and presses his nose into his crotch, causing Alex to emit a quick, high-pitched bleat and fall back against the doorframe.

Michael doesn't say anything; he just watches.

"Dewey, no," Alex says, more pleading than commanding. He reaches down and searches for Dewey's head, but the dog has achieved a clean entry and now his nose is buried.

"Trouble?" Michael says, arms folded.

Alex succeeds in getting a hand under the dog's jaw. He then wrenches Dewey's head away and positions himself so as to deny further access. Dewey stands, looking up at Alex for a moment, tail wagging. Then he turns and trots back into the living room. Alex straightens. "Jesus," he says. "I swear that dog's gay. Is he?"

Michael shrugs, watches as Dewey disappears into the kitchen, where Natalie is still on the phone. "I don't know. He does it to women to, if that means anything."

"Not to me." Alex enters the apartment and Michael closes the door behind him. "I'm pretty late, aren't I?"

"You were pretty late an hour and a half ago. Now you're way fucking late. And, she hasn't said it explicitly yet, but I think you might be a bastard, too."

Alex nods absently.

"Sit," Michael says. "Nat's on the phone." He drops back down onto the sofa as Alex takes his usual position in the director's chair along the wall. Alex is the only person who ever sits there; it provides no sight lines to the TV. "You look nice," Michael observes. "I should have told you you didn't have to dress up."

Alex looks down at himself.

"Where's your jacket? It's cold and rainy outside and you had it last night, and I can't believe I'm asking a grown man this question." Then something else occurs to Michael. "Did you bring anything else?" he says. "You know, we're not coming back until at least Saturday. Maybe even Sunday. I told you that last night."

"I've been walking around all night, thinking."

"Oh. How original. Did you do some soul-searching, too?"

Alex squints at Michael, cocks his head slightly. "What's your problem?"

Michael turns toward the TV, which Alex cannot see. Two men behind a desk are speculating about the playoff implications today's games might have. "Nothing," Michael says. "I apologize. What were you thinking about?"

"Robbing a convenience store," Alex says. "Seriously. I was walking past the Dairy Mart on Ellsworth. This was around three or four, somewhere in there—it's open twenty-four hours. And I was thinking, I should rob that place. What the fuck difference would it make? Eventually, I'll need the money."

Michael begins to laugh. It's a loud, sarcastic laugh—he can tell this even as he's doing it, but he keeps laughing. Then, when he figures Alex is not going to say anything more, he simply stops. "For Christ's sake, Alex. You just found out, not even a day ago, that you're getting laid off in, like, six weeks. What's the matter with you? You'll get a little severance package and be rid of Electro-Lite and you'll find another job. You're not a moron, are you?"

Alex just stares across the coffee table at Michael. "Thanks," he says. "Your sympathy is appreciated."

Michael can't help laughing again. This time the laugh is even harsher, almost sadistic. "Sympathy? You're not dying, Alex. You're about to experience a setback. Like we all do. Exactly how much sympathy—just a ballpark—is required of me here?"

From the kitchen, Michael can hear his wife talking—not the words themselves, but he can detect that rising tone of voice usually reserved for the moment just prior to hanging up. He looks over at Alex, who's now leaning back in the director's chair, looking up at the ceiling. Suddenly Alex, head still bent back, says, "Do I have to go along with you guys today?"

Michael watches him. "No."

Alex doesn't move. Perhaps, Michael thinks, he's mulling over his options. Then Alex lowers his head and he's again looking at Michael across the coffee table.

The clumsy rattle of a phone being replaced in its wall cradle is heard and then Natalie emerges from the kitchen. "Well, hello there," she says, heading over to Alex. "Happy Thanksgiving. You look like you're about to yell 'Action' or something." She heads across the living room to Alex as Dewey pads along behind her. Alex crosses his legs. When Natalie reaches him she bends down to give him a kiss, then stops short. "Whoa," she says. "Um, Alex. You want to, like, borrow our shower before we go?"

Alex, oddly to Michael, takes hold of his outrageous lighthouse tie, lifts it to his face, and sniffs it. "That bad, huh?" he says. "Do we have time?"

Natalie kisses her fingertips and touches them to Alex's forehead. "We'll make time."

After Alex hoists himself from the director's chair and is shown the closet with the spare towels, Natalie returns to the living room.

"We do?" Michael says to her.

"We do what?"

"Have time?"

Natalie sits down on the sofa next to him. "Yeah." She turns to Michael and takes his hand. "Listen, I'm sorry about being so pissy earlier."

"It's all right."

"No, it's not. It's Thanksgiving. You didn't do anything for me to get so bent out of shape about. I had no right."

She's still holding his hand. Michael looks into her face. He can hear the water in the shower turn on. "What did you and your mother talk about?" he says.

"Nothing. Hey, let's go into the bedroom."

"What?"

"While he's in the shower. Come on." She stands, still holding onto his hand, and gives a tug.

"What brought this on?"

She rolls her eyes. "Don't ask me that. Just come on." She giggles. "Hurry up. I want to show you something."

"Show me something. Nat, honey, what is it?"

"Get up." She pulls harder, jolting him forward.

He stands. From the bathroom around the corner, muffled by the fan and shower noise but still audible, Alex begins singing "Country Roads."

"Oh my God," Natalie says, and laughs. "Come on."

With his hand in hers, she leads Michael down the hall to the bedroom. She doesn't even bother closing the door.

✳ ✳ ✳

They had reservations for breakfast. Toby had trouble believing that any place in the city—any place in the world—was even open for breakfast on Thanksgiving day, let alone that reservations were needed to get a table there, and that he and his daughter and son-in-law were actually going there. For breakfast. But that's exactly what he awakes to find.

Toby was awake first. He went into the bathroom—long and narrow, decorated in black and white, with tub, sink and fixtures far too old for Toby's liking but that the kids nonetheless probably find charming—where he shaved and brushed his teeth; then, still in his bathrobe which he brought from home, he took his camera and went to the living room window. Eight floors below on West 77th Street the traffic was stopped completely, bumper-to-bumper, mostly taxi cabs. Toby lifted the window and stuck his head and shoulders out. The air was chilly but dry; the sky was overcast and showed no signs of clearing. The traffic, he suspected, was due to the parade, which, though mainly farther downtown, caused much of Manhattan to reroute itself.

Horns blew. Toby wasn't sure why, since there was nowhere for anyone to go anyway, but still, the horns blew one right after the other. Toby liked this vantage point: high enough to be detached from the action, yet low enough to see what's going on, to be a part of things in a noncommittal way. Though he works in a skyscraper himself, he's used to the ground floor; there's a certain stability in that. At one point a woman in a jacket the color of optic yellow golf balls got out of a taxi cab that had been stopped in one of the center lanes. She shook a finger through the open door, presumably at the person still sitting in the back seat, then slammed the door (which Toby could hear), made her way through two lanes of stopped traffic to the sidewalk, slung her purse onto her shoulder, and headed off in the direction from which the taxi just brought her, stopping only once, for about five seconds, to admire something in a store window.

Toby took her picture.

When the yellow of her coat grew small—the size of an actual golf ball—several blocks away and nearly lost among the duller colors of so many people around her, Toby discovered that his hands and nose had grown numb from the cold. He took one last picture, of the general street scene, objects buzzing haphazardly through the frame, then leaned back inside and closed the window.

The apartment was warm, in temperature at least. But the walls were white and bare, except for an occasional framed photograph—not of Ellie or Todd or of anyone anybody knew or anyplace anyone had ever been—usually in black and white. The sofa was gray and hard, as was the square carpet in the middle of the hardwood floor. Todd's guitars and cases sat up against two of the three walls—the fourth side bordered the kitchen, which was long and narrow and, again, black and white. Toby did not let any of this bother him. It was their place, it was how they wanted to live. The apartment's stark furnishings and chilly ambience was not an indication of his daughter and son-in-law's inability to afford anything better. It was all by choice. The fact that the feel of the place represented to him the exact reversal of the feel Toby and Ellie's mother had worked so hard to establish in their own home, for Ellie, was, he knew, irrelevant. This was his daughter's home, her life. He lowered himself into the leather upright chair by the window and sat listening to the dense murmur of the outside traffic. A car alarm sounded, wailing, changing pitches and patterns every few seconds until it suddenly stopped. Soon Toby settled into the outside sounds, watching the muted gray sunlight against the near wall, seeing it brighten and fade with the passing clouds, until the rhythm of those outside sounds was broken by a sudden medley of gurgling and sputtering from the kitchen. Toby picked himself up and moved to the kitchen where he found that, on the counter next to the stove, the coffee maker had turned on—by itself. He then remembered Ellie had been playing around with the thing before they went to bed last night, pushing buttons, and he made a mental note to look into one of these programmable numbers for his own kitchen. He was still standing there, watching the coffee drip down into the pot, beginning to smell it, when Ellie padded into the kitchen wearing gray (what else?) sweatpants-shorts, drawstring hanging down to mid-thigh, and a t-shirt emblazoned with a Camel cigarettes logo.

Toby's eyes fell to his daughter's feet. She was wearing white athletic socks pushed down around her ankles and he couldn't help turning from the coffee maker and giving them his full attention, even as he felt the quick kiss she planted on his cheek before silently continuing on to the refrigerator. He felt good, ready for something.

"Sweetheart," he says now, pouring the coffee that's waiting for him, "you know, I don't need to go out to breakfast. It's Thanksgiving. Why don't we ease into this."

Ellie is standing at the kitchen counter, washing one vitamin supplement after another down with a glass of juice that, judging from the color, is not orange and not grapefruit, but most likely within the citrus family. She swallows another pill, picks up two more, holds them in her palm. "This place is the best, Dad," she says. "We got reservations in September and even then this was the only day available for the whole weekend."

"But I'm saying it's all right," Toby says.

Ellie puts her now-empty glass down next to the remaining pile of pills. "You don't want to go." She opens the refrigerator again and removes the label-less container of juice. She stands there holding it. "I just, I don't know, I thought you'd enjoy it." She closes the refrigerator door. "Todd said it was a bad idea, too. He told me. I should have listened."

"It's not that, honey," Toby says. "It's not that I don't want to go. I'm just saying we don't have to go. That's all."

"Same difference." She pops some pills in her mouth.

"Ellie, are you sure you should be taking so many of those pills?"

"It's fine, Dad."

"What are they, anyway?"

"Just vitamins."

"Yeah, I figured that. But what vitamins?" He adds a spoonful of sugar to his coffee and stirs it. "I'm just curious as to what kinds of vitamins there are that you're supposed to take so many of them."

"Dad."

"Seriously. Vitamin C? Riboflavin? What? It can't be safe is all I'm saying. Did your doctor tell you to take so many?"

"It's perfectly safe, Daddy."

"Well, it's odd."

"Maybe." She takes the last of the pills and sets her glass in the sink. Then she picks up the phone. "I'll cancel the reservation."

"Ellie, please," Toby says. "You're misunderstanding me. Put the phone down." He takes it out of her hand. "I never said I didn't want to go. I just said it wasn't necessary. That's all."

"Of course it's not necessary. Nothing is necessary. It's just... I don't know."

"Where are the Sizemores again?"

"One of Mr. Sizemore's patients held him back. They may make it here Saturday, if thing's work out. I doubt it, though."

Toby can tell this is another sore subject for Ellie, so he drops it. "Let's get dressed and go," he says enthusiastically. "Is Todd up yet? What time is the reservation for?"

"Now you're just saying that. Now you're just giving in to be agreeable." Her hair is everywhere, and blonder than he remembers it ever being. Toby looks closely at her face and sees that she is pouting.

"Why would I do that?" he says. "Look, let's get dressed. Okay? I don't want to be this way with each other. I'm being totally honest when I say I really want to go. Really. Go get in the shower and I'll sit here and read the paper for a few minutes. All right? Where is the paper?"

"Just outside the door. If nobody's stolen it yet."

"Okay. Go on and get dressed. I'll be ready when you are." He puts his hand on her back and guides her gently out of the kitchen and gets her moving down the hallway toward the bedroom. She goes, but Toby can tell she's not convinced he's in total agreement. That's his fault. He's put her in a no-win position and he's sorry for it, but he also can't fight off the recognition that he and his daughter have had very similar conversations in their lifetime. The only difference is that those other conversations took place when she was about fifteen years old.

From now on, he decides, he'll just go along. Life's too goddamn short.

There is a story on page three of the *Times* business section with the headline, "Electro-Lite chairman concedes internal displeasure." It reads:

Thomas J. Corbett, Sr., Chairman and CEO of New York-based Electro-Lite Corp., admitted Wednesday in an exclusive interview to his "increasing displeasure" regarding the way various divisions have been handling the company's upcoming layoffs.

Most of his criticism was directed at the Power Generation Division, headquartered in Pittsburgh, Pa., where a majority of Electro-Lite's downsizing of 11,000 employees is scheduled to occur. Specifically, Corbett directed his irritation toward that division's handling of a recent press conference, at which time, he said, con-

fidential company information—some of which even he was not aware of—was released to the media.

"There will be some changes," Corbett assured. "From the top down."

The story goes on to discuss the collapsing market for nuclear power plant construction and service, as well as the increasing costs associated with all power generation, including fossil-powered plants. None of this is news to Toby. What bothers him is Mr. Corbett's comments regarding what Michael Dunne revealed at Monday's press conference, that Power Gen is going to miss its objective by such a large margin (sixty million dollars according to the story, though Toby seems to remember Michael saying fifty million) and the Georgia Power project that was finished by GE. What Toby wonders is: Is Mr. Corbett upset that that information was revealed, or is he upset that any of it ever occurred without his knowing? The distinction, Toby believes, is a significant one.

When he comes to the next to last paragraph, where the writer asserts that Mr. Corbett will be meeting over the holiday weekend with appropriate representatives of Electro-Lite management to address these new problems, and that an announcement regarding "the status of the corporation" and its "intended direction, both short- and long-term," will be forthcoming, Toby folds the paper and drops it at his feet, next to the hard gray sofa. He stands, goes to the window, then, without having looked out, moves away from it. He notices on the coffee table a magazine called *Details,* which he has never heard of. He picks it up and flips through the pages. He needs to get his mind off of things. Otherwise, he knows, he'll be horrible company. The magazine is heavy, the pages are thick and glossy and smooth. Inside are pictures of young men, sometimes accompanied by women, modeling what Toby understands to be suits even though none are wearing ties. Most of the pictures were taken outdoors and feature some degree of fall foliage, and most of the men are white and sport tangled wise-guy haircuts. He flips some pages and lands on an article titled "Increase your sexual endurance: ten easy exercises" next to which is a photograph of a man and a woman snuggling on top of the sheets. The man's wearing shimmering navy blue boxer shorts, she's got on a navy blue nightgown, very small. Toby closes the magazine and drops it onto the coffee table.

"Morning, Toby." Todd walks out from the kitchen carrying

a coffee mug. He's wearing jeans, a t-shirt and a tan, somewhat tattered-looking sports jacket. His hair is wet and combed back at the sides. "What's new in the world?"

"Nothing, unfortunately," Toby says.

"Sorry about this breakfast thing. Doesn't make a hell of a lot of sense, I know."

Toby waves this off. "Not at all. It'll be fine. Different."

"Yeah. Well, that's true." Todd goes to the window. He sips timidly at his coffee. "My folks were going to come, too," he says. "I don't know if Ellie mentioned that to you or not. But my dad's got this thing going on with a patient. Plus, my brother got some time off and they haven't seen him in a while so they decided to stay put so he could visit them. I guess he's bringing a girl."

"Well, maybe they'll make it out this weekend."

Todd shrugs, keeps his eyes on the street below. "I don't know. Something about plans. Changing plans, once they're made, in my family is like a huge deal."

"Well, that's too bad." Toby, feeling strangely on display sitting alone in the middle of the hard sofa, rises and moves over to the window. "We'll see what we can do about having a good time ourselves, though." He chuckles and likes the way it feels. "A Thanksgiving breakfast seems as good a place as any to start."

Todd looks up, smiles. "Yeah. I guess. Hey, Toby," he says, "I wanted to ask you something. You know how I like to mess around on the guitar a little, right?"

"Sure," Toby says. "You've mentioned it."

"Yeah, well. I'm performing Saturday night at this, well, it's kind of a bar, but not really. It's pretty classy. Well, maybe not classy, but it's an all right place. Kind of laid back. Anyway, I know it's not the best of nights, and ordinarily you wouldn't go out to a bar on Thanksgiving weekend, but a lot of people do so it's a pretty nice paycheck. So, like I was saying, you and Ellie can do whatever—hang out here or go someplace or whatever—until I'm done. But, what I'm getting at is, I'd like for you to come. If you want to. I think it'd be pretty cool if you came, and I think maybe you'd like it." He shrugs. "I don't know."

The heat kicks on, a gentle rumbling in the ceiling. Toby leans back against the windowsill, facing the room, in what he hopes is a casual posture, his elbows supporting him. "Perform? You mean like a concert or something? In front of people?"

"Yeah," Todd says. "Kind of like that. It'll be no big deal, though."

"Well, geez," Toby says. "Of course I'd like to go. Hell, yes. I think that's fantastic." He reaches out and gives Todd a slap on the shoulder. "Why didn't you say something earlier?"

"I just found out last week." Todd presses in towards the window, his elbows on the sill, too, looking out, so that he and Toby are now right-shoulder-to-right-shoulder, facing in opposite directions. "Apparently the guy they had—who's pretty good, a piano player from Philly, does a lot of bluesy stuff—he had to cancel. I'm just happy the owner thought of me. Like I said, Thanksgiving weekend, believe it or not, is a big bar weekend. So it's a pretty good payday, too. I'm lucky to get it."

"Well, I think it's great, Todd. Really." Toby wants to somehow touch his son-in-law again, to show that he means what he's saying, because he does, but any act of physical contact at this moment seems like it would be extraordinarily awkward. "I'm looking forward to it. But I mean why didn't anyone say something to me earlier about your performing in general? I didn't know you ever started. Hell, I didn't even know you were any good."

"Oh." Todd looks hard at something on the street, as if someone down there is trying to send him signals. "I guess you'll have to ask Ellie about that. I felt it was her place."

Toby doesn't answer. Suddenly he's wondering about the situation, trying to determine what question, if any, would be appropriate to ask next.

"But anyway," Todd says, nudging him, "I'm glad you're up for coming." He smiles. It's a real smile, Toby can tell, from inside, from the chest. No hidden agendas.

Michael leans against the inside of the Cherokee's passenger door and tries to concentrate. For some reason Natalie insisted on driving and now, having no specific purpose, it's all he can do to stay awake. The rain is steady. Sitting at the intersection of Murray and Forward Avenues in Squirrel Hill, waiting for the light to change so they can finally make their way onto the Parkway, Michael watches the windshield wipers glide gently back and forth. Occasionally they emit a labored squeal but otherwise the motion is soothing, too much so, in fact, for Michael. Traffic is tight and slow and tedious, but before too long they are exiting the Parkway in Monroeville and catching Route 30 for Greensburg and Ligonier. The rain never stops, and Alex doesn't speak. He sits in the center of the back seat, in the same suit as the day before (minus the jacket), tie pulled tight, hair wet from the shower, with one leg on either side of the hump, knees high in the air. Natalie isn't talking either, something Michael can't quite figure out. When they emerged from their bedroom, at the same time Alex stepped out of the bathroom wearing just his dress pants and drying his hair with a towel, she seemed to Michael to be in a fine mood, giddy even. As the three of them were putting on their coats and readying to leave, Natalie snatched the keys from Michael's hand and said, "Not on your life, mister. You're in no condition to drive." Michael wasn't sure to what aspect of his condition she was referring, exactly, but he didn't question it since he could tell by her joking, pseudo-sarcastic tone that he was supposed to know, and that, whatever it was, it was all right.

They pass by the empty parking lots of strip malls in North Huntingdon and continue on, stopping at lights every half-mile or so at the intersections of rural roads that seemingly lead to nowhere, to the Greensburg turnoffs where Michael, still fighting the urge to nod off, sees the stone, castle-like hospital, set up in the hills and off to the left, looking sinister in the mist beneath the dark, low-lying clouds.

"Man, I'd hate to get sick and have to be taken there," Michael says as Natalie guides the car around a bend, away from town. These are the first words anyone has spoken for more than twenty minutes. When no one replies, he adds, "So, is this fun or what?"

Within seconds they are beyond the maze of exits and off-ramps and are passing through another stretch of traffic lights, strip malls, car dealerships and steakhouses. Natalie pulls the Cherokee to a stop; she adjusts the windshield wipers to intermittent. To the right is Westmoreland Mall, which appears to Michael to be open, judging from the cars turning into the lot. The light turns green and Natalie presses down on the gas.

"What's the weirdest thing your family serves at Thanksgiving dinner?" Alex asks suddenly, to Natalie, Michael presumes.

"What?" Natalie says. She checks him in the rear-view.

"You know. Everyone's family has, like, one really weird thing they serve at every Thanksgiving. Like at mine, it doesn't matter if it's at my mother's place or my aunt and uncle's, somebody's going to make peel-and-eat shrimp. I don't know where it started or why, it's just always been that way. And it doesn't fit, you know? It's like, 'We got turkey, stuffing, cranberries, et cetera, and, oh yeah, there's peel-and-eat shrimp, too.' Shit, my mom and her boyfriend'll probably have it on their cruise today." He pauses, stares straight ahead. "So what's the weird thing we're going to have today?"

Natalie bites down on her bottom lip, signals, changes lanes.

"Those corn fritter things," Michael says. "Those are kind of weird."

Natalie looks at him. "No they're not. What's so weird about them?"

"I don't know. It's just a pile of corn fritters on a plate." He turns around to face Alex. "Looks like a big stack of pancakes. And everyone just picks one up and walks around eating them. I mean, what's with that?"

"They're just appetizers," Natalie says by way of explanation. She thinks some more. "I'd say the weirdest thing my mother makes is brisket."

"Oh, yeah," Michael says. "It's pretty good, too."

"Brisket and turkey?" Alex says.

"No. Just brisket. She doesn't make turkey. I don't know why."

"One year she did," Michael says. "Remember? She decided to try something 'different' and made a turkey and everyone just about went ape-shit. Remember that?"

Alex leans forward, pokes his head into the front seat between Natalie and Michael. His eyebrows are scrunched into each other and he's nodding. "All right," he says, as if they've all just uncovered something significant. "See, now that's what I'm talking about. That's fucking weird."

At around Latrobe, the rain lets up. The hills on either side of Route 30 are still hidden in a heavy mist, and Natalie has to leave the windshield wipers on, constantly adjusting their speed, because of the moisture in the air, along with the spray that is continually kicked up by the other cars. But, as far as Michael is concerned, it's good to know that the rain has seemingly stopped, at least for the moment.

Alex is again sitting back, staring out the foggy, water-beaded side window at the unassuming entrance to St. Vincent College and the muddy, rutted football practice field adjacent to the road. That field, Michael can't help noticing, would be nearly impossible to kick on in its present condition, and he waits for some comment to this effect to come from Alex. But he gets nothing, and a couple of miles past St. Vincent they stop at a light. On one corner of the intersection is a gas station with a letter-board out front that reads: YES WE dO HAvE FISHIN6 L1CENSES. Across the way is a burned-out building that looks to Michael as though it might have been a diner at one time, and directly to their left is a closed-down stand at which, during the summer, one can buy fresh corn, tomatoes and watermelon, according to the water-logged, hand-painted sign. Michael takes all of this in. It's all familiar, they've made this two-hour trip many times since moving to Pittsburgh. But, in spite of himself, he can't shake the feeling that something is going to happen to them on this particular trip. Something good or bad, he's not sure of the details, just something. As they sit at the light, in silence, it occurs to Michael that maybe he wants something to happen. Anything. A diversion, something to have to talk about, to address and comprehend and work out, something that can be worked out, if only the three of them would put their heads together and use a little common sense. Something other than what they have going for themselves now. It is then that Michael glances over to his right and, in the cleared-out area along the road, sees a dog, wet and matted and, it looks to Michael, shivering. It's standing in a patch of dead grass and leaves where perhaps a building once stood. The dog is the color of dust, medium height, maybe a collie or spaniel mix, with a little beagle somewhere in the bloodline. It is standing beyond the muddy shoulder, several yards off the road, yet it appears to be examining the traffic, as if waiting for the right opportunity to cross. The only thing that seems to be stopping it are the cars making turns onto Route 30. There are no houses in sight.

"Look at that dog," Michael says.

The other two heads turn casually, slowly.

"Mm," Natalie says.

"Pull over," Michael says. "Pull over there. Let's take him in." He puts his hand on the door handle.

"Yeah," Alex says.

"Are you crazy?" Natalie says. "I'm not putting that filthy, wet dog in this car."

"Come on," Michael says. "What are you, like, fifty now or something?"

She doesn't answer.

"Seriously. The light's going to change. Hurry up." Actually, now that he considers it, Michael can't believe the light is still red. It isn't red for long, though. Within seconds, it flicks to green and the car in front of them pulls out through the intersection to make a left turn. Natalie pulls out behind it, waiting.

"What are you doing?" Michael says. He looks back over at the dog, which is in the same exact place, still watching the traffic for some sort of opportunity. "That dog is lost and I want to help it. Do you hear me?"

"We already have a dog," Natalie says. "And our apartment isn't big enough for that one."

"Maybe your parents would want it. Maybe Alex wants it."

"Nope," Alex says.

The car in front of them, a big green Suburban, is still waiting to make its left-hand turn. On its rear window is a decal of the Confederate flag.

"Michael," Natalie says, watching for space to her right to swing around the Suburban, "that dog belongs to someone."

"Who?"

"There are houses just beyond those hills. And down that road there. You can't just take someone's dog." And with that the Suburban makes its turn just as the light turns yellow. Natalie steps on the gas and just makes it through.

"I can't believe you did that," Michael says.

"I can't either," Alex says.

"You shut up back there," Natalie says, and continues on, guiding the Cherokee confidently through the steady rain toward Ligonier.

Thanksgiving dinner at Mercy Hospital consists of two slices of stark-white turkey, a round, ice cream scoop of mashed potatoes, a block of stuffing, some corn nibblets the color of sawdust, a side salad of confetti-lettuce, and cherry Jell-O with pear slivers. And it is served just after noon, which is Newton Sarver's biggest problem since Maryann hasn't shown up yet with the real food. He is in his pajamas and seated in an orange vinyl chair by the window when the woman slides the tray out from the big metal heating unit.

"Already?" Sarver asks.

"Lucky you," the woman says, setting the tray on the table by the bed. She is thin and black. Her hair is pulled back and tied at the top of her head just behind her white nurse's cap and her heavy glasses are so far down the tip of her nose it's a wonder to Sarver they don't fall off. "Your room's at the beginning of my rounds." She checks something off on a clipboard. "Still raining out there?"

Sarver turns and looks out the window, as though he hasn't checked in a while. "It was. Not so sure about now. They got you working on the holiday, huh?"

"Uh-huh. I get off at four, so it's not so bad. I figure I got it better off than most of the people here. No offense."

Sarver smiles. "Can't argue there."

"All right then," the nurse says, taking hold of the big steel box and giving it a push. "You take care now, sweetie," and she pushes the cart out the door.

He isn't supposed to be here. The pain in his stomach that he had thought was caused by his prostate turned out to be caused by cancer in his right testicle, which he for several weeks refused to have examined and as a result he no longer possesses. The doctors told him his condition is extremely rare in men his age; it's much more common in younger men, which, Sarver suspects, is supposed to somehow make him feel better. Manly.

The operation was Monday afternoon. This is Thursday, and he isn't even sure he'll be able to go home tomorrow, although his doctor has told him if things stay the way they are now, he will. The problem, as Sarver understands it, stems directly from his having waited so long to put his goods out on display. And his age. Now, in addition to the trauma of emergency surgery, the doctors want to make sure the cancer hasn't spread; results from the last of the tests should be in later today, he's told.

This situation of his health, of course, hasn't stopped those he works with from wanting a piece of his time. The telephone in his room hasn't stopped ringing (he's even received some calls—from Marlene, from Dennis, from Diaz, from Marlene again—this morning). Everyone wants to know the next move, everyone's got a different opinion, and no one wants to go into a four-day weekend without knowing where they stand, where the company stands. What they don't understand, though, is that Sarver's entire lower torso is aching harder than it did before the testicle and its deleterious contents was supposedly removed—a phenomenon he can't seem to figure out—and he couldn't possibly give less of a shit about where anyone stands at the moment. He's not even sure he cares about where he stands, especially after this morning's interview with Corbett in the *Post-Gazette*, which it apparently picked up from the *New York Times*. One thing he is sure about, however, is that before he returns to the office, whether that's Monday or January or whenever, he needs to make some decisions—not about personnel or public relations or overhead reductions or any of the other matters his staff has been calling about for the past two days, but about himself.

The door to his room is pushed open and Maryann steps in cautiously, as if, still, after three days, she's not quite sure she's got the right room. She scans the room for a moment before her gaze lands on her husband. "Hi, there," she says, letting the door pull itself closed behind her. She's holding a white Hammermill box inside of which, Sarver presumes, is food.

"Hello, hello," Sarver says.

Maryann stands next to the bathroom door. She is a tall woman, historically five-nine, although earlier this month she reported to Sarver that it has begun: for the first time it is evident that she has shrunk an inch. She sets the box on the bed and lets her purse fall from her shoulder onto a chair beneath the TV. Her icing-white hair is damp, as is her overcoat, and now that she's closer Sarver can see that her tortoise shell glasses are fogged over. "Don't get up," she says, then crosses at the foot of the bed and plants a waxy kiss on Sarver's cheek.

"I wasn't planning on it, believe me."

"Still hurts?"

He nods. "Yeah, a little. A lot. Weird, huh?"

She shakes her head like she thought she'd seen it all, pulls off her coat and lays it on the deep windowsill. She's still angry with him, he knows, for never mentioning his problem to her. And he can understand that. Even now he's not entirely sure why he never mentioned to her that for the past few weeks his stomach and groin had been throbbing at an ever-increasing and painful rate, sometimes cramping to the point of him not being able to breathe, sometimes summoning waves of nausea. But, then again, that's exactly why he didn't tell her.

"So that's your feast," she says now, indicating the tray the nurse left.

"That's it."

"Looks tasty." She turns to him. Her glasses have cleared and she looks incredibly warm and comfortable in her fuzzy turtleneck sweater. "The kids wanted to come, too."

"I know," he says. "But it didn't make sense. It's better they just stay at the house and try to enjoy themselves until you get back. Then you guys can have a nice dinner and afterward everyone can come for a little visit, if they're up to it. It just doesn't make sense now. How are Cindy and Daniel. They all right?"

She sits on the edge of the bed. "Yes. I gave them the toys we bought last week. The little harmonica and the drum. They were making all kinds of racket when I left. And they both said they miss their grandpa."

Sarver smiles. "They can't talk yet, Maryann."

"Well, they were thinking it," she says. "I can read their thoughts." She narrows her eyes at him. She looks away out the window and then back. "We're grandparents now, Newton. Don't you dare go dying on me."

"I won't, Maryann."

"No," she says. "Listen to me. I'm serious. If you die on me now, I'll just hate you. I will."

He can't help smiling. "No, you won't, Maryann."

"Try me."

"So what do you got in that box, sweet thing?"

"Nothing." She reaches over to the night stand for the TV remote. She aims up toward the ceiling and turns it on.

"Ah, come on," he says, still smiling. "Don't be that way. What's in the box?"

She shrugs. "Just some things I cooked up."

He reaches out and touches her knee. He rubs his thumbnail across her stocking. "Like what?"

"I've been thinking," she says, ignoring his question, still looking up at the TV.

"You have?"

"Yeah. I've been thinking... I've been thinking that if you'd have died—gotten hit by a bus or something—way back when, like maybe a year or two after we got married, I'd have been devastated, of course. You see things like that on the news and you think, God, how tragic. But I'm relatively sure I could've come back from that and, you know, lived a life. Not that I'd have gotten over it, necessarily, but I'd have been able to go on, I think. I do. And, on the other hand, if we were like eighty or something—you know, old—again, you know, I think I'd be able to deal with that. On those terms. After all, one of us will have to, that's a certainty."

She looks down at him now. Her eyes behind her glasses are shiny, glassy, with tears welling up within the borders of her lids. Sarver can tell she's trying like the devil not to blink and bring it all streaming down her face. "But now," she says. "I wouldn't be able to take it now. Not now." She shakes her head as if trying to clear it. "Isn't that awful?"

"Which part?"

"All of it. I just—" Finally she blinks and the tears spill and tumble quickly down her cheeks and neck and into her warm fluffy sweater.

"It was just my balls, Maryann. They say I really only need one."

She pinches his shoulder, hard. "Don't you patronize me."

Sarver wrenches free of her grip; he doesn't know why he's still smiling, but he is. He can't help it. "I love you," he says.

She wipes at her cheeks with her fingers. "Yeah," she says. "That's what I mean."

The phone on the night stand rings. Sarver's hand is still on his wife's knee. They're looking at each other. She sniffles, clears her throat. "I'll get it," she says.

✳ ✳ ✳

The outside of the house is stripped. Stripped of paint, shutters, siding, pretty much everything. All that's exposed to the world now is wood and plaster, some red and black brick along the lower half. Even the walkway is missing, replaced by wooden planks that lead from the driveway to the front door. Beneath the leafless trees, and surrounded by the dense mud of construction, Michael can't help thinking that the house looks dead.

"I forgot to tell you," Natalie says as they negotiate the wooden planks, "they're redoing the outside of the house."

"Either that or—" Alex says. "Never mind."

"Let's just try and have a nice time today," Natalie says cheerily, as she leads them toward the front door. "Let's just enjoy the day and each other's company and try and forget our troubles. People do that. We can do that, can't we? That's what Thanksgiving is for. Am I right?" She stops on the plywood planks and turns to Michael and Alex, an expectant look on her face. It now seems to be raining, Michael can't help noticing, upwards.

"Yeah," Michael says. "Sure, baby. You're absolutely right."

Inside, a burdensome smell of beef bullion and burnt grease is in the air. Voices radiate from every room. Gil Winstead, Natalie's father, greets them in the entry hall and takes their coats. He gives Natalie a kiss and Michael gets a handshake, along with a half-hug with Gil's left arm. "Didn't think you guy's were gonna make it," he says. "You made it through the mine field in the front yard, too, I see." He then extends a hand to Alex. "Gil Winstead."

"Oh, I'm sorry," Michael says. "Gil this is Alex."

"Alex Quinby," Alex says.

"Good to meet you, Alex. Welcome." Gil Winstead is compactly built, thick but not at all fat, and Michael is sure that as soon as the man is out of earshot Alex will comment on this and suggest that, with such a build—sturdy, compact, low center of gravity—he would have made a good fullback. Or a nose-tackle, but for that he'd have to put on a few pounds and really hit the weight room. Natalie's father also is beginning to lose his hair in front and on top of his head in bizarre patterns, something like the North Carolina coastline (this began around the time that Michael and Natalie were married), and he hasn't given up on the mustache everyone tells him to shave off. He also likes to wear sweaters in the fall and winter and he pulls them down below his waist so that the sweater's bottom elastic is always awkwardly positioned halfway down his butt. "Let me just throw these coats upstairs on a bed. Dinner's almost ready I've been told. And, Michael, the game's on in the living room. Ralph and Marty are in there."

"Okay."

"I'll join you in a minute," Gil Winstead says as he weaves his way up the stairs, laden with coats.

It's been six weeks since Michael's and Natalie's last visit and already the place is different—the torn-up exterior not withstanding. Improvements have been made. Directly to the right of the entry hall is what used to be a mud room-slash-den and now is what Mr. and Mrs. Winstead now refer to as "the library." And, Michael has to admit, the name does—in the visual sense at least—do it justice. One wall is a gorgeous floor-to-ceiling oak bookcase, beautifully stained a deep amber. Unfortunately, the reason Michael can so easily appreciate the beauty of the bookcase is that there are very few books on it. As he glances in now he can see that there are a few more than the last time they visited, which was the first time they saw The Library, but not many more. There were a few picture books of San Francisco and New York (which Michael bought them for a Christmas gift a couple of years back), some self-help books, the Bible (which was displayed upright and facing the room), some old insurance guides (which is how Gil Winstead made his money), and a biography or two of well-known businessmen, Lee Iacocca and Warren

Buffett. Books with titles like *My Way* and *Discover Your Inner Power* and *Success: Grab It!* There also is a matching solid oak desk with a leather-trimmed blotter and a fancy pen in its brass-plated holder, the kind of thing Michael knows he'd lose within the week, if it was his. To the left of the entryway is the dining room: new table, new lighting fixtures (a chandelier with little diamond-shaped crystals dangling from it; when the air or heat kicks on in the house the crystals sway and spin gently, catching the light and reflecting it in piercing little bursts), new Asian carpet upon new pine flooring. Michael glances in and sees Natalie's Aunt Stephanie placing a big bowl on the table. She turns and gives a wave. "Hey," she says, brushing her sandy, brittle bangs away from her eyes. "Happy Thanksgiving."

"Hi, Stephanie," Michael says. "Same to you."

She takes a step toward the entry hall then stops suddenly when someone calls her name from the kitchen. She holds her index finger up to Michael. "Just a sec," she says, and disappears through the other doorway into the kitchen, which is where the newest batch of improvements has taken place.

When they enter the kitchen they are met, to Michael's amazement, by cheers. Actual cheers, as though everyone here has been held hostage and now Natalie, Alex and Michael are here to free them. The steam with which the kitchen is filled adds to this vision. Natalie's mother, a frail woman who relies too heavily on make-up to provide more dominant facial features and who is often self-conscious of her own voice, approaches from the stove, hands held out and up, palms inward, in order to frame each face for easier kissing. Lately she's been heavy into Jesus, referring to Him and His influence at odd, some might say questionable, moments. Her name is Sharon but insists everyone call her Shae. "We'd about given up hope," she says.

"Sorry, Mrs. Winstead," Alex says. "It was my fault."

"This is Alex," Michael says. "It was his fault."

She takes Alex's face between her hands and kisses it. "Now that's a tie," she says.

"Thanks."

"Good Lord," Natalie says, scanning the room. "What have you done now, Mother?"

Shae turns and regards the room with her daughter, as if seeing it for the first time, too, as various relatives—Natalie's Aunt Stephanie and Aunt Carly, Gil's cousin Ellen, and Nadine Something, who explains that she and her husband are friends of the Winsteads from Johnstown—approach and greet the three of them.

"What do you think of it?" Shae says. She has her arm around Natalie's shoulder.

"It's...interesting," Natalie says.

The floor is entirely new entirely: big squares of grainy cream-colored tile. Elegant is the only word that'll come to Michael's mind. The cabinets, which used to be a tan pseudo-wood, are now hunter green, shiny and solid-looking, with ritzy gold knobs. The countertops are a similar cream color to the floor, and the stove, Michael can see, is one of those numbers where the heating element is without the standard black metal spirals but is simply a circle that glows a vicious red. There is an oven above the stove and an oven below, and in the middle of the kitchen is a Formica island in the shape of a 7, with four stools around it.

"You don't like it?" Shae says, obviously hurt.

Natalie takes a breath. "I like it."

"It doesn't sound like you like it. What don't you like about it? The gold knobs? I was afraid that might be a bit much."

"Oh, for crying out loud," Aunt Stephanie says, rushing for a pot on the stove that is boiling over with water. She takes the pot and places it on a towel on the counter. Across the room, on another counter top, Ellen is slicing green peppers and Carly, spatula in hand, is transferring corn fritters from a skillet to a plate.

"No," Natalie says. "It's fine, Mom. Really. I like it."

"Very nice," Michael says, because he feels like he should.

"Thank you, dear," Shae says, placing a hand on his wrist.

"Come on," Michael says to Alex. "Let's check out the game." He doesn't want to be around this now. All the remodeling her parents have been doing lately has for some reason struck a nerve with Natalie. Her argument, which Michael has heard often as of late, centers mainly around the timing of it. Natalie grew up in this house. She was the middle child, a brother above and one beneath, and it bothers her that her parents have waited until the youngest, Marty, moved out before beginning any of these projects. To her, the concept is ass-backwards. Why not make improvements to the house while there were still some people in it? Not now, when it's just the two of them. It makes no sense, she says, and, frankly, it's insulting to those people who used to live here. There's more to the argument, though, and Michael suspects he knows what it is. It's frustrating to see her former family, that is, the one she used to be officially associated with before marrying Michael, swimming in cash, redoing the rooms of an already-respectable house, buying new cars and taking fancy trips (Mr. and Mrs. Winstead have visited Aspen, Vancouver and the Greek Isles in the past twelve months), while she, along with her new family, i.e., Michael, has to take cash advances on the MasterCard to pay the Visa bill. That's what's at issue here, and Michael would rather not stick around to watch it play out. So he and Alex excuse themselves, head toward the rear of the house, and step down into the mammoth, redone, window-lined living room. In the far corner is a big-screen TV. Michael can't remember if Gil, when he bought it last year, told him it was a fifty-two or a fifty-five-incher. Either way, though, it's big.

"Hey, Miguel," Marty says from the sofa. "Game's on."

A good-sized fire is going in the fireplace. Michael makes the appropriate introductions for Alex and each is given a Bloody Mary. Alex just looks at his, stirs the celery stalk around in it. Watching the game along with Ralph and Marty is Rich, a friendly enough looking fiftyish man with tiny, hairline-thin lips who reveals he is married to Nadine Something from the kitchen. The uncles, Michael is told, are in the basement playing pool.

Michael takes a seat on the floor next to Ralph, up against the fireplace ledge, the heat warming his back; Alex remains standing, drink in hand, eyes on the huge, hypnotic television screen. Michael's thoughts keep returning to what Natalie said on their way into the house, her suggestion that they try and forget their troubles for the afternoon. Michael has always had great respect for people who could do that. And, really, there is no reason not to do it. What was so hard about living in the moment? Enjoying the now? Anything Michael has to worry about isn't going to change, whether or not he has an enjoyable Thursday afternoon. But Michael, for as long as he can remember, has always taken the opposite approach: any enjoyment he could have today is automatically tainted, because once he leaves here he still has to deal with what he caused at that press conference Monday afternoon. That won't change. So why tease himself?

Ralph reaches out and taps Michael's leg. "Good to see you, man."

"You, too." Michael has always liked both of Natalie's brothers, but especially Ralph, who is two years older. He's going bald at thirty-four, but there is a softness in Ralph's face, a complete absence of tension in his high, curved eyebrows and lineless, constantly relaxed forehead—aspects that, until meeting Ralph, Michael has always associated with the notion of wisdom. He feels he could trust Ralph, though, if things ever came to that. "How's the job hunt coming?" he asks.

Ralph shifts his hips on the floor beneath him and sits up straight. He drinks the last of his bloody Mary and sets the glass on the fireplace hearth. "I'll tell you something, Michael. I'm beginning to think there are no jobs in my field. I mean, I apply for jobs I know I'm qualified for—some I'm overqualified for—and I'm not even getting interviews. So, theoretically, that means that there are that many people who are even more qualified than me applying for these jobs. And if that's the case, then they're way overqualified. See what I'm saying? Which leads me to wonder why they'd want such a job in the first place. I'll tell you, it's got me very confused. I go through these scenarios in my head, what qualifications the people who are getting these jobs have, and I can't figure it out."

"Well, keep at it. One'll work out." It's all Michael can think of to say. He's just hoping Ralph doesn't turn around and ask how his work is going.

"I did get in for one interview," Ralph says. "Last month. Listen to this. I go into the guy's office, right? The guy's seven feet tall. Seriously. He stands up to shake my hand and I, like, jump back. He scared the shit out of me. I mean, there he is sitting behind his desk, then he stands up, and whoa! That was my first mistake, I guess. Then—I'll tell you, Michael, I have to quit being so honest in these job interviews; it's killing me—then he asks me my reason for leaving my previous position. And I told him, it was because my former boss was insane. Well, this threw him off course, in terms of how he wanted to interview me and stuff, so he asks what it was that made me think the guy was nuts. Think! So, hell, I told him—Ah, bullshit, he had both feet down! That's a bad call."

Michael looks up at the screen. Two larger-than-life Minnesota Vikings are arguing, purple helmets in hand, with a chubby referee. Two words are very readable on the lips of the players: fucking, fucker or some distinct variation of fuck, and bullshit. Alex has sat down on the sofa, his drink still full, where he and Marty are watching the game together, silently. Gil Winstead's muted voice floats in from another room.

"So," Michael says. "The guy was crazy."

"Yeah." Ralph is still watching the TV. "My old boss was. But this other guy, the guy interviewing me, he wanted to know why I thought that. So I told him, well, one thing was the way he made us all sing 'You'll Never Walk Alone' at the conclusion of staff meetings."

"No way," Michael says. "Really?" Then it occurs to him to ask, "Solo?"

"No, as a group. Although sometimes he would sing it solo. He'd stand up at the head of the conference table and let fly."

"Was he any good?"

Ralph shrugs. "He wasn't bad."

Michael laughs, even though he doesn't find Ralph's story particularly hysterical. It just makes him feel good. "What else?"

"Oh, I don't know. Things like, well, one time I went into his office to talk to him, and the guy was blue, nearly passed out sitting at his desk. Veins popping out of his forehead. So I run up to him and slap him on the back and he gasps for a while and then he yells at me. Says he was holding his breath on purpose. Says he likes to see how long he can hold his breath for. Says it builds character. I'll tell you, the guy was gonzo. He was out there."

"And you told the guy you were interviewing with all this?" Michael is still smiling.

"Yeah. Like I said, though, I gotta tone down the honesty. I realize that."

"What kind of job was this for?"

"Human resources at a law firm."

"Oh. What's your field again?"

"Political consulting. Demographics research, specifically."

"Well, geez, Ralph," Michael says. "Maybe that's part of the problem."

Ralph takes a breath, picks his empty glass up off the hearth. "Yeah, I know. But that's the one I end up getting the interview for. You see what I'm saying? Now go figure that out." He leans forward with his glass, as if to stand. "I've been reading these books. The power of positive thinking and shit like that. *We Become What We Think About*, that's the name of one of them, off the top of my head. You know there are people out there who think you can control everything in your life, even your health, just by thinking it."

"I've heard that," Michael says.

Ralph shrugs. "I don't know. It's tough to swallow, don't you think? I mean, sure, I've always been sort of a pessimist by nature. That's true. My old man, he's always been into that positive thinking kind of stuff and I always thought it was a waste of time. I admit that. I figured, plan for the worst, then anything good that happens to you is gravy. But these books, I have to admit they make sense. While I'm reading them, anyway. Like, look at that guy there." He points to the television screen. A player jumps up after having been tackled and flips the ball to the referee. "He knows he's going to play well, knows he's going to get open and catch the ball when it's thrown to him. He doesn't just tell himself that. He knows it, down in his, you know, down in his soul. Confidence breeds success. That's a phrase I remember from one of the books. J.K. Tillinghast. And it's true. I can't argue it. But what if you just envision everything not working, because that's what feels right? Nothing intentional, just the way things feel, honestly. The natural course of things. How do you get confidence when you keep fucking everything up?" He looks around, lowers his voice. "Sorry, Mike. Pardon my language."

"No problem, Ralph."

"Ah, hell. How about you, though? Everything going all right with you? Job okay?"

"Sure," Michael hears himself say. "Fine. Full steam ahead."

Ralph makes like to get up, but he doesn't. He rubs the back of his hand across his chin, turns to Michael "That's great, man," he says. "Really. It's good to hear something's going right for someone, for a change."

Alex peps up some during dinner. He's beside himself with the whole brisket thing, and the strange combination of praise and utter bewilderment he continually directs toward Shea Winstead, for her efforts, brings out an obvious show of visual satisfaction in the woman. Michael, though, senses that Alex is running on fumes and could very well pass out from exhaustion at any moment.

The seating arrangement is pretty standard: Gil Winstead at the head; Shea at the opposite end, near the kitchen entrance for easy access; Michael and Natalie near the middle of the table; Alex across from them, a Winstead brother on each side; uncles, aunts, et cetera, scattered throughout.

"I apologize," Shea Winstead says to the Johnstown couple. "We don't have turkey on Thanksgiving. We have brisket instead. It's sort of a tradition with us."

Alex chuckles, shakes his head. "That's so great."

Again, Shea Winstead blushes. "Okay, Gil," she says, laying a lavender linen napkin across her lap. "Go ahead, honey. Say the Word."

Without speaking, Gil Winstead bows his head and closes his eyes. Everyone at the table follows suit, except for Michael, who bows his head slightly but does not close his eyes. Something inside him (aversion?) won't let him participate. He shifts his eyes, feeling them move in his unflinching head (aversion to what?). Alex's eyes are closed, his head is down. Quite possibly, he has fallen asleep. The Johnstown couple is holding hands under the table, Michael can tell by the positioning of their arms. As Gil Winstead begins with, "Heavenly Father, we thank You for these gifts," which, to Michael, though he hasn't been in quite some time, sounds like something right out of Sunday morning Mass. Michael glances across the table at Ralph and sees that his eyes are open, too. And he's smiling. A few seconds later, as Gil Winstead is touching base with all of the family members who have passed on and are therefore not present at today's festivities, Ralph—a thirty-four-year-old political consultant and, to Michael's way of thinking, an all-around good guy—leans way back in his chair, a big, silly grin still plastered across his face. Alex, groggy and listless, opens one eye, glances over, looks back down at his hands, then quickly turns to Ralph again, eyes wide. Ralph is now balanced back on his chair at a near-forty-five-degree angle. "We trust in Your divine guidance and look to You for answers in our daily endeavors," Gil Winstead says. "We ask You to look upon us with compassion as we continue to strive toward our individual goals and to bless our family bond, keeping it strong." His eyes are closed tight, as if, in addition to saying grace, he's exerting some sort of Herculean effort, trying to push the dining room table across the new Oriental carpet and into the kitchen perhaps. Ralph inches back farther. Natalie opens her eyes, looks up, straightens. Suddenly, Michael acknowledges a terrible and very real fear that he might start laughing. He feels it building in his stomach, warming like kindling, and he squeezes down hard in his gut, trying to extinguish the sensation. Then Ralph takes it that one inch too far. Michael can see it in his face. The smile vanishes and is immediately replaced by a look of such extreme horror that, if Michael hadn't known better, he would have suspected terrorists had just burst through the front door behind him, and Ralph, for the moment at least, is the only one who can see it. His eyes light and his arms shoot out to the sides for balance. Natalie stares in amazement. Others have caught on, too, and Michael is now free to glance around the table. Shae Winstead looks to her husband, who, eyes still squeezed shut, is appealing to God's knack for seeing the good in every situation, for help; Marty reaches his fork to the center of the table and spears a slice of brisket. (Why Alex doesn't simply reach out, take Ralph by the elbow and steady him, Michael can only write off to lethargy and disbelief.) When Michael turns his attention back to Ralph, he sees that his brother-in-law's arms are flapping wildly in what Michael imagines to be a bizarre, clownish imitation of a drowning man trying to do the backstroke. Now everyone's eyes are open but Gil Winstead's, and Michael finds that he is looking back and forth, from Gil to Ralph, in tennis match-like fashion, until, at the moment when Ralph teeters back just beyond the zone of gravitational indifference, Michael sees the antique, silver plated cart behind him, on top of which is an assortment of desserts—Michael notices, vividly for some reason, a big glass bowl of strawberries mixed with whipped cream—and Ralph's head disappears, replaced by the soles of his shoes as he goes over into the cart. The sound is less dramatic than Michael expected—more of a prolonged thud than a crash—and no desserts go flying spectacularly into the air, they just fall along with Ralph and the cart. Before the sound has dissipated, though, everyone at the table is standing. Except Michael.

After several seconds, it is Alex who breaks the silence.

"Whoa," he says. "Damn."

Natalie leaves the room. She cuts through the kitchen and into the hallway and then her footsteps are heard heading up the stairs. For a few moments Michael, still sitting, watches the other side of the table. He cannot see Ralph on the floor, just his feet and ankles in the air. There is some movement down there, the empty sound of platters, previously caught or suspended, falling the last couple of feet onto the carpet, a dull *whump*. Then, like a scrambled television show suddenly snapping into perfect focus, Michael sees that everyone else is now turned and looking at him; they are motionless, and he is laughing. He is laughing, he realizes, not because of Ralph's ridiculous chair-balancing act and its now-inevitable conclusion, but because of what he now believes to be the reasons behind Ralph's performance: contempt. Contempt, apparently, for every potential employer who overlooked Ralph's overqualified r sum , contempt for his own father, for God, contempt for a national holiday, contempt for the world. Because, Michael presumes, he can't find a decent job. He wonders what J.K. Tillinghast would say about Ralph's performance, and, for some reason, that strikes Michael as incredibly funny.

He keeps laughing, an uncontrolled, wheezing laugh, all breath, the taking in of air ill-timed with the laugh itself, and soon Michael is gasping and choking, his eyes blurry and, suddenly, filled with tears. The people staring back at him look as though they're submerged, like he's viewing them through the glass of an aquarium. Or they're viewing him. Regardless, someone quickly slips behind Michael, wraps their arms around him, pulls him up onto his feet, and squeezes three quick hard blasts of pressure into his chest. The result is anything but funny and Michael, having stopped laughing, coughs a couple more times, then sucks in a massive amount of air. He rubs his chest and turns around to see Gil Winstead step away from him, pulling the edges of his sweater back down below his hips. He says, "Sorry, son," as if he'd done something horrible and unexplainable.

Michael nods. On the other side of the table Alex and Rich from Johnstown are helping Ralph to his feet. There is pie crust and whipped cream in Ralph's hair, cherry filling hanging red and gooey from his ears and eyelashes. Michael doesn't find this funny. Not even a little bit. Ralph has a stunned look on his face, like a cartoon of someone who's just survived an explosion. He sways for a while then looks around the table at everyone, each person separately, as if taking roll. When he's gone around the table he says, "Where's Natalie?" Then, without waiting for an answer, he sits cautiously back down in his chair.

The rest of the guests follow suit, except for Shea Winstead who is busy cleaning up the fallen dishes. She takes a stack in her arms and stands, loose strands of hair hanging in front of her eyes. "Go ahead, Gil," she says. "Finish the blessing." Then she heads off into the kitchen. Everyone watches her go, and, to Michael at least, it's almost like a trick of the mind, an optical illusion, when, as his mother-in-law passes through the wide doorway into the kitchen and out of sight, her figure is replaced almost immediately in the doorway by that of his wife. She stands facing the table, looking down over it, arms folded across her chest, leaning her shoulder against the Winsteads' newly re-finished wood trim. Mahogany, Michael remembers being told.

"Hi, Baby," Gil Winstead says from the far end of the table. "Come join us. We're just about to bow our heads." He bows his head again.

"I need to talk to Michael," she says. "Michael, would you excuse yourself for a moment, please."

"Nat, honey, we're in the middle of the blessing," Michael says. He's looking across the table at Ralph who, despite the cherry pie filling that's still dripping from various parts of his head and torso, looks surprisingly natural and at ease. "Or we were at least. Come sit down."

Natalie straightens. A faucet turns on inside the kitchen, then the garbage disposal roars. "Again," Gil Winstead says, re-closing his eyes, "let us pray," and Michael, this time, is all-too happy to follow suit. He bows his head and closes his eyes and prepares himself with all he has inside of him for the sound of his father-in-law's steady, rehearsed voice.

But the voice he hears, from the doorway, is Natalie's. "I'm pregnant," it says.

Ralph's left eye does a funny squinching sort of thing, as if he'd been poked in the side by something sharp, then he turns his head quickly toward the doorway, spraying cherry bits onto Rich from Johnstown. Michael, though, does not turn. Not at first. He couldn't say how, but he knew this was coming. He waits for the sweats, the tightening in his chest, the shortness of breath and abdominal pains he experienced Monday while driving home after the press conference, but they do not come. He is calm, wholly calm, although he realizes that his ears are hot—almost unbearably hot. Then he turns toward the doorway. Natalie is looking at him, arms still folded across her chest. Over her right shoulder, back in the kitchen, Michael can see Shae Winstead approaching, hunched over, sneaking up on her daughter. She's actually walking on her tiptoes, holding a dishtowel; her forearms are pink and wet and dripping and on her face is a skeptical expression, mouth open, head tilted to the side, as if Natalie has just announced that she's become a magician and immediately proved this by making her own head disappear.

"Oh, sweetie," Shae Winstead says, reaching out, "that's wonderful. Oh, Natalie." She takes her daughter's hands in hers, the dishtowel wedged in between them. Then she says, "Wait. Are you serious?"

"Yes, Mom."

The near corner of Shea Winstead's mouth twitches. She says, "Oh, honey," and wraps her arms around Natalie's neck and then everyone at the table is up again. Within seconds a crowd has formed in the doorway between the dining room and kitchen; even the Johnstown couple are over there, offering their congratulations, pleased as can be. Michael watches his wife; she is trying to look back at him, to convey something, but soon the crowd envelops her and their sight line is severed.

Michael looks over at Alex, the only person, besides himself, still seated at the table. "Pass the brisket," he says.

Alex reaches for the platter. He stabs a couple of strips with the serving fork and sets them on his plate before passing the platter across to Michael. "Um, congratulations," he says.

"Thanks, pal." The brisket looks cold and unappetizing, dead on the plate; the dark reddish juice, already gritty and congealed, reminds Michael of blood and the fact that he noticed this is immediately embarrassing to himself. But what can he say? It does look like blood. It also reminds him, for some reason, of sweet potatoes and he decides he cannot share Alex's joyous opinion of brisket on Thanksgiving. The concept is just plain stupid.

"This calls for a celebration," Gil Winstead says, and heads off to the wine cellar, another recent addition to the Winstead estate.

Thanksgiving breakfast was at a place called Fairlane's on the Upper West Side, not far from the kids' apartment, and dinner was in a dark, cavernous restaurant by the name of Leiff, which Toby continually pronounced wrong (like leaf), on purpose. It was a new place, way down on 22nd Street ("in Chelsea," Ellie kept saying, as if this justified the place), and apparently quite trendy. They skipped lunch. Sort of a mercy omission, the way Toby looked at it. Now, riding back to the apartment in a taxi cab that smells like his sink when the drain clogs up, he wishes they'd've just skipped the whole thing: They had to wait for a table even though they had reservations; he was way underdressed (but not as underdressed as Todd, which obviously annoyed Ellie, who spoke directly to her husband noticeably infrequently); it was impossible to have a conversation above the echoes ringing throughout the cave-like atmosphere of the restaurant itself; the bill came to $239, before tip, and Ellie insisted, rather vehemently, on her and Todd paying it (even though, Toby thought he could tell by the look on his face, Todd would have been fine with his father-in-law paying it); then, while waiting for this taxi to take them home after dinner, there was an accident on the street, right in front of them. A Ford Explorer clipped the back end of a Volkswagen that was trying, carelessly, Toby had to admit, to change lanes.

"Oops," Ellie said, pulling on her mittens.

A man in a dark suit got out of the Explorer while the woman passenger stayed where she was, in the front seat. He walked over to the Volkswagen's driver's side door, opened it, reached in and took the driver—a young man, a kid really, seventeen or eighteen—by the collar, dragged him out onto the street, and put a quick, hard knee to his ribs. Then he went back to his car, got in, and drove away.

"I didn't see anything," Todd said, and laughed.

"Me neither," a guy beside them said.

The kid knelt beside his Volkswagen, coughing, while other cars honked their horns and tried to get past. Toby looked around him and realized something: There are too many people in the world. This New York city block was living proof. They were everywhere: some standing, some moving in and out of buildings, some walking this way or that. What there was a definite shortage of, however, was benevolence. Toby's thirty years with Electro-Lite had taught him something, though it really had nothing to do with his own job, per se, about supply and demand. The problem with the world was that there were too many people and not enough of anything else. This bothered Toby, of course, but what bothered him most, and perhaps was the reason for his own lack of benevolence, for his not somehow stepping in and helping the kid in the Volkswagen, was the raging fire behind his breastbone, caused by the quail or the pheasant or maybe the sauce one of them was served in, he couldn't be sure. It caused him to feel old. More specifically, though, it caused him to think of himself as an old man who has gone and spoiled the young folks' holiday fun. They were going to go ice skating somewhere (Central Park? Times Square? Madison Square Garden?—it was someplace he'd heard of before anyway). That was the plan, as it was explained to him. But Toby said he wasn't up for it.

"But, Daddy," Ellie had said, "it's tradition."

"Whose tradition?" Todd said. The kid in the street climbed slowly back into his Volkswagen and closed the door.

Ellie held up her arms up as if signaling a touchdown. "Everyone's tradition." Toby's vision fell directly on his daughter's yellow knit mittens, which caused an unexpected twist inside him.

"I've never been ice skating in my life," Todd said.

"Well, that's you."

"Ellie, honey," Toby said. "It's just not important to me." Immediately he knew he'd chosen the wrong words. He thought he would've known better, after this morning.

"Oh," she said. "Okay. I understand." Then a cab pulled up to the curb and Todd opened the back door and no one has spoken since.

The air outside is cold but Toby needs the window open several inches. The tinny smell of winter rushes into the cab. He can't remember ever having "heartburn." Not in his entire life. He sees commercials on the television for heartburn medicine and, though he assumes it's fairly common, he thinks, What is that? Well, now he knows. He shifts in his seat and hopes he doesn't break wind.

In front of him, the cabbie reaches up and adjusts the rear-view mirror; beside him, Todd pats the back of Ellie's mittened hands, folded on her lap. Those yellow mittens have done something to him, Toby has to admit. Fleetingly, he sees Ellie in his mind as a young girl, hooded parka pulled tight around her head, a straight line of light brown bangs crawling out of the hood toward her eyes, drawstrings tied in a bow beneath her chin. She holds up a hand—a yellow-mittened hand—as a signal that she's about to leave, then turns and reaches for the doorknob. On her back is a pink Barbie knapsack holding her schoolbooks. This is a typical memory, perfectly natural to invade his thoughts now, Toby tells himself. Predictable in every way. But after Ellie is out the door and on her way down the street to the bus stop, all that's left in his mind's eye is Carol, just standing off to the side, looking back at him as he watches the door. They're in their first house, in Churchill, which was just a short commute to the Electro-Lite facility in Turtle Creek, where Toby had landed his first job as a security guard. The house has a narrow entry hall; because of the heavy wood unit (which served as a place to hold keys and gloves and loose change) placed up against the wall opposite the closet, a full-grown man, like Toby, has to turn sideways to pass through. Carol's hips are still narrow, tiny, and she'd have no trouble slipping past if she wanted to. But she stays where she is, watching him down the length of the hallway. She touches the side of her head, where her long brown hair is pulled tight into a ponytail, checking for loose strands. She smiles. The tails of her plaid flannel shirt hang down nearly to her knees.

Toby does some quick subtraction: 27 years ago.

The smell pouring in through the window has changed. Now all Toby can envision is a mattress soaked with beer. He rolls up his window; the fire burning in his chest is steady, but not increasing. Todd, sitting on the other side of Ellie, sneezes.

"*Gesundheit*," Toby says.

"Thanks," Todd says, then proceeds to sneeze nine more times (Toby counts them) in rapid succession. The sneezes are loud, with considerable force behind them, and Todd, eyes closed to slits, rolls down his own window.

Toby now remembers that Ellie came home from school that day with what he and Carol thought was a cold but, when the symptoms wouldn't go away, and in fact grew worse over the next couple of days, they were told she had bronchial pneumonia. They admitted her into West Penn Hospital and, since the hospital was in East Liberty, a good thirty-five minutes from their house in Churchill, Toby and Carol took a room at the nearby Oakland Holiday Inn, just down from the university. They spent most of the next six days at the hospital, using the hotel room as a home base, a place to shower and to keep their things. Toby remembers packing those things, remembers the dead feeling in his chest, the same chest that now sustains the heat of a significant fire. He didn't know what he should bring. Carol was at the hospital with Ellie, leaving Toby to "see to the details." The suitcase was opened so that its lid fell over the far side of the bed. Toby threw in underwear, socks, a couple of shirts for himself. But when it came to Carol he stopped and stood in front of her closet, considering what was there. Dresses, blouses, pants, each on its own hanger. He reached in and removed a blouse. He held it up. It was sky blue, made from a velvety material, velour maybe, and it was tiny. At first Toby thought it might be Ellie's, in this closet by mistake. But that couldn't be the case. He'd seen Carol wear this very blouse. He took it, still on the hanger, and held it up to himself. He turned, and in the full-length mirror on the back of the bathroom door, he could see that the blouse seemed to barely cover half of his chest, and he realized how small his wife was, her physical size—how small, in fact, women were. It was something he'd never considered and it occurred to him suddenly that the reason behind it (he was sure of this, even then) was more sensory that physical. Carol was everything to him: the foundation on which he existed, and he figured the same was true for many men with regard to their wives, at least those men who were worth anything, who understood anything, and were man enough to admit anything. And what Toby understood was that, in a weird kind of way, he was intimidated by his wife. How could he not be? How could you not be intimidated, even a little frightened, by someone who has the power to so thoroughly, and seemingly without effort, know your fears, your weaknesses? How could you not be intimidated by someone whom you trust with this information? But, even more so, how could someone who occupied such a huge station in another's life be so physically small? It didn't fit. To Toby, Carol was a world in and of herself, a core to his world, his gravitational pull. This blouse could not possibly fit her. Then, as if he knew to look there at exactly that moment, he saw a blue jay fly into the bedroom window and kill itself. Why does he remember that now? Of all the things he's forgotten in his life, why does he remember that bird? That blouse? He, in fact, can remember everything, as if it were in slow motion: hearing the thud, seeing the bird's head bend sharply away from its body, the startling blueness of it in contrast to the white snow behind; he remembers how its wings flapped two or three more times before it fell to the ground below.

He put the blouse in the suitcase, along with several other tiny articles of his wife's clothing, then he headed back to West Penn. Twelve years later, Carol would die in that same hospital.

Toby reaches across the cab now and takes Ellie's left hand in his. He removes the yellow mitten and sets it on her lap. Todd sneezes some more but no one acknowledges him. Her hand is cold. The air inside the cab is cold, too, but the beer-mattress smell is gone; either that or Toby has become used to it. He rubs Ellie's left hand between both of his own, gently, as if to warm it. She lets him do this. In the palms of his hands he can feel his daughter's bones and knuckles, her thin wrist, the hard, smooth surface of her fingernails, which he knows for a fact she has done professionally. He looks down then and sees it all—the wrist, the knuckles, the nails—dwarfed by the monstrosity of his own man-hands. Hers is like the hand of a child, a doll even, not that of a grown woman, a married woman, an attorney. Toby brings the hand to his face and kisses the back of it. He suspects Todd is probably watching this, between sneezes, but Toby doesn't care. Todd, he knows, understands. He must understand.

* * *

While his wife searches the kitchen cabinets for some Pepto-Bismol hidden amidst the growing legion of vitamin supplements she keeps in there, Todd heads for the bathroom. He's afraid his nose may have started bleeding again. The again part is something Ellie doesn't know about, and this is not the time, with her father in town and her falling over herself to impress him, to hit her with it. The bathroom lights are white and harsh. They make everything look fuzzy and skittish. He leans in toward the mirror, elbows on the edge of the sink, and examines himself. He looks two-dimensional, flat. That's what his image is, of course, but he looks it. A picture of himself taken in bad, bad light. He tilts his head back and tries to examine his nostrils, searching the rims for signs of blood, dried or otherwise. Nothing, so far as he can tell. Through the wall Todd can hear Ellie tell her father that they don't have any Pepto, but that he should take three or four of these—they're all-natural—and they'll straighten him right up. Todd shakes his head. He laughs a short, breathy laugh, the force of which shoots two dime-size dollops of blood onto the mirror in front of him.

He's become a cliché; he knows that, but not even an up-to-date clich . Musicians are supposed to be into heroin now. Cocaine is old hat, totally out of style. He dabbled around with the stuff back in college, at Dickinson, where he met Ellie, when he was playing guitar for a cover band made up of four other guys, all students too. They played fraternity parties, pep rallies, spring and fall festivals sponsored by the college, and the occasional bar gig in nearby York, Pennsylvania. They even played a half-dozen shows in Philly, the five of them piling into the bass player's Oldsmobile, with a U-Haul, which they'd each kicked in ten bucks for, attached to the rear hitch to carry their equipment. Where the coke came from, Todd could only guess. Philly maybe. Or New York: it wasn't that far. In any case, one day, it was there, and, because they'd just driven four hours through the night to get back to campus, or because they were doing three shows in one night, or because he was feeling sluggish from finals and didn't want to slog his way through the set, or just because, he tried it. It wasn't much of a decision really. It just made sense, at the time.

But it was different then. He couldn't say exactly how it was different, if someone were to ask him now, if someone were to put a gun to his head and demand, Goddamn it, how was it so different? The only way he'd be able to defend his assertion would be to say that when he graduated college and married Ellie and the two of them got their jobs in New York and he quit playing his guitar, at least publicly, he also quit the white stuff. In fact, it wasn't even a matter of "quitting," technically. He just didn't even think about it.

Now, here he is, standing in front of the bathroom mirror, shooting blood from his nose all over his reflection.

It hasn't helped matters that this little career move of his hasn't gone anywhere. A couple of nights a week, if that, performing acoustic versions of songs by The Replacements and Peter Gabriel and REM and maybe a quiet Sinead O'Connor worked in there, along with a few blues instrumentals he enjoys playing and an original or two, in front of bar patrons who, for the most part, just came in for a few drinks and discovered, Oh yeah, there's some guy playing the guitar, too. He's not sure exactly what it is he's after, but he knows he's nowhere near it.

He considers his original compositions to be pretty good: Imagine Jimmy Webb if he'd grown up in Seattle, he tells people (some get it and some don't). Ellie, bless her heart, even thinks one of his songs is "beautiful." But they were meant to be performed by a band. They need drums, a backbone; they need density, texture. The problem, though, is no new bands want to take on a thirty-year-old guitarist. Why would they? They are doing their own thing. And a bunch of guys his own age? Well, what's that say about their potential for success?

Todd thought having Toby at one of his shows would be a good thing, for everyone. Now he's not so sure. He's in no condition to be the focus of anyone's attention, much less his father-in-law's. Outside the bathroom door footsteps move from the kitchen to the living room, and then the TV clicks on. Todd runs the water in the sink then removes the plastic contact lens case from his coat pocket, inside of which is what's left of what he bought the other day. He gives his nose a good hard blow to make sure the blood has clotted, then scoops out a small bit of the white powder with his pinkie and brings it up to his nose. He pauses. The worst part, he believes, is knowing full-well what he's doing to himself, and to Ellie. He's not addicted to this stuff. He could wash it all down the sink right now if he wanted to. But he doesn't want to. And that, more than anything, is what he'd very much like to understand.

When Todd shuffles into the living room Ellie and her father are sitting on opposite ends of the sofa. Ellie's shoes are off and her feet are tucked up underneath her; Toby is leaning back, knees apart, hands flat on his chest. On the television is, Todd presumes, a movie-of-the-week: Melissa Gilbert, all grown up

"I could play a little bit," Todd says. "If you want. I've been working on some things."

They turn and look at him. He's standing on the hardwood between the kitchen and living room, still in his coat. He hasn't been working on anything.

"Okay," Ellie says. She turns to her father. "Dad, what do you think?"

"Sure," Toby says. "Sounds good. Tune 'er up."

"All right." Todd slips out of his coat and goes to the corner for his acoustic. His fingers are beginning to take on that familiar numbness and his tongue doesn't feel comfortable in his mouth. Sometimes, though, you just do things. You do some things because you want to or think you should, and right now Todd wants to play a song for Toby. He's played with numb fingers before, with body parts that didn't feel right. Actually, looking at Toby, slouched on the sofa, hand across his chest, lips apart, it occurs to Todd that his father-in-law doesn't look all that right at the moment either. He takes the guitar from its case and sits in the chair by the window, lays the guitar across his knee. Ellie leans forward on the sofa, flicks the TV off with the remote, folds her hands under her chin. What's she expecting? Todd takes the pick and pulls it casually across the strings. Out of tune. Everything, it seems, is out of tune. Outside, a car alarm wails but is quickly silenced and it is in this sudden pocket of silence that Todd wishes a song would come to him, just materialize in the back of his brain and push itself forward and down through his arms into his numb fingertips. In fact, he expects it. He fingers a C chord—a point from which nearly any song could originate—with his left hand and raises the pick in his right. He holds it there, but nothing comes. He looks at his hand, suspended, bare, the hairs on his forearm making it look even more bare, more naked, more exposed, helpless. He lowers his hand, lowers the guitar to the floor, and says, "Toby, I quit my job. I'm playing music full-time now, and not very often. I'm bringing in practically no money and I'm making a mess of things and I'm meeting people who... who I otherwise wouldn't care to meet."

As he knew he would, he immediately wishes he'd kept quiet.

"Todd," Ellie says, a look on her face Todd can only remember seeing on the TV news—on someone standing out in front of her demolished home the day after a hurricane or tornado and being asked to describe it: a look of puzzled fear, with no roof to hide under.

"What kind of people?" Toby says. His hand is now rubbing his chest in a little circular pattern.

"Not bad people. Just frustrated. And I get that way too sometimes."

"Frustrated."

"Yeah."

"Please, Todd," Ellie says.

Toby stops rubbing and leans forward. "And what do you do with this frustration, son?"

"Usually nothing. It's just there."

"Usually."

"Yeah. Have you ever felt helpless, Toby? I mean, like the events going on around you, what's happening to you, is just totally beyond your control?" Suddenly Todd is frightened of himself; he's going to tell everything. He's going to keep talking until everything is out there. "Have you ever felt that way?"

Toby returns his hand to his chest. He leans back again. "Who are these people, Todd?"

"I don't want to talk about them, Toby. I'm asking you something here."

Toby lets out a long breath, then moves to stand. When he's up on his feet, right hand still across his chest as if saluting the flag, he sways backward, catches himself on shaky knees as Ellie reaches out in a rather pathetic attempt to catch him should he fall. "Daddy," she says. But Toby ignores her; he moves to the window and lifts it open. Immediately there is sound—the sound of nothing in particular; just a general whooshing of air and the hum of evening.

After a time, Todd wonders what Toby could be looking at down there. Thanksgiving, this time of night, there can't be much to see. Some cars. A few bums. Even the street vendors took the night off. Ellie, Todd notices, isn't looking at him from across the room, as it seems she should be. She's staring down at the floor, at a spot out beyond the coffee table. Finally Todd gets up and goes to the window next to Toby. He was right about what there is to see down there: cars, bums, parking meters.

"Not much to see," Todd says. He speaks softly. Ellie is only a few steps away on the sofa, but with his and Toby's backs turned, and the sounds pouring in from the window, she can't hear them—something Todd, though he can't say why, feels is necessary.

"Look up there," Toby says, and nods toward the building across the four lanes. The building is brick and about twelve stories tall. Todd looks straight across from their eighth floor window, and then lets his gaze pull upwards until, two floors from the top, he sees a man, leaning his elbows on the windowsill, looking right back down at them.

"How do you stand that?" Toby says. "People everywhere." The tone is not sarcastic or arrogant. Just curious.

Todd shrugs. "You get used to it, I guess."

"There're too many people in the world. That's the problem with everything."

"I don't know," Todd says. "Have you ever been to Nebraska? All kinds of room out there. It's just that it seems everyone chooses the same places to live is all."

Toby takes his eyes from the person across the street and examines Todd. He seems to be searching his son-in-law's face for something. "Yeah," he says. "I guess that could be." Then he says, "Is it drugs or is it alcohol?"

"What?"

"These people you know. Have they got you hooked on drugs or alcohol? My guess is drugs, since I haven't smelled anything on you for the past two days."

"How about none of the above? Isn't that an answer choice? It usually is."

Just then Ellie gets up from the sofa. "Fine," she says. "Don't include me. That's fine," and she heads off toward the back bedrooms, hand under her dress, snapping the elastic waistband of her pantyhose as she goes. Todd turns back to find Toby still looking right at him.

"Sure," Toby says. "All right. Or none of the above. Is that your answer?"

"No." There, it's out. Now what?

Toby nods. "Does Ellie know?"

"No. Just you."

"And your friends, of course."

Todd doesn't answer.

"Do you want help? Is that why you're telling me this?"

"I don't know," Todd says, because it's the truth. "I don't know that I need it. And I don't know what I'd do with myself if I got it."

"Are you high now?"

"I don't know if 'high' is the word I'd use, but..."

"Do you understand what I'm saying to you?"

"Jesus, yes, Toby. I'm not retarded. I haven't suffered a blow to the fucking head." Todd suddenly doesn't want to talk about this anymore. His annoyance surprises him, but it's there. "I'm not under anesthesia."

"Okay then," Toby says, turning. Todd can see his shoulders rise and fall in exaggerated breaths. "I'm going to bed now. Thank you for dinner. I'll head back to Pittsburgh in the morning and I'm going to suggest to Ellie that she come with me and stay with me for a while. I'm going to suggest it very forcefully. Good night."

"Huh?" Todd can feel his insides growing warmer. The heat behind his eyes and cheeks is nearly unbearable.

"I said Ellie and I will leave in the morning. Are you sure you didn't take a blow to the fucking head?" He takes two steps toward the back hallway before Todd grabs his arm.

"Why are you doing this?" Todd detects a whining tinge to his own voice. To offset this, he gives Toby's arm a hard shake, which makes him feel obscene.

"Because I thought you wanted my help," Toby says, looking away. "If you had wanted it, I would have given it to you, done whatever I could. But you don't, and that's fine. But I'm not going to leave my daughter here while you fuck around trying to figure out what's what and end up dragging her down with you." He shakes free of Todd's hold.

"Okay, then, fine. I want help."

Toby keeps going. "No, you don't."

"Come back here," Todd says, a harsh, hissing whisper. But Toby turns the corner into the hallway and five seconds later closes his bedroom door behind him. Todd turns back to the window and locates the man watching them—still watching them—from across the street. He holds his arms out and up, as if preparing to catch a baby falling down through the night sky. Under his breath, mouthing the words slowly and exaggeratedly, he says to the man: "Go... to... Neb... ras... ka."

So many sirens—one right after the other. What are they doing? Every time he hears the wailing erupt outside Toby expects red and blue lights to play across his darkened spare-bedroom ceiling, but then he remembers: he's eight floors up. Through the walls he hears Todd enter the bathroom, he hears the water running in the sink and, though he knows they shouldn't, his thoughts drift to Francis. Specifically, to something Francis said to him the first time they met, five years ago, in front of B&D's, a sticky August morning: "Want to know how you can help me?"

Toby was standing at the curb, waiting for the light to change so he could cross to the Electro-Lite side of Seventh Avenue, paper bag in hand. He looked around to make sure it was him that this guy was talking to. "How?" he said.

"Don't give me anything." Francis shifted his eyes from side to side, as if protecting a great secret.

"Okay."

"I mean ever," Francis said. "No matter how often you see me—'cause I'm gonna be around here now, for a while—no matter how much I beg, don't you give me anything. All right?"

"Yeah. Sure." The light changed. Toby took a step down off the curb but Francis grabbed hold of his shoulder and held him.

"'Cause it's true what they say, you know. You shouldn't help people like me. It only makes things worse. It'll just encourage me. I'll come to expect handouts, and that just hurts both of us—not to mention society. Dig?"

Back then, five years ago, Francis didn't look so bad: unshowered, certainly, but not filthy; wrinkled khaki pants, wellworn Hushpuppies, a white t-shirt with red block letters that read I ♥ MY SHIH TZU. A week's worth of beard, tops.

"Gotcha," Toby said.

"Okay, let's practice." Francis released Toby's shoulder and held both hands out to him, palms up. "Please, mister. Couldya spare a little, huh? I haven't eaten in, like, um, a month. Just a dollar, a quarter, whatever you got. I'm dyin'."

"No," Toby said. "Sorry, pal."

Francis smiled, eyes squinting through the morning sunlight. "Good."

Even as they grew to know one another, that first conversation contained the most words Francis ever spoke to Toby at one time. And, since then, Toby has handed over hundreds of dollars, which Francis accepted.

The bathroom sink shuts off and, through walls that Toby had no idea were so thin, Toby hears the clanging of Todd unbuckling his belt and then the hollow, porcelainic thud of his son-in-law sitting down heavily onto the commode. Thankfully, another siren begins to wail from somewhere in the city, drowning out whatever unwelcome sounds that might be preparing to permeate through the walls next. He doesn't want to know any more.

Ellie stands inside her bedroom closet, jackets and blouses hanging all around her. Her intention upon entering the closet was to find something to wear for tomorrow, but she's neglected to turn on the single ceiling bulb and now finds herself mesmerized by the strips of yellow light cast by the outside street lamps squirting through the vertical slats in the closet door. Besides, she has no idea what she'll even be doing tomorrow. The true reason she entered the closet, she now knows, was to avoid what's on the outside. She has no idea how she's become so obtuse. She is a lawyer, a pretty good one. She passed three state Bar exams, in three consecutive months, each on the first try. She's argued cases in federal courtrooms. She recently discovered a loophole in the New York tax code that allowed a prominent insurance company to continue to pay absurdly lower tax rates through the year 2016. Her time, outside of this apartment, is worth $175 an hour. Inside, though, she's clueless, and she has no idea how this came to be. There must have been warning signs—there always are, they say—but she missed them. She takes the sleeve of one of Todd's suits and feels the fabric between her fingers. She can't see very clearly, and the strips of fuzzy yellow light give everything a haphazard, stunted sort of luminance, but she knows the suit is his gray Armani, three buttons, a suit she used to like on Todd very much. She supposes the fact that this suit—like all of the suits that hang around her now—has not been worn in more than six months should have been one of those signs, but she refuses to believe that. People can change: they can change their desires and their ambitions and they can change what they love and they can do it completely on their own. Still, she feels stupid—not deceived or betrayed or offended, but just plain dumb. She thinks of her father, in the spare bedroom down the hall. He never did sleep well—she's retained that much knowledge of him and his habits at least—and she wonders if he's right now lying awake wondering just how far he's willing to push things in the morning. Extreme problems need extreme remedies. She's heard that phrase somewhere before—she thinks maybe the Buddha said it—but she doesn't know if the worthwhile thing to do is apply such wisdom to Todd or to herself.

Ellie reaches into the left pocket of the gray Armani and pulls out a piece of paper. It is folded into fourths and is soft with age. She opens it. Though there's not enough light in the closet to see clearly, she can tell the paper is a list of computer codes, complex and indistinguishable to her, in four columns. She turns the paper over and sees a series of scribbles in Todd's handwriting. She holds the paper up to a bar of light seeping in from outside. Barely, she can make out the names of songs, in different lists. She recognizes some of the names as Todd's originals: "Crunch," "Could Have Had," "B-Complex," "Wear Me Out," "Divebomb," "Happy Throngs," "Burn the Waste Behind You." Some of the titles are scratched out and sometimes the order is shifted around, and she recognizes at once that Todd had been devising various set lists for his performances—performances that he probably didn't yet have at the time but only hoped for—trying to find the perfect mix of fast and slow, the perfect progression. Ellie re-folds the paper and places it back in the suit pocket, then crouches down in the closet where she immediately is hit by an overwhelming scent of themselves. It is him and it is her: the quick fleeting smell of herself as she pulls a t-shirt over her head; the smell of him as she presses her face into the crook of his shoulder. A simultaneous scent. Both of them. She doesn't know why she didn't smell it while she was standing: maybe the shoes on the floor, the closet's air currents, but she finds this simultaneous scent both frightening and beautiful. She doesn't want to move. She doesn't want to move and let this feeling leave her without having something else to replace it. She figures she'll just stay here on the closet floor tonight, sleep here, curled up among the shoes, the hems of skirts brushing against her ear, and she is ready to do just this, has resigned herself to this act, when, from down the hall, she hears the toilet flush, and, completely against her will, it rouses her.

Teeth. They're all Michael dreams about lately. Sharp, pointy incisors so big that the mouth they're in is unable to close. The sensation of teeth ripping through soft flesh. Teeth scraping against one another until the enamel is gone and the nerves exposed. Tonight, baby teeth: the thick, hard permanent ones pushing upwards through the jaw, making contact with the child size roots' underside, taking the mouth hostage, wedging the little ones out of the gums one by one until they all lay dead and strewn across the tongue, white on red, casualties, to be spit out or swallowed. This is the sensation in Michael's mouth when he awakes, alone in the bed he and Natalie share upstairs in the back corner of her parents' "new" house, the newest addition, in what Natalie has, with much sarcasm, taken to calling the "South Wing." The clock on the wicker night stand glows a red and anxious 2:20.

He shakes his head, tries to clear it. His wife's pregnant. Natalie's pregnant. That's right. He remembers now: her announcement (not to him, but to everyone in the dining room), the congratulations (as if Michael already knew), the hugs, the ensuing talk, tips being passed around (Make sure you get that book, I forget what it's called; Magee Hospital is wonderful), Have you thought of any names? (Natalie said they haven't), Do you have a due date yet? (no there, too). It took over the day. Michael remembers a sudden loss of appetite, but he ate anyway. Then he went into the living room, laid down on the sofa and slept for a good long time. When he awoke, Shea Winstead was transferring the desserts (what little was left of them) from the now-upright silver cart to the table, and pouring coffee. So he had some dessert and some coffee, accepted some more pats on the back. Rich from Johnstown asked if Michael had started putting any money away for the child's education, which, to Rich's bewilderment, made Michael giggle.

At some point during the evening he lost track of Natalie. She disappeared as people began saying their goodnights and tracking down their coats. Michael stood by the door, shaking hands.

"You tell Natalie goodnight for us," Aunt Stephanie said in the entryway. She gave Michael a dry kiss on the cheek.

"I don't know where she is," he said.

"Oh, that's all right. She's probably tired. But she'll get used to it."

"I'm sure she will."

After everyone who was leaving had left, he found her upstairs in their given bedroom, light on, clothes on, lying on her back, wide awake. When Michael entered the room, she reached down and gave the hem of her corduroy skirt a tug.

"I have to tell you something," she said.

"Okay." He walked over and sat on the bed, by her knees. The room was sparsely furnished: just the bed, the wicker night stand, and a dresser. A vast expanse of new, eggshell carpeting. Sitting there, Michael could make out areas that had never been walked on.

"I tricked you," she said.

"I know." Actually this possibility hadn't occurred to him, but now, simply on the basis of those three words, it made perfect sense. He watched Natalie's face as she stared up at the ceiling; he could actually see the tears well up in her eyes, could see the level rise until the irises looked to be at the bottom of a shallow pool. "Honey," he said. "Listen to me—"

"No." She blinked, wiped the tears away quickly, violently, and sniffled once. "This is unacceptable. This..." She turned to him. "Do you hate me?"

"Of course not," he said quickly, and he didn't, although the truth was he didn't feel anything.

"I would. I would hate me. I do hate me."

"Don't say that, Nat. That's the worst thing you could do right now. We'll get through this."

"Oh, Mr. Optimism."

He didn't respond. She was right: he didn't believe what he was saying. He said, "How long have you known?"

"Just since yesterday. Last night actually. It was just one of those home tests. I took it while you were out."

"Oh. So you don't know for sure? You haven't had a real test yet?"

She turned away again. "You don't want me to be. I knew it. Oh, this is a bigger mistake than I thought."

"No, it's not. It's not a mistake at all. I just, you know, I just wish you'd told me."

She closed her eyes. "So do I. And I wish..."

She didn't finish, and they stayed silent for some time. Then Michael flicked off the light on the night stand and laid down with Natalie. Their faces were right up against each other, breathing in the other's breath. Michael remembers trying to coordinate his own breathing so that his inhales and exhales were the same as Natalie's. At some point, he fell asleep.

The spotlight above the garage is on now—Michael can see the yellow glare seeping in through the bedroom's far window, the one that overlooks the driveway. A rectangle of light extends across the floor, a block of white surrounded by black. Michael tongues his incisors. He listens. Outside, it's raining, or at least it feels like it, if there's such a thing as feeling rain. Downstairs, there's movement. He swings his legs over the side of the bed and then realizes he's still fully dressed, tie and all.

He heads down the long hallway and notes, like a private eye looking for clues, that light from downstairs spills upwards through the stairwell at the end of the hall. Slowing slightly, he hears murmuring, then as he picks up his pace his foot hits something and the next thing he knows he's on the floor, a face-plant into the eggshell carpeting; head and neck folded over his shoulder, a knee tucked into his chest, ass up in the air.

A cat glides around the banister and disappears down the stairs.

As he's picking himself off the floor, Michael realizes that his fall must have made a significant racket and, sure enough, Marty pads out of one of the bedrooms, bare-chested, sweat pants turned sideways on his waist. He looks around stonily. "Que fucking pasa, Miguel?"

"Nada, Marty. I fell over the cat."

Marty scratches his matted hair, closes his eyes long enough for Michael to suspect that he's fallen asleep standing up. Then he says, "There's a cat?"

"I hope so. I just fell over it."

"Okay," Marty says, then absently slips his hand down the front of his sweat pants and turns back into his bedroom.

At the bottom of the stairs Michael can make out several voices coming from the kitchen. When he turns the corner he finds Gil Winstead, Ralph, Alex and Natalie sitting on stools around the 7. Natalie and Alex are still dressed, as Michael is, but Gil and Ralph Winstead are in bedtime attire: Ralph in a t-shirt and sweat pants, Gil Winstead in red thermal underwear, shirt tucked into the pants. Mugs of coffee are set in front of everyone and they're pulling off pieces of what looks like a big sticky-bun, placed on the counter top within easy reach. Gil Winstead notices Michael first.

"Hey, Michael," he says and waves him over. "Another night-owl. Pull up a stool."

"When did you get a cat?" Michael says, standing in the doorframe between the kitchen and the main entry. He feels like a kid who's not supposed to be up. "I almost broke my neck on it."

"Is that what that was?" Gil Winstead says. "We couldn't figure it out. Yeah, Mrs. W. got that thing a couple of months ago from some farmer over by Derry. Name's—aw, heck, I forget the thing's name. I'm pretty sure he has fleas."

"Come sit down, honey," Natalie says. She's facing the other direction and has to turn her head around to see him.

"What're you guys doing up?"

"Conducting our first board of directors meeting," Alex says.

"What?"

"Come sit down, honey," Natalie says.

"Yeah, honey," Alex says. "Come sit down."

There are no more stools left so Michael takes one of the chairs from the kitchen table and slides it over to the 7 between Ralph and Natalie. The chair is much shorter than the stools, though, and when Michael sits, his eyes are barely high enough to see above the surface of the counter top.

"Coffee?" Gil Winstead says.

"No, thanks."

"It's decaf."

"This sticky bun's awesome," Alex says, reaching for another hunk.

Michael looks around the 7 and immediately comes to the understanding that these people are up to something. "So what's going on?"

"It was the weirdest thing," Natalie says. Her eyes the other faces for support. "We just all four of us got up and came downstairs—for a glass of milk or 'cause we couldn't sleep—"

"Or a scrap of brisket," Alex says.

"Yeah. Just, like, one at a time. And then, here we were. So Daddy fired up the coffee maker."

Michael looks down the length of the 7 at his father-in-law. "Mm."

"And we got to talking, you know. Actually it was Ralph who got us started on the subject."

Ralph raises his right hand. His thin hair is sticking out in many places, statically suspended. "Guilty as charged."

"Anyway, here's the thing." Natalie reaches for her mug.

"Mr. W.'s gonna back us to start up a little company," Alex says.

Nobody says anything for a moment. It seems to Michael as if they're all embarrassed. Their eyes are down and, from his low vantage point, he can see eyes darting back and forth, examining the workmanship of the new counter top, it seems. Except for Gil Winstead, who reaches for more sticky-bun.

Finally, Michael says, "Come again?"

Alex smiles. "Remember what you said to me last night when I suggested we should start our own company? You said, 'You gotta have a lot of capital to invest,' or something like that. I can't remember exactly, except for that word, 'capital.' Well, here it is, buddy: Capital City."

"What did you do, Alex?" Michael says, then turns his attention to Gil Winstead. "Gil, what did he say to you? You don't have to do this. He's overreacting."

Gil Winstead laughs. "He didn't do anything, Michael. Really. It was my idea. Alex just happened to be here and it made sense to include him."

"Include him in what?"

"A little interior design company," Natalie says.

The cat jumps up onto the 7, quite a leap, but nobody pays it any mind. It's a gray cat with flecks of white on its head and chest. It paws around on the 7 for a few seconds looking for a hand to pet it, then jumps back down onto the tile. For some suddenly foreign reason, Michael can't fathom the significance of an interior design company, where that idea came from, though he couldn't help but notice the repeated use of the word "little" when referring to it, as though such a distinction makes some profound difference that Michael is unable to grasp. He says, "What in the world..."

"I'm not so sure it's a good idea," Ralph says. "I mean, where do you start?"

"I know where," Natalie says.

"Okay," Ralph says. "Where do you put it?"

"Whoa, tiger," Alex says. "When did you become such the pisser? Five minutes ago you were all pumped up. 'Look where you're going, cause you'll go where you look,' or whatever. Who'd you say said that?"

"Emmet Fox," Ralph says.

"Yeah. Which book?"

Ralph doesn't answer. He gets up and crosses the kitchen to the coffee pot.

"Listen," Gil Winstead says. "Listen, if you kids are serious about this—and you better be—I'll get in touch with my real estate agent and my accountant on Monday. I'll have my real estate gal check commercial properties between here and Pittsburgh, just to cover ourselves, and we'll see what she comes up with. Also, I have to put a ceiling on this thing. Now I'm just glad we've been blessed with the ability to help you kids out in this way, but I can't just willy-nilly write out a blank check—not because I don't want to, but because that's nuts, you see. By the end of next week, if things go smoothly, and the good Lord willing, we'll have a couple of options, and I'll know what my maximum contribution to this thing can be. All right?" He reaches his cup out behind him for Ralph to fill it. "Now, what you folks have to decide in the meantime, amongst yourselves, is whether or not it makes sense for you all to be in business together. There are a lot of factors at play here. Nat, sweetie, I understand you'll be the creative element, so to speak, you'll run the day-to-day kind of stuff. Alex'll take care of the financial aspects. Makes sense. Now, where do Ralph and Michael fit in here?"

"Michael doesn't fit in at all," Michael says quickly, almost a yell. "I have a job. I don't even know what the hell's going on here. Let me try and get this straight. While I was up in bed for the past three hours, you guys were down here starting a company. Is that the gist, would you say?"

No response. Just hands reaching for mugs.

"Jesus Christ, is there anything else anyone wants to spring on me tonight?"

Gil Winstead frowns. From his lowered position, Michael has an upwards view of it and the angle makes the frown look particularly rankled, gives it a touch of evil. "We don't talk like that here, son," the older man says.

"What?" Michael says. "He said 'pisser,'" and points a thumb up at Alex.

Alex pops some sticky bun into his mouth. "Tattletale."

"Well, we can talk about it in the morning," Natalie says, rising. "I'm going to bed."

"Yeah," Alex says. "You need your rest now, you know. You're sleeping for two."

Chuckles. Michael looks across the 7 at Alex. He can't remember ever having seen him look happier. You can actually see his cheekbones. The lighthouse tie hangs from his neck with pride and he reaches for more-sticky bun, pulling off one hunk right after the other, tossing each into his already stuffed mouth.

"I'll be," Gil Winstead says, the frown completely gone now, arms crossed fatherly across his red thermal chest. "Would you look at that boy go to town."

The rain has let up, but there's a damp heaviness to the air, especially low, just above the asphalt, and as Michael walks along Derby Ridge Road, past darkened houses set back behind square front lawns, the Winsteads' neighbors, he feels as though he's pushing through knee-deep water. He ducked out as everyone headed, again, up to bed. For once, sleeping was the furthest thing from his mind. He had to answer to himself, on several fronts. First: Had he really made Natalie afraid to tell him she was pregnant? Was that his fault? Second: Why does he see the prospect of his father-in-law's helping his wife and best friend to start a business as a problem of similar scale? Third: When you throw in the situation at work, which problem should receive the highest level of worry?

The answer to the second question is the easiest. He sees the prospect as a problem because it doesn't make any sense for Natalie to begrudge her parents all of their recent good fortune, and then have no qualms about capitalizing on it herself. Somehow, that's not right.

He walks along the curb—there are no sidewalks. Gravel and ash crunch under his feet. He wants to start over—start everything over—and he has to admit that this is a perfect opportunity. Sure it is. New family, new career, new outlook. He can unburden himself from his vanquishment at Electro-Lite and, what's more, he can do it on his own terms. He couldn't have written a better script for himself, really.

In Michael's haste to duck outside without being noticed, he forgot to grab a coat, an oversight he now regrets. The wind's blowing into him and he walks down Derby Ridge leaning forward, hands stuffed deep into his pockets. Every now and then his tie flies up over his shoulder. This is not so bad, Michael thinks. None of it. It's not so bad. It's not, it's not, it's not, it's not, the cadence falling in with the sound of his footfalls. The wind whistles through the space between the houses around him, occasionally catching on a piece of aluminum siding and letting loose with a horrible groan. It is an empty sound that travels directly and deeply into Michael's bones. He feels exposed, vulnerable, a paper doll to the gods of inevitability. Off to his left he hears another groan, this one a little higher pitched, like sneakers scuffing on a basketball court, only more drawn out. The house from which the sound emanates draws to a point on top, the triangle enclosed in glass, which reflects, shiny and opaque, back out at the street. Then, Michael hears everything: the wind across the top of the water-sogged grass, the creaking mailbox posts, the gray clouds moving through the darkness overhead. To be this alone, one should learn a lot about himself. But, really, when you think about it, how much truth can one person stand?

Derby Ridge Road comes to an end; it just stops. No intersection, no cul-de-sac, nothing. Just mud and thin, black, leafless trees. Apparently the developers are not quite finished expanding the area. Michael remembers when he first met the Winsteads, theirs was one of only about a dozen houses (albeit a much smaller version then) in the plan. Now there has to be upwards of fifty. And, apparently, there are going to be more—as soon as the developers get the go-ahead to knock down these trees and extend Derby Ridge Road farther into them. Michael turns around. Though he likes living in close proximity to people, as they do in Shadyside, this is not what he's ever had in mind. Is this what it means to have children? Housing developments and contractors and waiting seventy-five years for the new trees to grow? At least the wind's at his back now.

The Winsteads' house is as dark as the rest of the street; Michael notes that no light is on in the South Wing. He turns into the driveway, and heads past their Cherokee, silent and still and unpaid for, to the side door (he's not up to the challenge of the front's wooden planks). Behind the house, about fifty yards back, is another house; and beyond that, through the darkness, is another street, on the other side of which is another house. Michael can feel the cold air drawing in and out of his lungs; he can feel the warmth inside him. He takes hold of the brass door handle and presses down.

Locked.

He tries it again, pulling back and forth as if there is some possibility of it giving way. The front door is surely locked, so he heads around back, through the soft, wet grass, his shoes making a sucking sound every time he lifts them out of the muck. Back here, surprisingly, there is some moonglow. He can see. The gas grill is still out on the back deck. So is the patio furniture, although the umbrella sticking out of the table's center hole is folded down. He walks up to the back door and looks in through the glass to the kitchen. Though it's dark in there—darker, certainly, than it is out here—Michael can see, his hands framing his face, the sticky bun carcass still sitting on the 7. He tries the knob, but of course it's locked, too. Then it occurs to him that, since no one knew Michael wasn't inside, Gil Winstead probably set the alarm system before going up to bed. So even if a door did happen to be unlocked, he'd set off a host of bells and whistles upon his entering. Which he doesn't want. So, before he can give it any more thought, he starts knocking on the back door's thin wood frame. He gives a series of quick, authoritative raps, then waits. When nothing happens, he knocks again, harder this time. Hands again framing his face against the glass, he sees the cat walk casually into the kitchen from the front hallway. The thing walks all the way up to the back door, sits, and stares out at Michael. He knocks again, pounds away this time, nonstop. Still, the cat sits and watches. Michael takes his left hand out of his pocket and starts pounding with it as well, attaining a sort of thunderous machine-gun beat.

He doesn't say a word, but inside, he's screaming: *Hey, let me in!*

SHOPPING DAYS TO XMAS: 21

Wednesday morning, 6:50, the middle of Crisis Week, as Marlene Stringer has come to refer to it. The alarm isn't set to go off for ten more minutes, but a strip of sunlight has skirted through the bedroom window of Jack Lipinski's Mt. Washington condo and settled across Marlene's face. Sunlight. The abnormality itself is enough to wake her.

Ordinarily, Marlene would lie and wait for the alarm to go off. This morning, though, she carefully peels back the covers and makes her way around the foot of the bed, wearing only a t-shirt of Jack's that barely comes below her hips, to the window. Far below and across the Monongahela River, the city radiates in this same sunlight. It appears to Marlene as though the glass and steel of the buildings are actually being warmed by the rays. If the buildings had arms, she can't help thinking, they would reach up to the sky in gratitude. Even the river looks blue. Or bluish. At least the far side does. The near side of the Mon, just below the mountain on which she is standing is still covered in thick shadows. A barge makes its way along that line of sun and shadow, from right to left, from West Virginia, having just passed under the Liberty Bridge, and heads toward the Point and the Ohio River and, beyond that, the Mississippi. She can see the Electro-Lite building from here, or part of it, the upper sections of glass catching and reflecting a significant portion of light, and she can't help her thoughts from drifting to Owen, who right now is probably already up, perhaps in the shower, in their own house out in Upper St. Clair, readying for his own drive into work. His last couple of days have been filled with problems as well, perhaps even "crises," relatively speaking. He has customers to appease and answer to, alterations in market strategy to devise. But he can't possibly understand her world—the sheer gravity of the decisions she must make. She, and the rest of Power Generation's division level management, must come up with ways to somehow salvage the entire organization—a tough task to say the least, especially when the division president has yet to bother showing up following the holiday. They've been working late, coming in early, so Marlene called Owen last night, claiming to still be at the office, and said she was going to just get a room at the Hilton, instead of negotiating her way, late at night, through the South Hills traffic, only to have to turn around and do the same thing in reverse about five hours later. Owen said he thought her idea made sense.

And actually, only part of her story was a lie. They really are busy. In addition to reacting to the turmoil of last week's announcement, they need to follow through with their promise and come up with names of several thousand people to lay off by the end of the month. And those notifications have to go out soon. What this entails is division management keeping up with the department heads, making sure each is following through on his reduction numbers. One of the many problems is that some managers are fighting the numbers dictated to them: I can't lay off that many, we can't run the department if we get rid of that many, blah, blah, blah. It's one of Marlene's responsibilities to say, Tough shit. It's also her responsibility to come up with a clean and effective way of getting rid of Michael Dunne. When she first broached the idea at a meeting late last week, it was met with skepticism all around. People were worried about perception, not to mention the possibility that Dunne would sue. But Dennis Tussy was not yet over the embarrassment last Monday's press conference had caused him, and it didn't take long for him to give the go-ahead. In fact, once the highlights and effects of the press conference were rehashed, and Tussy had some time to let the humiliation fester, he decided he didn't want to just lay Dunne off, didn't want him enjoying the benefits of an Electro-Lite severance package. He wanted him fired outright. "For insubordination. Or for revealing company secrets, or whatever," he said. "You figure it out, Marlene."

The alarm goes off behind her and she jumps. Jack rolls over and slaps the clock, then feels around on the sheets for her. She watches, the sun and city behind her now. When finally he realizes he is alone in the bed, Jack rolls over, away from where Marlene would have been, and rubs his face, hard, with both hands.

"Hey there," she says.

Jack looks over and blinks at her. "Hey yourself." He's not a particularly good-looking man, Marlene finds herself contemplating now. He's big, sturdy, with thick shoulders and forearms. When she touches his chest there's a sense of solidity there, of unbreakability, and she likes that. She also likes that, although he is, at thirty-five, four years younger than her, he already is known as one of the top orthopedic surgeons in the region. He has patients, wealthy ones, calling from as far away as Boston and D.C., and he recently operated on a moderately well-known actor to remove bone spurs from his hip. Fixed him up good as new.

But his big hands often feel awkward on her (sometimes she wonders how they could possibly attend to the intricacies of surgery), especially lately, and his face and forehead have an undeniably Neanderthal contour. He sniffles, coughs, looks back up at her. "You okay?"

"Yes."

"Is that sun?"

"It appears to be. Believe it or not. What time do you have to be in?"

He moves his legs in the covers and yawns, looking like a lion in full roar. When he's done he opens his eyes as if he's surprised himself in some way. "Eight," he says, and sits halfway up, head against his propped-up pillow. "Gotta do an arthroscopy later this morning. You?"

"Soon. Now." She moves away from the window and goes to her drawer. She bends over it, looking for undergarments to take into the bathroom with her.

"That shirt of mine fits you nice," Jack says. "Perfectly, I'd say."

It occurs to her then that, in her bent over position, the shirt has ridden up above her hips, revealing her bare backside. For some reason, she stands up straight.

"What?" Jack says.

"Nothing. I don't know." And she doesn't know. She's never been self-conscious with him about such things before. In fact, it surprises her that she's even wearing a shirt at all. "I've just got a lot on my mind. Sorry."

She goes to the bed and sits on the edge, bra and underwear balled up in her fist. She leans over and kisses him. His mouth is warm and stale from sleep and he reaches behind her neck and pulls her toward him. She resists, but only momentarily, and in the next instant he has deftly swung her over him to the other side of the bed and lays her in a new patch of sunlight, the crook of his one elbow behind her neck, his other hand beneath her, gently teasing the small of her back. The alarm goes off again, wailing like a truck in reverse, and this time Marlene, not looking, reaches up to silence it.

∗ ∗ ∗

Michael's not sure what's gotten into him, but all week he's been working like a man possessed. This morning, finding himself particularly invigorated by the sudden display of sunshine, he arrived at the office by seven-thirty and began sketching out a five-year public relations plan, prioritized. Over the last two days he has developed an intricate on-line filing system for every press release written dating back to 1990. The lack of interruptions is helpful: nobody stops by his office to chat; Drew next door has been curiously quiet. It's eleven-thirty now and he's on his fifth cup of coffee.

In front of him are three yellow legal pads, each representing a different scenario. One represents Electro-Lite Power Genera-tion Division in its current state—assuming no drastic changes occur anytime soon (fat chance). The second pad represents the division if it were to be sold to a competing company—that is, one that would seek to continue building and servicing fossil fuel-generated power plants and components. The third pad represents what Michael has chosen to call "other"—the division could get sold to a company that wants to continue only a por-tion of the Electro-Lite portfolio, or none at all, choosing rather to sell off the components of the business piecemeal. Of course the public relations approach for any of these three scenarios would be drastically different, and Michael wants to be certain that this knowledge is taken into account.

He works steadily through the morning, drawing up various situational flowcharts and making notes as to where background information can be found should it be needed. After finishing some hypothetical talking points that could be distributed to field sales personnel if the division is sold, explaining the ra-tionale behind this "decision," Michael sits back suddenly in his chair and, without thinking, reaches for the phone. He punches a sequence of twelve familiar numbers and listens to the phone on the other end ring four times before being picked up by an equally familiar female voice.

"Hi, Mom," Michael says. "How's it going?"

"Oh. Michael. Hello." She sounds genuinely surprised, perhaps racking her brain to come up with a reason behind this call that she should be aware of. "Everything's going fine. As usual."

"I'm sorry I didn't call over Thanksgiving. Things have been a bit hectic around here."

"Of course they have," she says. Michael can tell from her voice that she is settling into a kitchen chair. "You mean with work? Or at home?"

Michael is not sure how to respond. Of course "both" would be the honest and accurate answer. But he's not sure how deep he wants to get into this with her. "At work, mostly," he says. "So how was your Thanksgiving? Who said the blessing this year?"

"Your father said it himself this year. He was the only one left who isn't tired of that routine of his. I guess this year it finally dawned on him and he just went ahead and said it himself." She sounded pleased. And a little relieved.

"It wasn't so bad," Michael says. "I'm sorry to see it go."

"Well..."

"Listen, Mom," he says. "I have something to tell you."

"Oh? What's that, honey?"

He waits. Again, the honest and accurate statement would have been "some things," and now it seems as though he's worked himself into a corner from which he's not sure how to escape. Yet he suddenly wants nothing more than to tell his mother everything. Isn't that what she's for? He want's to tell her about the layoffs and the press conference and his excessive sleeping and Alex's situation and Natalie's father's offer and, oh yeah, the pregnancy. Maybe she'd be able to make sense of it all, give it some perspective, let him know there's nothing to worry about. He says, "I wish I could have been there, Mom. I missed you. And Mrs. Winstead isn't half the cook you are."

This gets a small laugh.

"I've told you they have brisket, right? I've told you that? No turkey whatsoever."

Another laugh: breathy, through the nose. "It is strange," she says. He can tell by the way her voice drops that she means to say more, but doesn't.

"I have to go now, Mom," he says, sitting up straight in his chair. Two women walk by his open door carrying white handled boxes filled with three-ring binders, staplers, pens, a potted plant in one. They look in at him, stone-faced, as they pass. "I have some things I need to do."

"Oh," she says. "All right. Why don't you call later this week, if you can. In the evening, maybe, when Dad's home."

"I'll do that, Mom. Actually, I was thinking maybe we'd make a trip out there in a couple of weeks, if you guys aren't busy. Maybe for a long weekend." He hadn't known he was going to say this.

"You mean before Christmas? That would be wonderful. Call in a couple of days. We'll check to see which weekend would be best. There's only 21 shopping days left, you know, and it's tough getting your father motivated for such things. I know it's not very traditional but I think he should have a say in the gifts we give jointly."

This, Michael hadn't been expecting. He says, "Okay."

"Oh, my," his mother says suddenly. He can hear the chair pulling away from the table. "That's Mrs. Borchardt at the door. She's here to pick me up for lunch. We're going to the—Come on in, Alice, it's open—we're going to the Avocado Room, downtown on Pine."

"I remember it," Michael says. "It's a good place. You'll have fun."

"Oh, sure," she says with over-exaggerated sarcasm, the intention of which Michael cannot place. "Like a carnival." There's some knocking around then and her voice fades in and out for a couple of seconds, like she's not speaking directly into the receiver.

"What's that, Mom? I can't hear you. Mom?"

" I said, Bye, dear. Call in a couple of days."

"Okay, Mom. Bye. Mom—" But the line's dead.

Michael sets the phone back in it's cradle and looks down at his lineup of legal pads. The absurdity of them becomes suddenly clear. When the phone starts ringing, as if it'd been waiting patiently for him to hang up, he just stares at it, listening to the computerized tone and watching the little red light above LINE 1 blink on and off, on and off. When he finally picks it up and says hello, he hears Natalie's voice, excited, breathless. Can you meet me? it asks. I have something wonderful to show you.

✳ ✳ ✳

Toby hasn't lived in the same house with his daughter in ten years. That's something he hadn't thought of at first but something that has, in the past six days, become painfully obvious. He wants her to be comfortable, that's the biggest thing. After all, she doesn't want to be here, if she had a choice—really had a choice. She'd rather be in New York, with her husband who, let's face it, needs her right now. But Toby wants to be smart. Ellie's being with Todd right now would be a mistake—her presence would only allow him to put aside the immediate need to work on his problem. Now, thanks to Toby, Todd has sufficient motivation.

Ellie, on the other hand, has the means, but lacks the motivation. She brought her laptop along with her and has set up an intricate little workstation on the dining room table, wires and cables and phone lines all over the place. Toby's not sure how, but apparently she's able to pretty much conduct her business right from 414 Tipton Street, Murrysville, PA. Everything, of course, but the face-to-face contact, an aspect that seemed to bother her at first, until Toby said, "Sweetie, you're a lawyer. You're selling bullshit, not vacuum cleaners."

When he thinks back, though, he can't figure out how he ever got Ellie out of New York. He expected Todd to fight him; he expected resistance and Toby has to admit to himself that if he'd gotten it he probably wouldn't have had the strength to follow through. But Todd didn't fight. He didn't argue or plead. He sat on the sofa in his bathrobe, hands on his knees, and as Toby and Ellie opened the door to leave he said, sarcastically, "I hope your flight's on time." And they left.

Now, Wednesday, mid-afternoon, the main lobby relatively quiet, he considers calling Ellie at the house. He's held off so far, hasn't called her all day. It's a promise he said he'd keep; or, rather, one she made him promise to keep, after four phone calls Monday and three yesterday. "Daddy," she finally said when he called for the third time yesterday, "when you call and ask me how I'm doing, all it does is remind me that I'm not doing very well."

He has no idea what's going on around him, what corporate wheels are in motion. He's out of the gossip loop—in fact he's removed himself from the loop—and he doesn't care. When again he considers the whole situation, as he watches a man and a woman click hurriedly across the lobby behind the front desk, holding loose sheaths of paper printouts to their chests and arguing through clenched jaws, Toby is able to see the sheer banality in it all. He reaches down beneath the front credenza for the phone and begins dialing his number, but before he can get the receiver to his ear, Ben returns from wherever he's been and casually announces, "There was a fire on five," before dropping into his chair.

Toby puts the phone down. "A what?"

"A fire." Ben leans back and locks his hands behind his neck, elbows out. He's a bit winded. "Just a little one."

"How did it start?"

"I don't know. You want me to find out?"

"That's our job, Ben."

"Oh." Ben stands, looks around the desk as if there might be some item there that could aid him in this task. He smooths down the front of his blue shirt. "All right. I'll just...I'll—"

"Hold on a second, son," Toby says. He leans back against the desk, folds his arms, puts a foot up on the chair. "Tell me what happened?"

Ben thinks for a moment. "It was in a conference room on five. Cigarette in the trash can."

"Oh. I thought you said you didn't know how it started."

"Yeah. I mean I don't know who started it."

"There's no smoking on five," Toby says. "There's no smoking in the building anymore."

"Right. Yeah. I said that. I told them—told the guy, Watkins, I think his name was— I told him there was no smoking. He said he knew that and that he'd take care of it."

Toby waits.

"So I left."

Ben shrugs, looks away. A man in a tightly drawn trench coat slides his card through the sensor and passes by the front desk. Toby notice the man's eyes. They are red rimmed and raw looking, as though he may have been crying.

"Did you see the fire, Ben?"

Ben looks past him, toward the revolving doors. "Yes, sir."

"Okay. And you put it out?"

"Uh-huh. I smothered it with..."

"Yeah?"

"I smothered it with the...with the Norwegian flag."

Toby smiles. He can't help it. He can't believe it either. But here he is, smiling. "What were you doing on the fifth floor with the Norwegian flag, Ben?" He's still smiling and now he notices that Ben's previously wandering gaze has again found him and that a puzzled expression is now playing across his young co-worker's face.

"We need it for tomorrow," Ben says. "I checked the sched-ule—trying to think ahead, you know—and so I figured I'd just get it out of the cabinet today so we had it here, you know, and then—I don't know—I guess I decided to take a walk around the building and I was on five 'cause, well, 'cause Missy Holbein works on five—" again he averts his eyes—"and I saw the smoke and a bunch of people looking confused and I guess I just re-acted. Sorry, Toby."

"And you say it was a cigarette in a trash can."

"Yeah."

"And you don't know whose cigarette it was."

"Aw, nobody's going to admit that, I wouldn't guess."

Toby nods. "You're probably right."

"I'm sorry about the flag, boss. You can deduct it from my next paycheck."

Toby stands up straight. He crosses to where Ben is sitting and puts a hand on his shoulder. "It's all right. We'll take care of it. It's no big deal." He gives the boy's shoulder a couple of gentle pats. "It really isn't."

Ben looks up at him, confused. He doesn't know what to say or do next and Toby feels for him. After all, how's anyone sup-posed to know the right thing to do? Ever.

Seated at his desk in his home office, Newton Sarver watches out the window as three workers unload railroad ties from a pickup truck and drop them roughly onto the driveway. On the side of the truck are the words RUSSO BROS. LANDSCAPING. This is his wife's project, replacing the ties. Why she couldn't wait till spring, he's not exactly sure, and it's none of his concern anyway. He's an observer, so that's what he does: observes.

One of the men—a black man with a full beard and wearing an orange knit hunting cap—is in the truck's bed, sliding each tie out to the other two men, both of whom are wearing short sleeve shirts, navy blue. Maybe, Sarver thinks, it's warmer outside than it looks. The sun's out, true, but there's a thin, weightless quality to the air. The barren, forked elm in the front yard stands abso-lutely still, rigid and tense, as though in a meat freezer. Yeah, it looks cold, but Sarver wouldn't know. He hasn't been outdoors since Friday, when Maryann transported him from the hospital to the house.

He watches the hands of the men, gloved, protected, as they lift and exchange and drop each railroad tie and then reach for another. The truck is a red Ford, mid-eighties model, it looks like. Behind the men, about twenty yards back, up against the back edge of the driveway, is Sarver's Lexus, silver, '95. He looks down at his own hands, placed side by side on the desk. They are white and chapped from the hospital's stale, dry air; if he were to rub them together bits of flaky skin would fall to the floor like snow. To their right is a stack of memos, to their left is a folded newspaper. Over the past three days couriers have been delivering various materials to his house from the office. Lists of potential layoffs for his approval. Possible approaches for fixing various problems. Other items requiring his signature. A confidential memo from Tussy explaining the basis behind his intention to terminate the employment of Michael Dunne. The newspaper was delivered by a neighborhood boy named Cyril.

After all of the new railroad ties have been unloaded, the three men (they couldn't possibly be brothers, of course) begin dismantling the old ones. They run one or two, occasionally three high along the entire perimeter of the driveway, and there is a section between the garage door and the front steps where a wall of two rows of six or seven is constructed. They do need to be replaced, Sarver has to admit. They're warped and rotting, taking in moisture like a sponge. The final straw was a couple of weeks ago when Maryann spotted a couple of mice setting up shop between two widening gaps in the wall.

Decay. It seems to be everywhere these days. Sarver picks up the twice-folded newspaper and looks at it again. It is the *Tribune-Review*. Sarver rarely reads it—the smaller circulation, generally less informed local paper—since Electro-Lite also pays for subscriptions to the *Post-Gazette*, the *New York Times*, the *Washington Post* and the *Wall Street Journal* to be sent to his house. His and Maryann's recycle box is an overflowing mess each week. Today's Trib has caught his eye, though, as it has everyone's at Electro-Lite, most likely. It's a front page, lower right story, written by a reporter named Patricia Cross, with the headline "Electro-Lite skimped on safety, source says." Again, Sarver reads the first few paragraphs:

Two Georgia Power Company representatives, who insist on remaining anonymous, have confirmed that the reasons behind the utility's dismissal of Electro-Lite Corp. service personnel this past

April from a job to repair an unspecified number of gas turbines at the Fernsdale power plant stem directly from Electro-Lite's "blatant disregard for proper safety measures."

"They put our people, and the people of the surrounding area, in serious harm's way," one source said.

According to utility representatives, Electro-Lite failed to package various unnamed hazardous materials in proper storage containers during transport, which could have exposed the plant, as well as approximately five square miles surrounding it, to "numerous" radioactive and cancer-causing elements.

"They're still doing tests," the second source confirmed. "That's all I know about it."

Apparently, the representatives added, Georgia Power did not report Electro-Lite's oversights to the Environmental Protection Agency or other watchdog organizations as required because, technically, the financially unstable utility could be fined or otherwise reprimanded as well, since it is the responsibility of the utility to monitor the safety standards observed by its outside vendors.

Representatives from Electro-Lite's Pittsburgh-based Power Generation Division, which had lead responsibility for the Georgia Power job, did not return phone calls. EPA officials would neither confirm nor deny the allegations.

Word of Electro-Lite's removal by Georgia Power first came to light when division representatives held a press conference at its Seventh Avenue offices last week to announce a massive layoff. When asked specifically of the company's reasoning for eliminating eleven thousand jobs, spokesperson Michael Dunne used the Georgia Power situation as an example, adding that Electro-Lite lost $5 million on the job, which General Electric finished. He did not mention the alleged safety violations.

What's happened is fairly obvious to Sarver. This Patricia Cross must have been at the press conference, heard Dunne talk, then went digging. He's not sure which is more embarrassing: what his division is being accused of, or the fact that he had no knowledge of it.

The Russo brothers start out by the entrance, next to the mailbox, using crowbars and what appears to be three-foot-long salad tongs to dislodge the old ties. When the first one gives way and they lift it out, the space beneath is dark and dead looking, a long, narrow strip of black decay. One guy—the black man—carries the old tie back to the truck while the other two men begin working on the next one, the shorter, heavier Russo brother standing in the grass with the crowbar, jimmying back and forth while the taller guy tries to get a firm hold with the salad tongs. There must be a reason, Sarver thinks, why they don't just bend down and lift the thing up. The ties can't be affixed into the ground that solidly. Can they? He just about has himself talked into changing out of his robe and going out there to help, maybe offer some suggestions—he is an engineer, after all—when he sees a red Acura come into view behind the workers. It approaches from around the bend and slows considerably in front of the house. The black man has rejoined the other two and now the three of them work on the second railroad tie, paying the Acura, which obviously wants to pull into the driveway, no mind. The car continues past the driveway entrance and parks along the curb. A few seconds later Marlene Stringer gets out.

She's wearing dark sunglasses and, beneath her thigh-length, vinyl-looking overcoat, tennis shoes. The most curious aspect about her appearance, however, is that she's not carrying a brief case, something Sarver's not sure he's ever seen. She walks past the workers and nods, perhaps even smiles (Sarver cannot see her facial features all too clearly from this distance). Once she's past, her back to them, all three men stop what they're doing and watch her continue up the front steps for about five seconds, then turn their attention back to the second railroad tie, which apparently has turned out to be a stubborn one.

When the doorbell rings, Sarver stays put, allowing Maryann to answer it. He pulls his bathrobe tighter around his waist. On the other side of the wall he can hear Maryann open the front door and then the two women talking in the entry hall. The sound of footsteps on tile is followed by a knock on his office door. Maryann opens the door a crack and pokes her head in.

"Marlene Stringer's here," she says. "You feel all right?"

"Yes, dear," Sarver says, leaning back in his chair. "I feel fine. Ask her to come in, please."

"You're sure?"

"Yes. Thank you."

She pulls her head away and then the door opens wide and Marlene steps into the room. She's still wearing her sunglasses and Sarver can see now that her face looks rather pallid. The corners of her mouth draw downward. She stands in the middle of the room, looking it over. There are two folding chairs on the other side of Sarver's desk, both with views of the driveway and the Russo brothers, and Marlene considers them for a moment. Her arms hang at her sides and, without her briefcase, it looks as though she's not sure what to do with her hands. Finally she says, "Newton, I'm so sorry to bother you at home, especially under the circumstances."

These words immediately draw Sarver's attention to his own crotch. He might as well be splayed out naked across the desk, goodies up. He picks up the coffee mug on his desk and sets it down. "It's okay, Marlene. Please, have a seat. It's good to see you."

She walks cautiously to the chairs across from the desk and, after pausing for a moment, sits in one, the vinyl of the coat making a curious squeaking sound against the metal beneath her, and crosses her legs. She doesn't say anything, just examines the books and pictures on the shelves above Sarver's shoulder. The general direction of her eyes lock on one particular spot and, though it's tough to tell, with her sunglasses still on, exactly where, Sarver guesses it's the framed autographed eight-by-ten of him shaking hands with President Clinton, taken a year ago at an international symposium on energy. He can't remember now who sponsored it. He waits another few seconds for Marlene to say something and when she doesn't he asks, "So how's everything?"

"Fine," she says, shifting the general direction of her gaze from the picture to Sarver, but before she can say any more she is interrupted by a crashing sound—a quick slap really—from outside. The Russo brothers have dropped a railroad tie onto the driveway and now they're standing around looking at each other, all three talking at once, most likely each blaming the others for the mishap.

"Maryann's little project," Sarver says. "I guess she felt I was in no condition to do the job myself."

Marlene is still looking out the window, watching the men now bend over and re-lift the tie and then begin shuffling over toward the pickup.

"What's the problem, Marlene," Sarver says. He's never seen her this hesitant, this reluctant to say what's on her mind. Usually it's her giving orders to him: sign this; speak clearly into the microphone, don't mumble; ten-kay is not enough for this project; you need to cut this speech down—it runs five minutes over and it's way too boring; the Quality Awards luncheon is next Monday, make time in your schedule. Even the notes she scribbles on yellow Post-its seem to have a commanding sort of tone. He's let her carry on in this way without comment because it has been obvious to him that she's comfortable in this approach. And, generally, it gets results. Plus, for all her annoying posturing, sometimes it's nice to have someone tell him what to do. Occasionally, if he's in the right mood, it takes some of the pressure off. He's not sure if this would qualify as one of those moods or not, but, either way, this dormant side of Marlene is a bit unnerving. "What's on your mind?"

Marlene turns from the window. She looks at her watch, then up toward the ceiling. "You have a nice house," she says, though she's never been here before and in fact has only seen the entryway and the driveway, which, at the moment, is being dismantled.

And of course now she's seen the office as well, which, admittedly, looks nothing like one would expect of a division president: light brown paneling; two carpets—one beige, one maroon—that overlap in the center of the room; a plywood desk Sarver's father built in 1943; a team poster of the 1976 Steelers and a blueprint diagram of the Wright Brothers' plane; fiberglass bookshelves cut into the walls that hold items such as Sarver's old fraternity paddle and mug, engineering textbooks and a couple of old spy novels, a clock with the word Stroh's printed across it, plaster indentations of his children's hands, a few framed photographs. And of course there's the folding card table chairs. No, this is not what his office should look like. It should look altogether heavier—big, heavy furniture; dark stained wood; thick brass and sterling silver paperweights; leather armchairs with ornate, hand-carved armrests that take two big men to move. For some time he'd meant to have the room redone to conform to his and others' expectations, but in the end he had to admit he didn't care what the room looked like, or what other's thought of it.

"Thank you," he says. "I didn't know you had an eye for such fine decor."

"You've received the material we've been sending over."

"I have." He touches the pile with his hand. "Never a dull moment, huh?"

"And you've seen Dennis Tussy's memo regarding Dunne?" she says, ignoring his latter comment.

"Yes."

She nods, waits.

"Have you seen today's paper, Marlene? The Trib?"

"No, I've been—Why?"

"No reason. Marlene, why don't you take off those sunglasses. It's rather awkward."

She reaches up quickly and, with both hands, slides them from her face. She blinks.

"So what is it, Marlene? What have you come here to tell me?"

She sucks in her lips, exhales them back out and she says, "Dennis has become dead-set on this thing—getting rid of Dunne. He says he's defaced the company, tarnished our reputation in the industry, that he's a loose cannon and there's no telling what-all he's capable of in the future. He says, from a public relations standpoint, we can't afford to have those kinds of potential problems, especially internally. External elements, he says, are to a certain extent beyond our control. And expected. But we have to take care of those things we can control." She pauses, blinks some more. "That's him talking now."

"What external problems is he talking about?"

"I don't know. None in particular, I don't think."

Sarver leans back in his chair and tries to cross an ankle over the opposite knee, but the pain beneath him is too much and he shudders and leans forward. "Okay. And?"

"And I've been looking into it some this morning. And the problem is—well, at least it's a problem if your objectives are in agreement with Tussy's—the problem is that we really have no adequate grounds for firing Dunne. Everything he said at the press conference should have been a matter of public record. There are no legal grounds for Electro-Lite to have withheld any of that information. Whatever the reasons for withholding it may have been, they were completely self-serving. If we fire him specifically because of that, all we can say is he released to the public information that we would rather have kept to ourselves. Period. Which makes us look awfully arrogant and secretive, to say the least." She turns back to the window and squints. The Russo brothers are working on the first double-layered section of ties. "Insubordination," she says, still watching out the window. "That's another possibility Dennis wanted me to try. But there isn't any insubordination. Michael simply answered questions from the press, something he didn't even want to do—something I didn't want him to do either—but Dennis insisted. It was as a favor to Dennis, for Christsakes. No, not even a favor. He was told to do it by his boss, and that's what he did. Technically." She shakes her head, turns her attention back to Sarver. "I'm telling you, Newton. If we let Tussy fire this guy, he'll take us to court and he'll have us for lunch. It won't only be a financial hit we'll take, our reputation will be wrecked. That's my opinion."

Sarver shrugs. "Okay. Fine. Then forget it. Michael's a good man anyway. Let's just move on to other things. It's not as though we're out of problems to address."

The door opens and Maryann enters, keeping one hand on the doorknob. Her hair is tied back tight and her face is streaked red and white, as if she's just washed it with incredibly hot water. "I'm so sorry to interrupt," she says. "Marlene would you like some coffee or something else to drink? I forgot to offer it before. We have Coke and club soda and a couple of different juices. Diet Coke, too, I think."

"No, thank you," Marlene says, not turning. "I'm fine."

With her free hand Maryann reaches over and spins the globe standing waist-high in its cradle next to the door. "Okay," she says. "Let me know if you need anything."

"Actually, I'll have another cup," Sarver says, holding up his coffee mug. "If it's already made."

"It's not," Maryann says, coming forward to take the mug. She smells of soap. "But I was planning on making another pot anyway."

"All right," Sarver says. "Thanks, dear."

Maryann takes the mug and then leaves the room, closing the door behind her. As soon as her footsteps begin to subside, Marlene says, "One other problem, though. Corbett called Tussy."

"He what? When?" The notion inflicts Sarver with a glut of sudden rage. "When did he call Tussy? And why? Why in God's damn name would he call Dennis Tussy?"

"Apparently he saw footage of the press conference. He wants Dunne fired. He's really pissed off."

Sarver leans back, hard, in his chair. This time, as he intended before, he crosses his ankle over onto his knee, in spite of the sudden shock of pain—welcoming it in fact—and one flap of his robe falls open across his thigh. "He's pissed off, huh? He's pissed off. Well excuse me, Marlene, but I couldn't give a shit less how pissed off Thomas Corbett is, today or any other goddamn day. It makes no difference whatsoever to me." He's surprised by his own indignity. Despite Corbett's position as Chairman of the corporation, Sarver believes it's none of Thomas Corbett's business who Power Gen hires or fires for mid-level positions, and he certainly can't believe the man would go to Sarver's own staff level PR manager and demand action such as this be taken. Although it makes sense: obviously Corbett knew about the Georgia Power situation, and Sarver supposes Tussy must have known as well. But still, a firing of this visibility, given the fallout of the press conference, should be discussed with Sarver himself.

"I'm sorry," Marlene says.

"It's okay, Marlene. And when have you taken to apologizing so quickly?" He's still yelling, though he hadn't meant to.

She takes a deep breath, lets it out. Something occurs to Sarver, and he can't help asking, "Marlene, forgive me, but does your trepidation concerning Dunne—the hesitancy you seem to be showing—does it stem from the logistics of it? The difficulty, as you've been describing, that would be involved in firing him? The legal ramifications? Or of, well, something else?"

She turns and looks back out the window. A wave of heavy gray clouds have has obscured the sun momentarily and a slight breeze has picked up—Sarver can see some movement in the elm's upper limbs. Across the street, Dave Bay, a retired neighbor, has descended his own steep, gravel driveway to check out the action in the Sarvers'. The Russo brothers have one whole side of the driveway deconstructed, the old railroad ties thrown haphazardly in the bed of the truck, and now the three of them are gathered in front of the high wall that separates the garage and the walkway, mulling things over. Wet leaves lay plastered to the asphalt around them. The taller, thinner man takes a blue bandanna out of his back pocket and mops his doughy, high-rounded forehead. Then he glances at the other two and, as if somehow signaling inherent stupefaction, spits.

"Maybe," Marlene says, "I'll have that cup of coffee now. If it's no trouble."

So basically the question, as Sarver sees it, is this: Does he want to fight Corbett on this Dunne issue, based merely on some sort of perfectly worthless, corporately contrived dignity, and risk opening himself up for criticism not only for what happened at Georgia Power, but for not knowing about it until now? Marlene was little help, strategically (since she didn't know everything), but was surprisingly helpful in terms of moral support. She offered relatively few of her famous proclamations of doom and simply tried to help Sarver see the situation in clear, well-informed terms, which is something Sarver did in fact need, seeing as how he hasn't been in the office for more than a week now.

At one point Maryann came in, this time looking much more assembled and less red, and refilled their coffee mugs. She asked Marlene how Owen was and Marlene said "Mm." After a time Sarver began explaining to Marlene the realities of layoffs, the reasoning behind them. We're actually operating in the red, he told her. Yeah, we're showing a net profit on the books, but that's because we've been having to dip into our reserve funds to pay salaries, benefits, debts, etc. Plus all the lawsuits we've been losing lately. The truth of the matter is, if we continue down the same path, we'll be bankrupt within ten years. Just look at the way the stock has been dipping. Sarver knew Marlene thought she understood the whole concept (though Sarver knew she did not) but she didn't interrupt his explanation, didn't take offense to his offering one, and the simple, straightforward explanation, moot as it might be, made him feel a bit better himself. She nodded, mentioned that she believed the division could use some fat trimmed away anyhow.

Now she pushes back the folding chair and stands, readying to leave. She sets her coffee mug on Sarver's flimsy desk and clears her throat. "You know how I feel about the whole Dunne situation," she says, although Sarver, actually, still isn't quite sure how she feels. "But, Newton, with all due respect, I'd think you'd be a little embarrassed yourself. The things he said—it doesn't make us look very good. And, well, it all reflects onto you in the end." She lowers her eyes then looks Sarver right in the face. "Forgive me. But am I right?"

Outside an engine coughs to life and the Russo brothers' pickup, loaded with spent railroad ties, a foot or two of each sticking out over the lowered tailgate, pulls out onto the street and drives away, trailing exhaust. The sun is on its way down now and the neighborhood is cloaked in that gray half-darkness between afternoon and twilight. Marlene waits for a response. Sarver knows she's waiting but doesn't know what to say to her. The truth is he wasn't embarrassed; it hadn't occurred to him that Dunne's testimonies and Sarver's his own ignorance were a reflection of his leadership. But she has a point, and Sarver feels his neck grow warm. He stands. "Thanks for your concern, Marlene. But right now all I'm really concerned about are the several thousand notices of termination I'm going to be signing during the next few days. That's embarrassing."

Marlene nods. "And about the Dunne thing?"

"Nothing. For now."

"Right. Okay."

He reaches across the desk to shake her hand. She looks at it for a moment, then accepts the offer and while they're shaking it occurs to Sarver how awkward the activity is: they've never shaken hands before, never had to. They see each other nearly every day. To mask the discomfort of the moment, he says, "So how is old Owen? He keeping those marketing folks in line over there?"

Marlene takes her hand away, as if it's been bitten. "He's fine. Thank you," she says, and then turns away and re-affixes her sunglasses, in preparation, Sarver supposes, of stepping out into the dingy coming twilight.

The address Natalie gave to Michael is in the neighborhood of Bloomfield, no more than three miles from the center of Shadyside. He takes his usual route toward home then guides the Cherokee up Fifth Avenue to Aiken, through stop lights and past apartment buildings, stone condos and pedestrians scurrying to bus stops. When he pulls up to the light adjacent from Shadyside Hospital, which has just turned from red to green, a car—a big white Mercedes with wide chrome rims and tinted windows— pulls out in front of him, traveling west on Centre Avenue. Now stopped, Michael watches as the car continues on for a couple of blocks and then suddenly makes a left-hand turn into the Food Gallery parking lot. Michael sits for a moment in the middle of the intersection, remembering, for some reason an old joke he heard once a long time ago: What's the difference between a Mercedes and a porcupine? (With the porcupine the pricks are on the outside).

He realizes then that his breathing is awfully heavy and strained; it feels as though he's breathing through a snorkel. Cars behind him start to honk their horns. Another Cherokee, nearly identical to his own, pulls out into the lane for opposing traffic and passes, the man in the passenger seat pressing his face up against the window and mouthing some obscene diatribe or another in Michael's direction.

After a couple of more breaths Michael continues on, up toward the Dodge dealership, then over onto Liberty Avenue, the heart of Bloomfield and the street on which he's to meet Natalie.

Bloomfield is busy, cars backed up for two lights. He creeps along past the Olds dealership, the animal shelter, the Buick dealership, and then finally into the business district, lined with diners and restaurants, ethnic food shops, a Woolworths, some lawyers' offices and shoe stores, and, right in the middle of everything, West Penn Hospital. He reads the address above the hospital's front awning, and sees that the location he's looking for is a block farther and on the opposite side of the road, on the left.

He didn't need to know the address, though, because in the next second he sees Natalie standing out on the sidewalk, hands in her coat pockets, in front of a used record store. When she spots the Cherokee she takes one hand out and waves, frantically, as if flagging down a ship.

Luckily, a car pulls out from an available meter just a couple hundred yards past where Natalie is standing, and Michael parallel parks and begins walking up Liberty toward his wife. Night is setting in. It always takes longer in the city, or at least it seems to, with all the buildings and cars and street lamps, which are just now turning on. And it's a bit colder than when he left the office; there's a chill in the air that at first is a bit misleading but then bites into any exposed skin all at once. He pulls his overcoat tight around him as he crosses at the crosswalk and then steps up onto the curb to find Natalie bouncing on the balls of her feet, her pink face curled up into an enormous smile. "So what's this all about?" he says.

She just keeps smiling. Then she flicks her eyebrows and makes a quick jerky motion with her head. "Found one," she announces.

Michael looks around. It occurs to him that at some point he (subconsciously, he assumes) decided not to participate. "Found one what?"

"Silly," she says, and giggles. "A place. We found one." She takes her thumb and points up. In a window above the record shop there is a sign that reads: FOR RENT— COMMERCIAL.

"Yeah?" he says.

"For us," she says. Her voice still has a teasing, urging quality to it and he wonders if there's anything that could knock her down from the high she's riding right now. "Hello?" She reaches up and knocks playfully on the side of his head. "Anybody home?"

"The business," he says. "Oh, right." Then he says, "You mean—what? Up there?"

"Yes, silly." She holds out a key. "Wanna see?"

"Where'd you get that?"

She turns away. "Real estate lady." She heads toward an unmarked door off to the side of the record shop's entrance.

"Where is she now?"

Natalie says nothing, but, as she's working the key in the door, he detects a shrug.

"Wait, Nat," he says, and takes her by the shoulder, turning her back around. "You can't just go in there without the real estate person. We have no right to be in there by ourselves. It's—I think it's against the law."

A car backfires going past and Michael jumps but Natalie doesn't. "My dad took care of it," she says. "Come on." Then she turns and the door opens and she disappears through it.

The stairwell is narrow and dark and Michael detects the faint smell of dog hair. The stairs themselves creak appropriately as he begins ascending and once he's taken a couple of steps the light from the door fades to nothing and he has to hold his hands out to the sides and use the walls as a guide. Natalie is out of sight, though he can hear a second set of creaks, coming from somewhere above him. Then a rectangle of bronze light appears from above, through which Natalie's darkened image passes, and he works his way toward that.

"Are you coming?" Natalie's voice sounds far away.

He steps up onto the floor and looks around. A single floor lamp in the far corner beneath a slanted ceiling splashes light across the room. The floor is some kind of wood, covered in dirt and what looks to Michael like paint shavings, and Natalie is standing in the center of it, chin held high and to the side in the manner of Napoleon. There are a few pieces of old, odd furniture scattered throughout: a heavy, unstained dresser; a loveseat that's been obviously reupholstered in blue and green plaid; the vinyl footrest to an unseen chair.

"Okay," Michael says.

"Okay what?"

"Just—nothing."

There are two windows side by side in the far wall and as Michael continues scanning the room he sees that there are two more in front, overlooking Liberty, one of which has the For Rent sign in it. Both, surely, will need to be replaced. The frames are warped and splintered and there appears to be a series of intricate cracks, like tiny spreading veins, in the one square of glass. The ceiling slants downward from front to back and, now that his eyes are beginning to adjust to the scant light, he can see cracks in that, too, along with a hole where a ceiling fan was once affixed. Michael takes a deep breath. The dog hair smell seems to be gone now, but the air here is so dry he can feel it along the inner walls of his nose. His lips go instantly chapped.

"I just love these," Natalie says, and walks over to one of the two four-sided posts running from floor to ceiling. "I like the way they look. Kind of Art Deco, don't you think? Like columns."

"Sort of," Michael says. "Nat, honey, is this definite? I mean, what's the deal here?"

She walks over to the rear windows and stands gazing out of them. "No. It's not a done deal. Not exactly. Not yet. Look, you can see the Cathedral of Learning." She turns her head around to face him. "Come here. Look."

He shuffles over, sensing the hollowness of the floorboards beneath his feet, and looks out the window. The land slopes away from them. There is a network of small, 1940s style houses along the roads beneath where they are and beyond the houses, she's right: you can see the Cathedral. And one corner of Pitt Stadium, too. And beyond that, the eastern edge of the downtown skyline. The USX Tower. He can't see his own building, though, and he takes some comfort in that.

"So what do you think?"

"You're right. It's a nice view," he says. "You wouldn't think you'd be able to see so far from just a two-story building."

"It's because we're elevated, and there's not much else to block the view. Not this time of year, with no leaves on the trees. Plus, it's not as far away as it seems." Then she says, "No, I mean, what do you think about the place?"

Below, from the record shop, he can make out muffled conversations, then the tinkling of the bell on the front door. "Are you sure we're allowed to be here?" he says. When she doesn't answer, just stares back at him, the single light in the corner casting the weird shadow of her own nose across her face, he asks, "Has anyone else seen it?"

She shakes her head. "Just me and you."

"And you want my opinion."

Again, no reply.

"In what capacity?"

She says, "Just your overall impressions. I'm going to fix it up, you know. It's not going to look much like this when I get finished with it." She laughs.

"Where are you going to get the money to fix it up?"

"Don't worry about that. It's taken care of."

"Natalie—" He walks over to the old dresser. It's covered in a layer of dust thick enough for him to write his name, if he wanted to. "We can't just keep piling on the debt like this. Everything you take in for the first who-knows-how-long will be going directly toward that. Don't you see?" Then something occurs to him. "How much is your dad fronting you? Did he get back to you on that?"

She walks over to him, reaches a hand around behind his neck and kisses him, pretty long, pretty hard. "It's a Christmas present," she says. Then she pulls away and stares up at him, as if to say, All right?

"Has Ralph or Alex seen the place?" he says.

She turns and walks toward the center of the room. "Didn't I say just you and me? Ralph's probably going to bail out. His heart's not in it, for some reason. I'm not sure what his problem is. And I can show it to Alex tomorrow." She lays a hand on one of the columns, turns back to him and waits.

"What do you want me to say?" he asks her, because he really doesn't know.

Downstairs, music begins to play; the pounding of bass can be felt beneath Michael's feet. The music itself is unplacable, all mud and fuzz. Michael finds that he is looking down at the floor and when he glances back up he finds Natalie watching him, smiling. It's a soft, genuine smile, originating from the inside; it is all pleasure and optimism and gratitude, and it confuses him terribly.

She comes toward him again. This time she reaches inside the front flaps of his overcoat, her fingernails deftly skirting along his sides, surveying his ribs. "Let's do it," she says.

"It's up to you," he says. "This is your...project."

"No," she says. "I mean, let's do it. Over there, on that love-seat. Right now."

"What?" He takes her by the wrists and holds her hands up between them. "What's gotten into you?"

She shrugs. "I'm excited, I guess. You got a problem with it?"

He has to admit, privately, that he does, though he couldn't say why. "No. It's just—it's so dirty here. Musty, I mean."

"So?"

Then a notion dawns on him as if for the first time, like a slap. "You're pregnant."

"Right again."

His collarbones begin to ache and he discovers a pain in his hips that make it difficult for him to stand. He says nothing but she must have read something horrible in his face because she turns away from him as though averting her eyes from some gruesome, unwatchable act and begins heading for the stairwell. He calls her name; she doesn't turn, just says, "I'll see you at home, Michael," and then disappears through the door. A few seconds later he hears the street level door open and close, and then more muffled music begins playing beneath him, the soles of his feet absorbing the oppressive, alien rhythm.

Dewey is lying on the sofa when Michael enters the apartment. The dog makes no move toward his master's crotch; he just lifts his head, as if simply to satisfy his curiosity, then puts it back down on the cushion.

"Nice to see you, too," Michael says.

Natalie is in the bathroom, door closed. He can hear the water running in the tub. It is the only sound in the apartment, and it makes Michael feel strangely more alone than if the rooms were deserted. The darkness might have something to do with this sensation: it must have descended completely after she'd already gone into the bathroom and now heavy shadows, from the rear hall light, crawl across the floor and walls. He should go in there—he knows he should. He owes her something, though not necessarily an apology. After shaking out of his overcoat and hanging it on the coat rack, Michael makes his way over to the table that stands between the living room and kitchen—the "dining area"—which is piled high with papers, envelopes, magazines and catalogs. He tosses his keys onto the center of it, flicks on the overhead light, then picks up what appears to be the day's mail and begins to leaf through the stack. Bills for Discover, Pier One, and a magazine subscription, *U.S. News & World Report*, which he has no recollection of ever subscribing to or receiving an issue. The registration for the Cherokee needs to be renewed: twenty-four bucks. Another *Victoria's Secret* catalog. On the cover is a very blond model in a short, sleeveless silver dress. She's getting out of the back seat of a shiny black car—perhaps a limousine—and this effort has caused the skirt to pull strategically up her legs nearly to her hips. She's smiling; she has thin wrists and sinewy arms, tiny and ribbed with muscle. Out of habit, he opens the catalog and flips through it. When he gets to the end he drops it onto the table and turns his attention to the last piece of mail, an introductory offer from Advantix Plus Gold MasterCard. He opens the envelope and sits in a chair, his hips—his entire pelvic region, in fact—still fatigued.

Dear Mr. Dunne, the letter reads, *our records indicate that you have consistently demonstrated an EXCEPTIONAL credit record. We appreciate conscientious people such as yourself and it therefore is with great pleasure for us to announce that you and one member of your immediate family have been PRE-APPROVED to receive an Advantix Plus Gold MasterCard, with a credit limit of up to $7,000. The Advantix Plus Gold MasterCard is different from ordinary credit cards in that it offers you EXTRAORDINARY SPENDING POWER wherever MasterCard is accepted, with a special one-time introductory interest rate of just 5.9 percent. Additionally, the features of the Gold card include...*

Michael doesn't read the rest. He searches the table for a pen. Behind the bathroom door, the water shuts off and then nothing can be heard except the quiet, wet sounds of Natalie moving around in the tub. Michael fills out the application completely, signs it, slides it into the enclosed envelope. He finds a crude satisfaction in the knowledge that no postage is necessary if mailed within the continental United States.

Alone in her father's living room, Ellie Sizemore fights back the giggles bubbling up in her throat. She's gone and rearranged the furniture. Actually, it's kind of a mean thing to do, she knows, given the routine-oriented nature of her father, but she couldn't help herself. Cooped up all day, Todd calling non-stop and leaving messages on the machine as she stood next to the phone and listened. She needed...something, and this is the best she could come up with.

But now, as she considers her work, it occurs to her that none of the chairs (sofas, La-Z-Boys or otherwise) face the TV. Not directly. Everything faces inward, toward each other, as if the coffee table were a campfire. The TV is in a far corner, in its cabinet, below the Regulator clock. She goes from the sofa to the loveseat to the chair to the other chair, checking sight lines. Awkward, to say the least. But that's all right, she decides, it's a living room, not an auditorium. Everything doesn't have to face the TV. Where in the rule book of life does it say every sitting apparatus has to face the blessed television? She stands, takes a few steps back, and reassesses what she's done. What she's done, she now realizes, is completely shift, albeit unwittingly, the focus of the room. Whereas until an hour ago the television was the focal point of any and all living room activity (in fact it had to be, given it's predominant location), an altar, the axis on which every other object in the room revolved, it now is just another knickknack, a doohickey, as her father might say, and the result is that any occupant of the living room will now be forced to manufacture his or her own entertainment. To talk to each other. No diversions.

Satisfied, she goes to the kitchen to fix something for dinner. Her choices are limited. When on rare occasions she has had to say out loud that her father's eating preferences consist of meat and potatoes, it always sounds like an exaggeration. It's just something you say to make a point, meaning, "He's a picky eater" or "He doesn't like to try new things." But with her father, meat and potatoes truly is the full extent of his range, although he does like corn on the cob in the summertime. So Ellie rifles through the stacks of frozen meat in the freezer, trying to pick out a good one. She's resolved to not push things while in Pittsburgh—a stay she's convinced will not be more than a couple of weeks. Thanksgiving Dinner at Leiff is an example that keeps playing through her mind. When she thinks about it, the recollection causes her face to heat up and tingle, even when she's alone—she can feel it. What was she thinking? Her father ate pheasant for her. And quail. And it gave him a roaring case of indigestion that he refused to blame on the dinner. No, while she's here she'll eat meat loaf and pork chops, and like it.

She finds some ground beef that's relatively free of freezer burn and sticks it in the microwave to defrost. Maybe she'll make chili. Standing there, she notices for the first time that, actually, her father keeps the house, kitchen included, pretty neat. Dishtowels and potholders hang from the corners of the oven handle. The squeegee for washing dishes is placed meticulously on the outer rim of the sink. The linoleum is clean, the throw rugs vacuumed. The table is clear and aptly reflects the light from overhead. She detects no curious odors. A pen, pencil and a note pad are arranged neatly on the counter next to the phone and the answering machine. Her attention having now fallen there, she goes over to the machine and presses the "play messages" button. The tape rewinds, hissing. A two second beep, then Todd's voice, tinny and submerged and far away: "Ellie, honey, pick up if you're there." A considerable pause. "All right, so you're not answering. That's okay. I understand. I probably wouldn't either. But I'd like to talk to you. Call me, all right? At the apartment. I love you, baby." Ellie looks down at the machine, watches the tape revolve through its little holes. Another beep. "Ellie?" This time the pause is shorter. "Okay, so you're not calling me back. That's understandable. I'd just like you to listen to what I have to say. We didn't have the opportunity when you left—your dad wouldn't let us alone for long enough and you didn't want to fight him, and I respect that. I just—oh, God, shit, I don't remember what I wanted to say. Let me call you back." The bell on the microwave goes off simultaneously with the third beep. "Here's the thing," Todd says right off. "It's an embarrassing situation for me. You can understand that, can't you, El? But that doesn't relieve me of anything, any responsibilities. I mean, I've hurt you. I've lied to you and I've hurt you and I'm ready to accept that. Okay? El? But what you have to realize—" He stops. There are several seconds of whooshing air, or the sound of it, coming from the answering machine. She can smell the ground beef now. Then Todd exhales—the sound he makes is not unlike that of a tornado on television—and when he resumes speaking there is a new, pallid emptiness to his voice. "Ah, hell," he says. "Forget it, Ellie. This is stupid. I'm stupid. Just stay there. I fucked up big, all right? I've been fucking up for a while now, just, now it's all coming down on me. I'm sorry. I'll call you when I have something to say and hopefully you'll want to...Wow, I just won't stop, will I? Well, I'm going to stop. I'm stopping now. Bye, Ellie. Bye." Then he adds, "I miss you."

The fourth and last beep is followed by airy blank tape, as if Todd is listening, or trying to listen, to the sound of Ellie listening to him. She can feel it. It lasts about fifteen seconds and then the machine clicks off.

This is the second time Ellie has heard Todd's messages (the first time being as he left them), but for some reason they seem more real to her now; she is able to gauge their progression more clearly and as a result they make more sense to her, have established themselves as solid components of her life. Especially the last one. She actually had the feeling that Todd was on the other end of the line, listening to her, and now—she's surprised herself—she finds she is crying.

Wiping at her face, she removes the ground beef from the microwave and sets it on the counter just as she sees her father's headlights sweep across the living room wall and pull into the driveway. She tears the cellophane off the meat and takes a skillet out from the cupboard. Her father's feet stamp a few times on the mat in the laundry room, knocking away the dirt and cinders from his shoes, then he steps into the kitchen and looks around. It is 6:15.

"Hi, Dad," Ellie says, choosing spices from the spice rack, averting her red eyes and looking busy.

"Hey there, yourself," he says. He pulls off his overcoat and carries it to the hallway closet, not glancing into the living room, sliding in sideways between the clumsy wooden storage unit across from the closet door. It seems they've never been able to find a hallway wide enough for that unit and she doesn't know why her father doesn't finally just get rid of it. After a moment he returns to the kitchen, loosening his solid navy blue tie, and kisses her cheek. "You okay?" he says hesitantly.

"I'm a little warm,." she says, and adds, "Kind of late, isn't it? How long does it take you to get home in the evenings?"

"Oh," he says, taking a couple of steps backward and leaning against the counter top, "I don't know. Depends on traffic through the tunnels. Usually about an hour."

She shakes her head in disbelief, drizzles some olive oil onto the bottom of the skillet and turns on the heat. "That's too long. Your back'll stiffen up." She pauses. "I thought you got off at four-thirty?"

"Yeah. I stopped off after to see, um, a guy I know."

"Oh. Well, anyway. Why don't you sell this place and get an apartment in town, close to the office? It'd be less work, less headache, less time in the car. And I could invest the money from this place for you. You could make a killing."

He shrugs. "Not really interested. Did Todd call today?"

She nods, cutting a clove of garlic and letting the bits fall directly into the pan where they sizzle and pop in the hot oil.

"You didn't have to cook dinner again. We could've ordered in."

"It's all right," she says. "Gives me something to do."

Her back is turned, but she can feel him looking at her; it's much the same feeling she had when she listened to Todd's messages.

"Did you get any work done today?" he asks.

She takes two cans of tomato sauce down from the overhead cupboard and slides them under the teeth of the electric can opener, thinking about her laptop sitting on the dining room table, one of the only things she didn't rearrange. "Not much," she says above the whirl of the tiny motor. "I moved a couple of things. Nothing major." She means stocks—for a client company she represents which is filing for bankruptcy—not furniture, and she finds herself smiling briefly at her unintended pun. After setting the open cans down on the counter she breaks off some ground beef and drops it into the skillet. "How about you?"

"Nothing much. A little fire."

"What? Someone got fired?"

"No. A fire. An actual fire. With flames and smoke. One of my men took care of it, though."

"Oh." She's not sure how to respond to this. "But everything's all right? I mean, nobody got hurt?"

"No. Well, a flag."

Ellie pokes at the lump of meat with a wooden spoon. She's never made chili before; she's feeling her way. "Well, that's good," she says. "That you're okay."

"Yeah, I'm fine. We're all fine. Except for any Norwegian sympathizers." He loosens his tie, watches her. "So what're you slaving so hard over?"

"Chili."

He nods, scratches his neck. "Good. I like chili."

She stirs some more, then it occurs to her that chili ought to contain more than ground meat and tomato sauce, so she opens the refrigerator and looks around. Not much: milk; orange juice; a six-pack of Iron City, one missing; ketchup; pickles; some left-over Chinese; three eggs, each in it's own little built-in groove in the door. Then, on the bottom shelf, she sees a green pepper in a clear supermarket produce bag. She slides the built-in cutting board out from the counter, sets the pepper on in, and turns for a knife.

"Maybe you want to turn the heat down a bit," her father says. "Smells like it's burning."

She lunges for the dial, slamming her hip against the cutting board.

"Ellie. Easy, honey."

Bent over, she feels her father behind her, hands on her upper arms, trying to get her to stand up straight. But the tears have returned; she can feel them in her eyes, and she doesn't want him to see her like this, doesn't want to have to admit to what has caused them.

"Stand up, sweetie. Let me see."

"I can't believe I did that," she murmurs, still bent over.

"It's okay," he says. "Just stand up straight, El. Your hair's getting in the pan."

She straightens, rubs her hip.

"You all right?" he asks.

"No." She starts crying again, trying, at least, to stay quiet, but it feels as though an air bubble's caught in her throat and she's afraid she might wail.

"Do you think it's bruised? Do you want me to get some ice for it?"

She shakes her head no. Behind her the meat burns; she can smell it—a singed quality.

"Well, all right," she hears her father say. "It'll be okay then."

"I can't do this," she says.

He nods, overly agreeable. "Sure, okay. We'll order in. It's fine." He reaches for the phone. "What would you like?"

"No," she says. "No." She rubs at her hip, a hard up and down motion. Suddenly she notices, in her other hand, she is still holding the knife. This frightens her and she drops it to the floor. "Oh, God," she says.

Her father sets the phone down. He walks over to her and retrieves the knife, then he takes her hand and leads her out of the kitchen, dropping the knife casually into the sink as they pass. He doesn't say a word but she can feel him pause when they step into the living room. Once they are seated together on the sofa—which was rather complicated in itself since she left little space to negotiate between the pieces of furniture—he says, "You said Todd called today."

She nods. Her hands are in her lap and she watches them.

"What did he say? If you don't mind my asking."

"Nothing. We just listened to each other."

After a minute he says, "What do you want to do, Ellie?"

Again, before she has time to think about it, to stop it, the tears roll. She's never cried this much. Not since her mother died. But that had been coming for some time and she didn't even cry this much at the funeral. It wasn't until about a month or so later when, one morning, something came over her suddenly and she cried for two solid days. She sniffs now, tries to compose herself. But the sniffle just catches in her throat and she begins to cough.

Her father pats her on the back. "Easy now."

"I can't do this," she says, and coughs some more.

"Okay."

"I thought I could. I thought I could be tough. But I'm not tough."

"It's okay."

"I just want my husband back," she says. "There's nothing wrong with that."

Her father nods. "I know. I know, sweetheart. But he's not your husband now. I mean at least, he's not the man you married. He needs to find that person again. He needs to—"

"Oh, what do you know about it," she snaps, surprising herself.

This stops him, and she's immediately sorry for it. He looks away, takes a breath. "I like what you've done with the place," he says.

"No, you don't."

"Sure I do. It's a good arrangement. Especially if I were ever to have anyone over. Everyone can see each other. Of course, I don't get many visitors these days."

She wipes at her eyes. "Who was the friend you went to see after work?"

"Oh. Just a guy I know." He leans back into the sofa, disappears from her peripheral vision. "He has lung cancer and, well, he..."

"That's too bad," she says.

"It's okay. I've never talked about him before, actually. His name is Francis. He's, well, he's just this homeless guy that hangs out on Seventh Avenue and we—I don't even know if you can say we've taken a liking to each other. I don't know if you could use that phrase. But we've sort of become part of each other's lives and I check on him now and again." He leans forward, as if being struck by a sudden revelation. "Oh, hell," he says, rising. "The stove's still on." He weaves his way between sofa and end table, end table and chair, and then Ellie can hear his dress shoes on the linoleum. A minute later he comes back. He's holding the skillet with the clump of ground meat. Ellie looks up at him. He smiles, then slowly, dramatically, turns the skillet upside down. All the meat stays in the pan, stuck to the surface. "For my next trick," he says. "Oh, hey, now *I've* put out a fire today."

Ellie smiles. "That's what you do, isn't it? Put out fires?" Then she says, "We don't eat much meat. And I don't cook much of anything."

"Is that right?" He heads back into the kitchen and returns a few seconds later with a handful of leaflets and flyers from local delivery joints. "Choose your weapon," he says, sitting back down.

"I see you've done this before." She takes a few from him and begins flipping through. Pizza, Chinese, sandwiches, Chinese, pizza, Dick's Diner. She finds she's not hungry. "You pick," she says, handing them back to him.

"If I pick something you don't like, you're not going to cry, are you?"

"I might. I can't promise anything. Tell me some more about Francis."

"What do you want to know?"

She shrugs. "Anything. What did you talk about today?"

"Today—" He stops. "Listen, honey. I asked him if he wanted help. Flat out. And in not so many words he turned me down. Maybe I need to tell you that."

"Francis did?"

"No. Todd."

"I'm asking you about Francis. Don't do this, Daddy."

She can feel the tears coming again, and he must have sensed their arrival, too, because quickly he says, "All right. Um, today—well, the fact of the matter is I've been trying to get him to call his wife."

Ellie swallows. "He's married?"

"Yes. Or he was. And she—his wife—doesn't know about the cancer, you see. And I think it's important she knows about it. I mean, she has a right—for her children's sakes, if nothing else—is the way I look at it."

"Absolutely."

They're silent for a moment. In the blank television in the corner, Ellie can see the reflection of her and her father sitting on the sofa. The angle is awkward, though, and their reflection looks like one rendered from a funhouse mirror, short and wide and skewed.

"And he won't tell her?" she says.

"It's complicated. He's losing his mind."

"Want to watch some TV?" she offers.

"Whatever, sweetheart." He reaches over and touches the back of her neck, moving the hair out of the way to get at her skin. "Whatever you want."

"I'll stay here with you, Dad," she says. "As long as it takes. I just—I just can't believe how weak I am." Then, in a contemptuous voice, one that she hopes matches the way she actually feels, she says, "A lawyer. Can you believe it?" She leans her shoulders back against the cushions. "I'm a child."

Her father's fingers work the back of her neck. She lets her head fall forward, chin to her chest, feeling it.

"You're my child," he says. "You're a brave woman."

He doesn't understand much—he'll admit that right out to anyone—but Todd Sizemore certainly doesn't understand why his wife found it prudent to return with her father to Pittsburgh, at a time when he most needs her. And the most difficult part, he's finding, is even as he tries to resent her actions, to locate some of the indignation to which he feels he's entitled, he can't. He could've stopped them. Even token resistance on his part would've kept her here, he knows—that's all it would've taken, but he was incapable even of that and he has no idea why and now he just misses her; he apologizes to her over and over again in his mind and on her father's answering machine, and grows more and more humiliated with himself. Even if she returned tomorrow, he's not sure he could look her in the face.

It's a little after two a.m. and the bar is nearly empty. Wednesdays aren't exactly the hottest nights at this place (Todd can't even recall the name—the Wooden Nickel or Nickleby's, something about a nickel) but it paid one-seventy-five and it got him out of the apartment. He played horribly, perhaps because yesterday he'd flushed the rest of what he had, and he hasn't been able to find any energy since. Nothing. His knees ache just to stand. His neck and spine throb with the undertaking of holding his head up. His breathing is long and drawn and even, like a sleeping person's. Sometimes, from his nose, he catches himself emitting a soft, gurgling snore.

He places his Alvarez guitar (just the one—he couldn't muster the energy to drag along the electric or the Martin 12-string) into its case, lying open across the beer-sticky floor. His heart does a light flapping thing in his chest and he sits up straight, holding still.

"You okay, Todd?" Juan, the bartender, is leaning over, lowering beer mugs elbow-deep into the suds-filled sink then transferring them to a draining board off to the side. He keeps his eyes on Todd, though, who is a few feet away, at one of the side tables.

"Mm-hmm."

"You look a little pale, my friend."

Despite his own listlessness, Todd has grown, over the course of the evening, to like Juan. He has a way of calling you "my friend" without it sounding phony or contrived. "Fine."

The fluttering in his chest has stopped but the resulting shock has not. Todd sits back in his chair, hands limp on his thighs and watches Juan continue to wash the glasses, like a machine: grab, dip, swirl, remove, grab, dip, swirl, remove. The air is cold now; both the front and rear doors are open to help circulate things, get rid of the stale beer smell. One last group of patrons lingers at a table across the room from Todd: three men and two women, late-thirties maybe. The women are pleading with two of the men to convince the third to do something. Todd can't tell what. Finally, though, the group staggers out, one of the women stopping briefly in front of the cigarette machine; she pats her pockets before realizing she has no change.

Sometimes people come up to him after one of his shows and tell him how much they enjoyed it; sometimes they even ask if he has a CD or something available, and if so where can they get it. But that doesn't happen tonight. Admittedly, he was sluggish and nonchalant in his performance. He played mostly instrumentals and achieved virtually no rapport with the meager audience, didn't try. Frequently, people got up and left, or talked loudly over him. But he doesn't blame them; he bored himself.

Juan has finished with the glasses and has begun wiping down the bar with a rag. He looks up at Todd without stopping and nods. Along the wall behind him there are bottles on shelves, stacked in asymmetric rows, surrounding a diamond-shaped road sign with the suggestion to YIELD. A set of lights flicker and click on, illuminating the place. Suddenly, Todd is somewhere else. This is not the bar he performed in earlier tonight; the aesthetics are all wrong. This place is bright and white and airy and expansive, not the dusky, remote setting he remembers. He sits up straight, feeling strangely on display.

His skin tingles. Juan clicks on the stereo beneath the bar and the Rolling Stones leak from the room's hidden speakers: "Miss You." The familiarity of the song, following closely on the heels of all the obscure stuff Todd played tonight, turns something inside him. The song's peculiar eeriness doesn't help things either, and Todd moves quickly. He flips his guitar case closed with his foot, takes the case up by the handle, slips on his jacket, and heads across the bar toward the open door.

"Hey, man," Juan says to him. "Hold up. Have a drink."

"No, thanks." He keeps going.

"Good set tonight. The boss'll have you back, no question."

Todd slows and turns, looks back at Juan's face, trying to detect sarcasm. Juan is still wiping down the bar; his long, angular face is splotched with shadows, but it is at ease, natural. "Thanks," Todd says.

Outside on the sidewalk, his check folded into thirds in his shirt pocket, Todd stands and, once again, considers himself. He's been doing this a lot lately—just thinking about himself— but his impressions change constantly, his present surroundings playing a large role in the construction of these impressions. Currently: it's drizzling. Tenements line both sides of the narrow, shimmery-wet street. Just one car—a cab, a half-block down, pulled over against the curb. The driver has his head out the widow and is talking to a man walking his dog on the opposite side of the street. He wants to know where the guy's scooper is. "I could report you," he says. "Just 'cause it's three in the morning don't mean your dog won't shit on the sidewalk." The guy tells the cabbie to kiss his Irish ass, mutters something about the cabbie's "good mind," holds up a finger, and continues on, the dog, a lab mix of some kind, leading the way. "That's it," the cabbie says, leaning farther out of the window now, "I'm turning your ass in. That's it." He seems confused by his own words, though, apparently having realized how ludicrous and, truthfully, impossible his threat is. When the man and his dog are out of earshot the cabbie looks around, as if in search of witnesses, then slowly (shamefully, it seems to Todd) lowers himself back into the car and sits obediently behind the wheel.

Todd's apartment—his and Ellie's—is a long way away. He's somewhere on the periphery of the East Village—East 9th, he thinks; the soft drone of traffic he can hear around the corner is probably Third Avenue. He considers taking the cab then immediately discharges the thought. The walk—some seventy blocks, all-told—will take him the entire night, but it might do him some good. What kind of good, he's not sure. His skin is damp already from the drizzle and he's attained that REM-sleep sort of breathing he's becoming accustomed to. The handle to his guitar case is slippery in his hand. He knows what he needs, but he won't let himself think about that, just keeps an eye on his surroundings. Across the street is a boarded-up newsstand. A sewer cover spewing steam. A red, white and blue fire hydrant. He turns to his right, toward what he believes to be west, and begins walking, guitar swinging at his side. Maybe he'll take a stroll through Union Square, if he can find it from here. He doesn't get downtown all that much anymore. Or maybe he'll stop in at one of those video-booth places, or a bar where the women will take their clothes off and pretend to be interested in him. He squeezes the guitar case's handle, hard. He keeps walking, passing no one. Water droplets from awnings and overhangs fall onto his head. At least he can feel that. The rain itself he cannot, though he keeps getting wetter. And where are all the people? Sure, it's two in the morning, but he hasn't seen a soul since the cabbie. It is his world, where he's in control, where every decision he makes is the right one and at this moment he's thinking that the right decision to make is for him to go home, take the stairs all the way to the roof of his building—fourteen floors—and throw himself off. A perfect clich d ending to the clich of a life he's apparently decided to lead: Run-of-the-mill addictions, run-of-the-mill fantasies.

Up ahead he can see an intersection—stop lights and street lamps and cars gliding past. He picks up his pace. That intersection, Third Avenue, he decides, is where he wants to be. If he could just get to that intersection—who knows?—things might start to make sense. He watches as the lights and passing cars grow larger in his blurred, bobbing vision. The lights are about three blocks away now and presently a car turns off and heads toward him. Todd stops. The car is a big one, a Buick or a Lincoln or an Olds. Its headlights are bright; the width of the beam traverses both lanes of the street. All Todd can see is the thick cone of light growing larger, cutting through the mist, pushing out to the edges of his sight. Then, before he can even account for its presence, the car is past him; it continues down the street spraying moisture from its tires. When it is gone Todd sits on the curb, sets his guitar beside him. He must, he knows, entertain the very real possibility now that he has lost his mind. He mulls this over for a moment. The mist keeps up in the chilly air, nearly soaking through Todd's wool coat. He wishes, briefly, that he'd worn his hat. The guitar sits next to him in its case and as he reaches a hand out to touch it, another set of headlights make the turn from the intersection and heads toward him. Actually, as Todd watches, he sees that it's just one headlight—the other must be burned out: What did his mother used to call that? A pedidel?

Again, Todd's eyes lock in on the light; it's not nearly as blinding as the first car's but fuzzy around the edges, as if forever traveling just outside of a heavy fog, and he finds that he's taken his guitar case by the handle and has begun walking toward the middle of the street. He feels these two cars, one right after the other, simultaneously ignored and intruded upon him.

He turns to face the oncoming car. The light blinds him. He heaves his guitar case back in preparation to throw it, cocks his arm. He hears a weird, timid beep, then again, and then the fuzziness around the light clears and he realizes that what's coming toward him is not a car with one headlight but a motorcycle, and in the next moment he finds himself airborne. He is laid out prone, facing skyward, an odd pressure in his chest, and then he comes down, hard, on his back. He feels himself bounce, his ankles knock together; then he comes to rest with his left shoulder pushed awkwardly against the streetside curb.

Todd lies still, waiting for what he's sure is his own death. He finds he's curious to discover just what it will feel like. A soft moisture surrounds him; an exquisite warmth originates in the small of his back and seeps outward, to his hips, shoulders, kneecaps, the empty area behind his collarbones. He can hear a steady, continuous squeaking sound. A voice says, "What the fuck, man?"

Todd moves one arm and then the other. He pushes forward with his hands and shifts his hips and soon he finds that he has managed to sit up. He scans the street. His guitar case lies, badly dented, against the opposite curb. The motorcycle lies on its side, front wheel spinning, its headlight illuminating the misty rain that's still falling. A few feet away a man in a red leather jacket and dark tinted face guard wobbles on his back like an overturned turtle. "Jesus fucking Christ," he says.

Todd sits up and, since he's able, figures nothing vital is broken.

The man rolls onto his side. Todd cannot tell if he is black or white, old or young. "Are you crazy?" he says. Then he says, "Hey, are you hurt? You're not hurt, are you, dude?"

"Maybe," Todd says. "A little," then realizes he's only answered the man's first question.

"No way," the man says. "You're okay. You're fucking nuts." He pushes up onto all fours and stays like that, looking, for all Todd knows, at the asphalt between his hands. "Oh my God," he says then. "My cigarette. Oh, fuck. I think I swallowed my cigarette. It's gone. I must've swallowed it." He begins crawling around the wet street.

Todd has no idea how this guy could have been smoking a cigarette while wearing that helmet. He imagines the entire inside filled with thick smoke. Perhaps, it occurs to him, because of the smoke, the guy couldn't see where he was going; perhaps his getting hit wasn't his own fault. Inspired, Todd positions himself on his hands and knees. When he's relatively certain everything is in working order, he scrambles over to the cycle, pulls it upright, and climbs on.

"Whoa, man," the guy says, stopping his search. With his complicated helmet and red leather jacket he looks to Todd like some sort of futuristic commando. "What the hell do you think you're doing?"

"Look at my guitar," Todd says, pointing. The outside of his hand, he sees, is badly skinned, glowing pink in the rain. "It's ruined. Probably. Look what you did to my guitar."

"What I did?" The man rises up onto his knees. "What I did?" His voice is dull and hollow behind the face guard. "What kind of guitar?"

"Alvarez."

"Oh." He examines the palms of his hands as though puzzled by them.

"Look what you did to it."

The man lets his hands fall to his sides. "Just hold the fuck on there, pal. You ran out in front of me. What was I supposed to—"

"Sorry," Todd says. "Fair's fair," then pops the clutch on the motorcycle and takes off down the street, back toward the club at which he just played. Remembering, somehow, to signal, he makes a right onto Second Avenue at the next corner.

He makes a series of subsequent turns—another right onto Houston, left onto Varick. Occasionally he has to wait for stop lights to turn green. Eventually, though, he finds himself waiting in line for the Holland Tunnel and then paying a toll and crossing under the Hudson River. He emerges into the dingy lights of Jersey, but he keeps going. The back of his head pounds. The rain stings his cheeks and he has to occasionally ride with his eyes closed. He passes by convenience stores and other brightly lit establishments until the road becomes something of a freeway, and then all he notices—his eyes now open to mere slits—are green exit signs. He is traveling by instinct now. He trusts himself. But his skinned hands worry him: they are cold well beyond the verge of numbness. He can feel the wind against his gums. The bottom of his coat is bunched up beneath him and torn at one of the cuffs. But he doesn't care; he keeps going. He doesn't want to stop. If he stops, he will hurt. At some point New Jersey becomes Pennsylvania and he is pleased with himself to discover that his only concern—the only thing that truly matters to him at this moment—is when he'll have to stop for gas.

At the bluest-black light of early morning, Marlene Stringer turns over in bed. She raises her head and supports it with her hand, then she gives her husband a soft poke to the ribs. She whispers his name.

Owen stirs, makes a chewing motion with his mouth. She pokes him again and he opens his eyes. "What is it?" he says. "What's the matter?"

"Nothing, honey," she breathes.

"Oh. Did you wake me?"

"Yes. I'm sorry."

He shifts beneath the covers. His prematurely white hair is puffed up like whipped cream piled on his head. "Is something wrong?" he says. "Is it that Trib story?"

"No," she says, and it's not. Not tonight. "Owen, do you think I command respect?"

He looks at her, blinks. "Command?"

"I'm just asking, Owen."

He reaches behind his head and props his pillow against the headboard, raises himself up. "Is something the matter, Marlene?"

"It's just a question, Owen. I'm just asking a question."

"Yes. I understand. And before I answer it—" he glances at the clock radio. "Before I answer your question, at 5:24 a.m., I'm just asking you if 'command' is the term you really want me to consider when answering."

"Oh, will you stop it." His ability to see through to the essence of things is the reason she decided to finally broach the question—which has kept her up most of the night—to him. But his use of this skill now is annoying to her.

He takes a breath, runs a hand through his mound of hair, takes her hand. "All I'm saying is your use of the word 'command' is, I believe, pertinent. Yes, I think you are respected in the sense that people respect your abilities. People respect your work ethic and what you are capable of, professionally. But, darling, when you say, 'Do I command respect,' well, I think that...demeanor about you speaks to something a bit deeper. Do you see what I'm saying?"

She does. "People don't respect me, they respect what I'm about."

"I can't say for sure. I'm answering your question on the basis of your question—the way you asked it."

She snuggles down into the covers, rests her head in the bow of her husband's shoulder and places her hand on his chest. "Corbett wants someone fired and I don't think it's a good idea. Especially now. I don't think it's wise for the company and I don't think it's fair to the employee. Even though I brought the issue up in the first place."

"Dunne?"

She nods, but there's no way he could have seen this. "The problem," she says, "is I certainly haven't done anything to help him in his career. I mean, I've—subconsciously, I like to believe, but I'm not so sure—at times gone out of my way to make him look incompetent. I think in many ways he is incompetent, but..."

She feels Owen turn his head and look at her. He doesn't say anything, though, and for this she is grateful. She thinks about how Jack would be instructing her as to exactly what she should do in this situation. He would become her therapist (a hobby of his: though he makes his money working on bones and tendons and ligaments, he considers himself quite adept at what he calls "matters of the mind"), advising and counseling, quizzing her in fact, making sure she was prepped, like a patient for surgery: First of all, wear a beige suit; now, when you walk in there tomorrow, be sure to keep out of your voice any indication of trepidation that might be inappropriately construed...Owen, though, just gives her shoulder a squeeze, fingers the wool of her nightgown. At Jack's she only keeps little teddies and silky negligees, and the thought of this, for the first time, causes a quick constriction inside her, like a screw tightening too far.

"It seems to me," Owen says cautiously, "that you have yourself an opportunity to gain some respect. Not to command it, but to earn it."

"Yes," she says.

"What are you going to do?"

She takes his hand and pulls his arm tighter around her. "I have forty more minutes to sleep," she says. "So I'm going to do that."

GOVERNMENT FOR HIRE

On December 6th it started raining again. It rained for two days straight and the local newscasters began putting forth various scenarios that the weather might cause, natural disasters and such, like floods and landslides. The rivers were rising and the mountains were softening. But after two days the temperature dropped enough so that the rain turned to snow and from that point on the only significant problems, weather-wise, that Michael could see, were the usual ones: slippery streets, slow drivers, frozen windowpanes, school delays, and, the morning after that first big snowfall, having to dig his car out of a drift, caused by a plow, on Belefonte Avenue.

Lately, he has been seeing his pregnant wife less and less each day. Today, for example, she and Alex are meeting with the contractors about the renovation work she wants done on the new studio. That's what she's calling it: the studio. She has a file folder full of sketches and swatches which she one evening held up in front of Michael and let him nod approvingly at. The contractor comes highly recommended, and paid for in advance, by his father-in-law—a consideration that Michael can't seem to put from his mind.

Another consideration of his is Alex. He wants to be supportive of his friend, of course, but he can't see what Alex has to gain by going into business with Natalie. Michael is skeptical of the whole idea on its own merits—it's something that he and Natalie will have to live with and, most likely, recover from for a long time; he just can't keep himself from expecting disaster—but the added responsibility (and that's the way Michael views it: a responsibility) of Alex's livelihood is a bit too much for him to come to terms with.

After the meeting with the contractor, Natalie has her first doctor's appointment. Michael is to meet her at Magee no later than eleven.

Leaving for work, though, he's not even nervous about the appointment. There's a new coating of snow on the ground and the cars are covered; he has to get the scraper out and clear off the windows. He knows just getting to the office—maneuvering up the hill at Negley Avenue and through the narrow Squirrel Hill streets—will be difficult, requiring his full concentration. At least it's something, a project, an objective. Lately it seems to Michael that everyone around him is engrossed in some project or another, everyone working to exact some sort of positive change in his or her life: Natalie, Alex, Ralph, everyone at work. He feels stupid all the time, out of touch. Even his mother has begun trying new restaurants and his father is now saying his own blessings. What next?

The snow is soft and light and all Michael has to do is brush it from the Cherokee. No scraping necessary. He switches into four-wheel-drive and heads out into the dim Shadyside morning. The challenge, he knows, will be a defensive one—trying to avoid being hit by other cars. By the time he merges onto the Parkway, though, he is disappointed. There is very little traffic and, because of the dry, downy nature of the snow, traction is relatively good. He pulls into the parking lot at work twenty minutes later, having achieved nothing.

Toby is not at the front desk when he stops for his temporary ID badge. Michael has to recite the required information for Ben, who, unlike his boss, does not know the social security numbers of forgetful employees by heart. The experience lacks the usual flippancy and spiritedness of Michael's exchanges with Toby, but eventually he gets his badge and makes it up to the tenth floor to his office.

On his chair there is a note from Dennis: "See me."

So okay. Eventually Michael was going to have to come into contact with his boss. He knows that, has known it. Actually, he can't believe it's taken this long. He thought for sure he'd be picking this note off of his chair the morning after Patricia Cross's Georgia Power article came out in the Trib. But, then again, Dennis always was late in getting back to people. He leaves the note where it is and slides out of his overcoat, hangs it on the back of his door. Looking around on top of his desk he tries to decide if he should bring anything with him. But what would he bring? He takes his suit jacket off and rolls up the sleeves of his shirt to create the impression of work. Why he feels he has to do this, he couldn't say. He expects nothing in particular with regard to this summons and convinces himself that there's no reason in the world why he should. Still, he unbuttons his top button and loosens his tie. He runs a hand through his snow-wet hair.

Out in the vestibule Michael sees Gloria, Dennis's secretary, lift her eyes to him as he pushes through the glass doors. Dennis's office is one of three set off of a waiting area complete with sofas, end tables, industry-appropriate reading material, and a coffee machine. The other offices belong to Diaz and Morton. Not long ago all three men had their own secretaries; then the cutbacks started and now Gloria, possessing the most seniority, is the only one left. Quite possibly she is the most overworked employee in the corporation, Michael believes. Right now she has the phone pinned to her ear with her shoulder and she's jotting something onto the outside of a file folder.

"Hey, Gloria," Michael says, a near whisper. "The boss in?"

She holds up a finger. "Uh-huh," she says into the phone. "No, not this week. It'll have to be next. Wednesday or later."

Michael puts his hands in his pockets and turns to glance into Dennis's office. Reflected in the far window he can see his boss sitting in his chair, leaning back, so he gives Gloria a look— he is unsure of the look's function but hopes she will interpret it appropriately—and walks toward the open door.

"Morning, Dennis," he says, stepping inside.

Snow is falling again, floating down behind Dennis, who still sits leaning back in his chair, motionless, crisp crimson handkerchief in the lapel of his gray pinstripe suit jacket. His computer is still switched off and his desk is nearly spotless, except for an unaddressed manila envelope and a cup of coffee on a brass Electro-Lite coaster. "Good morning, Mike," he says. "Come in. Close the door, please."

Michael does so, then takes a seat in one of the three chairs across the desk. He can see that, for some reason, the lights are on in Three Rivers Stadium across the cement-colored Allegheny. "So what's up?"

"Well, I thought we should talk," Dennis says. "Truthfully, I'm starting to feel out of touch. All the management training courses they make us take, all of them say you should maintain a consistent dialogue with your people. We work on the same floor, you and me, and what's it been, two weeks since we've seen each other?"

"I guess so," Michael says.

"Since the press conference."

Michael nods. "I guess that's right."

"So." Dennis swings his arms down from behind his head and leans forward, elbows on his desk. "What have you been up to?"

The snow swirls against the window. Michael stiffens. He places his hands on the desk, as if showing Dennis his rolled-up sleeves in response.

"What have you been working on these past two weeks?" Dennis says. "I have to admit I'm a bit curious."

"Well, I've—I've been working on some things."

"Marvelous. Such as?"

Michael does not answer. He keeps expecting, as each moment passes, to say what it is he's been doing these past two weeks. But nothing comes and he finds himself still sitting there, silent.

"You must have some pretty hot projects going on," Dennis says, and waits some more. The two men sit looking at each other until Dennis finally takes a breath and adds, "You see, I'm curious because, well, to tell you the truth, Michael, we've been working our asses off around here. And do you know what we've been working on?"

"The layoffs, I would guess."

Dennis nods. "That'd be a good guess. Yes, that's one of the things we've been working on. Certainly. But we've also been working on—" He pauses, scrunches his brow. "Where did you go to school again?"

"Miami."

"Ah, yes. Miami. Of Ohio, right? Yes, now I remember. Oxford, Ohio. Correct?"

Michael just looks at him.

"Well, Michael, back in Public Relations one-oh-one at good old Miami of Ohio U. they probably called what we've been up to here 'damage control.' You're familiar with that term?"

"What are you getting at, Dennis?" Michael finds that he's suddenly angry. He's being played with—by a man pretentious enough to stuff a hanky in his jacket and act like it means something. "I'd appreciate it if you knocked off the sarcasm."

"Fine," Dennis says. "Straight to the point. Indeed. That's why I hired you, if I remember correctly."

Michael waits.

"I want you to volunteer for separation," Dennis says. "Immediately."

"Say what?"

"I need to reduce my staff by one," Dennis says. "I'm sorry, Michael. You're it."

"Since when do you need to reduce your staff?"

"Since five minutes ago. Since two Mondays ago. What difference does it make? That's not what's at issue here."

Michael stands and sees Dennis recoil rigidly in his chair, as if he suspected that Michael were going to attack him. He sits back down. "You said 'volunteer.' If you have to make a reduction, why do I have to volunteer?"

This time it's Dennis who stands. He stands and actually turns away, toward the window. The snow is still coming down in fat, airy flakes. "Don't make this more difficult than it has to be, Mike. I want you out and I have that right."

"What are you talking about, Dennis? I mean where..."

"If you volunteer now you'll receive a severance package of one month's salary for every year of service. Plus unused vacation time and an option to continue health benefits. That's a pretty fair deal, one that, truthfully, I don't even think you deserve. How many years do you have with the company? Seven? Eight?"

"I don't know," Michael says.

"Well, either way it's not bad." Dennis turns back around. "Not too shabby at all."

"Are you kidding me?" Michael says. He figures he might as well play this out fully. "I mean, this is a joke. Right, Dennis? You're pissed at me for the press conference, because a reporter showed a little initiative and dug around into something I said. Maybe you're even a little embarrassed at how spineless and political you were—and now you're trying to teach me a lesson. Is that it? 'Cause if it is, okay, you got me. Good one, Dennis."

"What have you been working on?" Dennis says.

"Not much. You've closed me out of meetings. And Natalie's pregnant."

This seems to take Dennis slightly aback. He winces as though being pinched and then his eyes shift from Michael's face to his hands and then from Michael completely, wandering around the room. He takes the crimson hanky from his lapel and holds it in his hand. Michael is just glad to finally find some use for Natalie's pregnancy.

"We're very excited," Michael says. "Thanks for your concern."

Dennis says nothing.

"You'll understand if we don't name you as Godfather. I mean, you were up there at the top of the list, of course, but under the circumstances—"

Suddenly Dennis pushes his chair out of the way and snuggles up close against his desk. His fists are clenched. "Get out," he says.

"What's your problem now?"

Dennis takes two deep breaths; for some convoluted reason it reminds Michael of a woman preparing to give birth. Behind him a helicopter flies low over the West End Bridge. "Just get out. So help me, Michael, I'll phone security if I have to." He points at the phone on his desk for emphasis.

"What? What did I do?" Michael is still sitting casually. His heart, though, is beating so hard he fears it might just exhaust itself and stop. Then something occurs to him. "That's why you made me answer questions," he says. "You knew about the Georgia Power thing and didn't want to subject yourself to having to cover it up. Oh my God, what a fucking idiot I am."

"I expected resistance," Dennis says, ignoring him. "I expected indignity and maybe even denial. But I will not stand here and let you make disturbing things up and throw the lies right in my face."

"What? What are you talking about?"

"About your wife. I won't stand here and have you make things up to put me in an awkward position."

Michael chuckles. "Holy Christ. Talk about denial."

"That's it." Dennis reaches for the phone, dials four numbers.

"Hey, I'm sorry if I'm making this more difficult for you, Dennis. But my wife is pregnant. What the hell do you want from me?"

"Yes," Dennis says into the phone. "Dennis Tussy on ten. I need a former employee removed from my office." He's looking at Michael while he talks. "Well I don't know the procedure either, I would assume that's your department... What? I want you to escort him out the front door... Now. When do you think?... All right." He hangs up the phone.

"You can't do this, Dennis."

He sits. "It's already done."

"This is going to get ugly, you know," Michael says, though he has no idea what he might mean by this.

"Maybe. That's up to you." Dennis's face is red and puffy. Sweat clings to his mustache and he dabs at it with his hanky. "I'd advise you to not make it ugly."

"I don't have to. That'll happen all by itself. I always knew you were in over your head, Dennis. You're an ass-kisser in a ridiculous suit and you're not going to come out of this looking too good."

Dennis's lips are twitching; he's waiting for security to arrive, watching the door, each second probably seeming like an hour.

"I trusted you, Dennis," Michael says, though he's not sure he ever really did. "Who else knew the truth about Georgia Power?"

"Lots of people going out have pregnant wives," Dennis says. "You're not the only one with a pregnant wife, that I can tell you. I can't be—" He's interrupted by a knock at the door. "Come in, come in," Dennis says, standing.

The door opens and Toby the guard steps inside, looking around, confused.

"Hey, Toby," Michael says. "Missed you this morning. I needed a temporary badge, of course. That Ben kid doesn't play."

"I was a little late. I—" He looks at Dennis. "Him?"

"Yes, Toby. Please escort Mr. Dunne out the front door. He can come back at his convenience to retrieve his personal possessions. Under supervision."

"Just for the record," Michael says, "does this mean I'm fired? Because, I don't know—" he turns to Toby. "What's the procedure for escorting active employees from the premises? I mean, is that even done?"

Toby and Dennis look at each other.

"Oh, this is priceless," Michael says.

Dennis wipes the hanky across his forehead. "Toby, please."

Toby says, "Um, Mr. Dunne, I guess we'd better go."

"Sure, Toby," Michael says. He turns to Dennis. "I'd like to speak with Sarver about this."

"No. You've been separated. You're no longer an employee of this company and as such have no business in this building beyond the retrieval of your personal belongings." There is a hint of nervousness in his voice, a lilt at the end of each phrase that is negligible but that Michael nonetheless notices.

Michael stands, extends his hand. Dennis looks at it for a moment then takes it and shakes. Michael turns and leaves with Toby.

In the elevator Toby says, "I can't believe they canned you."

"Well, they did. He did."

"What are you going to do now?"

Toby's question strikes Michael oddly; it's as if the words formed inside Michael's own head and have seeped out audibly. He says, "Something."

The elevator stops at three and two men, both pudgy around their middles and both wearing short sleeve shirts with ties, step on. They're talking about the president. Clinton, not Sarver.

"Why don't you two just walk down?" Michael says, interrupting. "It's only two flights."

"Excuse me?" one of the men says good-naturedly.

"Nothing." Michael turns away. "Those are stupid ties."

∗ ∗ ∗

Todd returns from the Giant Eagle with a loaf of white bread, peanut butter, three apples, Band-Aids, a box of Entemann's oatmeal raisin cookies, some mini Ritz crackers, a jumbo size Extra-Strength Tylenol, and a pocketful of quarters for the Pepsi machine. The snow is a nuisance. Since he knew when he left the Monroeville Radisson he'd have a couple of bags to haul back he left the motorcycle—a Kawasaki—in the hotel parking lot, not trusting himself to maneuver the thing over the increasingly icy pavement and stop-and-go strip mall traffic of Route 22 while balancing two grocery bags on his badly bruised knees. Now he can't even seem to get across to the center median of the road's four lanes. He stands between the entrances of the Toyota lot and Chuck E. Cheese, a plastic grocery bag dangling from each hand. The traffic is bumper-to-bumper and never really stops, even though there is a light just a hundred yards down from where he is standing. The problem, so far as Todd can see, is that cars are backed up all the way from the next light, which is so far down the hill and around the bend that he can't even see it, which renders this light relatively useless; the cars just ignore it and continue creeping along as if this stoplight weren't even here.

Christmas shopping. Todd remembers this area of town at the holidays from his previous visits with Ellie and concedes to himself that he should have stayed someplace else. But this is where the closest hotels to Toby's house are, and, in this weather, he'd just as soon be riding that motorcycle around town as little as possible. The 349 miles here was one thing. He did that, he made it here, and now he's through.

After a few minutes he gives up looking for a break in the traffic and just stands there, eyeing the hotel across the four lanes like a prize that is so far out of reach he feels as though he should chastise himself just for wanting it. Behind the hotel is Monroeville Mall—actually the hotel and the mall share an immense parking lot—and that's where most of the cars are trying to go. Route 22 is nothing but a row of stores: plazas and strips, various shops in various groupings. Those outlets are fine but, in a town like Pittsburgh, Todd knows, you can't beat a mall. The whole place is done up for Christmas: wreaths on lampposts, lights strung across the building and hanging from the big Kaufmann's sign. Todd can see that they are on, glowing dimly against the off-white late morning sky. The sight makes him realize he hasn't gotten Ellie anything for Christmas. He hasn't gotten anyone anything. He does some quick calculations in his head to try and figure out how many more days he has, but, not knowing exactly what day it is, the best he can do is somewhere in the vicinity of fifteen to eighteen. Besides, what could he possibly get her? What manner of gift would be appropriate? Consider: she left him in his hour of need and his response has been to leave ridiculous messages on her father's answering machine, destroy his own eight hundred-dollar acoustic guitar, steal a motorcycle, and then setting up camp in a hotel fifteen minutes away and living off of her own credit card. Run-of-the-mill addictions lead to asinine actions.

He has stayed clean, though. There is that.

Todd decides he's had enough. He steps out onto Route 22, chin up, grocery bags at his sides. He can't move very fast: his knees ache and his hip joints are still stiff. Horns blare. Occasionally he feels—or perhaps senses—something brushing the side of his leg and then stopping short, but he keeps his eyes straight ahead and keeps going. When he gets to the center island he hears someone behind him slow down (he can actually hear the car slow down—a discreet but distinct change in tire to asphalt amplification) and tell him he's a fucking idiot.

"Merry Christmas!" Todd shouts, still facing forward, eyes on the Radisson's lobby doors. "Joy to the world!"

He needs a plan, a course of action. He can't just sit day

after day in his hotel room, watching ESPN Sportscenter and MTV and feeling close to his wife. This closeness to Ellie is merely geographical, he knows, not to mention one-sided and, truthfully, a bit psychotic. The thing is not to try and change her feelings—there's nothing wrong with them, after all —but to change himself. Yes, he needs to make changes. Six months ago making the change from computer network administrator to musician seemed like a good idea. It wasn't. But the change, he understands, went deeper than his occupation and what he has to do now is find out for himself exactly how deep that change has taken root.

More horns blare and he crosses the last two lanes and makes his way across the hotel parking lot. The motorcycle (it is a Kawasaki, light and maneuverable but not much for acceleration) leans on its kick stand near the front doors. There is no lock and anyone could steal it if they wanted to. But he's not concerned. He has the key and anyway he doesn't need it anymore. Toby's house is only seven or eight miles away; if he has to, he can walk from here.

She let Alex talk her into the painted walls. Blue and yellow: Panther colors, he said. Besides, he added, as they sat in their contractor's office, in the basement of his Swissvale home, sketches and blueprints scattered on the table all around them, it was the latest thing, painted walls. It was the new style. You didn't want to open an interior design company and have the studio lacking in the hippest current styles.

Natalie agreed, to an extent. Yes, walls painted in solid, darker colors were more popular lately. But for how long? Her goal going in was to design something that would say to the prospective customer: This person is in tune with what's going on. But she didn't want to have to spend the money to update the studio every two years as the styles changed. Besides, blue and yellow in combination spoke to her in a less than pleasing way. But Alex, she told herself, is her partner; he's going to keep the books, pay the bills, invest her earnings, keep them on target, look for ways to entice clients and, some day, to expand. Plus, he believes in her. Perhaps he's the only one who truly does. Sure, he has ulterior motives, but so does everyone, when you really think about it. Even her father, who, she can't help suspecting, is simply trying to buy her some time. So she figured out a compromise. Blue and yellow it would be, but with a twist. She talked Alex into a dark but muted blue, like acid-washed denim, and a deep, earthy goldenrod. One wall each: the high, back wall with the window would be blue, the wall to the left would be gold, and the other two would stay white, or an off-white, to better highlight some artwork. Alex liked the idea just fine.

Now, as they get out of Alex's car and walk across the Magee Hospital parking lot through the falling snow, Alex is positively gleeful. He's walking sideways, so he can face her—he looks to Natalie, who is scanning the lot for the Cherokee, to be performing some sort of side-stepping athletic drill—talking about the studio and time frames and where he can set up his workstation. His long, loping steps are completely out of sequence with the cadence of his voice. "I think we're going to save some money on the renovations," he says. "I really do. This guy's not going to screw us. So maybe we can get the upgraded software we were talking about. How many associates did you say you wanted to hire?"

"Two."

"Yeah. Okay. That won't be a problem. I set up a separate account for payroll. What do you think is better—to hire the people first, or establish a customer base? It's up to you. But I need to know because I have some ideas for both."

"Alex, I'm a little nervous." She hadn't expected to be, but she realizes she's spoken the truth. Perhaps the day's business and Alex's excitement camouflaged it, but she's just suddenly realized why she's here.

"Oh," Alex says, slowing his stride. "Sure. Okay. I'm sorry."

"It's all right." She reaches out and, though with his awkward sidesteps and twisted torso, it's difficult, she takes his hand.

They ride up the elevator to the fourth floor and follow the letterboard signs to Dr. Colick's office, suite 414. Something in her doesn't much like the fact that the man who is going to deliver her baby is named Colick, but guesses that the spelling is probably different and that also probably she's being paranoid, which, the doctor surely will tell her, is normal.

Michael is already in the waiting room when they enter, sitting in a chair, reading a magazine, a pregnant woman on each side of him. He glances up, smiles. "The little mother," he says.

She steps around the center table on top of which magazines are randomly scattered, hoping one of the other pregnant women will move to another seat; there are many empty ones. "Been here long?"

"Actually, a little while." He acknowledges Alex, who has just hung up his coat across the room. "Hey, champ. Arrange any doilies today?"

Alex opens his mouth to say something—probably something rude, Natalie figures, because he stops himself, takes note of the women throughout the room, then says, "No. They didn't have any pink ones. And that's all I'm into."

Michael nods. "Of course."

"How come you're here so early?" Natalie says, reaching down and touching his hair. "I mean, I'm glad. I'm just surprised."

"I cleared my calendar," he says. "This is a big event. I even had time to stop at home and have a talk with Dewey."

"Is that right?"

"Yeah. I figured he needs to prepare himself for when his new brother or sister arrives. So I gave him a little talking-to. He says he understands, he's cool with it, but I think he's still in denial." Again he turns his attention to Alex, who is bent over the coffee table shuffling through magazines. "What are you doing here anyway?"

Alex looks up. "I drove. Figured I'd stick around. Why? That a problem?"

"No. Just asking."

The receptionist slides open the glass window in front of where she sits and calls out a name. One of the pregnant women—the one to Michael's left, a big, round-bellied woman who needs to hoist herself with her hands behind her hips while Michael gives her a tug at the elbow to get up—meets a nurse at the door leading to the rear offices. Natalie sits. "I'm not going to get that big," she says confidently.

"Sure you will," Michael says.

"Thanks a lot."

He shrugs.

Natalie checks in with the receptionist. They wait. Alex selects a magazine—*Inside Sports*, a peculiar option, Natalie thinks, considering this particular doctor's clientele—and sits in a chair across the room, facing them. Natalie rests her hand on her husband's knee. There's no reason for this experience to be awkward, and she refuses to let it be. This is what people do, after all. They fall in love and get married and start businesses and have babies. The fact that she took her father's money to accomplish one thing and fooled her husband into another should have no bearing. Muzak seeps through a ceiling speaker.

The woman on Michael's other side is called back and a few minutes later Natalie's name is called. In the back area Michael watches as Natalie is weighed and measured (she's four pounds more than she thought she'd be, but they made her keep her shoes on). Then the nurse takes her blood pressure, temperature and pulse, then they give her a plastic cup and show her the bathroom. When she emerges a couple of minutes later, holding the cup down below her hip, like something she's ashamed of, the nurse leads them to an examining room and says, "The doctor will be right in."

"Do I need to take any clothes off?" Natalie asks.

"Not necessary," the nurse says and closes the door.

Again they wait. Something about all this doesn't seem quite real to Natalie. It's as though she and Michael are browsing in a new car showroom, checking out cars they know they can't afford. It's okay, though, because when the salesman gets down to business, wants to talk about making a deal, they can say, You know, we changed our minds. Thank you very much. Yeah, that's the way it feels now: they can talk to the doctor, but in the backs of their minds they know they're not bound to anything.

She slides up onto the examining table. "This is exciting, huh?" she says.

"Yeah." He picks up a tongue depressor from a metal dispenser and looks it over. "I think I'm hoping for a girl. Boys can be such little pricks."

She laughs. "That's true."

"They have these egos, you know?"

"Yes. But everyone has an ego."

"Men let it rule them. Boys, I mean. Boys and men both. They want to intimidate, to govern. I'm as bad as anyone." He puts the tongue depressor in his mouth and closes his lips around it. Then he takes it out and taps his chin. "If we have a boy, I'd want to rid him of that, or teach him how to avoid it. But I'm not sure I'm capable. It would be hypocritical."

She shrugs, swings her feet back and forth, scissorlike. "Well, then we'll have a girl," she says. "But I don't think you give yourself enough credit. Who do you want to intimidate?"

"I don't." He takes a deep breath. "You're right. I think I fall short even in that regard."

"Girls mature faster," she says. "Maybe that's what you mean."

"Yeah. More mature. Exactly. That's probably what I'm getting at. Maybe." He tosses the tongue depressor in the waste basket and comes to her. He takes both of her hands in his and holds them. "This is okay," he says. "This is good."

The door opens and the doctor enters. She's been waiting anxiously but now she wishes he'd have made them wait a bit longer. She feels as though Michael has more to say to her, and she wants to listen to him.

"Good morning," Dr. Colick says. He's wearing a suit, jacket and all, and has a file folder in one hand. He holds the other out to Natalie and then to Michael. "Don Colick."

"Nice to meet you, Doctor," Michael says.

Dr. Colick folds his arms across his chest, folder held out to the side, and leans back against the little counter top, like a model in the JC Penney catalog. "Well," he says. "You're pregnant."

Michael and Natalie are silent.

"It was my understanding that you hadn't had a formal test yet," Dr. Colick clarifies. "We just wanted to make sure."

"Of course," Natalie says.

"And this is number one, right?"

"That's right," Natalie says.

"Well, the baby is about eight centimeters long. Maybe a hair under."

Out of the bottom corner of her eye, Natalie can see her own feet dangling above the floor. She swings them gently back and forth. Her attention, though, is on Dr. Colick. The doctor's face is intelligently lined, with just the right amount of baggage under the eyes to show that he's a hard worker, but not a fanatic. His hair, too, pleases Natalie. He's got a full head of it (Dr. Colick appears to be in his mid-forties) and it is unkempt just enough to suggest an easy casualness, but not enough to indicate flat-out indifference. Natalie thinks maybe she could grow to like this guy.

"We're hoping for a girl," Michael says.

Dr. Colick raises an eyebrow. "Really? That's interesting. Usually couples—or at least the men—want boys first. When they do have a preference. I've never known why. My suggestion, however, would be to not get all geared up one way or another." He flips through the pages in the folder. "Natalie, you're thirty-two?"

She nods. For some reason she fears it she might look a bit overly agreeable.

"Good. That's a good age." He steps forward, sets the folder down on the counter top. "Now let's have a look at you. I just want to check your vital signs and such today, take some blood, give you a squeeze, answer any questions you have—I know you have a million of them. Then we'll set up an appointment for four weeks."

Her husband steps back and watches as Dr. Colick prods Natalie, uses various gizmos to look into every facial orifice. The doctor talks about his own kids—two boys, the oldest of whom will be entering his first year of Little League this summer (he's already excited about it) and the youngest of whom was born with a freak degeneration of the spine that restricts his physical capabilities a little more each year. Dr. Colick is pleasant about it, though; he's simply telling about his sons like any father would. These are just the facts: his son could just as well have been learning to ride a bike or gotten sick eating insects on the school playground. When he finishes his examination he pronounces Natalie to be in tip-top condition and asks if either of them has any questions.

Michael and Natalie look at each other.

"It's all right," Dr. Colick says, apparently having gauged their stupefaction. "They'll start popping into your heads the moment you step off the elevator. One right after the other. That's okay. Just give my office a call. It's no problem whatsoever."

"Thank you, Doctor," Natalie finds herself compelled to say. "We've been so busy, Michael and I, and this baby, I'm ashamed to say, has become somewhat of an afterthought." She hates the word she's chosen: afterthought. But it does the trick.

"Sure." Dr. Colick touches his hair, a habit. "The farther along you get into this, though, the more it'll just... be there. The whole thing. But it'll be a good thing. You'll grow into it, just like it's growing into you."

Natalie can tell this is a line Dr. Colick has used before, many times. His stock phrase, perhaps. But she lets it slide without counting it against his character. It's achieved the effect he was going for, after all: she feels the urge to hug someone, to be embraced.

"July fifth," Dr. Colick says.

She hears Michael clear his throat. "What?"

"It may change a few days here or there the next time you come in, after the sonogram and such. We'll know more then. But, based on the first day of your last cycle, that's the due date we'll go with for now. For fun." He approaches Natalie, hand outstretched. He wants to shake again. "Take care of yourself now," he says. "René at the front desk will make an appointment for you to come back in four weeks. All right?"

He turns to offer his hand to Michael now, but Natalie doesn't want to let go. She likes the pleasant pressure it exudes, she likes what she believes is behind that pressure. Finally the doctor breaks free and shakes hands with Michael. On his way back, past the examining table, he gives Natalie a pat on the thigh before going to the door. He stands there, holding it open for them.

In the car, Michael says, "I quit my job."

They're stopped at the corner of Forbes and Craig, and Natalie watches Michael as he watches the museum entrance off to their right. She is driving, and it is this fact—not the one that Michael has just revealed—that registers in her mind now. Now it makes sense: why he didn't feel like driving, that is.

"Why? Did something happen?"

He raises his hands and touches his forehead with his fingertips, as if checking himself for a fever.

"Michael." The light turns green and she continues up Forbes.

"Nothing happened," he says. "I don't know. Me and Dennis had it out."

"Had it out over what?" she asks, but then realizes she really doesn't want to know, and she hopes Michael will just drop the subject, as she should have done.

"I've been wondering what religion we should raise this kid," he says.

"Since when?"

"All right. That's not true. I just thought of it now."

"And this is important to you?"

"I don't know. You and me, we've never, you know, followed anything. Your folks are Catholic, which is kind of, well, antiquated. But they don't act like Catholics anymore, really. They act more like..."

"Like what?"

"I don't know. Like born-agains or something. Billy Graham types. Bible-thumpers."

"They do not."

"Jesus this and Jesus that. Bless you. And they've started saying 'him,' you know, with a capital H. Have you noticed that one? You can hear it in their voices."

can hear are her heels clicking along the tile, until her heart begins to pound; she can feel it banging away in her temples. When she gets to Dennis Tussy's table she stops and bends down, her lips right to his ear.

"I'm going to be trouble for you," she whispers.

His mouth is full of something. With a quick shift of her eyes Marlene can see slices of something on his plate—chicken maybe; a pool of yellowish gravy. He wipes his mouth with a napkin. "Pardon?" He tries to turn to face her but she stays right up alongside of him.

"If he comes to me, I'll back him."

"Marlene, sit down." His voice is pleasant. He motions to the open chair to his right.

"Just consider yourself warned."

She straightens and continues on toward the rear of the cafeteria. Behind her she hears Dennis's voice, then she hears chuckles. Her skin is hot. There is a satisfying ache in her knees as she walks. She thinks, vaguely, fondly, of Owen. When she passes the last row of tables, Marlene sets her untouched tray on the revolving dishwashing belt and watches it disappear through the stainless steel chute.

✳ ✳ ✳

The biggest problem—or, annoyance really—that Newton Sarver has had to deal with during his first three days back at the office is that people don't want to accept that he has other responsibilities to this division beyond the immediate task of laying off employees. Business still has to be conducted, plants need to be serviced, gas turbines need to be built and sold and installed, lawsuits need to be settled. That's the most recent quandary: a new lawsuit, this one filed on behalf of Carolina Power & Light. It's a dual suit naming two Electro-Lite divisions as defendants and claiming that the steam generators built by Power Gen and installed by another division were sold to CP&L, in 1988, with "known defects in design and construction" and that Electro-Lite management knew at the time of sale that the steam generators would never last the thirty years for which they are guaranteed. In fact, they already need to be replaced, a necessity that could cost the utility hundreds of millions of dollars, when costs from the time lost on the current steam generators is factored in.

"Michael, stop it. It's not the way you make it sound."

"Okay."

"And what if it were? Is that, like, the worst thing ever?"

He doesn't answer. Snowflakes are falling onto the windshield again, but they could just be blowing off of the big barren trees lining the road. Natalie cuts over to Fifth and makes a right toward Shadyside. As she guides the Cherokee past a synagogue and then a big old house in the process of being remodeled—scaffolds and ladders draping off of it, translucent plastic pulled across two upstairs windows—the stifling conditions of their life descend full upon her and she finds suddenly that she can't breathe.

"My dad's a Methodist but my mom just sort of goes along with it," Michael continues. "But you and me, we've never had, you know, a religion of our own. So I was thinking we should come up with one that—"

"Stop," she manages.

Michael turns to her. "What?"

"Shut... up."

A car behind them blows its horn and Natalie realizes, though her sight has become blurry and she can't see the speedometer, that she's reduced the Cherokee to a mere crawl in the left lane.

Michael reaches for the wheel. "Nat, what is it? Pull off the road."

But she's just worried about her breathing. Her chest is all heaves and twitches. If she could just settle into a natural rhythm she'd be okay. Michael grabs at something between them and the car comes to a sudden halt, throwing Natalie hard against the shoulder harness. She waits for the impact of being hit from behind, but there is nothing and the blurriness in her vision leaves her as quickly as it came. "Oh," she says. "Oh, my."

"Are you all right?"

In the rearview mirror she can see drivers behind her looking over their shoulders for an opening that might allow them to pull out into the right lane. She's still breathing hard, but regularly now. She leans back in her seat.

"I'm sorry for that crack about your parents," he says. "It just came out that way."

"See that house," she says, indicating the one being remodeled. "How much do you think it would cost to buy a house like that and remodel it?"

"Nat, honey, we're stopped in the middle of traffic."

"I mean, it was a dump when whoever bought it, I'm sure.

Remember it? It was all run down, vines growing all over. It's big, though. And I'm sure there are a lot of possibilities inside, classic fixtures and stuff."

Michael reaches across and touches her forehead with the back of his hand. She brushes it away. "Don't do that, Michael. I'm asking you a question."

The honking horns have stopped. Apparently everyone is now resigned to the fact that there's a disabled vehicle up ahead of them. Michael shifts his eyes nervously. "You mean landscaping and all?"

"Everything."

"Well, I don't know." He sighs. "It's a great old house. You've remarked about it before. Perfect location. Corner lot; lots of space for an urban neighborhood." He looks it over some more. A group of men are using some sort of hoselike tool on the wood area above the front porch, scraping or sanding. "Whoever bought it might have had to pay some back taxes, too. Plus the remodeling and the landscaping. Maybe half a million when all's said and done."

She nods, senses her breathing subside. The feeling she had earlier, to be held, is gone. "That's what I was figuring." She turns to him. "Is it wrong for me to be resentful of that?"

"Resentful? Natalie—"

"I just want all the time, Michael. When is that going to stop? I mean, I want everything. Not necessarily possessions, but stuff. I walk around during the day just wanting, and it drives me crazy. Why can't I just appreciate what I have?" She waits for a response from him, which doesn't come. There is a pained expression on his face, twisted somehow, as if her comments were directed squarely at him, which, she thinks now, they may have been. "I'm sorry."

"It's okay," Michael says. He clears his throat. "You're right. It is a nice house."

She puts the car in gear and steps lightly on the gas.

* * *

Marlene finds out about Dunne while she is in the cafeteria line, fretting over the assorted shades of beiges and tans that have overrun the lettuce in the salads. She hates eating in the cafeteria to begin with. It's amazing how those old junior high school tendencies come rushing back at a grown person whenever group meals and trays are reintroduced into their lives. Who's sitting with who becomes an issue. Groups of people actually have their "turf": The engineers sit at the far end of the dining hall, near the big window overlooking Seventh Avenue; secretaries and service personnel at the near end, right next to the check-out lines. Financial types have the market cornered on a group of four or five tables in the center of the room. Marlene likes to watch the heads turn whenever Sarver or some other Big Man on Campus emerges from the food lines into the dining hall, carrying his tray and looking for an open seat. What an event! It's priceless, the looks on all the faces. Priceless and sad.

Today she's in the cafeteria by necessity. The fact is she's incredibly hungry—so hungry she's not sure a salad will do the trick, even a green one. She had a fitful night's sleep, and awoke feeling more tired than when she went to bed; then she didn't eat any breakfast. Into her overworked, empty stomach she poured four cups of coffee this morning and now she feels jittery and hollow. She needs to fill herself. That's all she's thinking of when she overhears the man to her right, who's waiting patiently as she holds up the line searching through the salad trough, say to the man on the other side of him, "So they did it, huh? Whacked Dunne. I'll tell you, I didn't think they'd have the *cojones*."

"Are you kidding me?" the other man says. "That Trib article was the writing on the wall." Then, giving up on Marlene, the two men step around her, trays in hand.

She picks a khaki-colored salad from the sea of shaved ice, grabs a bottled water from the cooler, then waits patiently in the checkout line. As she creeps closer to the woman behind the register, Marlene sees, at a row of tables along the left wall, just before the engineers and over from the accountants, Dennis Tussy. He's wearing his gray suit jacket at the table and is sitting with two other public relations people and Harriet Coombs, a tomboyish marketing rep for advanced technology who everybody knows he's sleeping with.

The sky outside the big wall-sized window is gray; all the lights are on across the ceiling. There's a hushed murmur of conversation in the cafeteria today, as if people are talking in a wind tunnel. Marlene pays for her salad and water, selects a packet of lite ranch dressing from the basket and takes a few steps out into the seating area, surveying.

She's not hungry anymore; her stomach seems to have gone flat. She carries her tray down the left side of the room. All she

But nobody wants to hear about that. Sarver stares down at his desk now, at the stack of separation notices he has to approve and sign, which should have gone out already. Four from financial planning. Eight from accounting. Three from communications. Several from each and every engineering department. A third of the secretaries. Three from shipping and receiving. Nine from quality assurance. Four from graphics. Seventeen from marketing. He's taken to just signing the forms, blindly, one right after the other. What difference does it make? The numbers are set; the only question is the names, and even if he disagrees with one, then that department has to come up with another. He even needs to get rid of one of his own staff managers. Which one is to be determined. The main thing is to make sure that the responsibilities of whoever goes out can be divvied up accordingly. It will probably be Stan Harvey, the division's strategic planning manager. He's been with Sarver the longest but unfortunately the work he does—the particulars of which, Sarver has to admit, are sketchy at best—is of far less immediate necessity than anyone else's on his staff.

Sarver pushes his chair out and stands, waiting, by habit, for the pain at the base of him to wash away, as if draining down through his legs and out his toes. But there has been no pain for several days now. The pain has been replaced by nothing. Numbness. Which, in its own way, is significantly more frightening than the pain ever was. Out of his twenty-sixth floor window he can see well beyond the city, where urban gives way to rural. From tall steel buildings to steam-spewing factories and then to hills and grass and clouds. The window faces west and, when he was first given this job and this office he was told that he could see Ohio from here. Since that time Sarver has tried to gauge the spot where Pennsylvania ends and Ohio begins, but he has no idea. He has always been much more impressed by the fact that, from this height, he can actually see, on the other side of the Allegheny, patches of the Crayola-green Astroturf of Three Rivers Stadium. Today, for some reason, the stadium's lights are on. During Pirates day games he can sometimes even see the players running around down there. It's impossible, from this distance, to tell exactly what's going on, of course, but Sarver has always understood and appreciated the fact that something memorable could be happening as he watches, some fantastic play could be being made, some record set. Out there, beyond his big window of four-inch-thick glass, who knew? Things could be happening.

He takes the stack of separation notices and places them in an expandable file folder. It's one-thirty. He has a half-hour until his meeting with the lawyers to begin discussions of how to proceed with the CP&L lawsuit. Then he has a meeting with Morton (he doesn't know why; Morton called it) and then tonight he's scheduled to have dinner with a group of Taiwanese diplomats. They'll discuss the series of power plant construction contracts that were awarded to Electro-Lite in 1987, how the plants were never built. He walks around his desk. Directly above him, the round speaker in the ceiling softly oozes adult contemporary standards. He goes to his private bathroom—just an unmarked door, the same beige color as the wall; to the uninitiated eye it could be a closet. He closes the door behind him and, with the lights still off, unbuckles his belt and sits down to pee. Since getting out of the hospital he's taken to sitting for this purpose. It's just easier, as he's come to expect a considerably long stay.

Sitting in the dark he waits for his eyes to adjust. It's a small bathroom—he could easily touch each wall if he reached out to the sides—but he's nonetheless always been embarrassed to have it. Why should he have his own personal private place to relieve himself? What an odd perk, he's always thought. In the past he used the regular men's room on twenty-six, using this one for storage and to brush his teeth before meetings. Only since he's had to start sitting down for marathon pee sessions has he been using his own.

He thinks he may have something: a brief reverberation down there that often indicates the beginnings of some minor flow. Or the possibility of one. Then he hears a noise at his office door, shuffling footsteps on the carpet, voices. The sensation is gone.

The voices are those of his secretary, Iris, and Dennis Tussy. "I don't know where he is, Mr. Tussy," Iris is saying. "I didn't see him leave his office. And the light is off in his washroom. I—hmm... I'm sure I would have seen him leave."

More movement, perhaps some rifling around on his desk.

"He has a two o'clock," Iris says quickly; there is some sharpness in her voice. "I'm sure he'll return beforehand. Mr. Tussy, please."

"All right, Iris, all right. Goddamn it. Tell him I'm looking for him, would you."

"Of course, sir."

Sarver holds still. He finds it painfully difficult. The tendons in his legs are starting to cramp up something awful.

"Mr. Tussy, please, put that down. Those are Mr. Sarver's personal materials. I don't think you should—"

"Why hasn't he signed these? These need to go out. These here should have gone out last week."

"I don't know. Please—" More movement, shuffling. Things being picked up and set back down on his desk.

"All right—here." Tussy is striving for anger is his voice, but Sarver detects panic in it, too. Fretfully, he fears he may never pee again. "But tell him I've got two—no, three things I need to talk to him about. ASAP. Okay, Iris? Got it?"

"Yes, fine. Now, please, leave."

There is a pause, and in that pause Sarver pictures himself as he is, sitting on the can, suit pants at his ankles, waiting nervously in the dark like a thief to urinate. He's about to end the charade, just zip up and show himself, put an end to this nonsense, when he hears Tussy say, "I'm sorry, Iris. Here. Come here, sit down."

Another pause. Then, "I don't think it's appropriate. This is Mr. Sarver's office. And he—he's not here. We should go out in the lounge."

"What? We're just waiting for him to come back. Have a seat."

"But... his phone."

"It's right here. Calm down, Iris. For Christsake."

He must have said something, or gave a look, that pacified Iris because there is a new pocket of silence inside of which Sarver senses the maneuvering of chairs, the acts of sitting. He also hears something—something from inside the bathroom; a faint dripping sound: pat-pat-pat. It seems to be coming from somewhere around his left foot and ankle and, judging from its muted, almost echoy quality, might be inside the framework of the bathroom wall.

"Listen, Iris," Tussy says, breaking Sarver's concentration, "You like working here, right?"

She doesn't answer at first. Sarver tries to imagine the expression on her face but can't. Her glasses are halfway down her nose; that's all he can be sure of. "You mean—what? For the company? Or for Mr. Sarver—in this office?"

"Yes. All of the above."

"Why, of course I do. Did somebody say something? It's a lie."

"No. Iris, listen to me. I'm going to give you some advice now, okay? Maybe I shouldn't do this but I'm going to, because—well, just because. Things might get a bit messy around here in the coming weeks, and you should do whatever is necessary to avoid getting caught in the crossfire. Do you understand?"

"I certainly do not!"

Sarver nearly stands. In fact, if he hadn't lost all feeling in his legs he might have. He's not sure what Tussy is up to but his tact—or lack of it—with Iris is inexcusable. The old girl is oblivious to the political spider webs that surround a division president of a major corporation. It's the reason Sarver hired her. She works like a demon from seven-thirty to four-thirty then goes home to her carpenter husband where they live like happy little sharecroppers, growing their own vegetables out in Penn Township or where-the-hell-ever. To approach her in such a manner is unfair.

"All I'm saying, Iris, is that you might want to take steps to protect yourself." Tussy's voice is considerably lower. "I'll tell you that I—well, I know some things, some rather ugly things that I can't go into too much detail about, but I know them from a good source. Do you see what I'm saying to you, Iris?"

"No. No, I don't." Sarver can hear her voice moving around now. His eyes have adjusted somewhat to the dark and he can make out shapes around him: the faucet, the towel rod, the air vent in the wall. These familiar shapes place him, they acknowledge his once-hidden presence; he feels as though he's back in the world, and it is oddly disconcerting. "Please leave now. I'll leave a message for Mr. Sarver that you came to see him."

"You do that, Iris. And remember what I said to you." His voice is mobile now as well, floating. "But, listen. That was just between us. Right?"

"Yes, yes. Okay. Now go. Please."

The voices stop and the door closes and again it is quiet. Except for this new sound, this dripping, this hollow *pat-pat-pat*, the source of which Sarver can only imagine.

✳ ✳ ✳

At Doc's, after dropping Natalie off at home, Michael has been matching Alex drink for drink.

"Now you gotta come and work with us," Alex says. They are at the bar again, in pretty much the same spot Michael found Alex dripping wet the night before Thanksgiving, and Michael has just revealed to Alex the real story—not what he told Nata-

204 CHRISTOPHER TOROCKIO

lie—of what happened with Tussy. Angel is serving them again— shots of Jack and plastic cups of IC Light. But Michael doesn't feel drunk. Not really. He feels... disenchanted. But in a faraway, looking-at-oneself-from-the-outside sort of way.

"All right," Alex says. "See that girl over there by the dartboard? The blonde? I've been watching her. Every time she tucks her hair behind her ears, we do a shot. Okay, captain?"

"Alex, you're thirty-three years old."

"Yeah. So are you. And just like when we were thirteen, neither of us has a job."

"I'm only thirty-two, asshole."

"So, you playing?"

"Yeah."

They signal to Angel to refill their shot glasses but before he can get the bottle over to them, the girl grabs a strand of hair and tucks it neatly behind her ear.

"Whoa, yes!" Alex says. "Hurry it up, Angel, my man."

The game doesn't last long. The girl does the thing with her hair about every thirty seconds and very soon motivation is lost.

"God damn," Alex says. "Fuck it, I quit."

"I'm thinking of 'Penelope' as a name," Michael says. Long ago whiskey stopped tasting good to him, but tonight he has to admit it isn't too bad. He motions for another round.

"Huh?" Alex looks, and sounds, exactly like he must have twelve years ago, as a Pitt junior, sitting at this same bar, or one just like it over in Oakland: Jeans, sweatshirt, tennis shoes, a raging case of bed-head. He's talking loud. "Nah," he says, "you don't wanna do that."

"Why not?"

He turns and scrutinizes Michael. "'Cause it's a stupid-ass name for a little boy is why. Penelope. The little squirt'll get his ass kicked. Daily."

"It's not a boy," Michael says.

"How do you know?"

"Didn't make one."

Alex laughs. He laughs long and hard, bent over at the waist. Finally he straightens, takes a napkin and blows his nose into it. "You jobless son of a bitch."

Michael decides to work on his beer for a while, forget the whiskey. He takes the cup in his hand and fixes his eyes across the room, zeroing in on the girl whose hair was the object of their earlier game. She is pretty and he almost says this to Alex, but he doesn't want to hear what his friend has to say about her—it'd probably just ruin the moment. The girl is perhaps in her mid-twenties, short, five-two or so, and her hair, now that Michael has a chance to really look at it, is not so much pure blonde but more of a reddish blond. She has a tiny nose with a slight upwards lift on the end and big dark eyes that look black from this distance; whenever one of her dart-playing friends says something funny the eyes go sleepy with her smile. She's thin and sure of posture and Michael is certain that underneath she has a gymnast's body and a terrific laugh.

She does the thing with her hair again, tucking it behind her ear, and as she does this her eyes catch Michael's and he experiences a sudden, undeniable blast of longing—longing for his life before now, before today. He turns away in what he is sure is visible shame.

"You should see what Natalie's got planned for the place," Alex says. He's still blowing his nose, one napkin right after the other; when he finishes with each one he places it on the inside edge of the bar. He's got nice a little pile going. "I talked her into Pitt colors. It's gonna be killer."

"Do you even know what you're doing?" Michael says. "Do you know the first thing about interior design?"

Alex shrugs. "Don't have to." He reaches into his jeans pocket and takes out a small rectangular box, about the size of a sardine can, gift-wrapped, with a red ribbon. "Merry Christmas, buddy."

Michael looks down at it. "What's this?"

"Don't say 'What's this.' That's so ordinary. Take it and open it."

Michael takes the box from Alex and does another ordinary thing: he shakes it. Whatever's inside rattles dully. "Christmas isn't for, like, two weeks."

"All right, so it's a middle-of-December present. Just open the fucking thing."

Michael tears away the paper and sets it on the bar, then lifts off the lid. Inside, sitting on a bed of synthetic cotton, is a little gold-plated piece of metal into which his name is engraved. Next to his name is an icon of some sort: a thick, curvy, tri-colored D, the bottom of which wraps clockwise all the way around itself in a swirling fashion. The colors are dark blue, yellow and silver, the series of individual lines making up the D shape. "Well, huh," he says.

"It's your nameplate," Alex says. "It was going to be for your door, but we don't have doors. Natalie wants a more open, airy feel, or some shit like that."

"My—huh?"

"We had the logo designed last week and we just picked the plates up yesterday. I went ahead and made one up for you and wrapped it, in case you changed your mind by Christmas. I'm just glad it was still in my car."

"Yeah. Me, too."

"It's a pretty cool logo, don't you think? That's a funky looking D, for 'Dunne,' in case you hadn't figured that out. I figured since Natalie is the creative brains behind the whole operation that that would be okay."

"That's mighty big of you."

"So, do you like it?"

"I like it. What's not to like?"

Alex claps a hand around Michael's shoulder. "This is gonna be so great. Your wife is a goddamn decorating genius. Did you know that? It's weird—you'd never guess it from your apartment. No offense."

"We have no money."

"Oh. Yeah. Anyway, lookie here—" he raises his plastic cup of beer. "To us—two schmucks who're through with all the corporate shenanigans. No more mind-numbing meetings for the purpose of setting a meeting, no more doctoring the numbers, no more layoffs or busy work or floating holidays—"

"No more 401K," Michael says, raising his cup to Alex's. "No more medical, no more dental, no more free theater tickets. No more paycheck."

Alex smiles, touches his cup to Michael's. "You're not going to bring me down." He takes a drink. "Do you hear me? Can't do it. So don't even try."

Somewhere toward the middle of the evening, with a hockey game on the big screen and the patrons starting to push to the back of the bar and funnel upstairs, Michael begins to feel as though he might have drunk himself sober again. But then, from the same bar stool on which he's been sitting for the past six hours, he sees something that couldn't possibly be real, must certainly be an alcoholic hallucination: Toby—Toby the security guard—walking through the front door of Doc's Place.

"Hey." Michael jabs an elbow at Alex, who is stretched halfway across the bar trying to explain to Angel why field goals tend to drift off to the right on natural grass but get yanked left on Astroturf.

"I don't know," Angel is saying. "A lot of kickers just kick the damn thing straight. Why didn't you do that?"

"Listen to what I'm telling you," Alex says. "It's the texture of the ground surface. You need a certain amount of cushion between—"

"Hey." Michael gives another poke. "Isn't that Toby?"

Alex looks, squints. "Well, I'll be. I think it is. Barney Fife."

Toby stands just inside the door for a moment, head shifting back and forth. He's wearing a snow parka, unzipped, over his dress shirt and tie. No hat. He pushes through the crowd a few steps, stops, then pushes forward some more, past the coat rack. When he shuffles to his left to let someone by, Michael notices a young woman behind him and sees that she has a firm grip on Toby's jacket. When the two of them reach the bar they slide to the right, away from Michael and Alex. Michael calls out, "Hey, Toby!"

But Toby doesn't hear. He and the young woman continue around the square bar area. When they're directly across from them, both Michael and Alex stand and wave their arms like madmen hailing a taxi. This catches the woman's attention. She taps Toby on the shoulder and points; Toby gives a nod and then the two of them continue around the bar until they arrive at Michael and Alex's spot.

"Good evening," Toby says, extending a hand.

Alex shakes it first. "Hi, Toby. What are you doing out so late on a school night?"

"Looking for you actually. Or for Michael rather."

"Looking for me?" Michael shakes Toby's hand. The woman behind is looking around the place; she's met no one's eyes.

"What can we get you to drink, Toby?," Alex asks, swiveling.

"Oh, well, a beer I guess couldn't hurt." He turns to the woman. "How about you, sweetheart?"

"Nothing, thanks," the woman says.

"Guys, this is my daughter, Ellie. Ellie Sizemore. She's in from New York for a while."

"Hey, New York," Alex says, handing a bottle of IC Light to Toby. "How're things up there?"

"Alex and Michael used to work in our New York office," Toby clarifies.

"Oh." She nods. "It's pretty much the same. Hard to breathe."

She has sandy blonde hair, short, perhaps recently cut, and, in this light anyway, tight, unblemished skin. You don't often notice skin without blemishes, Michael considers, but for some reason, hers, you notice. Maybe it has something to do with the short hair, which is damp looking and combed back away from her face the way a man might, that calls attention to the decided femininity of the rest of her. There's not much to place her as Toby's daughter. There is a softness to her—in her features and her mannerisms—that Michael could never apply to Toby. She seems unsure of herself—eyes continually scanning the place, hands moving all around, fixing the collar of her jacket, touching her chin, her hair—but he can't shake the suspicion that, when the occasion feels right to her, there is considerable passion in there. But that's all it is: a suspicion.

"Ellie's a lawyer," Toby says.

"Oh, really?" Alex is still talking too loud. "I never would have guessed."

Ellie tilts her head slightly at Alex. "Surprise."

"It's the reason we came looking for you, actually," Toby says, to Michael is seems. "I called you at home and your wife said you were here. I left a message but then Ellie felt like getting out of the house and so here we are."

"Yeah," Michael says. "Here you are."

Toby takes a drink of his beer. "The thing is, I mentioned your situation to Ellie, and she thinks you may have a pretty strong case against Electro-Lite. If you're interested in that kind of thing."

"Hell yes, he's interested," Alex says.

Toby looks away, toward the big screen. It is between periods of the hockey game and one of the local announcers is doing a piece about a North Side bar and grill famous for its kielbasa and chicken wings. Toby takes a deep breath and lets it out. "I feel pretty awful—what they did to you, what it looks like they're doing in general. It's not right. It tears me up when I think about it. I was there at the press conference, heard what you said to that reporter woman, and, I don't know. I've been with this company thirty years now and—goddamn it. I've been trying to think of how I might be able to help and I came to realize that I can't. But maybe my daughter can."

Michael turns to Ellie and, as he does this, he realizes that the other two men have done the same thing and now all three of them are looking at her. She lowers her eyes, briefly, then raises them to Michael and says, "I work for a firm that ordinarily defends corporations. We're not very big so we often take on cases regardless of the circumstances, as long as the company in question is big and powerful and loaded down with assets. We're a government for hire, and so are our clients. But I'd be willing to see how I might be able to help you." She shrugs. "For the heck of it. If you'd like."

"He likes, he likes," Alex says.

"Alex, can it, man."

A group of people push by behind Ellie, single file, trying to make their ways to the door. Each bumps her accidentally and she give a series of quick jolts forward with her shoulders.

"Sorry about that," Michael says, standing. "Here. Sit here."

She doesn't argue; she slides by Michael and takes his seat at the bar. "Thanks."

"So what you're talking about is a lawsuit, I gather. Punitive damages, the whole nine yards."

"I know," Toby says, making a sour face. "Got an ugly ring to it, don't it?"

"If that's the route you'd like to go," Ellie says. "We could meet sometime to talk about the particulars. Daddy just knows what he's seen, and from what he's told me it sounds like maybe we could pass you off as a whistle-blower. But I'm sure there's more to it."

"Well, not really. What you see is more or less what you get in this case." Michael feels light on his feet. And tall: six-foot-four tall. He feels as though he is looking down on all these people around him, packed into Doc's, these strangers living their lives. The feeling is in no way metaphorical—he actually feels as if he can look down at them. His chest feels big, too. Like it could withstand significant force if it had to. "Alex, get me another beer, would you?" He turns back to Ellie. "Are you sure you wouldn't like anything."

"Yes, I'm sure."

"Okay. Let's do that. Let's get together and talk about a lawsuit. Why not? Does tomorrow sound good? I could call Toby and tell him where. Let's not talk about it now, though. The atmosphere leaves a little to be desired. And I've had quite a few of these." He takes a fresh cup from Alex.

"But don't you live in New York?" Alex says. Michael could strangle him.

"Yes. But I may be here for a while. And if I go back—when

I go back, I mean—I can handle things from there. They have telephones and fax machines these days." Her voice trails off and Michael can barely make out these last few words.

Alex and Michael look at each other. When she gives a giggle, self-conscious as it is, they figure it's all right to go ahead and laugh. Man, am I drunk, Michael thinks.

"I can't believe I'm doing this," Toby says.

"You look like you could use a shot, Lieutenant," Alex nearly shouts.

"I believe I could." Toby turns to his daughter. "Is that all right with you, sugar? You don't need to get back for anything, do you?"

She doesn't answer right away. She raises her eyes to the ceiling and studies the dark wood beams. Then she, very gently, touches the top of her head, which Michael is sure confirms his suspicion that her hair has been recently cut. "No, Daddy," she says. "It's fine. In fact, on second thought, I think I wouldn't mind one myself. What're you drinking?"

"Jack," Michael and Alex say in unison.

She swallows. "Okay."

Alex leans out over the bar, all smiles. "Angel," he says, "we need you, my man."

✳ ✳ ✳

Todd's shoes are soaked through. And he doesn't remember his father-in-law's neighborhood as well as he thought he did—not in the dark, and not on foot.

The moon, dull and spongy, spreads a vague half-light through the clouds above the line of pine trees to Todd's right. He's been following this tree line, believing it will lead him to Toby's backyard. But there are more houses now; they've cut farther into the trees and built more pre-fabs, and now he's not sure if this tree line is in fact the same one that once separated the rear of Toby's neighborhood from... whatever.

It's strange: he assumed that when he quit using the cocaine he would crash, have no energy, lay around like a slug until his body readjusted to running on natural air. And, at first, that was true. But now he finds he can't sleep. The last time he slept—really slept—was six nights ago—the night after his show at Nickleby's, or whatever that place was called, and the subsequent road trip that has brought him here. Since then he's been able to talk his body into periodic naps of fifteen or twenty minutes, but that's it. And the thing is, he feels fine—being run over by a motorcycle notwithstanding. He keeps waiting for the sweats or headaches, or fatigue of one kind or another, but the truth is, except for occasional ache in his knees, he's beginning to feel pretty damn good, physically.

But now he needs to make a move. By his count Ellie has had five days to herself (though he admits he could have misplaced a day or two somewhere), to think, to regroup—no phantom phone messages, no badgering on his part—and now it's time for some decisions to be made. That's his purpose tonight. He rode the Kawasaki up the strip in Monroeville and into the comparatively quiet town of Murrysville; he turned off of Route 22 and, once he got his bearings, he walked the bike off the road into the woods and left it lying on its side next to a creek's stone retaining wall. Then he cut up the hill through the woods. It was dark and he had no idea what he might be stepping on—wet leaves and mud and logs, a jagger bush every now and then—and occasionally a low branch would catch him across the face. He kept going, though, until he came out the other side and saw the backs of all the houses.

But he's been wandering for quite a while now and nothing is looking familiar. There are the woods on one side of him; porch lights, driveways full of minivans and pickup trucks on the other. A scent of spiritual mildew permeates the heavy air. Clouds, wind, soil. Rural suburbia. The ground is wet and mushy but the blades of grass growing out of it are frozen, so that with each step he hears a combination squish and crunch beneath his feet. Sometimes he trips over toys—trucks and baseball bats, cap guns, shovels and pails alongside little mounds of snow—and he finds himself becoming strangely angry at these children—not for causing him to trip, but for their irresponsibility of having left the toys so far away from their houses. What he's angry about is the neglect.

At one point he hears barking, close and strong and deep: a big dog. He takes off running, at first continuing along the treeline and then cutting between two houses and running across the street and into the yards of the adjacent row of homes that, on the other side, border another patch of woods. When he stops on an unlit lawn and begins walking, catching his breath, its like he's just stepped through the magic wardrobe. He knows where he is. Toby's house should be right up here.

He walks down the driveway of a small Tudor then reestablishes his position along the tree line, a mirror image. Then, there it is: the brick two-story that Toby and Ellie's mother picked out from a choice of four different plan options and Toby claims to have paid $24,000 for in 1975. All the lights are out. He's not sure what time it is but, certainly, somebody should be home. He approaches the house from the rear and then makes his way around to the side. There is no car in the driveway. Todd stands for a moment. He goes to the detached garage and lifts open the heavy door, chains and pulleys grinding. Except for Toby's workbench in the far corner and some tools hanging on hooks, the garage is empty.

The side door is locked. He tries the front and back doors. Both locked. Then he goes around trying all the windows and finally finds some luck with the kitchen window—the short, side-sliding one over the sink. Toby's foresight is a blessing as well: no screens. Todd lifts himself onto the windowsill then pushes through with his elbows and flops down into the sink which (lucky again) is empty. His legs are still hanging out the window and he finds he does not have enough space to bend them—the window is too small—so he pulls forward over the edge of the sink until he is through past his knees and can bend his legs. Before he can brace his feet against something, though, he drops headlong to the floor.

He stands and listens. The house is quiet—an empty sound, heavy with time, memory. Todd walks around the kitchen, fingering the tablecloth, opening cupboards, allowing his eyes to readjust; then he takes a stroll through the living room. He sees a table set up in the corner with Ellie's laptop on it. On the chair is her briefcase. He touches that, too, then goes to the sofa and lies down on his side. A wondrous exhaustion sweeps over him. Soon he is asleep, and he knows it. He can feel his eyeballs rolling back in his head, can sense the cloudy murk of sleep enveloping his brain. His dreams are of himself, of himself as a sleeping person: he sees himself lying on Toby's sofa, mud on his shoes, mud which he's probably tracked all through the dark downstairs of Toby's house, hands folded prayer-style and tucked up under his head. He can feel every cell of his body, can feel the indentation his body makes in the sofa cushions; he can feel every hair follicle, the roots growing into his head. He can feel the weight of his eyelids and his knees and his pelvis and his liver and kidneys and heart inside him. He can feel the weight of himself.

Then, suddenly, Todd sits up straight on the sofa, drops his feet to the floor. Fully awake now, he stands, heads back to the kitchen, turns on all the lights, and begins rummaging through the cupboards and drawers. He checks every one, then opens the refrigerator and takes a quick mental inventory. From the fridge he takes out half a head of lettuce, half a tomato, a stub of cucumber: salad stuff. He also selects five eggs from the grooves in the door, a produce bag of sliced raw mushrooms, and some Velveeta.

Everything laid out nicely on the counter, cutting board nearby, he sets to work. He sprays a skillet with Pam, chops the vegetables, beats the eggs in a big green plastic bowl. He is focused, but not hungry. He beats the eggs with a wire whisk until his shoulder aches, then he pours half the mixture into the skillet and sprinkles in some vegetables. While that's sizzling away (a wonderful sound) he works on the salad. A salad doesn't go with eggs, he knows, but he decides he's pretty much past the point where considerations like that should make any difference. At just the right moment, he folds the omelet over and scatters some cheese on top. When it's finished he spoons the omelet onto a plate and repeats the process using what's left in the big green bowl.

When everything's ready Todd sets the table: dinner service for two. Candles, linen napkins (which he finds in a drawer) and red wine (under the sink). He stands back and looks at the table. He turns out the lights. The candles flick heart-twisting shadows across the wallpaper and in this dim light it occurs to him that the omelets look like little half-moons on the plates. He cleans up his mess—rinses off the skillet and wipes down the cutting board, replaces the unused vegetables in the refrigerator, grinds the eggshells up in the disposal—then, candles still flickering, he climbs up onto the sink and leaves the same way he came in. As he drops from the kitchen window to the ground he can't help feeling as though he's just been expelled by Toby's house. Or, perhaps, it occurs to him, standing, brushing off the fronts of his pants, regurgitated.

Newton Sarver is crouched down next to the toilet, in his undershirt, using a wrench to loosen the section of pipe he's isolated as the cause of the leak in his office bathroom. He's already used a small ball-peen hammer to break through the plaster in the wall, leaving a hole of about one square-foot in diameter. Then he went down to maintenance to get more tools. The guys down there wanted to do the job for him, or at least help, but Sarver would have none of that. He also had to run out to a hardware store and buy a new elbow section of pipe to replace the cracked one. He started working on this little project after his meeting with Morton and after canceling his dinner with the Taiwanese diplomats (blaming his health), about four hours ago.

He's worked up quite a sweat—he can feel it under his arms and behind his neck and the small of his back and it feels terrific. His joints feel lubricated and nimble, his muscles are loose. He breathes in through his nose and out his mouth, attaining a sort of whistle that reminds him, sharply, of his father. Nathan Sarver was an engineer, too, of sorts. He was a carpenter. He built houses, for people as well as for dogs, birds, rabbits. Whoever wanted a house, he'd build it for them. He had a workshop in the garage and Newton, when he was younger, often would help out. With Nathan Sarver, "help" meant "hold things," and Newton was glad to do just that. Especially if his father were close to completing a project. Newton liked to see things come into fruition—he didn't much care for the beginnings. When his father was about to start a new creation, Newton usually found somewhere else to be: nailing a couple of two-by-fours together that you had to imagine one day being the foundation of an elaborate two-sectioned doghouse in the style of a nineteenth century Victorian mansion held very little appeal for Newton Sarver as a boy, and still does. His father, though, could see things becoming something else.

Nathan Sarver designed and built homes, places for living creatures to do their living. Newton designs (well, designed—he doesn't design anything anymore) mechanisms that attach to things to which other things are then attached. A valve which is attached to a tube which connects to a flange, all of which combine with other elements to run a compressor which, along with a hundred other mechanical contrivances, contributes to the operation of the gas turbine. Like his job now, there is no beginning. There is no end either, just a world of middles, and, though it displeases him in some far, indiscernible corner of himself, he, for the most part, likes it that way.

He will fix this pipe, though. He will see that through to the end. Perhaps, he thinks, he should have called Maryann, let her know what's up. But she wasn't expecting him home until later tonight anyway, because of the dinner he was supposed to attend, so he supposes it doesn't really matter.

The old elbow joint is corroded and refuses to turn. Along with the tools he was given, however, there is a spray can of WD-40. He takes it out of the tool box and gives the pipe a good shot, stopping only when he sees the brown liquid drip down onto the plywood inside the wall. Now it should come off, he thinks, leaning back against the toilet to let the grease do its job. As he's sitting there he considers himself, and he feels a smile form on his face. He likes the way he must look: sweat-stained undershirt, ruined dress slacks, head up against the commode in his personal-private-confidential restroom, darkened hallways and offices beyond his door, in a twenty-six-floor building which, more or less, he runs.

He takes the wrench and clasps the pipe, which turns and dislodges easily, spilling dirty water onto the linoleum. The act of the pipe coming loose in his hand, to his surprise, causes him to gasp. He sits there now holding the ugly rusted piece of metal, holding it out away from his body as if it were a human ear, swollen and bleeding and newly detached from its head.

Shaking this from his mind he sets to work installing the new section of pipe, consciously modeling himself after his father, right down to the nose whistle. Once the pipe is in position he tightens the flange on each end by hand, then he gets the wrench going again. When everything is water-tight and secure he reaches up and flushes the toilet (a terrifically loud noise) then stands and runs the faucet to get some more water flowing through the pipes. No leakage. He cleans up his mess, replaces the tools in the box, brushes the damp plaster crumbs back inside the hole he made in the wall. That, he will let the maintenance guys take care of.

Sarver slides off his undershirt and unfastens his belt and lets his slacks fall to the bathroom floor. Before he knows it he's peeling off his socks and then he's stark naked. He steps out of the bathroom and walks around his office. He goes to the window and looks out. There's not much happening down on the street, just headlights and stop lights and storefronts and car tops, so he walks around the office some more, wandering, like he's browsing through a store. He turns and notices himself in the darkened glass; he can see himself, and he realizes he has the body of a carelessly squeezed tube of toothpaste. Then he gets an idea: he goes to his chair and sits. The cool leather against his scar is something next to heaven, seeping through the numbness to soothe, and when the leather warms he shifts himself around searching for another cool spot.

Sometimes one's actions don't make any sense the next morning, but Sarver believes this one will. In fact, it's something he should have done long ago—canceling an important business dinner to mess with his bathroom pipes and sit in the dark, naked in his leather chair. The coolness on his body seems to revive him, as if his remaining testicle were a re-chargeable battery to his mind. Somehow, Sarver thinks, he will take care of things here, fulfill the responsibility he assumed when he accepted this job. Find out what happened at Georgia Power and fix it, make it better. To partake in petty personal skirmishes with the likes of Dennis Tussy will do no one any good. So, yeah, he'll see to things. He'll see to those things that most need seeing to.

Natalie Dunne has never been one to pace. It is something on which she has always prided herself. Even as a child she found little difficulty in blocking out potentially discouraging events and moving on with her day. The trick is to stay busy. When she was eight and her dog, Triangle (so named because of the white patch of fur on her forehead), or Tri for short, ran away, she organized a neighborhood kick-the-can tournament that ran until bedtime. When she was twelve and that same dog died she read books—eleven of them in three days: Jack London, Agatha Christy, Salinger, Shel Silverstein; biographies of James Dean and Olivia Newton John.

And the night before Thanksgiving, just a couple of weeks ago, while her husband was lost in disgust and doubt over his situation at work, over what he'd done, and on the day she first suspected (and later confirmed) that her, well, plot (yes, that's an appropriate word) to get pregnant had in fact worked, even then she found it possible to take a nap.

So why is she pacing now? Not only pacing back and forth, but doing laps around the apartment? She wants to go to Doc's; she wants to see what's going on over there. Michael is drunk, no doubt, but maybe he shouldn't be. Maybe all of his faculties are required of him tonight. This Toby, who she has heard Michael speak of before, sounded serious: "I have a proposition for him," he said. He even suggested that he might drive in and talk to

Michael tonight. And Alex will be no help. He'll be as drunk as Michael, maybe drunker.

Natalie walks around the back of the sofa and loops in front of the TV. Her mouth has gone dry again and she goes to the kitchen for the Evian bottle. Her problem, she thinks, taking a drink, is she doesn't believe her husband. It has nothing to do with anything specific he has said to her. Not really, though if she took the time to consider it, it might. She just doesn't believe him, doesn't believe in him. She doesn't believe what he's about, doesn't believe it's Michael—her Michael—inside that shell, behind those eyes, behind those words speaking to her. *I've been wondering what religion we should raise this kid.* Who said that? Not her Michael, surely.

She does want all the time, though. She meant that when she said it to him and she still does. That was honest. That, anyone can believe. But she doesn't know what she wants. No idea. Money, power, health, a successful business, a few good friends, this baby, a really cool pair of sunglasses, a twenty-three-inch waist, a stretch of sunny days in December, an endless supply of Fontanella cheese, strength. Who knows? She replaces the water bottle in the refrigerator and paces the kitchen, dish towel in hand, wiping the counter as she goes. Then she thinks: There is love. She wants that. She has it, in fact, or had it, and she understands that this fear—the possibility that love, the love she once had with Michael, the love she counted on, that has always been there, and now might be leaving them—is the source of her pacing. She wants it back.

Realizing this, she feels better. Or at least she has something to focus on now. To hell with her business. To hell with this contraband baby, if it comes to that. She's not sure what's happened with Michael at work—that's one particular aspect about him she does not believe—but she doesn't care. She hasn't been particularly approachable for confessions lately. But she will be, from now on.

She finishes wiping down the countertops, then takes some Formula 409 and cleans off the stove, getting underneath the heating elements and around the edges of the dials. When everything around her sparkles (or seems to sparkle, like some demented television commercial) she decides to go for a run. It will feel good, some late-night exercise, better than pacing. And it's good for the baby, too, she suspects.

✳ ✳ ✳

She's done it again. She told herself she wouldn't, but here she is, dressing in the bedroom of Jack Lipinski's Mt. Washington condo and trying to devise an explanation to give Owen when she gets home, after midnight, again. She's not that busy at work. Owen is a bit sharper than that.

Moonlight sweeps in through the window and lies across the bed, just missing Jack's closed eyes. For some reason, Marlene feels the sudden urge to wake him. She thinks about slamming a dresser drawer, or dropping a shoe, but what she does is take hold of the palm-size crystal ashtray sitting on the dresser—the one Jack had made for him special by a guy in Vail, to ash his cigars in—and throws it across the room, hard, at his head.

It's dark, but the ashtray appears to sail just above Jack's ear. It skips across the night table and smacks against the wall, surely leaving a mark, perhaps a dent. Jack sits up quickly, thrashing, covers flying everywhere. "What the—Marlene? Marlene!"

"I'm right here, Jack."

"Where? Are you okay? Did you—what are you doing?" He squints at her.

"I have to get home. Go back to sleep."

"Didn't you use the overnight-at-the-Hilton story?"

"Owen's not brain-dead, Jack." She pulls her skirt on, zips it up and spins it around. "We both work for the same company, remember? He knows where things are."

"Where things are," he repeats, as if he's never heard these words said in just this sequence before. "Yes, but—hey, is something wrong?" He rubs his eyes. He's just a little boy, Marlene thinks. A little boy who gets to cut into people and feel around inside them and then gets a big allowance for it.

"Nothing's wrong, Jack."

"Okay. So you're coming over tomorrow night?"

"I'll call you." She buttons her blouse then checks herself in the mirror. Her appearance could be the result of a hard night's work. It's not inconceivable. But she's not sure if the blue-black light behind her is helping or hurting what she sees. She applies some lipstick.

Jack swings his legs out of the covers and sits at the edge of the bed.

"Don't get up," she says.

He looks at her. His face is blank, pale. His big chest looks grotesque. It's too much.

She has made a decision: She will follow through on her threat to Dennis Tussy. She's not sure what disturbs her more, what reportedly happened in Georgia or the fact that she didn't know about it. But in any case, she'll fight him and her own company over it, and over their treatment of Michael Dunne. If, after thirteen-plus years with Electro-Lite, proving time and again the worthiness of her opinions and the accuracy of her instincts, they don't want to listen to her advice, then she'll put it to use elsewhere. It will not go to waste.

"Come back to bed, Marlene," Jack says. He pats the mattress.

"Get a hold of yourself," Marlene says. She puts on her earrings and slides into her shoes. "Bye, Jack," she says, slinging her purse over her shoulder and heading out into the hallway. She doesn't even want to stay, doesn't want to kiss him goodbye, to taste the sleep in his mouth, or hold him for a second or two. Each thought makes her swallow, a necessary act.

✳ ✳ ✳

Two A.M. Snow falling outside, snow falling inside. At least that's the way it feels to Michael, who has once again stumbled into his apartment, drunk and wet and confused, to find his wife still waiting up for him. She is wet, too, but it is a clean sort of wet, shimmery. As she sits in the corner armchair, with light from the single floor lamp pouring down on her, Michael can see that her cheeks are flushed with a warm moistness. The tips of her hair curl into tiny ringlets in front of her eyes. She looks tired but content—no, not content, resigned—a thoroughbred who's just been washed down and stabled. But still, there is a hint of precipitation in the air, a front moving through, and Michael keeps his coat on.

"What're you still doing up?" he asks. On the table is a new stack of mail. He doesn't want to see it.

"Waiting for you." She's wearing thermal pajamas which Michael recognizes but hasn't seen for years. "You're my husband, aren't you? I'm your wife. I have the right."

"Sure you do. Of course. But let's go to bed now. You've got to be tired." He takes his coat off, though he still doesn't want to—he's awfully cold—and lays it on the back of a chair.

"Michael, did you really quit your job today?"

He looks at her. Between them, he actually believes he can see falling snow; it has a flickering, grainy quality, like old movies.

"Come over here and sit down," she says. "Sit on the sofa across from me. I know you're drunk, but I want to talk anyway."

"I'm not that drunk."

"I don't care. Please come over here on the sofa."

He does as he's told. When he gets to the sofa he just lets his legs out from under him and falls back into it. "They fired me," he says; it just comes out. "Dennis did."

"Because of the press conference?"

He shrugs. "Pretty much. Yeah, I guess so. Turns out the beans I spilled about Georgia Power was more, um, there was more to it. We—did you see the paper today?" Before she can answer he says, "I don't want to talk about it. And I don't want to talk about money either. Please, don't make me do that."

"No. Okay. And, well, what about this Toby guy who called tonight? Did he find you?"

"Uh-huh. His daughter's a lawyer. She's gonna help us fight it in court. Her name is Ellie. She's very pretty."

"What?"

"She's sad, though. I'm not real sure what the deal is with her. We're meeting tomorrow."

Natalie nods. "I'm coming with you."

"No," he says, a touch of lunging in his voice. "I mean, it's not necessary. It's gonna be messy and ugly and embarrassing and you have other things to do."

"Like what?"

"Like being pregnant."

She lifts her feet off the floor and tucks them beneath her; it occurs to Michael that her bare feet represented the only skin, other than her hands and face, visible to him, and now they're gone, too. "It's important for me to come with you tomorrow, to be a part of this with you," she says. "And that's what I'm going to do. Can you understand that?"

"She has this hair," Michael says, "This... and skin. Her skin, too."

"Who?"

"Ellie."

"Ellie does? What—do you *like* her or something?"

"I like her, yeah. I like her... vigor, which I really didn't see but I can tell is there. I'm just guessing."

Natalie is silent. Perhaps, Michael thinks, she is allowing his words to settle in the room, with the rest of the snow, so he can see how ridiculous they are and then they can sweep it all away. But he's just talking, just saying.

"I wish I could buy you nice things," he says.

"I have nice things." Her voice is softer now, withdrawn, and it occurs to Michael that he might, unwittingly, have hurt her.

"Yes, you have some nice things. Yeah. But we didn't have the money to buy them when we bought them and now we're still paying for them, we'll always be paying for them. Don't you see? I wish I could give you something."

"I have everything I need," she says.

"Don't talk stupid."

"Stupid? You think that's stupid? All right, then give me something. What's stopping you?"

"You want everything," he says. "You said so."

"No. I said I want all the time. It's different. It's a completely different thing. I would hope you'd have known that."

He doesn't answer. He remembers how tall he felt at the bar earlier. Right now he feels as if the sofa is swallowing him.

"Do you want this baby?" she asks him then. She's sitting forward in her chair, leaning toward him; she pulls at the neck opening of her pajama top.

"Nat, don't," he says. "That's old news. That's done."

Her shoulder is partially exposed now, exposed to the snow. "Done?" she says. "Done? You heard the doctor. An inch long. July something. Only one thing is done. Now, sweetie, I'm not trying to harp—honest, I'm not. But I need to know. We need to know. I'm coming with you tomorrow, either way, but tonight I need to know: Do you want this baby or not?"

Michael feels something in him rise—from his toes, through his legs and chest and into his throat. "I'm going to be sick," he says, standing.

In the bathroom he throws everything up; he empties himself out, one heave on top of another. With each wave he believes his body will break apart, it comes that much closer, piece by piece. Then he feels Natalie's hand on the side of his face, or believes he does. The hands are cool and soft and simple: a mother's hands. But how—how could they do this? He can't even take care of himself. Between the two of them, they can't even seem to take care of each other anymore. A baby? He heaves again.

Natalie's hands work their way around his face, his forehead and cheeks, the back of his neck. She gently rubs his eyelids and smooths back his hair.

"It's snowing out there," he manages between gasps.

"Yes," she says. "Now, sshh."

SHOPPING DAYS TO XMAS: 8

Employees are leaving daily now, hourly, heaped with boxes and plants and framed photographs. They nod at Toby as they pass by the front desk, but they do not meet his eyes, they do not look back; it's as if they are carrying something other than books and staplers. It's as if they're carrying their misfortune, solid and heavy and smoldering. At first Toby thought: Shame. They are carrying their shame. But that wasn't it. They did not feel ashamed; at least that's not the sense Toby got. They felt unlucky, forgotten, contractors of a freak, random ailment. Toby cannot find boxes fast enough: supply cannot keep pace with demand.

Occasionally Toby must do what he did with Michael Dunne and escort a separated employee to the door. This is required when an upper-level manager is separated. Toby's task is to make sure the employee properly disposes of his files and does not leave with any information that he could shop around to a competitor. Today's unlucky escortee is Stan Harvey, director of strategic planning.

Mr. Sarver is in Stan Harvey's office when Toby arrives. The two of them are sitting at the little round conference table, ankles crossed over knees, talking casually. Mr. Sarver is wearing a suit; Stan Harvey is in khaki pants and a yellow golf shirt. The room is empty, except for the furniture. It looks as though someone's preparing to repaint it.

"Everything's fine, Toby," Mr. Sarver says. "Stan's okay. There's no need to go through any search. It's not necessary."

Toby nods from the doorway. "Okay. Would you like me to come back a little later? The memo said ten o'clock..."

"No, Toby, it's all right," Stan Harvey says. "I'm ready to go." Then he says, "Thirty-one years..." and lets it trail off.

The two men shake hands. Then they stand and embrace each other. Maybe it has something to do with Stan Harvey's clothes—Toby has never liked seeing his bosses in their street clothes; it makes him uncomfortable—but all at once this man looks as though he does not belong. Could a jacket and tie be so psychologically powerful? Toby isn't sure, but he knows that this man, Stan Harvey, who has been with this company for one year longer than Toby has himself, which means one year beyond forever, and has been a division-level manager for more than a dozen years, suddenly doesn't look right here. In his own office. He doesn't have that... what? Managerial aura? Is that the term he's looking for? All Toby knows is that when guys like Mr. Sarver, or Morton or Diaz or, at one time, Stan Harvey, walk down the hallways, people hush up; they avoid eye contact but they look, as if these men were celebrities, and, within the context of this world, this government for hire, as his daughter refers to it, the Republic of Electro-Lite, they are.

But now Stan Harvey is just a balding guy in a golf shirt, and there's something not entirely right about that.

Toby, carrying a box (thirty-one years, just one box), leads Stan Harvey to the front door. They revolve through the doors and when they're outside Toby sees that Mrs. Harvey has pulled their Oldsmobile Ninety-Eight up to the curb and is waiting, both hands on the wheel.

After setting the box in the trunk, Toby shakes Stan Harvey's hand, tries to think of something to say, can't, then turns and walks back into the building. And then, like his son-in-law, whom Ellie has not heard from in nearly two weeks now, these people simply disappear.

Ben is sitting behind the front desk, leaning back in his chair. He holds a slip of paper out to Toby. "You got a call about some guy named Francis?" he says, more of a question than a statement. "You're supposed to call this person at Allegheny General. I wrote it all down."

* * *

The worry is beginning to lift, like a fog. For some time, Ellie was concerned. Concerned, yes, as anyone would be. The last contact she has had with her husband was many days ago—the message on her father's answering machine when they listened to each other.

Except, of course, for the omelet. The omelet and the candles. The sight, she has to admit, creeped her out. Creeped her out and broke her heart. And injected a sad pang of finality to the situation.

But now she has this case—Michael Dunne's case. She arranged an extended stay in Pittsburgh with the partners at her firm so that she would work on it for a percentage of the award (an award they fully expect). Her firm, by Manhattan standards, is a small one—three partners and thirteen associates, including herself—and her caseload, prior to skipping town, was embarrassingly light. She just hadn't been taking on anything new and her sixty-hour workweeks had over the past couple of months dwindled to less than forty, a slump she chalked up to Todd's mysterious, deepening despair finally taking its toll on her. They could do without her, Mr. Linville supposed, so long as this Electro-Lite thing amounted to something, for everyone.

She began riding into town with her father in the mornings (now she has her own Toyota Corrolla, an Enterprise rental) and taking her files and laptop to Hillman Library in Oakland. It's big, close by the law school, and easily accessible to Michael, who she's been meeting with every other day or so, to "strategize," as he likes to facetiously call it.

Today, Michael is coming by to watch a tape of the press conference, as it previously was broadcast on Channel 2, which has just been delivered to her by courier. She sits in a small room on the second floor of Hillman Library, designed, she supposes, for study groups to congregate. The walls are bare and beige; six undersized chairs surround a small, rectangular conference table. In one corner she has wheeled in a VCR and monitor, which she had to reserve. The room smells oddly of fireplace ash.

Fact is, she doesn't miss Todd the way she thought she would. The first week was bad, but now...She cut her hair and took on a new case—a case of her own—and she's starting to look at her options objectively: Should I stay in Pittsburgh, my father's home, and get a job here, start over from the beginning? Should I look elsewhere, make a clean break, Atlanta or Denver or Seattle? Should I do nothing for a while, live with my father, who is lonely, and let the days wash over me? And a secondary option, an alternative: Should I go back to my husband, wherever he is? After all this time, is it her place to do that, her choice?

There is a knock at the metal doorframe; there are no doors to these rooms. "Is everything all right, Miss Sizemore?" asks Kathy, one of the librarians, who has hair down past her rear end. "Can we get you anything else?"

"No, thank you, Kathy," Ellie says from her chair. She touches her own newly shorn hair. "I'm all set."

"Are you expecting Mr. Dunne today?"

"Yes. If you could just let him know which room I'm in, that would be wonderful. In fact, maybe later today we could work out some system so that I can have the same room every day. I think that'd make things easier on everyone."

"Surely," Kathy says. "Stop by the reserve desk before you leave today and we'll work it out," and then she walks away between two high stacks of books to the stairs, hair swaying behind her.

Michael Dunne has become another factor. With her husband's whereabouts unknown, his condition quite possibly deteriorating, quite possibly needing her now more than ever, she can't seem to stop thinking about Michael Dunne. The thing is: he looks at her. He looks at her as if he's trying to decipher something strange and necessary in her face; he looks into her and breathes and she feels as though he's trying to pull something out of her that, if she knew what it was, she believes she would give him. There is a curiousness in his gaze that makes her want to answer questions that haven't been asked. He looks at her, she feels, because he is interested in what he sees, in what he might find, if only he had the time to keep looking. She would never tell him this, but there is something, well, womanly in the way he looks at her—or perhaps sisterly is more accurate—and it is comforting. Beyond comforting: heartening. She takes heart in his gaze.

The first time they met to talk about the case, his wife, Natalie, came along. They met at the Elbow Room in Shadyside and they ate grilled chicken salads and talked. Much of what they talked about had nothing to do with the case. At one point, after their plates had been cleared away and the three of them sat drinking coffee, Natalie, a pretty, athletic-looking woman with straight, shiny, shoulder-length brown hair, leaned her shoulders in over the table and, apropos of nothing, said to Ellie, "I think you would have a talent for parenthood. It's just something I sense about you." She also said that under different circumstances, they probably would be friends.

When Michael arrives, Ellie, apparently, is asleep. She feels a hand on her arm, something, a touch, and then she sees Michael looking down at her, smiling. There it is: that look. First thing.

"I've heard of burning the midnight oil," he says. "But it's eleven in the morning. It's mid-day."

She blinks. "My goodness. I guess I conked out. I've been falling behind on my B-complex."

"That'll do it, I suppose." He sits. "Watch the tape yet?"

"No. I was waiting for you."

"Already seen it," he says. "I'd give it two-and-a-half stars. Worth seeing, but I wouldn't pay the admission twice."

Ellie doesn't answer; she stands and fights off a dizzy spell, then goes to the VCR and sets everything up. She hits play and sits down next to him.

The footage opens with KDKA's financial reporter standing out in front of the Electro-Lite building, the glass reflecting dully behind him, a dreary, overcast afternoon. He's setting the stage: Electro-Lite announces it will lay off eleven thousand employees, etc., and one company representative gets a little loose-lipped (the reporter's word) regarding some company information. Cut to Michael, answering a question—or volunteering the answer to a question never asked—concerning the reasons GE took over an Electro-Lite job for Georgia Power.

His eyes, though. Ellie does not know whom Michael is addressing, but his brown eyes register that same curious comprehension she has discovered gazing at her (strange for the circumstances). I get you, it seems to say, and I'm letting you in so you can get you, too. Soon, Ellie loses track of what's going on on the screen before them.

When it's over she says, "Darn it, they were supposed to send all of the footage, the unedited version," and turns to him.

He is already looking at her. "Yeah, I've tried. For other things, I mean. Not this particular newscast. They won't give you the raw footage without a court order. It's considered, like, their private possession. Copyright something-something. They'll only give you what aired. But, hey," he says, eyes still fixed, "that was all the incriminating stuff anyway."

"Oh, they'll give it to me," she says. "I'll make sure of that. And besides..." But she can't remember what she was going to say.

He sits back in his chair. "I want to thank you," he says.

She gets up to stop the tape machine. The monitor has gone black. "You're quite welcome," she says, then realizes she should have asked him what he wanted to thank her for. Maybe it was something other than the obvious. But it's passed. "You know, you've never asked me how much we should try for."

"Oh." He lays his hands on the table. "Okay. How much?"

She puts the tape back in the case, snaps the lid shut. "Ten years salary, plus compensatory damages, plus payment for defamation of character, adjusting for inflation. Nine hundred and seventy-five thousand." She turns and looks at him. "We thought about going for an even million, but decided it would sound too contrived, too random."

For once, he is not meeting her eyes. He is looking at her left shoulder and, slowly, his head tilts to the side like a bewildered Irish setter. It's as if he does not understand anything: who she is, why he's here, the English language. Finally he says, "God damn."

"Yep." She walks over to one of the adjacent chairs and takes up her coat. Suddenly, she feels good, at ease with herself. "Welcome to the deep waters, kid," she says. "Want to get an early lunch? I'm buying—for now."

✳ ✳ ✳

Natalie, for all her efforts, can't seem to keep Alex on a short enough leash. Actually, hog-tied is what he needs to be. Strapped down. Anesthetized. Here they are in a tile store (tile and wood floorings, that's all this place sells!) and Alex is asking the salesman question after question, about additional charges for upgraded hardwood and protective coatings and oil finishes.

They've narrowed their choice down to some sort of pine—Natalie believes it is the most successful of all the woods at attaining a look that is both enduring and contemporary. The contractor isn't here. They're supposed to pick out the flooring they want and place the order under the contractor's name (he'll bill them for it later, of course).

"So, you're saying if we add this stuff, this coating, we'll get an extra few years out of it?" Alex asks. "Like, how many?"

"Several," the salesman says. "Maybe more, depending on wear and care." He is a painfully thin man of about forty; stringy, side-swept hair and pointy, geometrically precise facial features: nose, cheeks, even his eyebrows are pointy. He is wearing a plaid sport coat that hangs on him as though it's too heavy for his shoulders to support. The store smells like sawdust and vinegar.

"Well, we ought to get that then," Alex says. He turns to Natalie. "Don't'cha think?"

"No, I don't," she says. "I think my father's money could be put to better use elsewhere."

"Elsewhere," Alex repeats. "Okay, scrap the coating stuff. What else you got?"

The thin man leads them around the showroom. He points out the molecular makeup, durability and cost of each piece of flooring. "Now this—" he says—"this is a nice piece of floor." He uses the word "floor" with particular relish, like a chef might use the word "dish."

"Okay, hit me with the numbers, chief," Alex says, and the thin man rattles off some prices.

Natalie has already seen the flooring that she wants, though: a simple, moderately priced light pine, which they saw a while ago. Maybe a couple of years ago she'd have gone for something darker, richer, but now—now, the light stuff will do. Why she doesn't speak up and tell Alex she's found the one she wants, she's not sure. She feels it's important to let Alex and the thin man carry on their charade, standing back and out of the way. It's fine with her; she has no place special to be this afternoon, and she's grateful to Alex for shouldering the aspects of the business she knows nothing about: insurance and copyrights, incorporating a limited partnership and establishing a payroll. Truthfully, she'd be lost without him.

"...cleans up with a damp rag," the salesman is saying.

After the choices have been made, Alex and Natalie step out onto the sidewalk. They're on a side street in the South Side section of town, known more for coffeehouses and blues clubs than flooring shops, certainly. It is mid-day and the cold air clears the sawdust smell from her nose. The sky is the same color as the road. She takes two deep breaths, then coughs.

"Well, little mother, looks like we're off and running now, huh?" Alex buttons his coat. "We've got something to stand on. That's key."

She looks up at him. "I guess we are then."

"Michael says you're having a girl. That true?"

"Yeah. That's what he says."

"You haven't been puking or anything, have you? Don't you be getting sick on me now. Bedrest and shit like that. I don't have any maternity leave policies in place yet."

"I won't," she says.

Then Alex turns and faces her. He holds out his long, spiny arms. "Could I give you a hug?" he says. "Would you mind terribly if I embraced you right here on the sidewalk in the middle of the South Side?"

"I wouldn't mind."

"A buddy hug, of course."

"Either way."

He is much taller than her and she presses the side of her face into his chest. A car, passing slowly, honks its horn. Alex says, "I'm what you call your 'professional life' now. We're a team. I think it's good this way 'cause now Michael is the private life for both of us—in different ways, of course. But he's our recreation. You see what I'm saying? So it's good, I think, that we're each other's professional lives. Don't you think? It's like a perfect circle."

Natalie keeps holding on around Alex's waist. His overcoat on her cheek is warm and scratchy.

Ordinarily, Newton Sarver would not have come in today. It is his and Maryann's twenty-ninth wedding anniversary and he would have preferred to spend the day with her. But today Thomas J. Corbett, Sr. is in town, and Sarver has a plan.

He sits on the sofa in his office, leaning back, knees wide apart, relaxing. Marlene Stringer, who should arrive any minute, is his partner in matters. Over the past week the two of them have devised a plan. With some extraneous cuts elsewhere, he and Marlene believe—well, he believes—Power Gen can stop the layoffs where they are. Some people will have to be reassigned, and those people who already have been given notice will be highly pissed off, but, in all, about a quarter of the jobs scheduled for termination will be saved.

The one question Sarver can't seem to answer is why Marlene has been so helpful in this effort. On more than a few occasions in the past she's expressed to him the opinion that layoffs would be a good, healthy thing. The more the better. Trim the fat, that's the cliché she's fond of. Yet, there they were, day after day this past week, eliminating the annual customer meeting in Boca, reducing the per diem for field sales, cutting back on advertising, getting creative with the pension plan.

The other items of business Sarver has with Corbett surround the issues of why he was kept in the dark regarding the Georgia Power situation, and of Michael Dunne: word of a lawsuit has been circulating. Sarver wants some answers.

When Marlene arrives, a bit disheveled, but, thankfully, her dark-lined eyes still holding their usual feistiness, they move to the adjoining conference room, where they are to meet Corbett at one o'clock.

Outside, the sky is strangely without sun or clouds. Marlene sets out the bound volumes containing the details of their proposal, then goes to the side credenza and pours some coffee into a Styrofoam cup. Her silver-blond hair frames her face; she is slouching considerably.

"You okay, Marlene?" Sarver asks.

She puts the cup directly to her mouth, without even setting the coffee pot down, and tilts her head back, like a fraternity brother pouring beer down his own throat. Finally, she swallows. "Fine. I'm fine, Newton. Just fine and dandy."

"Well, today's my anniversary," he says.

"With the company?"

"With my wife."

"Oh." She holds her cup out to him, expressionless. "Here, here."

Neither speaks for a while; they are just waiting. In the vestibule, through the cracked-open conference room door, Iris is talking to someone about a movie she's recently seen, which she liked, though she has never heard of any of the actors and there was a little too much swearing and one "naked scene," as she put it. Then the conversation stops and Sarver can hear her say, "Yes, Mr. Corbett. I'm fine, sir, thank you. They're waiting for you in the conference room." Marlene comes to the table and puts her coffee down. As the conference room door opens wide Sarver's gaze lands on a framed photograph of a rock climber adjacent to the marker board, a wide shot, meant to be subconsciously motivating. What Sarver notices now, though, is that the climber (his face is not visible, just his back and the wall of rock) has no place to go. There's nothing to grab onto and probably, after the photographer got the shot, the climber had to be removed from the rock face by a helicopter. What, he'd like to know, is so motivating about that?

Corbett steps in and looks around. "Newton, hello, my boy," he says. He's not wearing a suit jacket but his sleeves are properly clasped at the wrists with silver cuff links. His thin, gray hair, usually pushed back strategically across his bald spot, hangs messily in his eyes, a la Red Skelton.

"Nice to see you, Tom," Sarver says, approaching with his hand outstretched. Then he sees Dennis Tussy enter the conference room. "Oh. Dennis. Hello. This is a surprise."

"I asked Tussy here to join us," Corbett says. "I hope that's okay."

"Sure. Fine. Have a seat, everyone," Sarver says. "Tom, you remember Marlene Stringer."

"Of course." Corbett sits. No handshake. "How we doing, Marlene? All right?"

"Fine, sir. And yourself?"

"Tendonitis in my knee. Too much standing. Thanks for asking. Now—" he turns his attention back to Sarver—"you have something for us. Something you want to discuss."

For us, Sarver thinks. Corbett and Tussy? "Yeah," he says, "we do. It's right here in this package." Sarver indicates the bound copy on the table and takes one up for himself. "If you'll just turn to the first page I think we can walk you through—"

"Why don't you just tell me about it."

Sarver looks over at Marlene, who seems to be staring at the black speaker box built into the center of the table. "Okay. Well, Tom, I think Marlene and I have come up with a way—a few ways actually—to cut down the number of layoffs."

"That's done," Corbett says. "Old business. Move on." He gives a wave of his hand as if shooing away a fly. "What else you got?"

"Yes, well, a little more than half of the layoffs are done. We think we may be able to at least delay the remainder of them. About twenty-eight hundred positions."

Corbett looks over at Tussy.

"First of all," Sarver continues, feeling a patch of sweat form between his shoulder blades, "we've considered eliminating our Boca meeting in the past. There're some real drawbacks to it anyway. Attendance is dipping and our surveys show our customers aren't getting much out of it. It's too expensive and time-consuming for them to attend. And we could save about a million-five by cutting it. It's all in this chart here. Secondly—"

"Newton, please. That'll do."

Sarver looks up. "Is there a problem?"

"A problem? Hell yes, there most certainly is a problem. Several, in fact."

"Well, okay. What?"

Corbett pushes his chair out and stands, letting out a soft groan, like oh-uh. Then he steps away from the table, holds his arms out in front of him and performs a slow, awkward series of deep-knee bends, bones and cartilage popping with each dip. When he's finished he sits again, groans once more, leans back in his chair. "Let me tell you a story," he says at last. "Marlene, this'll be good for you to hear, too."

"Tom," Sarver says, interrupting. "I see what's going on here. I really don't think I need to be told stories with morals so I can—"

"Shut up and listen, Newton."

Sarver folds his hands in his lap. He swallows.

"Now then. This story. It has to do with me, of course. Not too terribly long, actually. I was in Spain, Madrid, and I had one mother of a hankering for Chinese food. Now that's a predicament, let me tell you. Not impossible, but difficult. I don't often like Chinese food, but when I get in a mood, watch out. I get a craving for that General Tso's, you know, that chicken. Very sweet. I suppose it's not particularly CEO-like, but, there, now you know something intimate about me." He chuckles, smooths some of his flyaway hair down with his palm. "So, yeah, anyway, I'm in Madrid craving General Tso's chicken. Also, I'm there with some fat boys from the Spanish government—they were showing us around—and some Japanese utility guys. Remember that partnership we had a few years ago with Mitsubishi to build that plant in Spain, Newton?"

"I remember."

"Yeah. Good. Well, long story short, you know what I did that day?" He waits, looks each person in the eyes individually. "Anyone?" No one answers. Only Tussy is even looking at Corbett now, feigning interest. "I ate a fucking bean and cheese tostada, or some damn thing, is what I did. Then I went back and sat on the can for three days straight. Pardon my vulgarity, Marlene, but that's what I did. It's a fact."

She coughs, looks out the window.

"With all due respect, Tom," Sarver says, "I'd like to—"

"I don't know if you catch what my story's getting at or not," Corbett says. "But this horseshit about canceling your Boca meeting and all the rest—by the way, have you checked all this stuff out with Morton or any of the financial boys, or marketing for that matter? Or field sales? Or anyone but the two of you?"

Sarver is ready for this. "I didn't see the need to get the whole division worked up until I checked it out and felt comfortable myself and ran it by you. There's always time to work out the details."

"Yeah, well, whatever. In any case, all this putzing around makes what I'm about to say a lot easier for me."

Sarver sits up straight. "Which is?"

"I'm going in a different direction. The board wants it and I support it. Sorry, Newton, but I'm afraid you're out. I'd like your resignation."

Sarver feels the fluorescent lights on his skin—quick, thrumming compressions. A clock on the wall the size of a large pizza reads one-twenty. "What?"

"The lawyer-snakes wanted to be here for this," Corbett says. "But I told them we could iron this out like professionals."

"Iron out..."

"This is a difficult decision for me, Newton, I won't try to hide that. For me more so than the board of directors anyway. I picked you for this job, remember? You were my choice. But let's be honest: the division—this corporation—is going down the shitter, on your watch. And mine, of course. And here you are, sitting across from me, for crying out loud, trying to prolong the agony, applying Band-Aids where amputation is necessary. The long and short of it, Newton, is I thought when I appointed you to this position that you would be a strong leader. Or at least would become one. You seemed sharp and ambitious and the common employee seemed to relate to you. You were liked. That was something I noticed right off and I guess I fooled myself into thinking that would be enough. But it's not. You're just not a strong leader and history will prove it. You don't have that...what? That extra lining of steel in your stomach that is just plain essential today. Take this Georgia Power rigamarole, for example. You didn't even know what really happened down there, did you?" He doesn't wait for an answer. "And, when you finally do find out, instead of going after someone's ass to chew on, well...let me put it to you this way, Newton: I feel pretty confident that, given the same situation, you'd have gone out of your way to find a take-out carton of General Tso's chicken. Am I right?"

It occurs to Sarver now that he hasn't taken a breath since Corbett started talking. He tries to take one now, watching the long, thin second hand glide around the pizza-clock, but something slips in his throat and he makes a bleating sound like a clown's horn.

Marlene clears her throat. "Tostadas are Mexican," she says, coldly. "Not Spanish."

Corbett ignores her. "You'll see this is for the best, Newton," he is saying now. "We'll take care of you. You won't leave here empty-handed. The lawyer-vermin and H.R. folks are working up the papers as we speak. So buck up."

Sarver looks over at Marlene. Her lips are slightly apart. "Did he just say 'buck up'?" he asks her.

She just stares back at him.

"Get out of my conference room, Tom," Sarver says. "You, too, Dennis. This meeting is over."

"Newton," Corbett says, rolling his head around dispassionately on his neck, "you can fight us on this—God knows everyone else is—and you may win, and we'll dish out whatever we have to dish out. But you won't win. In the long run, we'll end up ahead. I'm confident on that count, and so is the board. We're willing to chew off a leg to save our life, and we'll survive. A three-legged dog is still a dog. It just has to learn how to run differently."

"And what the hell does that mean?"

Corbett shrugs. "One of my writers put it into a speech I gave last week. I like it. I think it might be a famous quote."

"Get out," Sarver says.

"Newton, come—"

"I said get out." He thinks about standing and then thinks better of it. "I'm still the president of this division, am I not? This is still my personal conference room and I want the two of you out of it." Then he says, "And by the way, Dennis. What the hell are you doing here anyway? I meant to ask that before but I was being polite."

"I asked him along," Corbett says. "You can never have too much public relations."

"Get out!" He's raised his voice and, to his surprise, it seems to have worked. Everyone stands. "Not you, Marlene."

She sits, but Corbett and Tussy head for the closed conference room door. "We'll talk later, Newton," Corbett says. "When you see the package you're offered, I think you'll come around."

The second hand on the clock seems to freeze between the 6 and the 7, then continues its glide.

Tussy opens the door and steps out; in the vestibule Iris, ignorantly, it seems to Sarver, is watering the plants. Corbett stops in the doorway and turns back. He says, "If it's any consolation, no one here is going to get your job. The board wants to bring someone in from the outside. Maybe a utility guy." Then he says, "Please give Maryann my best wishes for the holidays."

"It's our anniversary," Sarver says.

"Hey, well that's great. Unusual, though. Getting married a week before Christmas."

"We wanted a Christmas honeymoon," Sarver says, thinking, Why am I telling him this?

"Well, okay," Corbett says. "Give her my best on that count, too," and then he leaves, pausing to give Iris a sort of half shoulder-hug before proceeding through the vestibule and out the glass doors to the common offices and cubicles.

"Jesus," Marlene says. Sarver had forgotten she was still here. She looks over at him like, Oh, man.

Sarver stands and goes to the window. He looks out, again noticing the curious sunless-cloudless sky and says, "It seems I'm always standing at windows anymore. Why do you suppose that is?"

Marlene's voice comes from behind him. "I don't know," it says. "I've been doing it a lot myself, actually. It probably doesn't mean anything."

"Probably not," he says. Then he says, "I'm sorry. He's right, you know—it's my fault."

She doesn't answer.

Locating a homeless man, whose last name you do not know, in a large urban hospital, is not an easy task, as Toby is discovering. At the main receiving desk he asks for Francis, but that just gets a shrug from the chubby receptionist; she has a telephone pinned between her shoulder and ear and is trying to make adjustments to a patient's file. So he asks for Dr. Lee and is told there are several Dr. Lees at Allegheny General and then is directed down the hall and through a set of double doors where he is told he'll find a nurses' station. He doesn't like being here, of course, so he busies his mind with the simple task at hand and with random details: the sound of his rubber-soled shoes on the tile, the neutered voice over the loudspeaker, the faint smell of urine and antiseptic.

There is less traffic here, in this corridor, fewer people blowing past and asking questions; and this new nurse, though a bit confused by Toby's inquiry, is far more helpful—or is trying to be.

"Francis," she repeats, flipping pages over the metal loops of a clipboard. "Dr. Lee." She is a slight woman with a thin face and long fingernails, which Toby is surprised to see on a nurse. "Oh. There's a Francis Doe here. Dr. Bobby Lee is acting physician." She looks up. "I'm afraid he's in Intensive Care."

"Is it possible for me to see him?" Toby asks.

"Depends. You'll have to ask at the ICU. Sixth floor. You can take the elevator."

"Thank you." Toby heads down the hall and steps onto the elevator. He has to wedge himself into the corner to make room for a gurney, carrying a boy of about twelve or thirteen and pushed by two male nurses, big guys. The boy's skin is pale and dry, scaley; he lies on the gurney and stares up at Toby. Every few second he blinks.

On six, outside the big brown double doors leading to the Intensive Care Unit, Toby asks yet another nurse if it would be all right for him to see Francis Doe. "He was admitted today," Toby says, trying to be as specific as he can, hoping the nurse will appreciate his clarity. "Dr. Bobby Lee is his physician."

This nurse is enormous, two hundred-fifty pounds if she's an ounce, dark-skinned and red-lipped. "Dr. Lee is on call today; he's around here somewhere," the nurse says. Her voice is as big as her body, though it seems to be somehow ashamed of itself. "Let me page him. He makes the decision of whether or not to allow visitors. You can sit there." She points.

In the hallway against the wall facing the nurses' station are four plastic chairs, one of which is occupied by a very pregnant woman. She's leaning back, feet wide apart; her head is resting against the wall and she's staring straight up at the stark-white ceiling. Her stomach seems to be pointed upwards as well.

Toby sits, leaving an open chair between him and the pregnant woman. Here, people walk by casually, occasionally stopping to chat with each other. The doctors and nurses, all clad in either blue or white, seem oddly cheerful, considering that every few minutes another unconscious person, IVs dangling, is wheeled through the automatic doors of Intensive Care.

"You're here to see Francis?"

Toby turns to his left to see a blue-scrub-clad man, youngish, Asian, the rubber tube of a stethoscope flung across his shoulder the way a cowboy might carry his lasso. Toby stands. They are about the same height. "Yes," he says. "Yes, Doctor, I am."

"Bobby Lee," the doctor says, extending his hand.

The hand—the entire arm actually, up to the elbow—has a pink tint to it, looks too clean to touch. But Toby takes the hand and shakes it. "Toby Avellino."

"Francis is a friend of yours?"

"Yes. I don't know much about him, though, I'm afraid. He hangs around outside the building where I work. I've known him a few years."

"Well, Francis isn't doing so well."

"His lungs?"

Dr. Lee puts his hand on Toby's shoulder and guides him toward the ICU doors. "I believe so," he says. His English is perfect, naturally flawless, without even a hint of regional dialect. With his face and build and full head of hair, Bobby Lee could have been a news anchor if he'd wanted to. "One of them has completely shut down. Collapsed. He's on a respirator now. An ambulance brought him in this morning off of after an anonymous 9-1-1 call. They found him on Seventh Avenue. That's where you work?"

"Yeah. He has cancer in his lungs," Toby says. "They diagnosed him a while back. At the free clinic."

Dr. Lee nods. "We haven't run those tests yet. Probably won't. But I suspected."

"Can I see him?"

"If you want to. He's not conscious."

"I understand." Then Toby thinks to ask, "How did you know to call me? I mean, he hasn't been conscious at all, has he?"

They stop in front of the double doors. Dr. Lee takes his hand from Toby's shoulder, steps back and examines Toby's face. "No," he says. "He's been unconscious the whole time. But he had a bunch of little scraps of paper stuffed in his pockets. Most were just gibberish. I mean, the handwriting was actually quite meticulous. But the words themselves—couldn't even make them out, hardly. One, I remember, said, 'chicken wire: wrapping the beds of oranges.' I remember that one exactly." Dr. Lee catches himself. "Well, anyway, one had your name—just 'Toby'—along with a phone number, which turned out, I suppose, to be your office number." When Toby offers no response Dr. Lee says, "Come on," and leads him through the doors of the ICU.

Inside beds are lined up, two rows, separated by curtain-walls. Toby averts his eyes from any of the patients, focusing on the blue center of Dr. Lee's back. Then the blue starts getting larger in Toby's vision and he realizes Dr. Lee has stopped. To the right, Francis lies in a narrow bed, head slightly propped, feet pointing toward the aisle. A wide, plastic tube snakes it's way into Francis's mouth and is connected to a big accordionlike machine, the pleated bag of which pumps up and down and exhales a mechanic sort of breath with each repeated motion.

"Francis," Toby says, though he knows it is a waste of his own breath.

"I'll stop back in a minute," Dr. Lee says. "Visits have to be brief here."

"Sure," Toby says. "Okay."

Then Dr. Lee disappears, but Toby does not watch him go. He is watching Francis's beard, marveling at its sheer depth and unruliness, like an overgrown field of crabgrass. The whiskers growing from his neck wind their way down and mingle naturally with Francis's chest hairs. It is something.

Toby feels himself sway. He stands before Francis a little longer, listening to the deep, mechanical breathing, watching the machine pump the air, though Francis's chest does not seem to rise and fall. Suddenly, Dr. Lee is back at his side. His stethoscope is no longer across his shoulder.

"Doctor," Toby says, "you know this man has no insurance."

"That was an assumption I went ahead and made, yes."

"He can stay, though?"

"He's going to die soon, Mr. Avellino. It won't cost much. I hate to sound cold about it, but it's the truth. Let's just say the hospital has hidden funds for such circumstances."

Toby nods, looks down at his shoes. There is a ring of gray salt dust around the edges.

"Does he have any family, Mr. Avellino?" the doctor asks.

"Not that I know of."

* * *

As usual, Ellie left Hillman Library and walked up Forbes Avenue in Oakland, looking for a suitable place to have lunch. Perhaps today she set out on her search a little earlier than has been her norm; that was a bit odd, sure. The other abnormality Todd noticed—the first thing actually, before the time—as he followed along, slightly behind, on the opposite side of the street, ducking behind parked cars and lampposts when necessary (for that is how this is done), was that she was not alone.

He began a week ago: waiting for her to leave her father's house in the morning, then following behind on the Kawasaki, through the Squirrel Hill Tunnels and into Oakland. But that got a bit tiring so he switched home bases, taking a room at the Oakland Hampton Inn so as to be that far ahead. As he watched Ellie and this guy cross Forbes at Bigelow Boulevard, catty-corner from the Cathedral of Learning, he wanted to say he'd seen this guy she was with before, entering the library, or perhaps exiting, some other time.

A cold day: it didn't exactly feel like snow but the wind was blowing and as they passed by the Mellon Bank, Todd saw Ellie slip her hand through the crook in this guy's elbow. It's cold. Here, keep me warm.

They continued up Forbes less than a block before ducking into Hemingway's, a little bar-restaurant with wooden booths and brass railings and hanging stained glass lamps that Todd had seen Ellie go into before, by herself.

Now, he stands on the street, looking in. They are seated in one of those wooden booths, smiling, pointing at each other's menu. When the waitress comes she laughs at something he says, and there (he swears!) is some vague sense of pride in Ellie's face, pride in the fact that this man she's with is capable of making a joke.

He knows he should move around a little. Remaining stationary like this, even though his face is well hidden by the painted glass of the front window, is asking for trouble. But he can't help it. He is no longer willing to be held responsible. Is it his fault all he wants to do is feel the sun explode and spray all over his face, that he wants to feel his spine light up and sizzle inside him? Is that so bad? Is that some sort of sin? And anyway, he stopped for her. She didn't even ask and he stopped. For her. What more does she want from him? What more can he give?

They eat. They chew and they swallow and they stab at things with forks. They butter rolls. They take careful sips from their water glasses. This surprises Todd perhaps more than anything else: he's never seen her drink ordinary, untreated tap water, ever. There is a lemon wedge in her glass—he can see it slide down and bump against her lips when she drinks. She's wearing her wedding ring; sometimes, when her hands aren't doing anything, she twists at it. At one point she puts her elbows on the table and leans over her plate, positioning her face close to his so she can say something no one else can hear. Her lips barely move. When she is finished she listens to his response, and, even though he can only see the back of this guy's head, Todd can tell he is looking at his wife—looking at her. He can tell by the way Ellie's face accepts his gaze, lets it take her in, relaxes in a way that he can't ever remember seeing, or at least not for some time, and this is when he throws open the door to Hemingway's and walks in.

He is all breathing, breathing through every pore in his body, in and out in thunderous, wheezing blasts. He walks toward the table, but Ellie does not even look his way. His vision seems to be shimmying from side to side in warped 8-millimeter clarity, covered in gauze, but he keeps coming, at one point bumping a candlestick on an unoccupied booth with his hip, knocking it to the floor. Her elbows are still propped on the table when he takes the guy by the collar and jerks him upward.

Ellie is leaning forward on her elbows, hovering above the table. A smile forms at the corners of her mouth. She licks her lips and, says, "I really want to win your case. Not for you, though. For me. It would be really good for me."

"It would be good for me, too," Michael says.

"Tell me something nice," she says then. "Tell me you like me. Just for kicks. Tell me I'm pretty."

He doesn't say it, though. He believes the words themselves would somehow ruin something. So he just looks across at her—she is propped on her elbows and her skin is flawless, like something molded and smoothed by hand—and he wonders how long this can go on, how long she'll let this go on before she needs words. Her eyes are still, full, reflecting himself back at him, and then they flick out to the side, to her right, and widen, and then he is being lifted out of his seat.

"Todd," Ellie says, almost a question. Then, louder, "Todd!" as a fist is pulled back.

Michael doesn't feel the contact—it happens too fast. There is a sharp pain in his neck from his head having snapped back and then a tingling sensation, like tiny bells, a thin band starting and ending at each corner of his mouth—wrapped around his head. He finds himself seated in the booth again; their glasses are overturned and bits of lettuce are scattered about the table. Ellie is standing.

She has her palm on the scruffy cheek of this man, this Todd. This Todd is wearing a black ball cap, no logo, and an unbuttoned wool shirt, like a lumberjack's, over something dimpled and thermal. He's unshaven by a week or two. The man's eyes, though, are dry and calm, languid, perhaps even sleepy, which Michael finds strange for a man who's just attacked someone.

Ellie has her hands on either side of Todd's face now, talking to him in soothing tones, eye to eye, like one might talk to a hyperactive puppy; then she hugs him, hard, around the shoulders, squeezes, and pulls quickly away, talking to him some more, though Michael can't make out what she's saying. All the while Todd's arms hang at his sides, as if they were extra appendages he doesn't need or know how to use.

Then Michael hears her say, "Tell me," words that cause something to twist inside him. "Tell me."

But Todd isn't telling. He shrugs a shoulder, not in response, but to scratch his chin with it. As he does so he looks over at Michael with a narrowed expression that is both submissive and calculating; his shoulders and chest heave with one big breath.

Waitresses and manager-types start coming around, asking if everything's all right. Neither Ellie nor Todd answers so Michael begins to dismiss the event but when he goes to speak he just mumbles something that is incomprehensible even to himself and the waitress who had been waiting on them says, "Oh, shit, someone get some ice. He's bleeding."

The blood, Michael finds, is leaking from the corner of his mouth and within seconds, after moving his tongue around, he realizes that a tooth is loose—his left upper incisor—hanging by a single root, in fact.

"Oh," Ellie says, and takes a step toward him, hand extended, and when she does this Todd turns and heads for the door. Ellie stops short, lowers her hand. "Todd!" she calls, but Todd doesn't stop, doesn't turn. Ellie regards Michael for a moment.

"You're very pretty," Michael gurgles through the pain, and with that Ellie's eyebrows raise slightly on her perfect, high, blemish-free forehead, and she whirls around toward the door, picking up speed as she goes.

* * *

Todd has crossed over Forbes and now is passing by the School of Law, walking as if into a stiff breeze, hands stuffed in his pockets, legs churning beneath him in quick, busy steps. Ellie crosses, too, ignoring traffic, and sets off after him.

She's forgotten her coat and the chill soon hits her. Todd's pace is impressive, especially because it looks so effortless, and it takes her some time to catch up, though she finally does, in front of the sheltered stop for the 74D. She takes hold of his sleeve but he keeps walking. "Todd," she says. "Todd, look at me. What's going on? How did you get here? What the hell's wrong with your ear? It's all—what is that?"

He turns his face to her, only briefly, as though he were idly checking out a funny haircut (which, it occurs to her, he might be) then turns away. All at once she knows it was him who broke in and made the eggs. In fact, she feels stupid now. How could she not have known? Her father called the police. He filed a report and she let him. She is embarrassed now—wholly embarrassed. Comically so.

"Todd," she says, "honey. Are you hurt? I listened to you on the answering machine. I did. I listened to you listen to me. That's got to count for something. Are you feeling okay? Todd. I have a case here. We can live here with my dad for a while, get out of New York. That would be good for us. Todd, listen to me. I haven't been taking my vitamins. I don't know what to do. I feel ragged. Todd, goddamn you."

They turn onto Bigelow, back toward the library, and then Todd crosses the street and heads in the direction of the public parking lot.

"You're starting to piss me off," she says. "You made me leave. You gave me no choice. Don't you understand that? It's what—it's what you're supposed to do. Listen to me! I cried for you, you son of a bitch."

He stops in the middle of the street; she takes an extra step or two, her momentum taking her, before stopping as well. Cars slow around them. Todd is looking off toward the naked, swaying trees that surround the parking area.

"Todd?"

His eyes are still, steady. Then he squints. "I don't have—" he says, and stops.

"What?" she says. "What?"

But he has started walking again. He cuts through the dead, spongy grass to the parking lot where he uprights a red and purple motorcycle that was lying on its side.

"You don't have what, Todd?" she says, trying to keep up. "Where did you get that?"

He walks the motorcycle back past her, in the direction from which they've just come. Apparently he's going to bypass the lot's toll gate. She turns. "I want you to fucking stop right now. I'm you're wife, who supported you—in every possible way you can support a person. I supported you all the way until—"

This stops him again. They are standing along the patch of trees separating Bigelow Boulevard from the parking lot. "I wanted to feel the sun inside me," he says. He's not looking anywhere, just past the trees and the cars and her. "I wanted to feel it explode in me and course through my veins. And I wanted to share that with you. I wanted it all to melt over us and make us glow like Christmas. That's all. But I can't. It's impossible."

She looks at him, in his ratty flannel shirt, torn at the cuffs, and week-old beard. His eyes land on her briefly, but they slide away and settle on something over towards the library.

"Are you that dumb?" she says.

His eyes move back to her, acknowledging. He blinks once, slow and pronounced, then continues pushing the red and purple motorcycle to the sidewalk and onto Bigelow Boulevard where he swings his leg over and, as she watches, her feet frozen in the soft grass, hugging herself to stop the shivering, he starts the motorcycle with a flick of his wrist and pulls out into traffic. He accelerates through the light at the first intersection, which, she can't help noticing, is blatantly red and has been for some time.

✳ ✳ ✳

A single bird, the most pathetic looking pigeon Marlene has ever seen, keeps following her around the non-operational fountain at Point State Park, as if she were dropping popcorn from the hem of her skirt.

"Shoo," she tells it, but the pigeon just cocks its ratty head indignantly and keeps after her.

The bird's head is nearly bald; bits of feathers poke out haphazardly like loose threads of a mangled sweater. One of its legs appears to be longer than the other and with its wide, glazed over eyes, it looks drunk, or like a bigger, prettier pigeon has just beaten the crap out of it.

"Go away," Marlene says. "Shoo."

The three rivers coming together in front of her are a swift-moving gray. If you were to dip your toe in this water you would be sucked in and washed away, your body eventually being spit out into the Mississippi.

Marlene continues around the inert fountain. Across the Mon, up on Mt. Washington, she can see the sloping roof of Jack's condo. At least she thinks she can. When she gets to the far side of the fountain she seeks out a bench and sits, looking out over the water. Blowing leaves tumble across the cement. Off to her left she hears cars moving across the Fort Pitt Bridge, their tires moaning. The bird is still there, swaying at her feet.

"Get the hell away from me, you filthy rat!"

She looks around, afraid she's spoken as loudly as she thinks she might have, but there are only perhaps a half-dozen people in the entire park, none of whom seem to be taking any interest in her. She can't stop thinking about Newton Sarver's spineless-ness, the very aspect of his character she has always despised, the very aspect which has led her to believe he should have been replaced long ago, the very aspect that has not only caused him to lose his job but to lose it without the slightest hint of dignity. Get out of my office. That's the best he could manage? That's the best he could do, when he had Georgia Power and Michael Dunne, like two loaded six shooters laid across his lap, cocked and ready, and Marlene herself sitting right next to him, pre-pared to toss grenades on his behalf? Pathetic. She turns to the bird. "Pathetic."

The bird stares blankly, not at her but seemingly to either side of her. It wobbles for a moment then rights itself. She wishes it could blink.

A man sits down next to her—she has no idea where he even came from—and begins tossing bits of bread at the pathetic bird. The bird doesn't even try for them; it just stands there, swaying, while the crumbs land all around it. The man is large, bearlike (his face even has a dark, bearish quality to it—pulled out away from his skull like a muzzle), with heavy, sloping shoul-ders and a high, rounded chest. Marlene imagines a layer of thick fur beneath the man's nylon jacket. On his head is a red, white and blue knit cap, pulled way up above his ears, sort of balanced there. Graying, strawlike hair pokes out from underneath. He keeps reaching into a clear plastic baggie and tossing out bread crumbs, which rain down on the uninterested bird, with a natural flick of his wrist. Then he yawns, big and wide, and Marlene can see his tongue flopping around in his cavernous mouth.

Finally the man quits with the bread crumbs and looks down quizzically at the bird, as though it might be defective. Then he takes a deep, groaning breath and says, "Rivers are gonna flood over."

She nods; he has no way of knowing this.

"Too much precipitation," he continues. He looks up at the sky, then back down. "Rain, snow, this, that, the other. Too much. Yeah, they gonna flood up, all right." He turns to her. "You don't live along one of the rivers, do you, lady?"

She shakes her head no.

"That's good. I learnt my lesson the hard way. I used to of lived down Sharpsburg." He points northward, toward the Allegheny. "Basement got flooded out a bunch of times. Now I live up New Ken. The river goes through up there, too, that's true enough. But I'm on a hill. Looka here—" He leans to his right to extract his wallet from his back pocket and as he does a raucous fart escapes. Marlene jumps. "Pardon," the man says, unfazed. "I'm a bit gaseous. Anyhow, looka here." He flips through some pictures in clear plastic sleeves. "I built this here retaining wall at the base of my property. The water'll probably never get that high, but if it does, it won't erode away my property none."

Marlene examines the pictures but they are of very poor quality and it's difficult to tell what's what. "And you took pictures of it?" Marlene says, since that seems to her the most amazing aspect of all this.

"Hell, yes, I took pictures." He looks at her. "You know about erosion?"

"I know what it is."

"Well then, all right," the man says and replaces his wallet. Marlene braces herself for another of his gaseous releases, but there is nothing. When he has his wallet put away the man nods toward the bird, which now is staggering around inside of a one-square-foot area. "What's with him, you figure?"

"He's pathetic," Marlene says, eyeing the bird.

"Aw, that ain't nice."

"Maybe. But it's true. Look at it."

The man leans forward, doing what he's told. He rests his elbows on his knees. "Yeah?"

"I could step on him, if I wanted to, and he wouldn't even try to move out of the way. I would, too, if I didn't mind ruining these shoes." She looks down at his feet. "You should step on him."

He sits back. "You a lawyer?"

She clicks her tongue disgustedly against the roof of her mouth and shakes her head. "Oh, how typical is that," she says. "Of course, I think people should stand up for themselves, I think weakness is just that: weak—look at him!—so I must be a lawyer. Of course."

"A banker?" The man folds his arms, with some effort, across his expanse of chest. The baggie hangs from his fist in front of him. Marlene hears a squeaking sound, then a sound like twisting leather, and she can't be sure if these sounds are coming out of this man or not. The real question, though, which occurs to her now is: Why don't I leave?

"And what do you do, Mr. Meteorologist-Dam -Builder?"

"It's not a dam. It's just a sort of protective wall."

"Yeah. Whatever."

"Well, criminy. You're a feisty one, ain't ya? I'll bet you got quite a career ahead of you."

"I'm waiting," she says.

He waves a hand in the air, dismissing. "Ain't never worked a day in my life. Not since high school. I got caught with some shrapnel over in Vietnam—I was just nineteen—and they had to—or thought they had to—take a mess of my large intestine out." As if to demonstrate, he leans to the right again and releases another thunderous burst of gas. Even the pigeon jumps.

"Oh—" Marlene gasps. "Oh..."

"See? It's rude as hell, but they don't stink none. It's just air. Anyway, I been getting checks from the service. Yeah, I got a nice little arrangement going."

Marlene tries to recover herself. She smooths her skirt in her lap and re-crosses her legs, which, she can see through the stockings, are goose-pimpled. A man in a black wetsuit rides by on a jet ski and Marlene feels a sudden jolt of panic for him, riding on that choppy, gray water. Quickly, she turns to the man next to her. "So why should I listen to you?" she asks.

He does a thing with his shoulders that, if they weren't so stooped, may have been a shrug. "Why should you listen to anyone?" He reaches back into his baggie and starts tossing more bits of bread at the sorry, sorry pigeon.

The bird just stands there, leaning, mangled feathers everywhere, getting pelted.

∗ ∗ ∗

It's not until Toby is already back behind the front desk at Electro-Lite, phone in hand, having already dialed 555-121—, that he realizes there is no possible way, now or ever, to contact Francis's wife by telephone. He has nothing to go on, no place to start. And even if he did find her he might be putting her in danger of acquiring unwanted hospital bills. He hangs up the phone and pulls out the yellow pages from beneath the credenza. What he'll do, he decides, is arrange for a funeral—the cheapest affair possible—and put a notice in the newspaper about it, along with his own name and phone number as a contact. If she lives in town, perhaps she, or someone she knows, will see it and show up. That way, he hopes, things can be kept quiet, confidential. It's worth a shot, he figures.

What he discovers, after four or five phone calls, by way of a talkative mortician in Lawrenceville, is that when homeless, nameless people "expire" their bodies are ordinarily cremated in the hospital morgue. A death certificate is issued for a John or Jane Doe, given a number, and filed away, courtesy of each and every taxpayer. What this guy—Nicholas Schurr, Jr.—says he'd be willing to do, however, is to hold a reception at his funeral home, with a photograph of the deceased and an empty urn ("No one will know the difference," he says) at a "minimal" cost to Toby.

"Is that—I don't know—ethical?" Toby asks.

"It's legal, yes," Nicholas Schurr, Jr., says.

"Oh."

"Do it all the time. Occasionally."

Toby says he'll get back to him (after all, Francis is still alive) and then calls the house, hoping Ellie is at home. She's not—he gets his own recorded voice talking back at him, telling him he's not home—so he sits back in his chair and listens to himself breathe.

"Did you hear?" Ben's voice, from behind.

Toby swivels around in his chair. "Hear what?"

"They canned Sarver."

"They—what? Who?"

"The big cheese has been shredded. The king is dead. The—"

"Where'd you hear this?"

Ben leans back against the rear credenza, hands behind him. He's bouncing his stick-thin leg all around with nervous energy. "Down at the fitness center. I was just down there, you know, checking things out, making sure everything's secure and all. And anyway, yeah, Susan told me. You know, the personal trainer down there. The brunette? Sweet—"

"I know who Susan is, Ben."

"Yeah, well, anyway." His leg is still vibrating anxiously." That's what Corbett was here for."

"Corbett was here? Today?"

"Yeah," Ben says. "Geez..."

Suddenly and thoroughly, Toby is proud of his daughter, for what she is doing with Michael Dunne. Somehow, while Toby's back has been turned, it seems, victims have been created all around him, mistakes have been made, and sooner or later, someone has to take the blame for it all. Maybe Ellie can assign some of that blame. It would be a start.

"Here," Ben says, reaching into his pocket. "Want some gum?" He extracts a big rectangular purple slab. Even the wrapper looks fructosey. He tears it open and holds out an individually wrapped cube. Toby accepts it, turns it in his fingers. Hubba Bubba, the inner wrapper says, and when that is peeled away the cube of gum reveals itself as the deepest, purest shade of purple Toby has ever seen, like a tender Technicolor bruise. Toby pops it into his mouth and works his teeth around it. The sudden sugar-jolt nearly sucks the air from his lungs. He fears he might be buzzed.

Ben nods confidently, chomping on his own wad of Hubba Bubba, as if the two of them are in cahoots with something wonderful and forbidden. "Good shit, huh?"

Toby flattens the gum out in his mouth, presses his tongue into it, then watches, cross-eyed, as the silky lavender bubble emerges in front of him, expanding.

✳ ✳ ✳

On his way home from the office, Newton Sarver pulls off of Ohio River Boulevard outside of Sewickley to get a bouquet of flowers for Maryann. Getting out of his car, feeling the wind of passing cars and trucks, Sarver considers the old adage that men only buy flowers when they've done something wrong, or are about to. Does his situation apply? He hasn't really done any-thing—at least, certainly, not to her—but he is sorry. Sorry he won't be president of Electro-Lite's Power Generation Division for much longer, sorry for his failure, sorry he doesn't feel like go-ing to the Georgetowne Inn for their anniversary dinner tonight, as was originally planned.

Inside the flower shop the air is moist and excessive; the smell is of almonds and overripe fruit. There is a red tint to the place— the walls and the carpeting—and plants hang everywhere, creat-ing that manufactured lush feel for which Sarver supposes all flower shops strive.

The woman who appears from the rear of the store even has red hair. She also is stumpy and white-skinned; glasses hang from her neck by a chain. He asks her if the long-stems are fresh.

"They sure aren't!" the woman says in a curiously cheerful, positive tone. "This is a bad week for long-stems, all colors, all around. So sorry."

"That's okay," Sarver says. "Could you just work something up for me then? An arrangement. Something nice, anniversary-like."

"How much you figuring to spend?"

Sarver thinks a moment. "Five hundred dollars," he says.

The woman stares blankly at him. "'Scuse me?"

"Six. Six hundred," he says. "I want to barely be able to fit the thing in my car."

The woman slides her glasses on and peers around Sarver toward the front window. "What kind of car you got?"

"Range Rover."

"Oh, well my great good gracious. All right then..." The wom-an begins scurrying around behind the counter, tearing off pieces of tissue paper and collecting various accessories. "This may take some doing," she says.

Sarver flicks a hand as if her concerns are completely incon-sequential. "Take your time," he says.

The entire project takes nearly two hours and it is dark outside when Sarver, the woman (whose name is Martha) and another girl Martha called in from home to help with the ar-rangement, carry it to the car. The foliage has been placed in what looks like the bottom portion of a halved wine barrel and consists of bushes and vines and leafy vegetation interspersed with various flowers all planted loosely in a straw- and shredded Styrofoam-like pseudo soil. Actually, the whole shebang is not as big as Sarver expected. Apparently it can only be so big or the components won't hold together. Simple engineering. The cost ($577.93, including tax) was a result of combining size along with selection. Martha put all manner of their most rare and expensive plants and flowers into the arrangement, stuff Sarver never heard of. Some didn't even have English names, just Latin.

They slide the barrel into the back of the Range Rover and, in addition to the cost of the arrangement, Sarver gives Martha an extra forty bucks and the other girl and extra twenty, gestures which, for a time, make him feel pretty good. But as he works his way up the dark, winding, gravely back roads of Sewickley Heights, closing in on his house, all he can think is that the inside of the car definitely reeks of something awful, something like guilt.

As she often does, Marlene drives up to Mt. Washington on her way home from work. This evening, though, parked on a side street around the corner from Jack's condo, she empties her aerobics clothes onto the back seat of the car and carries the empty gym bag inside with her.

"Hi, baby," Jack says when he sees her. He is sitting in a chair by the patio door, in jeans, t-shirt, and heavy woolen socks, ankles crossed, reading the *Post-Gazette*. His eyebrows do a predictably confused, inward-pulling scrunch as she turns on her heel and heads toward the bedroom.

He stands in the doorway and watches her stuff her things into the gym bag. There are not many, but the items are significant: bras and underwear (stuff Owen has never seen), perfume, earrings, bracelets, spongy shoulder pads, little glass bottles that clink together in her palm—each item seeming to flaunt its femininity, its intimacy.

"Marlene," he says. "Marlene? What..." but his voice fades. He will not humiliate himself. Not Jack.

When she's finished in the bedroom she goes to the bathroom where she removes toothbrushes and tweezers and bubble bath and tampons and hand cream and the shower curtain. This takes a couple of minutes, disconnecting it from the rod, but she picked it out, she bought it, she's taking it.

She pushes past him into the hallway. The last thing she takes is the waffle iron she brought from home and left in Jack's kitchen. Owen has been asking about it (two weekends ago he had a craving for blueberry waffles—he gets them twice a year) and Marlene has been feigning ignorance, shrugging. (Tonight it will magically reappear in the drawer under the stove.) She does not stop to say anything to Jack; she does not look at him as he follows her from room to room, no longer curious, just watching to see how far she'll go with this. On her way out the front door, gym bag stuffed and flung over her shoulder, shower curtain trailing free in her left hand, she hears him call out from behind her, as groping an effort as she will ever get from him: "What did I do?"

The drive back to Upper St. Clair is a blur of headlights and turn signals and exhaust. Even as she's driving she's thinking, *How am I doing this?* When she finally makes it to their driveway she transfers the gym bag to the trunk (she'll put everything away later, some time when Owen is out) and heads inside, noticing Owen's car in the garage on her way up the front walk.

He is at the kitchen table, eating a plate of spaghetti, papers strewn all around him. "Oh," he says, glancing up. He is wearing his glasses and his thick white hair has the mildly disheveled look it gets when a shirt has been put on and taken off over it. "Thought you were going to be late again tonight." He motions toward the stove. "There's more."

The kitchen smells of garlic. Marlene steps out of her heels and kicks them aside.

"Hear about Sarver?" he asks.

She nods.

"Poor bastard."

Through the opening below the row of cupboards, Marlene can see that the lights are out in the living room. In fact, the kitchen light seems to be the only one on in the house. A Chris Issak song plays on the clock radio on the counter. She reaches back and unzips her skirt and lets it fall to the floor. Owen stops chewing. Then she removes her pantyhose—a clumsy process, but when she finally gets them off she finds that Owen is still watching her. She walks over to him, in just her white blouse, and swings a leg around him and sits on his lap, facing him. Behind her, Owen drops his fork onto his plate, clanking. She pulls his face toward her, to her chest.

"Well," she hears him say. "Hmm."

On the sofa, where they ended up, numb and spent, a blanket printed with covered bridges wound and tangled between them, he says, "So who were you seeing?"

Her temple is pressed against the nook of his shoulder. She thinks to lift her head and look at him, but she doesn't. She can hear the wind rattle past the chimney outside. Then he takes a breath and she thinks, Here it comes, but he doesn't say a word.

They lie in the darkness, music from the clock radio floating in from the kitchen. Her back and behind, once sweaty, now sticks pleasantly to the sofa's leather. Finally she says, "I'm going to call Michael Dunne tomorrow and volunteer my testimony on his behalf—I hear he's suing. I'm going to—" She pauses. "I'm going to fuck some people up. I'm going to make a mess of things and I can't wait."

"Good for you," Owen says, and she can tell he means it, even before he kisses her forehead and pulls her close to him.

"I'm not seeing anyone," she says.

"Okay."

She can feel the house settle around her—a creak here, a chill there. Then she hears, coming from the kitchen, a strange flapping sound. The sound startles her and she gives a shiver; then she recognizes the source of the flapping: It's the stove, which is in need of replacement, the electric heating coils beginning to cool down. She settles into Owen and listens to it—*whit-whit-whit-whit-whit*—and it is not at all annoying.

* * *

Ellie swings her rented Corolla into her father's driveway and finds him bent over at the shoulders near the far, shadow-enveloped side of the house. When she steps out of the car she can distinguish the hum of a motor of some sort, and when she gets close enough she can see that he is trimming away the tall dead grass from the base of the house with a weedwhacker.

"Daddy?" She approaches him, briefcase in one hand, a plastic grocery bag in the other. "Daddy, what are you doing?"

He glances up as if he's been expecting her and Ellie sees that he is wearing protective goggles. He reaches down and adjusts a lever and the trimmer quiets somewhat but does not shut off entirely. "Hi, pumpkin," he says.

"Dad, what are you doing?"

He looks down at the trimmer. "Just—I don't know. Tidying things up a bit. I felt things needed to be tidied."

"It's nighttime," Ellie points out. "It's December."

He lifts his gaze and examines the starless sky, as if it were the source by which Ellie has come to her conclusions. "That's true," he says. He pushes the lever forward again and the trimmer roars fully back to life. He positions the bottom against the edge of the house and Ellie hears the synthetic cord snap crisply through the tall blades of grass. Then he shuts the motor off altogether and lifts the goggles, positioning them on his forehead. "I guess that'll do for today," he says. He looks at her. Ellie, even in this dim hazy light, can see bits of grass stuck in his eyebrows. "So how is the case coming?"

The question, quite unexpectedly, causes her to swoon. Where to start? After Todd disappeared on the motorcycle, crossing Fifth Avenue and up into the big old mansion-like homes she remembers seeing in that area, she walked back to Hemingway's, cold and numb and dumbfounded, to find that Todd had knocked Michael's tooth out. Well, he didn't exactly knock it out but he sufficiently loosened it so that while Ellie was out chasing after Todd, Michael was able to worry the thing the rest of the way out with his tongue. He was sitting there with it on his open palm, studying it, when she came back in.

Then to the dentist, where he was cleaned up and fitted for a replacement of some sort. It has to be specially made, though, and at present Michael Dunne is without an upper left incisor, a condition that, curiously, fascinated Michael but did not seem to concern him. Since then, she's spent the past two and a half hours at Paula's Health Hut in Squirrel Hill, stocking up on supplements and protein powder and herbs and a facial scrub, all of which are in the plastic grocery bag she's now holding in her left hand, and talking to Paula herself about the debilitating circumstances of chance. It made her feel much better, for a time, but the temporary relief is gone now and she feels weirdly short of bone marrow.

"Ellie?"

She believes her heart had stopped beating for a while and now is rushing to catch up. "I saw Todd," she says.

"Oh?" Her father shifts the trimmer from one hand to the other. He is not surprised.

"He left."

Her father says nothing, and his silence is exasperating. She could scratch him.

"He knocked out one of Michael Dunne's teeth and then he left on a motorcycle. It was like a movie, only sickening."

Her father reaches out and takes her hand, causing her to drop the bag from Paula's Health Hut, and it is only now that she notices he is wearing yard gloves. "What can I do?" he asks.

"Nothing." She pulls her hand away. "I don't want you to do anything or say anything or help me or sing to me or give me a speech with a moral."

"I don't do most of those things," he says. "I never have."

"Good. Keep it that way." It feels as though there's a bubble in her head, between her brain and skull, expanding, filling with air. She drops to her knees and begins tearing through the plastic bag. "Where's my beta carotene?" she says. "Oh, God, I'm getting an aneurysm." She checks bottle after bottle but it's too dark to read the labels. The ground is cold and wet.

At some point she feels herself being lifted and when she refocuses her eyes she finds that she is standing again, looking at her father, who has his gloved hands on either of her shoulders, bracing her.

"Ellie, honey, please listen to me," he is saying. He waits for a moment, to make sure she is listening. "You don't always have to let things go," he says. "Sometimes it's best for us to just swallow our pride and do what feels right."

"God, Daddy," she says. "I asked you not to do that and you do it anyway and that's the best you can come up with?"

"I think you should take him back. I'm afraid this was a big mistake, my mistake, and you should take him back."

She thinks for a moment. "Daddy, that's advice."

He makes a confused face, all eyebrow-wiggling, which causes the goggles to fall down and dangle from his neck. "You never said no advice."

"Yes, I did."

"No, you didn't," he says, sure of himself. "You said not to sing to you."

"Well, it doesn't matter anyway. He's gone. I can feel it." It begins to snow. Not much, but big, isolated, slow-floating flakes. She picks up her bag and her briefcase. "I want to help you," she says.

"Help me what?"

She looks around. Her eyes have adjusted well and she sees,

in among the soggy mulch and browning pine bushes between the front door and the side of the house, an unruly mess of weeds and roots and decay.

"Weed," she says.

"Huh?"

"This all needs to be cleaned out, weeded. Tidied, like you said. We'll do it now and then you'll be that far ahead of things in the spring."

"Ellie," he says, "I really don't, you know, weed very often. Spring, summer, whenever."

"You're telling me? Wait here while I change into something warmer. It's cold out here."

She heads across the lawn, feeling an occasional snowflake touch down on her neck or nose or the back of her hand. Behind her, as she reaches for the front door, she hears her father give two sputtering tugs on the trimmer's starter cord; and then, with the third pull, the motor catches and, after an initial phlegmy growl, settles into a steady, relentless buzz.

Todd has gotten rid of his motorcycle helmet. Fuck it, was his attitude at the time, and still is. What's inside his head, he figures, ain't worth protecting. After punching out Ellie's luncheon companion, cutting his knuckle on the guy's tooth in fact, he drove the motorcycle around aimlessly, ending up on some bridge or another—the Highland Park Bridge, he remembers now—and pulled over to the side. He unhooked the helmet from the back of the bike and tossed it into one of Pittsburgh's infernal, omnipresent rivers, heaving it over the suicide-prohibitive chain-link fence and actually saying, out loud, "Fuck it," as the helmet disappeared beneath him.

Then he headed for downtown (which he could see in the distance from the bridge), found a sign for I-79 South, crossed another bridge, another river, and opened the throttle. He's now wearing his black ball cap backwards and passing exit signs for Fairmont, West Virginia—hometown of 1984 U.S. Olympic gold medallist Mary Lou Retton, a sign informs him—and he keeps going, paying little attention to the vague and sporadic lights of the town. He likes the state, though: West Virginia. Who'd have thought? The winding, mountainous roads are exhilarating, and challenging. His hands, now healed, are frozen to numbness, as are his ears, also healed. He thinks, Frostbite: that's next for me.

The lights of Fairmont slide away and again the road goes dark, save for the single cone of light the motorcycle throws out before him. Todd imagines critters—people even, mountain men—in the forest watching him speed past, cursing him for who he is and what he's done and the thoughts that might be in his head.

Up, down. Lean into the turns. Without his helmet as a buffer the tractor-trailers are loud, monstrous, and at some point, West Virginia gets old: an awfully long state, from top to bottom. But at least, he concedes, everything's down hill now.

He stops at a 24-hour Bob Evans off an exit in Wytheville, Virginia, a mess of gas stations, hotels, and truck stops just over the state line. It is four a.m. He goes into the restroom and allows warm water to run over his hands. Soon he can feel the inner flesh swell and press against the newly warmed skin, as though ready to burst through. His face is red and raw and blistery in the mirror. He smiles at himself, shows his teeth.

At a table by the window overlooking I-77 he orders coffee and an egg sandwich. He's trying to conserve funds, use Ellie's credit card as little as possible, prolong the time it takes for her to get wise to him. Plus, he's going to need the card to get him set up when he gets to where he's going, which right now appears to be Columbia, South Carolina, as, according to the framed wall map outside the men's room, that's where I-77 ends.

The waitress brings his order. She is a straight-backed, shapeless woman with tired eyes and a mouth that seems to never want to close completely. Her lips are white and chapped and her nametag identifies her as Perle. "So, y'all heading home for the holiday?" she asks, making a note on his check and tearing it from the pad.

Great, Todd thinks, I suppose these people are going to be y'all-ing me to death down here. "No, ma'am," he says, all cheer. "Matterafact, I'm on the run from the po-lice. I reckon they'll never find me here, in—what's the name of this exit?"

"Wytheville," Perle says, narrowing her gray eyes at him. "And we're more than just an exit."

"Well, that's real good. Yes, ma'am. You don't happen to know a good place I could hold up—I mean hole up—for a while, do you? An apartment of some type? A trailer maybe?" He shifts his eyes around. "Something, you know, out of the way. Off the beaten path, so to speak. I ain't real particular."

She drops the check on the table. "Mister, I think you better finish up and then leave."

"Sure." He picks up half of his sandwich. His hands ache. "I's just bein' neighborly."

Perle turns and retreats to the kitchen, shaking her head. Todd chews his sandwich and sits back, watches out the window. This Bob Evans' is set off the road and at the top of an embankment. Headlights crawl past silently on the interstate and disappear around a bend. Just below, an occasional car, its roof loaded with luggage and Christmas gifts, everything strapped down tight, pulls into the Amoco station across the street. Sometimes the people get out of the car, put their hands on their hips, and perform a series of stretching exercises. Maybe, Todd thinks, this thing with Ellie will blow over. To be sure, the problems between them are slippery, perhaps even partially manufactured. He's not sure where or when this started but, now at least, everything seems uncorrectable. A horrible feeling. Perhaps what he's most disappointed about is the way things fell apart with Toby, a man he trusted and respected—oddly, a man he still trusts and respects. Todd feels to blame, of course, but shouldn't he get points for that? For taking the blame? That, certainly, should count for something.

Todd sips his coffee. He'll get set up in an apartment in Columbia—a co-op or furnished room, the cheapest thing he can find. Then he'll pick up a piece-of-shit used guitar at a pawn shop and that'll be the last he'll use of the credit card. Then he'll just start trying to get gigs. And this time, if he makes a mess of things, if he gets thrown out of his apartment and eventually dies homeless and penniless on some South Carolina street corner, well, at least it'll be his failure, solely. He won't be dragging anyone, much less the woman he loved—loves—down along with him.

And, if things go well...

He pays his check and leaves a fifty percent tip (only a buck seventy-five, but still). He gasses up at the Amoco across the street, buys a pair of cheapo cotton gloves and three Dutch Masters cigars in the gas station convenience store, and by five o'clock he's back on the interstate, heading south. When he gets to Columbia, he thinks, maybe he'll call his mother. Then again, maybe he won't. The thought of being the cause of further disappointment to anyone close to him is more than he can take right now. He only hopes that when the sun comes up, in an hour or two, certainly before he hits Charlotte, he'll be able to see it clearly through the narrow slits of his wind-streaked and watering eyes.

* * *

Some time shortly before dawn Toby rises from his bed and slides his feet into his bedroom slippers. He pads through the dark, down the stairs, and goes to the closet where he puts on a heavy goose-down coat and a knit cap. From the hall cabinet he takes his camera and hangs it around his neck. Outside, he goes to the garage, lifts open the heavy door as quietly as he can, and feels around against the near wall in the dark until he finds an old lawn chair. Cottony spider webs cling to it; he can feel them. He takes the chair to the back yard, feeling the dampness beneath his slippers. The air is damp, too, and cold, although he cannot see his breath. The barren tree branches creak and snap—a settling of sorts, as there is no wind tonight, this morning.

Toby unfolds the chair and presses its metal legs into the soft earth. The tree branches before him reach into the gray-black sky. He likes to take photographs of these branches at this time of morning, sometimes out of focus; the result is often weirdly exhilarating—a labyrinth of shadows. He raises the camera now, checking to make sure the nighttime setting is turned on, and snaps a few pictures, trying to frame the branches and the sky behind in equal proportions. The flash illuminates the entire area around him, like little explosions, with each click of the shutter. Then he lowers the camera to his lap and just sits.

The time must be somewhere between five and five-thirty, Toby figures, the most unusual combination of dark overlaid onto light. He hears a rustling in the patch of trees then. The air here carries with it the smell of wet leaves and mold, but also a... smell isn't the right word; perhaps breath is more appropriate: he detects a breath of the sky; he can sense it when he breathes in himself, a cool mix of clouds and air, thin and crisp and immediate. He breathes in again, deeply, feeling his nostrils expand, and he thinks of Todd, his daughter's husband, who is, according to her, gone. Toby hasn't asked questions. He has assumed the worst—that Todd is not coming back, and that Toby himself is responsible. There's some blame for you. But how does one possibly begin to own up to something like that?

Again, leaves rustle in front of him and then he sees a pair of yellow eyes looking out at him from the underbrush. A raccoon,

Toby assumes, and he stares back at them for a while and then the eyes suddenly disappear, as if they simply blinked themselves right out of existence.

"Carol," Toby says aloud, but then stops himself. He's never talked to his wife since her death, and he's not about to start now. Before he knows it he'll be talking to her all the time, in front of people, and then, inevitably, beginning to think she's really there, and that's not the way he wants to go through life. But the awful truth is that he'd like to talk to her, to seek out her consolation, her empathy, to share with her the mistake he now believes he may have made with their daughter, with her life. "Carol," he says again.

Then he turns around in his chair. He doesn't know why he turns around, or what it is that suggested this course of action to him, but when he does he sees a silhouette in the upper, far right window. It is Ellie's old room and he can't make out anything past the shape that is framed there—no expressions, just black on gray, like the tree branches and sky in front of him. The silhouette stays put, watching him, and it occurs to Toby to take its—her —picture, so, still twisted around in his lawn chair, he raises his camera, again makes sure the nighttime setting is activated, centers the silhouette in the viewfinder, and brings her into focus.

But he doesn't snap the picture. He'd rather have the memory itself, which would lose something, he believes, if documented in this way, would lose this hint of dreamy reality and become something literal, tangible, a photograph, not of this world but of every world in which the picture were subsequently viewed. He wants to feel it when he remembers. And so he lowers the camera.

H.M.O.

Today, two days before Christmas, pre-dawn, Ellie waits for the front doors of Hillman Library to be unlocked. Soon she is in her "office" and at around nine she receives by courier documentation informing her that a pre-trial hearing in the civil case of Dunne v. Electro-Lite Corp. has been scheduled to begin on May 17, 1997, at Allegheny County Courthouse, Judge Trudy Sobocinski presiding, depositions to be scheduled as necessary, etc., etc.

Her firm in New York has been tremendously supportive of her efforts (despite denying her reimbursement on some of the expenses for which she's filed). After all, they could end up getting some pretty good publicity from it—Electro-Lite is a recognizable name in New York, too. But she wonders how long she can keep this up, if sooner or later there will be a time when she has to decide between going back or staying. Not that she expected to, but she hasn't heard from Todd since he left. Their marriage is just, sort of, going away, which seems to her as weird as it is heartbreaking. At some point, she knows, they'll have to start considering logistics: who gets what, who owes what to whom. And the longer they put it off the more each will be responsible for.

And, to top everything off, for some reason, her father seems to be taking the impeding death of some homeless guy pretty hard. Where does all this leave her?

She has files lined up on the thinly carpeted floor of her study room, stacked along the wall next to boxes of library stationery: transcripts, possible angles to play, potential depositions and precedents. Her first big score came when Marlene Stringer called to volunteer her testimony, if needed, saying she was involved in the decision to fire Michael (she had advised against it, she claimed), and that the decision was purely personal and purely Dennis Tussy's, the result of a blast to the ego from which he apparently still hasn't recovered. Ms. Stringer also hinted that Newton Sarver, who recently "stepped down" as president of the division, might be willing to testify as well, particularly with regard to the lack of knowledge he had regarding Michael's firing. Perhaps, Ellie hopes, he'll be able to confirm that Michael had no prior knowledge of the Georgia Power fiasco, that Michael was not knowingly trying to point that reporter in the direction she eventually went with the story. "I'll look into it," Ms. Stringer said.

Electro-Lite has been making its presence known, circulating information to the press (apparently Michael was offered the opportunity to "volunteer" for separation, an offer he reportedly turned down and then neglected to tell Ellie about) and seeing to it that bits of the press conference are re-broadcast alongside flat denials of any wrongdoing at Georgia Power. But these things Ellie can deal with. She only wishes she had an assistant, someone watching her back, picking up on anything she misses.

She suspects her office—this room—is beginning to smell like her, like her perfume, like her shirts when she slides them over her head. She wheels her chair over to one of her expandable file folders where she extracts Michael's past five performance evaluation reports, the last two of which are signed by Dennis Tussy. She leafs through them again, thinking, I wonder if this new fixation with my own smell is a result of the absence of Todd's?

Michael's performance evaluations are exceptional—nothing here to support grounds for him to be fired. But they're charging insubordination, so that's where she needs to focus. The company has the tape of the press conference in its corner. Okay. It has the rejected offer of a voluntary separation. Fine. Ellie needs to concentrate on finding examples of contrary behavior in Michael, incidences where he went out of his way for the good of the company. Having settled on a plan of attack for today, Ellie stands, thinking, Protein—I need protein, and Lesithin, to find Natalie Dunne standing in her doorway.

"Oh," Ellie says, startled. "Natalie. Hi."

Natalie smiles like, Yeah, it's me. Here I am.

"Come in, please." She positions a chair.

"Thanks." She is dressed in a yellow jumpsuit beneath a heavy, unbuttoned parka. Duck boots. Gloves stick out from the coat pockets and her hair is frayed at the edges. "Actually," she says, "I was thinking maybe we could take a walk, go for a cup of coffee or something. If you're not too busy."

"Coffee? Oh sure." Ellie gathers some papers on the table. It is unnecessary, just something to do with her hands. "But, um, should you be drinking coffee?"

"Okay. Decaf."

"Yeah. Of course. It's funny, I was just thinking how I could use a protein shake."

"How is that funny?"

"Well, I don't know. I guess... Well, yeah, okay. Um, I found this place over on Craig that has both." She grabs her coat. She is all random movement. "Coffee and protein shakes, I mean."

"All right, so let's go there."

They leave the library and walk down Forbes to Craig in relative silence. They touch on the weather (cold, getting colder), the holidays (doesn't feel like Christmas, does it?), the gender-related quirks of babies, and the most annoying thing about Pittsburgh that Ellie has rediscovered: one-way streets. All Ellie keeps thinking, though, is that she doesn't want her relationship with Natalie to be adversarial. Why should it be? So Ellie likes the way Natalie's husband looks at her. Big deal. What's that prove? Even she knows the feelings are a product of her own husband skipping out. And anyway, maybe he's not even looking. Maybe it's something in the way she translates his gaze. So it makes her knees feel weak, her joints sticky. God, she needs some protein in her.

At the coffee bar Natalie takes a seat by the window and immediately slips out of her coat. She sets her purse on the window ledge.

"Let me get it for you," Ellie says, perhaps, she realizes, a bit too cheerily. "Decaf, right?"

Natalie nods.

"Coming right up."

For herself, Natalie selects a banana-tofu concoction with protein powder and alfalfa along with a dash of espresso. The coffee bar looks more like an ice cream parlor: muted pastels, glass countertops, floral patterns on the walls. When the drinks are ready Ellie carries them back and joins Natalie around the white, tire-size table.

"Here we are," she says, setting Natalie's decaf down.

"Thank you."

Ellie takes a sip of her drink. It is thick and pulpy and as soon as she swallows she believes she can actually feel the protein rushing into her, each tiny molecule setting out in a different direction in search of something to adhere to and galvanize. "So," she says.

Natalie pushes her mug around in front of her. "Oh, shit," she says. "I can't believe— I'm a little embarrassed." She glances up and then Ellie can see that, indeed, Natalie's forehead and ears have gone red.

"Embarrassed? Why?"

"I don't know. It's just—just something I—just how I feel right now. How I've been feeling. The truth is I came here to thank you."

Ellie fills her mouth with her drink and swallows.

"We don't have the money to pay for a lawyer. We'd never have even thought to hire one, if you hadn't come along." She pauses, lifts her coffee cup halfway to her mouth and holds it there. "Actually, what probably would've happened is we'd have been miserable for a couple of weeks, felt sorry for ourselves for a while—we're famous for that—and then Michael would've gotten another job. Eventually. His severance gives him close to a year's pay. Maybe he'd even have found something he actually enjoys..." Though she appears to be finished, Natalie's words contain an odd, trailing off quality. Outside on the street a young boy holding a blue, helium-filled balloon follows his mother up the sidewalk. "Do you know, originally, that first day, Michael told me he quit his job. I mean, it wasn't until he found out about you, and court, that he even told me he was fired. I don't know why that matters." She sets her cup down, tilts her head importantly. "But don't you think it should?"

"Well," Ellie says, "in his defense, all of that happened the same day. Maybe he viewed it as something that wasn't worth saying outright, at first." The stupidity of this statement is not lost on her, but for good measure she adds, "Like common knowledge."

Natalie's coffee is no longer steaming, nor has she drank any of it. Ellie sips her shake and hopes Natalie will not ask her what in God's name she's talking about. "I like your hair," Ellie observes, and she means it. "The, I don't know, the texture of it. Sometimes I wish I hadn't cut all mine off."

Natalie doesn't answer.

"My husband left me."

Natalie looks up. "You don't have to do that," she says.

"Do what?"

"Explain anything to me. This is not confession."

"I wasn't confessing. Or explaining. I was just saying."

Natalie touches her belly then, the first time Ellie has seen her do that.

"What's it like?" Ellie asks.

Natalie takes a deep breath and lets it out. "Being pregnant? Oh, I don't know. And that's the truth. I don't feel pregnant, not like I thought I would. I don't know what it feels like."

"Mm," Ellie says.

"It makes me cry sometimes. That's about the only thing that feels right to me anymore. Crying." Then she says, "No, scratch that. I'm sorry. That's a lie. About the crying. I don't cry—I haven't cried once. I have no idea why I said that."

A man walks in the front door then. He stops just inside and looks around, eyes wide, as if expecting to find something unpleasant and inevitable here. He's wearing an old-time fedora which he removes cautiously from his head, revealing tightly curled salt and pepper hair. He steps up to the bar, still glancing around suspiciously. Ellie lowers her hand and slides it across the table, thinking maybe she'll give Natalie's forearm a supportive squeeze or something. But then she stops halfway.

"I've changed my mind," Natalie says. "Would you tell me about your husband. Actually, I think I would like to hear about it."

"I told you—he left me," Ellie says, suddenly annoyed. "First I left him and then he left me and I don't know why either of those things happened. And now I don't even know where he is. The end."

Natalie leans back in her chair. "That's never the end."

Ellie kicks her under the table, a quick shot to Natalie's shin. Then she slugs down the last of her shake and sets the glass on the table. Natalie has not reacted to being kicked, at least not outwardly. Her back has straightened, and her mind is turning like crazy beneath that hair, Ellie can tell, trying to determine if she has in fact been kicked, and, if so, if it were intentional. "I'm sorry, Natalie," Ellie says, "but I don't have time for this." She stands and takes her coat from the back of her chair.

"Wait." Natalie reaches up and takes her by the wrist, not a very firm grip. "Please. You're right. I deserved that. Just stay for a

few more minutes." Then she blinks up at her, just once, and Ellie
can't help it: she imagines those eyes and Michael's staring back
at each other, what that must be like. "Please," Natalie says again,
and Ellie wonders if her shin will bruise. "Tell me about our case.
Michael's so close-mouthed anymore."

Ellie sits, as if she's been waiting for just this invitation, her
coat piled on her lap. "Why is it, do you think," she says, "that men
think that if they don't become men they become nothing?"

Natalie shakes her head. "I don't know."

"What do you want to hear about the case?"

"Anything. Just talk about it."

"Well—" Ellie thinks for a moment but nothing comes to
mind. "I'm not sure what to say about it. We're—well I'm used to
saying we; actually I mean I—just found out that the preliminary
trial—that's the trial to determine if there's enough evidence to
have a trial—is set for May seventeenth. So there's that, which is
good news."

"Wow. That far away?"

"Oh, that's nothing. We were lucky to get it then. Apparently
there was a cancellation. If it had been set for next fall it wouldn't
have surprised me."

Natalie takes her first sip of coffee. "I never wanted to be a
lawyer."

"Good," Ellie says. "There are too many of us already."

"I don't think I could've been a lawyer," Natalie goes on. She
dips her index finger in her coffee then sniffs it. "Truth is, I'm not
very good at many things. I'm okay at lots of stuff, but not, you
know, like, an expert at any one thing. Except maybe for getting
pregnant behind my husband's back. I'm one-for-one there. This
coffee tastes funny."

"Let me get you another cup," Ellie says, grateful for the sudden change of subject, for the opportunity to do something. She
stands.

"No, it's fine," Natalie says. "It's probably just me. Sit. Let me
tell you—since we seem to be confessing here—that when I first
realized I was pregnant I was horrified at myself. But then—and
I hadn't even admitted this to myself until recently—I felt it was
something that Michael had coming to him. Nasty, isn't it?" She
picks up the sugar dispenser and holds it upside down over her
mug for a good five seconds, then picks up a spoon and stirs her
coffee. "What makes us do these things, do you think?"

Ellie finds she is suddenly offended. She doesn't like being included with the group of "us" to which Natalie is referring. "I thought you wanted to hear about the case?"

"I do," Natalie says.

"Then tell me what you think of this: My father says that sometimes you have to do what feels right. He was talking about something else, of course, another situation, but...."

"Sometimes what feels right isn't what you want," Natalie says. "Sometimes I feel that retribution is right. More and more lately I feel like what we all need is a bit of our own medicine. Myself included."

Ellie slugs down the last of her shake. "Retribution," she repeats.

"I'd like to hold a press conference about them. That'd make me feel better."

"Yeah. Wouldn't that be—" Ellie stops. "Oh, my God."

"What is it?"

"That's a pretty good idea." She straightens. "Holy shit."

"Oh, no. I was just—"

"No, Natalie, it's good." She stands, puts an arm into her coat sleeve. "It's perfect. They've been pushing re-broadcasts of the first press conference, saturating the media with releases. So we'll hold a press conference. Today. We'll trot out all our dirt—well, some of it. Throw it back at them, and then watch them scramble around over the holidays trying to save face—and, inevitably, they'll come out looking even worse. Public relations is the one place that company can't afford to take another hit. The more dirt that gets out the more people will start looking into what really happened in Georgia last spring. Yeah. They'll want to settle for the full amount without a trial, to guard their precious reputations, their egos, which is what got them into this to begin with. Come on," she says. "I have to make some calls. Can you get in touch with Michael?"

"Today? You want to do it today?"

"Absolutely. Last minute press conferences are always the best attended. They figure it must be something big. Can you get ahold of him?"

"I think so. I think he and Alex are over at the studio." Natalie is still sitting comfortably, one shoeless foot tucked up against the inner thigh of her opposite leg.

"Good," Ellie says. "Tell Alex to come, too. We could use his... his... acrimoniousness."

"Ellie, are you sure about this? I was just talking. I was just playing your... you said—"

"I'm sure, yes. Come on." She steps over to the door and waits for Natalie, whose hand moves to her stomach again, to get her coat on. "Are you taking Echinacea?" it occurs to her to ask. "It's really good for the fetus."

* * *

Back at Hillman Library Natalie watches Ellie make preparations. Ellie flips through various hardcover books and manuals in search of contact names and phone numbers. She calls all four network television affiliates, both newspapers, several radio stations, *The Pittsburgh Business Times*, the local outlets of AP and UPI and various other wire services. She arranges the press conference for four-thirty; that gives the TV stations enough time to put something together by six. She says these things to Natalie, never looking her way—as if simply thinking out loud really—as Natalie sits on a loaded cardboard box in the corner rubbing her belly, which, very subtly, has begun to feel a bit unsettled, like wings of a tiny bird opening and closing in there, preening its feathers.

Ellie calls Marlene Stringer and Newton Sarver. She starts to call her father, decides not to, calls him anyway, then hangs up without speaking when someone else answers. Natalie is impressed with her organization. She thinks back to times over dinner, better times, when Michael would tell her about the intricacies of his day, many of which included planning press conferences. The Monday before Thanksgiving was the first and only time he had to speak at one, but he'd planned many. At Hillman Library, Ellie is saying. First floor auditorium. The scene is somehow all too familiar to Natalie, a sort of convoluted déja-vu, and soon she finds herself leafing through a heavy volume titled *Issues in Jurisprudence Vol. 24*, Jan-June 1988.

"Natalie," Ellie says, the phone's receiver cradled against the side of her neck. Her index finger is poised at the keypad. "What's the number over at your studio?"

"Oh. We don't have a phone yet."

"Shoot. Can you get over there? Tell Michael and Alex both to be here by two at the latest to go over the stuff I'll be preparing up until then. Tell them not to come before two, 'cause they'll just get in my way. But tell them not to be late. Tell them two o'clock exactly. Can you do that?"

"Sure," she says. "I can manage it," though she still, for the life of her, can't figure out what good such a production will do. Why would a company the size of Electro-Lite be intimidated by a little dirt flung by an ex-employee and his lawyer? But Ellie looks confident, and, anyway, what could it hurt? "No problem," she says.

"Thanks." Then Ellie begins flipping through another book—a catalog, this one—and she is gone. Tuned out.

On her way back through the library Natalie searches out and locates the books on pregnancy and infant care. There are many racks, in the rear of the library near a tall window overlooking the brick remains of Forbes Field's outfield wall. She walks between the stacks as if through a museum, glancing at the spines, the call numbers. The smell here is of dust and old carpeting. Taking a fat book down from an eye-level shelf (the only red spine among a mess of blues and grays and blacks) she feels a fragile breeze on the back of her neck, almost like a breath. She examines the book's cover, which features big yellow block letters: *The Complete Prenatal Encyclopedia*, co-written by five different doctors. She flips the book over. On the back cover publications such as *Newsweek*, *Us* and *Parent* praise the book as containing "everything first-time parents need to know about the birthing process," claim it to be "lovingly written," and the authors to be "the most highly respected physicians in their field." Natalie opens the book, hearing the spine crack with worry and disuse, and thumbs through it. The drawings are old-looking, but graphic. She turns to the front and checks the copyright date. 1983. Then she turns to the index in back and scans the Bs, for "bird"; the Fs, for "flap" or "flapping" or "feathers"; and the Ws, for "wings."

Nothing.

Strike three, she thinks, glancing out at the Forbes Field wall.

"Yer out," comes a voice from behind her. Natalie turns and sees a young woman coming lazily toward her through the stacks of books. The woman appears to be of Hispanic descent and she looks extraordinarily bored. Her dark hair hangs curly and casually across her face and her green hooded sweatshirt hangs from her shoulders, unzipped. Beneath the sweatshirt is a plaid button-down, untucked, and beneath that is a belly that appears to Natalie to be about ten months along. At first Natalie wonders how the woman does it, carries it all, since she's not wearing maternity clothes. Then she notices the sweat pants, drawstring tied low, way below her hips, the bottoms tucked into silver-buckled motorcycle boots. The girl pads through the racks slowly, not bothering to lift the heavy boots from the carpeting.

"Pardon?" Natalie says. "You were speaking to me?"

The girl shrugs, holds out a hand and skims a row of books with her fingertips. "You say 'strike three,' I say 'yer out.'"

"I said that?"

Again the girl shrugs. "You know anything about these books?" She's eyeing them, both sides of the aisle, with disinterested awe.

"Not much," Natalie says. "Are you looking for something in particular?"

"Yeah. I wanna know why this little devil won't come out. My doctor says be patient. I say to hell with patient."

"How far along are you?" Natalie asks.

The girl waves her hand at this preposterous question. "'Bout five years, seems like."

Natalie chuckles, which seems to catch the young woman off guard, though she, a bit late, laughs too, as if joining in on something she's missed. "Well, I don't know if any of these books can help with that." She indicates them, a grand gesture.

"No. Guess not," the girl says.

"If you can find it, there's a pretty good book called *What to Expect When You're Expecting* that they might have here. I forget the authors."

The girl brushes away this suggestion as well. "Oh yeah," she says. "Everyone's got that one." After a moment, looking toward the window at the end of the stacks, she says, "What this little bastard needs is a daddy." She pats her stomach as if she's just finished a big, satisfying meal. "I'm gonna name him Jimmy, after his creator." Then she adds, "For spite."

"Oh, my," Natalie says.

"You knocked up, too?" the girl asks, with a little head-bob toward Natalie's stomach.

"Well, yes." She touches herself, her stomach, though she realizes she hadn't intended to.

"You ain't too bloated up yet. Ain't so swelled around the edges and butt-ass fat, like me."

"I'm only about thirteen weeks along," she says. She wants to say more, something like, No, you're not so fat; if you'd just wear different clothes... Something. But she doesn't.

"So what do you do?" the girl asks. She puts her hands on her hips, with her fingers wrapping around to the small of her back, and sticks her tummy out, as if settling in for a long stay.

"I'm an interior designer," Natalie says

"Oh, wow," the girl says. "That's so cool. I could use one of those. Listen, so, I got this crib, from Ikea. The one out in Robinson Township? My mother drove me out there a couple months ago. So I get this crib—white plastic piece of shit—and me and her, we spend, like, *days* trying to put this thing together. I mean, who built this thing, you know? Probably some drunk, shitheel, best-friend-banging *man*. And Mexican, too, I'll bet. I'll put money on that right now." Her dark eyes, which have been scrunched together as if belonging to something in the reptile family, relax. She takes a breath. "So, anyway, what I'm getting at is, you don't know who designed that Ikea stuff, do you? You don't know the secret to putting it together or anything."

Natalie shakes her head no. "Sorry. Actually, I think it's Swedish."

"Swedish?" She says the word as if she's eaten it and doesn't like the taste. "Huh."

"Yes. You know how to use those little, like, ratchet things they give you, right? Those little metal—"

"Of course," she says. "I'm not stupid. My mother is. And the creator of this baby is, of course." She points at it. "But I'm not stupid."

"No," Natalie says. "No." Then she says, "Well, I hope that little guy decides to come out soon. I'm sorry, but I have to go see my husband. I need to tell him something." She replaces *The Complete Prenatal Encyclopedia*, which she has been holding like a prop this entire time, back on the shelf.

"Yeah," the young woman says, waving her hand again as if brushing away a dull thought. "You go do that. Go see your husband." Then, as Natalie turns to leave, the girl says, "Hey. You don't happen to have a library card, do you? I don't got a driver's license and they won't give me a card without one."

Natalie unzips her purse and starts digging around. She seems to recall filling out some forms to get one and, at some point, receiving it in the mail. If she could only remember where she put it. She keeps digging, digging.

* * *

"Just listen to what I'm saying here." Alex clomps across the room to the far wall, east-facing. The paint has been stripped and the plaster is exposed in patches. He holds his hand out toward it like a mime and looks back over his shoulder at Michael, who is leaning up against one of the support beams, hands in his pockets. "Just hear me out," Alex says.

"Okay."

"You ready?"

"Ready."

Alex turns toward the wall and back again. "An aquarium."

Michael smiles. He can feel the room's chilly air hit the exposed area of his gums where his top left incisor used to be.

"I'm serious," Alex says.

Michael nods. "I know you are."

"You can't see it? Are you kidding me? A big-ass honkin' fish tank? Fifty—no eighty—gallons? Saltwater? Sharks and eels and spiny puffy things? Big, bright, colorful motherfuckers? Come on, get with me on this, Michael."

Building materials of various sorts (wood, windowpanes, cans of paint and turpentine and tubes of caulk) lay piled and scattered across the dingy wood floor. After the holidays, their contractor has assured them, is when some serious work will get started. As he looks around, Michael can't help thinking how everything his father-in-law gets his nose into involves some sort of renovation. The crack in the rear window at some point in time became a hole and now a bird has made its nest up in the rafters. Michael kicks at an empty pint-size milk carton left by one of the workers. "Can't do it, kid," he says.

Alex drops his arms, as if he's been shot in the back. "Aw, come on. Use some imagination."

"Alex, you know perfectly well—hell, I even know this—that Nat has that wall set aside for the bookshelves."

"Yeah. And that's another thing." He takes a couple of steps away from the wall and removes a pint bottle of Jack Daniel's from his big coat pocket. He unscrews the cap. "What in the world is with all these books? I don't get that." He takes a drink, screws the cap back on, and tosses the bottle to Michael. "It'll look dopey," he adds. "I thought we were going to be, you know, hip. Cutting edge and all that."

"I don't know anything about that," Michael says. "What I do know is that Natalie has, like, a thousand books on order. When someone comes in off the street and doesn't know what they want—or has a vague idea—you have to have something to show them." He takes a drink of the whiskey. "That's what she says. And besides that, a big fish tank would be so incredibly dumb—so around the bend and beyond dumb I don't think I can even come up with a word for it. Wait, hold on: Asinine, maybe. Moronic. Ludicrous. Lumpheaded. No, maybe I can come up with a word for it."

"What're you, a fucking thesaurus?"

"Bovine. Witless. Doltish. Addlepated, dimwitted, horse's ass—"

"That's it." Alex lunges at him across a pile of lined-up two-by-fours, driving his shoulder into Michael's chest. The Jack Daniel's goes flying and the two come crashing down on top of a stack of paint trays and rollers. Quickly, Alex flips Michael over, forces his face down, and tries to pin his wrists up behind his head. Michael's coat is twisted around him, constricting his arm and upper torso so he bends his knee and kicks up and backwards, as if trying to kick himself in the back of his own head. Alex gives a yelp and freezes. Then he falls off to the side of Michael and rocks back and forth next to some cigarette butts that have been swept into a neat little pile, tucked up into a tight, wrapped fetal position. He moans.

"What the hell?" Michael says, sitting up.

"You got my balls, man," Alex groans. "Shit, how did you do that? From *behind*. God damn, that was weird. Ah, man."

"Sorry." Michael stretches out for the bottle of Jack, which, miraculously, didn't break. He unscrews the cap and offers it to Alex.

"Hold on a sec," Alex says. "Jesus Christ. I swear, that's much worse than a straight-on shot. *Ungh*."

Michael takes a drink. "How come everyone's trying to kick my ass lately?"

Alex opens an eye and looks at him. "'Cause you're an asshole maybe." He takes two quick breaths. "When're you gonna get that tooth fixed anyway?"

Michael touches his tongue to the hole. "I don't know. Maybe never. I kind of like it." He lies back on the floor.

"I meant to ask you: How'd he get that side tooth like that? Roundhouse?"

"Huh-uh. My head was turned a little."

"Oh. What the fuck's 'addepeldated' mean anyway?"

"Dumb."

They lie on the floor for a while, passing the bottle back and forth. Slowly, Alex uncoils himself and even sits up on his elbows. "I don't know a damn thing about interior design," he says.

"Me neither." Michael shrugs. "But, hey, we didn't know anything about fossil-powered gas turbines either."

"Yeah. But there were thousands of us. You know? A huge buffer. We weren't involved enough to really fuck things up too much."

"I did."

Alex takes a drink, swallows, wipes his mouth with the back of his hand. "Yeah, that's true." After a moment he says, "Do you really not like the fish tank idea? Or are you just taking Natalie's side 'cause she's mother of your children? Some cockamamie angle like that?"

"I really, really, really don't like the fish tank idea."

"All right, fine." Alex hands the bottle over. "Consider the idea officially dropped."

Michael feels a raw sensation in his throat: the dryness in this room, the dust. He coughs. "Did you ever—" he begins, and then stops. "Let me ask you something. Have you ever considered disappearing?"

Alex takes another drink. A strange, whitish shaft of mid-morning light has crept through the rear window and now lays across the floor with them. "You know, I'm starting to actually like this stuff," Alex says, holding up the bottle for inspection. "That's scary. It actually tastes good to me now. Huh. That's a new thing. Just in the last couple months."

"Ellie's husband, he disappeared."

"Yeah?"

"I'll tell you what: I envy him."

"Oh, boo-hoo. There's nothing quite as nauseating as yuppie angst."

Michael looks at him. "You better guard those nuts, buddy-boy."

"Look—" Alex sits all the way up. "You're wife's pregnant, you got no money, maybe a little crush on your attorney, blah, blah, blah. Oh, dear me, I'm so distraught!" He gives a scornful, mock-masturbatory flick of his wrist, hand twisted into a claw. "I was the same way, remember? 'I'm unemployed! I'm gonna rob a convenience store!' But you know what? It's bullshit. Here." He hands the half-empty bottle to Michael. "Drink."

"It's, like, not even eleven a.m., Alex. I've already had some."

"Hey, you wanna lay your woe-is-me shit on old Alex here, you play by his rules. Drink."

Michael takes the bottle, drinks. "You know what I want. All I want is for my life to just get out of my way. That's my goal."

"Let's be honest for a second," Alex says, ignoring him. "A kid ain't so bad. It's something. You see what I'm saying? You think my lifelong dream is to keep the books for some frilly-panty furniture joint? Fuck, no. But here I am. I'm doing it, you know? Look around you at this mess. Pitiful. But I can see it. Natalie talks about it and I can see it and it's something to shoot for—for now, which, really, is all we ever should have the right to expect. Shit, I'm getting all tingly just thinking about it. I'd have me a woody if you hadn't just neutered me before. Gimme," he says, reaching for the bottle. Michael hands it to him. "I'll tell you what I really wish," he says. "I wish Nat's brother Ralph had stuck it out with us. Now that sour-ass son of a bitch could use this. More than you. You think you got problems. That sorry sack a shit's problems go way-deep, and nobody even knows it. They're up here." He taps his temple with his index finger. "I feel bad about that. I didn't before, but I do now. Him and his positive thinking." He makes a face. "Over-thinking is more like it. At some point you gotta just stick your ass out, take your whoopin', move on to something else. You stop to consider it, and that's when you're dead. You know—" he pauses, cocks his head as if listening. "I think there's a lesson here: that fucker died without a fight." He thinks about what he's said then, and, apparently satisfied, tips the bottle.

Michael hears the street level door open and close. The sound is followed by footfalls on the wooden stairs. Alex hurriedly screws the cap back on the bottle and stuffs it into his coat pocket. The footsteps on the stairs grow louder until the door to the studio opens and Natalie steps in, surveying. Beneath her coat she's got on a yellow jumpsuit Michael has never seen before and the expression on her face is squeezed into a look of muddled purpose.

"Hi, boss," Alex says.

She looks around, her head moving systematically, like a searchlight. "What're you two doing on the floor?"

"Just messing around," Alex says. "I tried to kick Daddy's ass, but then he kicked mine. Literally."

"Oh," she says, disinterested. "I need to tell you guys something. Both of you."

* * *

According to the electronic message board mounted on the back wall above the front desk, the call comes at 11:41 a.m. Francis has "passed."

"I'm sorry," Dr. Lee says through the phone. "I thought you'd want to know."

"Of course," Toby says. "I would. Thank you, Doctor. Thanks for calling me yourself."

Toby went to see Francis two more times since the man was first admitted to the hospital, but there was not much point. He never woke up, never stirred. He looked peaceful at least and the only request Toby made of the nursing staff was to perhaps shave Francis's face, which they gladly did. The result, to Toby anyway, was simultaneously joyous and spooky. Francis shed ten years with that shave, along with, seemingly, the weight of the world. The new, pronounced cheekbones underscored what Toby imagined to be renewed light behind the eternally closed eyelids. And the chin—his chin—was slightly squared at the bottom and dimpled in the middle, and Toby could see some red bubbles of ingrown hairs where the nurse who shaved Francis apparently had had some difficulty cutting through the mass of tangles. Toby stared at Francis's face for more than an hour, without looking away. Then he left, knowing he would never come back.

Toby calls the Post-Gazette and tells the person in advertising to go ahead and run the ad he'd reserved; then he calls Nicholas Schurr, Jr., to book the funeral home for the middle of the week between Christmas and New Year's. There is no rush, Toby figures, as Francis's body will be cremated by the hospital immediately anyway. This way, it gives anyone who is so inclined to read his ad enough time to make the necessary preparations to attend his service.

Then he figures, What the hell, he might as well have the thing catered, too. So next he calls Giant Eagle, the one in Lawrenceville. He speaks with a gruff-sounding woman in the deli department who, first thing, wants to know how many people the "arrangement" is for.

"I don't know," Toby says.

"Ten? Twenty?" comes the voice. "A hundred and twenty?"

"I don't know."

Toby thinks. A man in a burgundy suit approaches him, wanting a visitor's badge. Certainly, it's better to be safe than sorry, he figures. But what's safe? With his free hand he spins the visitor's log around for this man, who obviously is in a hurry to sign in, judging by the way he keeps looking at his watch and making popping noises with his heavy, flesh-colored lips. "Um, I don't know," Toby says into the phone. "What would you suggest?"

"What would I suggest for what?" the voice replies. Toby can hear metal clanking together in the background.

"For a wake," Toby says. "A funeral."

"How many people are you expecting?" The woman is angry now. Toby is just one more idiot she has to deal with today.

"I guess it all comes back to that, huh?" Toby says.

She doesn't answer. Then something makes Toby say "Twelve," though he dreads in his heart the true exorbitance of that figure.

The woman at Giant Eagle releases a slow, leaky breath. "Twelve. Okay, that's good. Twelve. Now, what we could do—" Toby hands the burgundy-suited man a visitor's badge, marks the badge number down next to the man's signature in the log book— "is a general luncheon meat platter. You'll have your baloney, salami, turkey, ham and capicola. Plus some cheese and two kind of rolls. And we were throwing in a half-pound of mixed olives but I'm not sure if that special's over. I'll check. Is that what you're looking for?"

Toby says, "Yes, that'll do fine." He gives her the address of the funeral home and she, scoldingly, tells Toby Giant Eagle doesn't deliver. He'll have to come pick it up some time after ten a.m. on that day. He thanks her and hangs up the phone. He can't believe he's doing this and he has to sit down and think about it for a moment. What he's deathly afraid of, of course, is standing alone in a Lawrenceville funeral home, organ hymns piping through the ceiling speakers, just him and a photograph of Francis (and where is he going to get that? he wonders) and a loaded-up tray of deli meat, pink and brown and beige and red. He can smell it in his mind: the meat and the cheese and the incense.

Toby is in the middle of filling out the holiday schedule for the security personnel—a horrible duty; everyone wants off the same days—when Ellie calls, her voice an overload of sound; she is pure excitement. He has to interrupt her by saying, slowly, "Ellie, slow down, honey. Take three deep breaths."

She does: Toby can hear all three. Then she goes on about a press conference at Hillman Library how she thought it was a really good idea at first but now she's not so sure because the perception certainly could be misconstrued or seen as posturing, which in a sense it is, or even desperation, which would be worse, and, besides, now that she sits down and looks at all the material she's not sure what to focus on anyway because she keeps thinking about political elections and ads and negative campaigning and smear tactics and she doesn't want her or her client, who by the way she thinks she may be falling in love with although it might just be her mind playing tricks on her as a result of Todd leaving, to be tagged as a bloodsucker and the last thing she wants to do is involve her father because after all he still works for the company and is going to be subjected to enough once the trial starts, what with his daughter the attorney for the plaintiff and all, but—

"Ellie, honey," Toby interrupts. "What time's the press conference?"

She takes another breath, and another. "Four-thirty," she says.

"Okay. I can be there by three."

Marlene Stringer makes her way westward along Ohio River Boulevard, following the curvature of the river itself off to the left, until she comes to the town of Sewickley. At the main stoplight she turns, away from the river, and cuts past antique shops and real estate offices, then out of town and up through the winding, tree-lined back roads that lead into ultra-posh Sewickley Heights. She's made this drive before.

The first thing Marlene notices when she pulls her Acura into Newton Sarver's driveway, is that the project that had been going on during her last visit here is finished. New railroad ties form a neat border around the entire driveway, and a wall stacked six or seven high encloses a patch of growth between the walkway and the house. The ties are a deep, earthy brown, but their solidness defines them. Marlene gets out of her car and ascends the front steps.

Sarver answers the door himself. He's wearing blue jeans (blue jeans!) and a white cotton dress shirt, untucked and open at the collar. Unable to avoid scanning him from top to bottom Marlene also notices he's wearing glasses she can't ever remember seeing on him—round, wire rims—and white tube socks, no shoes.

"Marlene," he says, in a pleased tone. "What a surprise. Please, come in."

She steps into the entryway. "Hello, Newton. I'm sorry. I guess I just can't seem to leave you alone lately when I have a problem. I'm not sure what to make of that."

"Well, let's go into the living room and sit down and we'll see what we can figure out. Here, let me take your coat."

She surrenders her coat and follows Sarver down the hall and into the kitchen. When he turns left and heads for another wide, wood-framed doorway, Marlene stops short. "Newton," she says. "I'd just like to ask you something." He stops and turns. "Could we not make a huge production out of this?"

"Well, sure, Marlene," he says. "Certainly." He steps over to the kitchen table—a white, clothless number with a bowl of wax fruit on it—and pulls out a chair. "Here. Have a seat here."

She sits, folds her hands in her lap, and waits for him to settle adjacent to her. Pots and wicker baskets hang from wood beams along the ceiling. Through the doorway to the den she can see a huge pot—a barrel really—of plants: ferns and flowers and crawling, viney things. "You know about the press conference today," she says.

He nods.

"Are you going?"

Sarver sits back in his chair, his knees apart, and clasps his hands behind his head. "No," he says. "No, I'm not."

"Why?" She can't help it—the word comes out effortlessly, blurted. "I mean what have you got to lose at this point?"

Calmly, he says, "I have plenty to lose, Marlene."

A vacuum cleaner turns on somewhere upstairs. Through the kitchen's sliding glass door Marlene can see a beehive-shaped birdhouse hanging from a leafless tree. The vacuum shuts off and Marlene places her hands flat on the tabletop. Finally, Sarver says, "I know it's difficult not to pass judgement on me, given my situation. Someone like me. I know that. But—" He lifts his glasses up onto his forehead and rubs the inside corners of his eyes with his knuckles. "But—let me see how I can put this—the thing is, I've been forced to give credence to one or two considerations that I might otherwise overlook. One is my wife and the other is my future, which, now, is one in the same thing." When Marlene doesn't respond he continues, "Look, Marlene, the fact of the matter is Maryann and I are looking to buy a house on some land along the North Carolina Outer Banks. Okracoke Island, to be specific. The package Electro-Lite is offering me—ah, hell, it's a buyout is what it is—it's generous enough so that I can just hang it up and forget about working, which is what Maryann wants. What I want. I mean this... surgery—it was difficult on her—she's not as heartened as me by the fact that it's a young man's cancer—and I think I owe her this much. Certainly, I owe it to her. Do you see where I'm coming from? Can I get you something to drink?"

She shakes her head no, clears her throat but doesn't speak.

"All right," Sarver says, as if owning up to something. "There's also a—I forget the wording but there's no denying what it is. It's a gag order. If I speak out in any public forum, or position myself in such a way that is against Electro-Lite or any of its management, shareholders, board of directors—there's a whole list—I could lose everything." He pauses. "And, I'm sorry. I'm sorry for you and for Michael Dunne and your families and for whoever else gets caught in the middle of this. But I'm not going to sacrifice my wife's peace of mind. Not for anything. Not after what I've already put her through." He flips his glasses back down onto his nose. "I have got to see to those things that most need seeing to. And if you can't accept that reasoning then I understand that, but I won't apologize for it."

He looks at her, waiting. She says. "I understand."

"Do you?"

"Your lawyer would never allow a gag order like that. You do have a lawyer, don't you? Because there are ways around—"

"I appreciate your concern, Marlene. But this is done. A done deal. Now—" He leans forward on the table, arms folded in front of him. He glances up toward the hanging pots, then back down. "Having said all this, your next question to me, I would assume, is if you should attend the press conference, associate yourself with all this. Am I right?"

She nods. She's not sure if it is or not, but she'd like to hear his response anyway.

"Well, I can't answer that, because, either way, it would sound hypocritical. It's something you have to decide. Now, if you ask me what I would do, I would like to say, yeah, I'd show up and do what I could to help. I'd like to say I'd be pissed off enough about the inappropriate actions of my company—not only what it did but the way in which it buried the true extent of those actions—to show up and be counted in opposition, regardless of whether or not I thought such a press conference would do a lick of good, which I'm not completely sure it will. And, to be honest, I think I would. I really do. But that's hypothetical. That's in a perfect world. In reality, it's what I like to think I would do. But who knows? My short answer, Marlene, is I don't know. You've been a source of great support to me as of late, and I can't help you. I'm sorry for that, too. Add that to the list."

Marlene is struck by Sarver's apparent surety of mind, and it strikes her as quite sad. Where were these powers of articulation when Corbett kicked his ass, when he found out he'd been lied to and abandoned? Then, they could have been worth something. It seems to Marlene that Sarver (poor soul!) is one of those people who can summon incisiveness and conviction when it is needed to convince themselves of something or another, i.e., that giving up and purchasing a nice little swatch of land along North Carolina's Outer Banks, whiling the days away and telling themselves Boy, that was close, is the right and honorable thing to do. These people think the same logic will work on others as well. So they rehash it, a sort of regurgitation; all the while, she suspects, trying to convince themselves all over again. Because they need to.

"But, please," Sarver says now, with disturbing joviality, "stay for lunch. Whatever you decide, you have a couple of hours. I believe Maryann has some eggs boiling over there that should be ready soon. Do you like egg salad?"

"I can't, Newton. I have to get back. Frankly, I'm surprised you haven't been in the past few days. I'd have thought a division president would have more loose ends to tie up."

Sarver drops his elbows from the table and focuses his gaze on her forehead. "You'd be surprised how little there is in the end," he says.

She thanks him and pushes out from the table. At the front door he hands her her coat and takes a step back. "I hope," he says, "when this is all over, you'll be as comfortable with your decisions as I am with mine. And, for what it's worth, I am comfortable."

"I doubt it," she says, though it occurs to her she's not sure to which of his "hopes" she is responding. Then she thanks him again, shakes his hand (a touchy handshake, all fingers, meant to somehow convey more than just the common societal norms), and steps out onto the front porch. When the door closes behind her she notices, across the street, a man descending his gravel driveway and heading toward the mailbox. The man's house is not visible—the driveway disappears as it snakes upwards into a dense agglomeration of trees and scrub, all branches and pine needles, hiding even the hill itself, as well as the upper driveway and the house, from the road. The man, who is older but not old, mid-sixties maybe, recently retired-age, in corduroy country-club pants and pink sweater, no coat, opens the mailbox and reaches inside. He extracts a stack of correspondence and sorts through it, standing there at the roadside, breath visible, transferring the top piece of mail to the back of the stack, then repeating the process. When he appears to be through everything, the man drops his hand holding the mail to his side and looks downward, at the ground, showing to Marlene the fleshy top of his head, which, in the cold, has turned nearly as pink as his sweater. Then, after five or ten seconds, he turns and slowly, methodically, begins the climb back up to his unseen house.

✳ ✳ ✳

Everyone is looking at Ellie. For direction. For answers. It's three-thirty, an hour before the press conference, and those involved want to know what's what. She sits at the center table in her "office," a pile of material in front of her, just trying to think. There are problems. Michael and Alex are drunk—that's one. Marlene Stringer is hesitant—she wants to know exactly what's going to be said before agreeing to this. Newton Sarver is not going to show. He's out, a non-factor.

"Let's just fuck 'em," she hears Alex say, from somewhere behind her. "Nuke the sons-of-bitches. Just lay into them. So this is gonna be on TV?"

Marlene is saying, "If those bastards had listened to me in the first place and not put you up on the podium—" apparently she is talking to Michael—"this all could have been avoided. And if they'd have listened to me the second time and not fired you, we could—"

"You told them not to fire me?"

"What in God's name do you think I'm doing here? Do you think I'm here for the pure thrill of flushing my career down the—Hey, have you been drinking?"

"Earlier. Teensie wee bit."

"Oh, great."

"Hey, Nat." Alex's voice again. "We should hold a press conference for the business. You know? Get the word out. These are great."

Ellie can't make out the reply. Everyone is talking at once

now, a rising nervous murmur. Then she hears her father's voice, very distinctly, say, "Just settle down everyone, and listen to your attorney, and we'll get through this fine."

Ellie stands. In the near corner of the room, just left of the door, she can see that a spider has begun making a web in the nook between the ceiling and wall. Have I been here this long already? she wonders. "Okay, folks," she says. "Let's get organized here."

"Thank you," Marlene says.

Ellie ignores this. "Now, first off: if any of you are worried about having to say something, relax. I do not want anyone to speak. You got that, Michael?" The six people are scattered throughout the small, square, windowless room, but all faces are turned toward her; she holds eye contact with one person, then, when that person blinks, moves on to someone else. "I want to thank all of you for your assistance here today. Especially Marlene and Toby—" her father's name feels odd in her mouth—"who have quite a lot at stake. And I want everyone—especially you two—to rest easy. If Electro-Lite in any way makes your life uncomfortable as a result of today, then we'll do to them exactly what Michael is doing now. I want that understood." She looks from Marlene to her father (holds his eyes for a moment) and back.

"Now, for the most part, today's press conference is going to be rather general and unspecific. Companies the size of Electro-Lite fire employees all the time and sometimes those employees sue. It's not much of a story. It just so happens, however, that in this particular case Electro-Lite chose to fire the employee who stood up at an earlier press conference, in front of reporters and television camera crews, and spoke in regard to a major layoff that came on the heels of accusations of questionable business practices on the part of the company—which was broadcast and subsequently re-broadcast. And we know the rest. Our intention here today is to level the playing field. We're simply going to inform the public that there is more to the firing of Michael Dunne than meets the eye; that in fact no insubordination or releasing of company secrets took place, that he had no prior knowledge of the incidents at Georgia Power last spring and his mentioning the situation at the press conference was from a merely financial perspective, that he in actuality is a whistleblower and a credit to society, and that we intend to subpoena Electro-Lite's books, as well as Georgia Power's, as we are entitled to do, and prove this in court."

"They'll never give you the books," Marlene says. "At least, they won't give you what you're looking for, something that can help you. They'll have plenty of time to fix them before the trial."

"Well, then we'll release that information as well, when the time comes. Another advantage I hope to secure involves bringing Georgia Power's name farther into the fray, establish them as something of an unofficial co-defendant. It's my hope that Georgia Power will pressure Electro-Lite to settle, so as to keep its own name out of litigation. Expand Electro-Lite's down side, that's what we're all about here today, and I feel good about it. Again, I want to thank everyone for their assistance. Especially you, Marlene. I am going to point out in my remarks how you advised, based on your research of the legal ramifications, the company not to fire Michael. Your being here makes things a lot easier. Lends a wealth of credibility to the statement." She takes a breath. She knows she's forgotten something but she doesn't know what. "Are there any questions?"

"So, we are going to be on TV, though, right?" Alex asks.

"Yes. I want you all lined up behind me. Behind the podium. Michael, I don't want you in any more of a prominent spot than anyone else. These people are not here supporting you, they are supporting an ideal, of which you are a major part. We're a group. It's us against them. Okay?"

There is silence for a moment.

"Is there anything else?" Everyone looks at each other, and then something dawns on Ellie. "Oh, one other thing. After today. You're going to be getting phone calls. Please, refer everything to me. Everything goes through me. Alex, I don't care if they promise to put you on TV. You refer all inquiries about the case to me. Understand?"

Alex shrugs, nods sheepishly.

"And Marlene and Toby—please do not discuss the case with anyone at the office, okay? Most likely you both will be subpoenaed for a deposition by Electro-Lite's attorneys. Come directly to me if and when you receive anything in writing." Then she says, to everyone, "I'm going to take care of you."

Soon the murmurs begin again and Ellie sits down. Has she forgotten anything? Has she overlooked some aspect? What, really, are the odds of this blowing up in her face, of her coming off looking like an amateur publicity hound? She figures she'll soon find out. As she glances around the room her gaze falls on Natalie, standing in the corner by herself below the spider web, a faraway look on her face, arms folded low across her midsection. From the opposite side of the room she again hears Alex's voice: "Hey, after this let's all meet at Doc's."

✳ ✳ ✳

While watching Ellie deliver her address at the press conference, Natalie, standing along the back wall of Hillman Library's low-ceilinged lecture hall, behind the cameras and tripods, observes in her husband's attorney an air of innocent intellect, an almost apologetic forcefulness in her mannerisms that, she has to admit, has the audience, herself included, engrossed. Ellie begins by thanking everyone, rather coldly, for showing up, then nonchalantly slips on her glasses, providing her with a well-conceived scholarly edge, and dives right in to the matter at hand.

The event, for all Natalie knows about it, appears to be well attended. She counts twenty-one bodies in the room, not counting her own or those behind the podium. She wonders if the woman from the Trib, Patricia Cross, is here, and figures she must be. Why would she miss this, the product of her own creation? The podium itself is laden with microphones, above which Ellie is barely visible. As she speaks—clearly, categorically, making certain there is no mistaking what is said—she routinely gives her newly shorn hair a coy little flick with her fingers. Between flicks, her hands brace either side of the lectern, and behind her black, rectangular, New York-ish glasses her eyes bounce from one reporter to another. "We want it understood," she is saying, "that Mr. Dunne in no way knowingly revealed what Electro-Lite is calling 'confidential company information' and that, in fact, this information should have been made public previously, for safety reasons if for nothing else, and was withheld, concealed, by the company knowingly, which in turn put lives of plant workers and area residents at serious risk. We will acquire this information through court procedures and apply it to our case accordingly and appropriately."

Natalie feels the bird inside her flap its wings again. At first she thought, Maybe this is what a baby kicking feels like. But she is far too early into her term for that. Months too early. She wonders if she should perhaps call Dr. Colick and ask him. But what would she say? There's a tiny bird flapping around inside me? She watches Ellie, who again goes for her hair, an act that could be viewed as insecure, Natalie supposes, but for Ellie helps to convey a sort of casual humanity that is altogether appealing and comforting. She talks some more. She introduces the people standing behind her, all of whom continue to stare stoically into the cameras when their names are announced—except for Alex, who smiles wryly and flashes a quick peace sign.

Ellie plows through the information in front of her, taking, in all, about ten minutes. Simply put, as far as Natalie can tell, Michael is a hero, Electro-Lite is a conniving villain trying frantically to cover its mistakes, and Georgia Power had better have a good explanation for its role in this. When she's finished she thanks everyone for coming on such short notice and announces that she will field questions—only her, she wants that understood up front—as long as she is not asked to speak in detail about what she calls "specific issues or as-yet-undisclosed aspects of the case, or any confidential information as is dictated by the courts." She has a way of saying this stuff, Natalie concedes, that makes you want to listen. Or, at least, makes you not so quick to tune it out.

"Oh, one last thing," Ellie says then, and goes on to say she has neglected to introduce Michael Dunne's wife, Natalie, who, by the way, is pregnant with "the couple's first child." She points to Natalie and all twenty-one heads between the back wall and the podium turn in unison. Natalie has no idea what she is doing with her face—a smile, a grimace, an eye-popping look of pure horror?—and flash bulbs explode like enormous demon fireflies. Then, suddenly, it all stops, and Ellie is answering a question, saying, "Yes, we are implying—no, we are saying outright—that the information Mr. Dunne divulged at November twenty-fifth's press conference is true and accurate to the best of his knowledge, but at that time that knowledge was limited and the information that came out subsequently is a result of one reporter's own initiative. If anything, Mr. Dunne's comments were understated."

"Can you offer any proof, Ms. Sizemore?" A voice, male.

"We will disclose the proof in an appropriate setting, in a court of law."

"Ms. Stringer, what information did your research uncover to lead you to—"

"What did I say?" Ellie cuts in. She waits for a moment. "Again, to reveal such specificity would serve to provide details to the opposition. It also could, legally, render the information inadmissible in certain situations." Ellie looks away, off to the side, then back at the mass of reporters. When and where she acquired this marvelous cache of self-confidence, Natalie wouldn't even want to guess. Ralph, though, she suspects, would be proud. Or pissed; it's always hard to tell with him. "So I'll ask you one last time to refrain from such questions. And to address your questions only to me."

The bird in Natalie's abdomen gives two quick, powerful flaps of its wings, then does a curious thing: it makes a digging motion, as if poking around for worms in the lower reaches of her insides. Then the digging and flapping subsides and her bird settles into what feels like a soft, steady preening gesture, a mild vibrating.

"That is not the case," Ellie says. "Our intention is to quell Electro-Lite's shameful use of propaganda and its unabashed manipulation of the media. The fact that we had to use the media to do this is unfortunate. It also is unfortunate that, because of the circumstances, this case was born in the media. But it does not belong there. At one time it did—when the people of Georgia should have been made aware of the health risks in their area. But that time has come and gone—Electro-Lite management saw to that. Our sole intention now is to level the playing field so we can settle this matter in a court of law, where it does belong."

There is a clock on the wall to Natalie's left—a big, round, sterile moonpie of a clock with big black numerals. She watches this clock, which reads four-fifty-one, and then, as she turns back to the podium, she hears Ellie say, "Nine hundred seventy-five thousand, that's correct," and the bird inside her—her bird—flaps once more, then again and again, with force, big, awkward, flight-taking flaps, a heron or an egret or an osprey, it must be, and Natalie loses track of her breathing, the pace of it—she forgets how, it seems—and the movement of Ellie's lips have somehow slowed, as if she is speaking from a far-off distance, a sort of deranged Doppler effect, and then Natalie realizes that she is sliding downward, her back still up against the wall, her bird flapping and flapping and flapping.

She is on the floor now, lying on her side. It is not a pain she feels so much as an irritation, a muffling of functions that saps her balance. Then Natalie thinks, No, it is a pain; and then, Okay, all right. A warm, seeping sensation washes over the bird. She cares not a lick about the specific goings-on inside her—confusion is not an issue—and she is just beginning to experience this warmth, this liquid ease, just beginning to accept the bird's presence, when she becomes aware of the people gathered around her, kneeling, bent at the waist, hands on knees. "Michael," she calls out, or thinks she does. She means to, at least. People are asking her questions. Now, she thinks, all inquiries are to be directed to me. "Michael," she says again, and then she sees him push through the huddle of people, screaming, "Turn those fucking cameras off!"

He falls to his knees and touches her forehead. His tie lays across her face and he brushes it away. "You're okay," he says. "You're okay."

Without another word Michael lifts her. A second later he is standing, cradling her. "Get out of the way," he says, and Natalie presses her cheek to his shoulder, though she refuses to close her eyes.

∗ ∗ ∗

Michael was watching as Natalie, in the back of the lecture hall, slunk down the far wall. At first, beginning to zone out Ellie's voice, which was surprisingly sure and strong, he thought Natalie was just tired and had decided to have a seat on the carpeting and listen to the rest. That seemed plausible, even understandable. Then she cried out—a combination groan and wail and gasp for breath—and he felt something pop inside him, like an inflated paper bag slammed against an open palm, and then he was pushing through the crowd of reporters—which he previously had been so pleased to see—until he found her, crumpled, in her beautiful, spanking-new yellow jumpsuit, her face twisted with pain and dawning knowledge.

He picked her up—he didn't know what else to do. He knew he had to get her to a hospital and figured the quickest way to accomplish this would be to do it himself, take her in their own car, the Cherokee, parked out on Bigelow. As he carried her through the main lobby of the library, past the card catalogs, he had Alex fish the keys out of his pants pocket and when they got to the car Alex opened the passenger side door. "I'll meet you there," Alex said.

"Magee," Michael clarified, getting in.

"Yeah, I know. Can you drive all right?"

"Yeah. Can you?"

"See you there," Alex said.

Now, accelerating through a yellow light on Fifth Avenue, Natalie looks relaxed, leaning back in her seat, knees squeezed together, hands in her lap. She stares straight out though the windshield. There are no lines in her face; the tight, squeezed-in quality is gone.

"Baby," Michael says, turning left down an alley that will re-connect him with Forbes. "How are you feeling? Where does it hurt? Are you all right?" It's way too many questions, he knows, so he adds, "You're going to be fine."

"It feels like a bird," she says dryly, from her throat. "Flap-ping."

"A bird?"

"Yes. Flapping and flapping. Like crazy."

"Like you're going to be sick?"

"No, not like that. I'm sorry, I don't want to talk. I'm sorry."

"Listen—don't you apologize for anything." He swings around onto the Boulevard of the Allies. He can see Magee Hospital a couple of blocks up. "Just think positive. What would—what's that guy's name?—what would J.K. Tillinghast say?" Michael pauses. "He'd say, 'Think positive,' or some-fucking-thing like that." Then, suddenly, almost before the last words are out, he is angry, furious. He knew something like this was going to happen. He just knew it—down deep, as Ralph said to him on Thanksgiv-ing, in his soul. And now Michael is angry. His eyesight is blurry with it. "Hold on, baby," he says. "We're here."

He pulls up in front of the Emergency Room doors and starts screaming. When he has the attention of two orderlies—one male, one female, smoking out along the curb—he returns to the car and opens the passenger side door. "They're coming with a wheelchair or something," he says. "Is it still flapping?"

She shrugs vaguely.

"All right. All right." He takes her hand, but the gesture seems so small. He releases her hand then and touches his thumb to her eyebrow and rubs gently against the grain. "Here they come."

Two altogether different men, white-clad, crash through the automatic doors and wheel a stretcher up to the car. They appear to be paramedics or some such specialists and it occurs to Michael that, in his earlier screaming, he must have alluded to the nature of his wife's condition. They lift Natalie from the car and position her on the stretcher. "Where are you taking her?" Michael asks.

"Ask inside," one of the men says. He is a burly guy with curly, disco-ish hair and a diamond stud earring. "Who's her physician?"

"Colick," Michael says, astonishing himself. "Dr. Colick."

"We'll call him," the man says, then Natalie is quickly wheeled away through the automatic doors. As Michael reaches for the car door to close it he sees, on Natalie's seat, a small, dark dollop of what he immediately understands to be blood seeping into the Cherokee's charcoal gray cloth interior.

Nurses everywhere. One instructs Michael to sit across from her and fill out a bunch of forms, many of which have questions he does not know the answers to. A second nurse tells him to watch his tone or he'll have to wait for his wife in the waiting room. A third nurse—a large woman with truck-driver hands and wrists—at one point takes him by the shirt and forcibly sits him back down in the chair. "We've called Dr. Colick," she says, as if walking an idiot through a simple process for the thousandth time. "He is on his way. When you finish filling out these forms we'll take you in. You dig, sonny-boy?"

"But she's already a patient here," Michael says, also for perhaps the thousandth time. "This is our hospital. Don't you keep, you know, records of this stuff?"

The truck driver nurse glares at him. Her eyes are much too small for her face, and gray, and Michael picks up the pen. He feels like a child, helpless among a world of older, wiser, stronger, better equipped beings. He scratches words onto the lines in front of him but he's lost all comprehension of what he's doing. If "no" is a choice, he checks it; if there is a line he simply writes "no" on it. When he finally finishes he hands the forms across the desk to a woman with absurdly thick eyelashes who smells strongly of nicotine and baby powder. She looks the forms over, then turns to the big nurse and blinks.

"Okay," the big nurse says, to Michael it seems.

He stands, and again she takes him by the shirt, his sleeve, and leads him through a door that reads "No Unauthorized Entry" and out into a hallway the color of French vanilla ice cream which winds and bends at surprisingly sharp angles. The tile is tan and white squares. He wonders if he'll be required to put on one of those funny paper outfits, with the hats and the sterile shoes. Then he thinks, No, she's not having the baby; that's not until July, and his hips go numb with sudden dread and the hallway's fluorescent lighting gives him an immediate headache, a pulsing, dark-around-the-edges-of-his-vision sort of headache. "Oh," he says, reaching his hands out to the wall for balance.

"What is it?"

"Could I have a Tylenol?"

The nurse's rubber soles squeak the tile, walking away. "Come on," she says. "Your wife needs you."

He follows. He must be following because her white back doesn't seem to be getting any farther away. They turn a corner in the corridor and the hallway opens up—the ceiling lifts higher and the walls push out and the lighting is hot and white. A nurses' station sits in the middle of the space, sectioned off on all four sides, like the bar at Doc's. Unoccupied chairs line the walls between rooms closed off from the outer area by what looks like big shower curtains. On the other side of the nurses' station a woman in turquoise polyester wearily works a mop across the tile.

For some reason, Michael looks at his wrist, expecting a watch to be there.

"In here," the nurse says and takes hold of one of the shower curtains with her big truck driver hands.

Michael steps past her, into the room. At first he thinks there must be some mistake. All he can see is a stretched wall of bed sheets, propped up along the near end of an elevated cot. "Ma'am," he says, turning, but the nurse has gone. When he turns back he sees the sheet-wall move, and when he steps to the side he sees Natalie looking up at him and he realizes that the sheet is covering her legs, which are set up in stirrups, and the rest of her had been hidden by the elevated nature of things, and by the sheet and by the angle at which she is lying. The realization—the stirrups especially, the wide-open position of sheer physical vulnerability that his wife is in—stops him. He turns away. A jar of cotton balls on a side table blurs together into a block of solid white. A tightness in Michael's chest is followed by a constricting sensation in his throat. When he turns back to Natalie and manages to take a step toward her, and then another, he sees that her face—her cheeks especially—are damp and shiny. She blinks apologetically. Michael hears a moan escape from his own throat and he tells himself that he must stop that—such actions are of no help. He reaches out to Natalie and touches her hair with both hands, sweeps it away from her face, where it had adhered to the moisture.

"Michael," she says calmly. "I can't feel it anymore, Michael."

"You can't feel it," he says. "Honey, it's all right." In his peripheral vision he can see the imprint of her knee in the sheet. "You mean you could feel it? Before?"

She doesn't answer.

"Nat, honey, why didn't you tell me you could feel it?" Then he says, "What—what could you feel?"

She blinks again, looks straight into his ever-tightening chest. "Nothing specific," she says. Her voice is soft, strained. "Just a general sense. I can't explain. I don't want to explain now. Please, Michael."

"Okay."

"I just know it's not there now. Whatever it was."

"Yes. I understand."

He touches the back of his hand to her sticky cheek and she struggles to pull her own hand from the tangle of sheet and touch it to his. There is no longer a sense of emergency in Michael's mind. He's used to the sight of Natalie lying in this position now—she seems comfortable enough—and there is a calm between them that he'd almost forgotten could exist. Whatever's done is done. All they have to deal with now are themselves.

"We're going to be all right," he says, and when he says it, her eyes snap upwards with a forcefulness he didn't know she had available to her, from his chest to his face, and in this look he reads a question, one which seems to ask, How in the world could this possibly make things all right?

He says, "I love you," and she, without pause, says, "I love you, too," and once that is over they wait. Every now and then the smell of rubbing alcohol drifts in and then fades. It reminds Michael of the free flu shots Electro-Lite gives each October, and he supposes he'll never get another flu shot again.

The room is stark and white with silver metal furnishings. It reminds Michael of what the euthanizing chamber at the dog pound must look like, though he has never seen one. Beyond the blue shower curtain occasional voices can be detected, directions given, shoes squeaking on the floor. Basketball game sounds, Michael thinks. He tongues the hole where his incisor once was. Surprisingly, for the first time, he wants that tooth back.

"You know," Natalie says, quietly, forcing Michael to lean down towards her, "my stupid fucking asshole brother—" She says these words as a matter of fact; there is no malice behind them. "I'll tell you, he's really on to something, trying to adjust his thinking and stuff." She takes a breath, then another. "The problem with him is that there's a warped misdirection in there. There's a place where—oh, I don't know how to say it—where his thoughts and his words don't line up and he comes off looking like a total fucking moron when all's said and done with. It's like, he'll say, yeah, the glass is half-full, but it doesn't really matter because sooner or later you're bound to spill whatever's in it anyway." Her voice is beginning to gain strength. She's staring straight up at the ceiling. "Let's take you, for example."

"For an example of what?"

"Let's take for example your reaction to getting fired. You didn't want that job, you thought you needed it, and you didn't like the way something you thought you needed was taken from you. But I have everything I want and need both. I—I mean we—we don't have money. Well, that's not entirely true. We have it—it's just that as soon as we get it we have to give it right over to someone else. But I don't need it anyway, and to want it is..." She trails off. When she begins talking again her voice is soft and even, like a recorded voice giving instructions over the phone. "I thought I needed a business of my own," she says. "I thought that would fix the other things I thought I needed and didn't have. But I don't; I just want it. And this baby. That baby. I thought I needed that, too. But there's a fine line somewhere that I'm just now becoming aware of. Like, when are we satisfied? So, if you want and need to pursue this thing with Ellie, well, then I might as well remind you that her husband left her. You know that already, of course. It's just a reminder. She has no idea where he is and I feel bad about that because I like her and I'm thankful for her. I told her that today. So if you want and need that, who am I to stand in your way. Me, who has just said she has everything she wants and needs. For now. I don't want to talk," she says, her voice suddenly losing the strength it had somehow acquired. "I don't know what I'm saying and I don't feel like talking; it's tiring and I suspect it's hard to be taken seriously in this position." She moves her legs around beneath the sheet. "Dr. Colick was in just before you got here, by the way. He poked at my stomach, listened to it, and told me to relax—he actually said that; he said, 'Just relax'—and then he left. I suppose I should have told you that right away. But I forgot. I was thinking... I don't know what I was thinking. I don't want to talk anymore."

Michael continues pushing the hair back from his wife's face. She takes hold of his wrist, just holding it, and then the two of them once more wait together in the pocket of cold hospital silence, waiting, it occurs to Michael, to be told what to do next, how to proceed with their lives. And the simple truth is that he wants to proceed. No, he needs to. He needs to not exactly reestablish what once was pleasant and familiar to him, but to redefine the parameters—to borrow a phrase from a press release he once wrote—of that familiarity. He needs Natalie; and at least, for now, she's still here.

The shower curtain parts, making a terrible metallic screech across the rod, and Dr. Colick steps in, suit-and-tied, file folder in hand, hair flying. He pulls the curtain shut and walks over to the side table. "Hello Mr. Dunne," he says, without looking at him. "Televised press conferences for the purpose of suing major corporations can be a bit trying on a pregnant woman." He sets the clipboard down and pulls the sheet partially from Natalie's legs.

Michael turns away. "Yes," he says. "I realize that. I mean, I should have realized that."

Dr. Colick snaps on a pair of surgical gloves and bends down at the other end of Natalie, disappearing. Natalie winces; Michael pulls her face to him. "You've hemorrhaged," Dr. Colick says, standing suddenly and pulling off the gloves. "And the hemorrhaging caused you to go into a series of minor episodes—not really contractions, technically, but we'll call them that for the sake of argument. Very rare—not only for a single fetus, but for someone in your physical condition." He snaps off the gloves and drops them in the wastebasket. He is visibly angry and, whether or not the anger is justified, Michael is having trouble believing a doctor, especially this one, who Michael liked, could be so callous under the circumstances. Dr. Colick picks his folder up again and begins writing on one of the pages inside. He takes frequent deep, exhaustive breaths. Behind him, the tongue depressors and Q-tips and cotton balls look like props; a doctor of his expertise and preeminence has neither the time nor use for them in his daily endeavors. "I want to run some tests, Natalie," he says. "I assure you they are necessary." He looks up. The lines below his eyes squeeze together. "I'm not going to lie to you. The tests are to establish whether or not the baby has undergone any trauma as a result of the hemorrhaging, and to what extent. Such things, even in the first trimester, can lead to various birth defects. Down Syndrome, low birth weight—"

"You mean—" Natalie breaks in—"the baby is... is still... there?"

"Why, yes. Of course. Didn't I say that earlier?"

"No," Natalie says. "You didn't. Oh, my God."

"Well I certainly apologize," Dr. Colick says. "But I assure you that if what you feared had occurred, I'd have wanted to make absolutely certain before telling you."

"But you are certain that... that..."

"The baby is, at this point, presumably unharmed. Yes."

"Oh," Natalie says, stunned. She lays her head back and closes her eyes. "Wow."

Dr. Colick sets the folder down with a metallic clank and leans against the steel storage unit. He crosses his arms across his chest. "I want to apologize," he says, looking past Natalie to Michael. "I didn't mean to be cross with you. I feel you've learned a valuable lesson here. At least I hope you have. Natalie is an expectant mother and as such must guard against any unnecessary anxieties. Now you know. And we can go on from here, if that's all right. There's no reason we can't." He turns to Natalie. "I do, however, want to conduct those tests. Immediately. We're not out of the woods yet."

"Um, can I take my legs out of these things now?" Natalie asks.

"Absolutely," Dr. Colick says, though he makes no move to help her. Michael runs his hand down the length of the sheeted leg to her ankle, trying to coordinate her movements. Finally Natalie raises her head, knees bent, ankles together, propped up on her elbows. "I'll send a nurse in with instructions to schedule the tests for later today." Dr. Colick glances at his watch. "I hope you don't mind spending the night." He reaches out for Michael's hand. "No hard feelings, right?"

"Right," Michael says, shaking.

"We understand each other, though. Good. I'll send that nurse in momentarily." Dr. Colick then touches Natalie on the forehead, as if blessing her, before disappearing behind the blue shower curtain.

For some time Michael and Natalie do not look at each other.

"Do you think it's all right for me to put my clothes back on?" Natalie says finally.

"I wouldn't," Michael says, remembering the blood he saw on the car seat and figuring the clothes are probably not wearable. "The tests. Better wait and see what they're all about."

She doesn't answer. Michael suspects she has nodded.

"How do you feel?" he asks.

"Okay," she says. "A little weird."

"Mm. Well how about that, huh? It's really something. What he said."

"Yeah." For the first time since Dr. Colick left Michael can feel his wife's gaze on him. He turns to her. "Michael," she says.

"I think he's wrong. I mean, I don't feel anything in there. How could this be?"

Michael, dizzy, carefully lifts the sheet and reaches his hand underneath. There, Natalie is wearing only the little white cotton t-shirt—barely more than a half-shirt really—that she'd worn under the yellow jumper. The sudden feel of her skin, so much of it, surprises him for a moment but he keeps his hand there, on her stomach, just below the bottom of the shirt. "That's my fault," he says. Her skin is warm. "It's my fault you don't feel anything there. But I'll—"

"Oh, Michael, stop." She grabs him around the wrist, not hard, but certainly with the intention of removing his hand. He holds it there, though, and, after a time, she lets him.

Michael helps to get Natalie situated in her private room on the sixth floor— wondering if their Electro-Lite hospitalization benefits, the H.M.O. or whatever it is these days, are still active and, if so, to what extent—then decides he should check down in the Emergency Room waiting area. Alex might be down there, looking for news, maybe others, too. He kisses Natalie on the mouth, pulls her head in close to him and tells her he'll be right back. She says okay and turns onto her side. She says she's tired, she'll rest a minute. Her dark hair splays across the white pillowcase.

He takes the elevator all the way down, then begins negotiating the sharp-angled corridors. When he turns a corner he sees, tucked into a tiny alcove off to his left, the hospital chapel. He finds his pace slowing. The faÁade sticks out awkwardly; it is positioned on a slant and the heavy, double wooden doors, which proclaim, simply, CHAPEL, stand with an ill-at-ease precariousness. Still, Michael slows. He walks to the doors. By the entrance is a waist-high black letterboard on a metal post that announces, "All Welcome No Services Scheduled Today." He pulls open the door, which is much lighter than he anticipated.

Inside, he is hit by the scent of candle wax and ammonia and ash. The place is empty. The tiny pulpit is separated from the four rows of pews by a padded railing; the floor is carpeted in what appears in this light to be a thin, all-purpose burgundy. Candles burn on either side of the altar, the room's only sources of light. The place, really, looks to Michael like someone added some pews to a living room in lieu of sofas and chairs. There are no crosses, no statues of anyone holy-looking, no stained glass (no windows). But, he reminds himself, this is a hospital. What should he expect? Against the back wall there is a narrow table on which prayer cards featuring ancient-looking paintings of saintlike men and women—wearing robes, holding staffs, herding sheep—are neatly stacked. Michael picks one up. On it is a painting of a robe-clad bearded man raising his hands, palms up, to the heavens, thoroughly airbrushed. He flips it over. On the back:

My heart is not proud, O Lord, my eyes are not haughty;
I do not concern myself with great matters
or things too wonderful for me.
But I have stilled and quieted my soul;
like a weaned child with its mother,
like a weaned child is my soul within me.
                                        —Psalm 131.

So okay, Michael thinks. Okay.

He puts the card in his shirt pocket.

He pushes open the big chapel door and continues weaving his way through the beige labyrinth of hallways. He's looking for the Emergency Room waiting area—Alex is probably there by now, anxious for news. He's lost, he knows, but he figures that sooner or later, as long as he keeps searching, he'll come across someone who can put him on the right track.

* * *

At a stoplight in the middle of the University of Pittsburgh campus, Christmas lights blinking at her from all four corners of the intersection, Marlene Stringer calls her husband from her car and asks him to meet her for lunch.

"It's five-fifteen," Owen observes.

"Dinner then."

"I'm still at work. I have work to do." Owen lowers his voice. "What's up, Marlene?"

"Please, just do this," she says. "I'm on Forbes. I can be at Pamela's in Squirrel Hill in fifteen minutes."

Owen hesitates, clears his throat, then says he'll be there. Marlene tosses her cellphone onto the passenger seat next to her and proceeds through the stoplight. She continues up Forbes into Squirrel Hill and finds a rare parking spot on the street a block or so before Pamela's. The sidewalks are packed with after-work

Christmas-shoppers. As she swings her door closed the rain begins and she has to quickly unlock the door and fish her umbrella from the floor of the Acura's backseat.

Marlene pulls the belt of her overcoat tight around her waist. The rain is cold; her fingers feel thin and brittle. She pushes the umbrella open and starts up Forbes. She's hungry and she thinks that when she gets to Pamela's she's going to have chocolate chip pancakes for dinner. As she approaches a narrow alley a garbage truck backs noisily into her path, to empty one of the dumpsters between blocks. She could go around, but that would mean venturing part-way out onto Forbes, which at the moment is bumper-to-bumper with anxious drivers. So she waits, exhaust from the garbage truck rising up around her. To her left, she notices, is a shop called Raven's Nest, a rather funky-looking clothing boutique, and in the window is a pair of knee-high boots—two subtle tones of deep red, almost burgundy, in a cubed, quilt-like pattern. Three-inch heels. On the top of each foot is a gold sun. Though they appear to be leather they probably are fake. There is no way in the world, it occurs to Marlene, that she could wear those boots to the office. But where could she wear them? And what would she wear them with? She coughs once from the exhaust that has begun seeping into her lungs, then enters the boutique and buys the boots.

Owen is waiting for her outside Pamela's when she comes up the street carrying her bag. It is dark; the streetlights are on. He is holding a golf umbrella, huge, in one hand and blowing warm air into the other. "Closed," he says.

"What?" She glances inside the front windows of the restaurant. The room is dark, empty, but she can see the chairs stacked on top of the tables. "What time does it close?"

"Sign says two. It's a breakfast place, Marlene. What were you thinking?"

She looks at him. His skin, his lips, his hair, are white. Stark white. The outer rims of his eyes are red like little veins. A droplet of rain catches his eyelash and he blinks several times. "I was thinking—" Across the street, a woman in a cream-colored fur coat, her tiny head poking out of the top, exits Adele's with a dress wrapped in plastic lying flat across both arms. She looks up into the sky, then down at the arm of her coat, which is getting soaked. A silver sedan pulls up in front of the store and stops, holding up traffic behind it. The trunk pops open and the woman goes around and lays the dress carefully inside. Horns blare. "I was thinking I might want to have a baby," Marlene says.

"Okay."

"I still want to work. But I think I might want to do this, too."

"All right."

"Just like that? You're forty-five years old," she says.

He shrugs. "That's true."

"But we're past this."

"Apparently not."

She sees that Owen's tie—which is burgundy, a similar shade to the boots she's just bought—is still knotted tight beneath his chin, just above the top button of his overcoat. "But I'll be a terrible mother," she says. "Doesn't it bother you that I'll be a terrible mother?"

"No," he says. "It doesn't." He takes his handkerchief out from his coat pocket and wipes it across is nose. He's coming down with a cold; this rain can't be good for him.

"So did you hear anything about the press conference?" she asks.

"I heard there was one. Did you have to talk?"

A man passes by on the sidewalk. He bumps into Owen and keeps going. It occurs to Marlene that, just standing there, they're taking up too much space on the crowded sidewalk. She takes a step toward him; their umbrellas knock against each other, spilling water down on them. Marlene closes her umbrella, shakes out the excess wetness, and joins Owen beneath his. "No," she says. "I didn't have to say a thing."

✳ ✳ ✳

Tomorrow is Christmas Eve—no work—and from the looks of things Ellie's father plans on taking advantage of his day off by not going to bed tonight. It's already after eleven but he's gotten the old movies out, the eight-millimeters, clickety projector and all. Though she says nothing, Ellie wishes he'd refrain. She doesn't want to see these things, doesn't want to acknowledge the past.

A problem: Ellie's furniture rearrangement has made her father's favorite wall for home movie projection inaccessible. He looks around the room, scratching his cheek.

"Why don't we just talk," Ellie suggests. "You have a bottle of sherry in there. Let's open that and get drunk and tell ugly confessions to each other."

"I think if we move the end table over here and stack some magazines on it, that will work okay."

"Daddy."

He looks up at her. "Huh?"

"Do you hear what I'm saying? I'm trying not to be blunt, but you don't seem to be reading between the lines."

"Sure I am. Okay, break out the sherry. That sounds good. But I'm putting these movies on. I want to watch them." Down on one knee, he takes some magazines from the rack and flops them down on the end table.

Ellie goes to the kitchen, which, she remarks to herself, is spotless. She and her father have taken to cleaning it—the whole house but the kitchen especially—constantly. Whenever someone is home and in possession of a spare moment, he or she can be found in the kitchen, sponge in hand. Now, though, she goes to the cupboard where she knows the sherry is. Then she digs the corkscrew out of a drawer, banging utensils around. As she's doing this she finds, infuriatingly, that she is jealous. Of Natalie. Good Lord, how awful! How absolutely devious. She pulls the cork from the bottle with a pop, and pours two glasses. She thinks—and now that she thinks about it it's not so bad—that her jealousy is not directed toward Natalie's physical condition but toward the potential she and Michael have to mend things and move on. She wants that, or a similar, opportunity to be available to her.

Back in the living room the projector is set up. Her father is sitting on the floor, an arm's reach from the on-off switch, elbows propped on his upright knees. Ellie goes to him and hands him a glass.

"Christmas, seventy-one," he says.

Ellie sits on the sofa. "Daddy, you know I don't want to watch these, right? I really don't. You are aware of that?"

"Yes." He takes a sip of sherry. "Sit back and relax, counselor. Oh, can you reach that lamp next to you? I forgot where it was."

She leans across the sofa and flicks off the lamp. The house goes dark save for the shadows skirting the carpet from the light in the kitchen she forgot to turn off above the stove, and the moonlight drifting in, like a gray mist, from the front window. Her father turns a knob on the projector and after a series of hummy *click-click-click*s, a square patch of light is thrown onto the side wall where it flickers for a moment or two before being enveloped by the image of a young girl in footed pajamas of blue or gray or yellow or pink, moving jerkily across a room barely known to Ellie now. Dark carpeting. A radiator in the corner. A closet with no door. Paneling on one wall, two, but not the others. A sliding glass door; in front of it a Christmas tree. A little dog (Tammy or Princess?) runs through the frame, brushing the young girl's legs. She staggers but does not fall. She looks at the camera and laughs, laughs. Then she bends down and begins tearing open the wrapping on a large, square gift. A woman, hair pulled back, robe drawn around her waist, stoops down to help. The picture jumps. The woman and the child hold the now-unwrapped gift up to the camera. It is impossible to decipher what it is. The picture jumps again, then jerks horizontally for a moment. Ellie turns. The bulb from the projector lights the near side of her father's face; his glasses reflect it, sparkle. In this light, from this angle, Ellie can see how people must sense an awesome banality in her father's efforts to be a good man.

On the wall, the young girl tears open another package; the woman holds a shy palm in front of her face, trying to hide.

"Is this your way," Ellie says, "of trying to get me to stay?"

Her father's brightly lit eyes stay frozen to the wall. "No. I do this every Christmas. Just before you and Todd get here. It's just something I do."

The young girl on the wall sits down on the carpet, holds her arms up as if to signal a touchdown, and then the picture flickers and disappears, the film on the projector slapping around in circles. Ellie's father settles the roll, removes it from the clip, and snaps another into place. He laces it through the machine and hits the switch that sets the projector clicking. Once again the square of light is thrown onto the wall. "Halloween, seventy-two," he says.

The same house. The entry hall this time, at the bottom of the stairs. A lighting fixture hangs from the ceiling into the frame, partially obscuring the woman, who stands on the first or second step and keeps turning around and back in quick staccato bursts of motion, as if demonstrating something for the camera. She's wearing thick-framed glasses, perhaps tortoise-shell, though the film's graininess and absence of color make it difficult to tell. She says something. It looks like You're bad, with bad drawn out in feigned offense. Then she laughs, all top teeth, head turned back slightly.

Ellie takes a sip of her sherry. It is sweet and warm in her mouth and she holds it there for a moment. The woman on the wall wags a you've-been-naughty finger, steps down off the stairs and swings around and watches as a young girl descends the staircase, hand cautiously gripping the railing slightly above her head. When she gets to the bottom she turns and laughs, eyes closed tight, and bounces up and down. She's dressed as a bear cub. A pajama-like suit is fashioned with snaps up the front and a snug-fitting hood. On her face, drawn with makeup, are whiskers and lines to accent her jowls. A doglike nose, attached via an elastic band around her head, fits on top of her own. Suddenly, she crouches and holds her hands up in mock attack, showing her paws, which are extensions of the suit's sleeves. Following someone's direction, she then turns around and shows the round, stubby tail on the back of her suit. She wriggles her rear end. The woman kneels and fixes the little girl's snaps. The little girl looks up at the camera like, Oh, well.

His eyes still on the wall, Ellie's father reaches for his glass on the coffee table. He takes a drink, sets it back down. The woman on the wall hands a big plastic pumpkin to the little girl. Ellie's father takes a deep breath—a sigh, Ellie thinks at first, but it is not, it is just a deep breath. "Young people today don't know how to be happy," he says. "It's become blasé, for some reason. The whole concept bores them." He turns to her. The light leaves his face. A tiny flicker of white reflects in his glasses. "I think that's tragic."

She keeps watching him. "I do, too."

"Why is it, do you think?"

She says, "I think—" and then stops. The scene on the wall has moved outdoors, summer, a jump forward in time. A backyard. A plastic swimming pool with a picture of Scooby-Doo painted across the inside. This time there is a man in the picture, shirtless, Bermuda shorts, sandals, standing with a beer and a hose, filling the pool as children run around him, in and out of the picture, revolving around the man like drunken planets around a proud sun. One of the children is the young girl from before. She does not stop to pose for the camera. She chases a little boy around the plastic pool, around the smiling man. The man turns toward Ellie now, who is sitting on the sofa, taking another drink of sherry, and waves her over with the hand holding the beer can. His lips say, Come on, and then he gestures again, jerking the hose so that the water misses the pool, and then the man rises out of view as the camera is lowered to the grass. All that can be seen on the wall now are enormous blades of gray grass and, in the background, the man's sandals. Then another set of feet enter the picture. They are bare feet. They enter the frame and sidle up next to the sandals. They raise up on their toes and then lower again. The projector clicks and clicks. Still the feet are on the wall, in the background behind the grass, and Ellie's father watches from his seat on the living room floor. But Ellie closes her eyes. Through the clicking in her mind she can see the future, or believes she can. Todd comes back to her. Or he doesn't. She returns to New York and makes a clean go of things. Or she stays here with her father. A baby is born. It cries. She cries. She falls in love all over again, her heart breaking all the while. She attends a funeral. She buys a gun. She adopts a dog from the Humane Society but it runs away. She learns to drive a stick shift and a man she's never met before tells her that she has skin so lovely it makes his chest empty itself of air and he would like to paint her. She develops her mother's eyes, her way of standing, with one hip pushed out to the side. She misses Todd. She grows to hate him. She learns to sleep at night, on her back, like a corpse. Maybe she learns to be happy. One day—maybe it is a summer day, a holiday—she plays tennis with a stranger in the rain and she finds that a continual effort to be good should never be viewed as banal, or trite, or ordinary.

She opens her eyes. Her father is lacing up another reel. "Virginia Beach," he says. "Seventy-four." Realizing her glass is empty, she stands in the dim, flickering light. She would like more wine, but she does not immediately head for the kitchen. She doesn't want to miss anything.

SHOPPING DAYS TO XMAS: 361

Dewey is playful today. He's not used to both Natalie and Michael being home all the time like this, for so many consecutive days, and he is beside himself with exuberance. Natalie is sitting on the floor. For Christmas, Michael gave her a yoga instructional video for pregnant women, and she has been trying it out. It's difficult, though. She's never been very flexible and just the effort of stretching has caused her to break into a mild sweat. It's good for her to sweat, though, Dr. Colick says. It keeps the blood circulating, especially in this weather. Another of his favorite sayings is, Yes, it's true you are eating for two now; but remember that one of the two weighs less than a pound. Translation: Don't go crazy; fat is fat. So she's been trying to watch what she eats. But she feels hungry all the time, empty, hollow, as if nothing could possibly fill her. All that wanting. It's a dangerous thing.

She lies back, flat on the floor, hands above her head, stretching her spine, pointing her toes straight out like the tape tells her. She's still in the gray mohair sweater and black skirt she wore to the funeral for Toby's friend. A strange affair but also strangely enjoyable. Well, maybe not enjoyable, but certainly pleasant, as funerals go. Perhaps ten people showed, including a flaky-skinned woman and her two adolescent sons—Francis's family, everyone presumed, though nobody asked. They all stood around the funeral home in Lawrenceville and remarked on the weather, which, since the flooding, has been pretty standard for end-of-the-year-Pittsburgh: gray, windy, snow every few days, the remains of which cake in the corners of lawns and curbs, harden, turn brown and won't entirely melt until April. There were cold cuts set out on a folding table off to one side of the orange-tinted room—odd, yes, but Natalie helped herself, which seemed to give the green light to everyone else. There was no coffin but an urn of elaborate, ornate configuration, pewter, like something from the Middle Ages. Probably a loaner from the funeral home because it was empty—Natalie knew it was empty because she, at one point, when curiosity got the best of her, reached out and touched it with her index finger, under the guise of examining the carvings, pushing forward. It moved too easily (she almost pushed it right over, actually), was far too light to have contained enough ashes to form a person. But, she rationalized, that doesn't seem to be the point of this gathering, though she couldn't have said exactly what that point was. Toby seemed nervous, continually checking on everyone so as to eliminate gaps in conversation that might be conducive to sneaking out. It was kind of sweet, so Natalie did what she could to help. She talked about ultrasounds and morning sickness (her lack of, thankfully) and water retention and name possibilities (Michael likes Penelope, which got a good laugh). She and Ellie discussed the act of labor in great detail and when she mentioned epidurals Alex, to much laughter, feigned the sudden upheaval of his cold cuts. Even Michael, at one point, said, "Honey, tell them that thing you just read to me yesterday out of that book. About how the facial features form, or whatever that was."

Near the end of the affair, she and Michael took Alex and Ellie aside and told them that they would be unreachable until at least the middle of January and that in the meantime they were leaving their respective projects—lawsuit, business startup—in their capable hands. If that was all right. Both Ellie and Alex were only too happy to oblige. ("Yes," Ellie said. "You should do that. Get away for a while. It works wonders.") The reasons, Natalie suspected, were that Michael, now that the background had been established, was not yet a necessary aspect of the case: there was still paperwork to file, research to conduct, that he did not need to be a part of, in fact he at times could be an outright distraction. And Alex, well, to arrange things on his own was what he wanted all along.

Now Natalie raises her head off the carpet and watches Dewey and Michael—still in his suit, still without his left incisor—run laps around the living room, twice nearly knocking over the Christmas tree. Every now and then Dewey makes a pass at Michael's crotch and Michael spins away at the last minute. It's like watching some sort of alien bullfight.

They need to pack. Three days ago, just after Christmas, a new MasterCard came in the mail. How they even were approved for such a thing Natalie has no idea. But that day Michael took the card and called a travel agent and booked two weeks in an out-of-the-way bed and breakfast in north-central Vermont. They thought about someplace warm—the Bahamas maybe, or Cancun—but decided against it. They wanted to be snowed in, trapped, forced to depend on each other for survival. So they will spend the New Year, and the following twelve days, in Vermont. They will get to know each other again, the people they have mostly become, and they will get used to the idea of how their lives will be from now on. Or, perhaps, how their lives could be, can be. Maybe they'll cross-country ski. In any case, Michael made the reservation, booked the B&B with the new MasterCard (they will drive up in the Cherokee) and then he cut the card in half with a pair of scissors. Snip, gone.

They do not watch TV anymore. They take showers together and there is a weird mix of ease and uncomfortableness in the apartment that Natalie, though she suspects she's probably wrong, thinks might be healthy. Michael has taken to touching her stomach. It gets a little annoying but she lets him do it because she understands it's something he feels he needs to do. He says he wants to officially switch their religion to Unitarian— "Smack-dab in the middle of the Christian road: not batshit fanatical, but not sissies about it either." Other than that, they wait. They're eager to take their trip. They tell each other this.

Natalie sits up and fixes her legs in the lotus position. She breathes in through her nose, out her mouth, as instructed. With her exhale she tries to feel the "release" that the woman on the video is talking about.

"All right, Dewey, okay. That's enough now," Michael is saying as he makes his way over to the sofa. Dewey keeps at it, though, jumping up against Michael's thigh and pushing off. He has no discipline; neither she nor Michael knows how to administer it. "That's enough, boy," Michael says, and sits.

She can't concentrate—not with him breathing like that, all out of breath, behind her. It throws off her timing. She switches off the tape. He sits with his hips forward, arms spread out like wings. His tie is loose and his shirt is coming untucked in places. Dewey goes to the kitchen in search of his water dish. Soon they can hear him lapping.

Michael's breathing subsides and he says, "So."

She turns off the TV, swivels around on the floor to face him. "I ate too much of that processed turkey." She puts a hand on her stomach, makes a face.

"Yeah. I couldn't eat it," he says. "It didn't feel right, you know?" He shrugs.

"You mean the turkey itself? Or the circumstances—eating it in a funeral home?"

"Both." He slides down onto the floor, leans his back against the sofa, facing her. "I've been thinking about writing a book," he says.

"Yeah?" Hands propping her up, she stretches her black-stockinged feet out toward him. She touches his legs with her toes.

"Yeah. Nothing too hoity-toity. Sort of, I don't know, a peon's view of Corporate America." He shrugs. "I haven't thought it through very far. I'm not even sure I have enough of an attention span for something like that."

"Well, you'll know a lot more about your attention span after two weeks in the middle of Vermont. With just your wife for company."

"That's true."

She flexes her toes along his pantleg.

"Wanna hear something?" he says. "When I was younger—like high school—I wanted to be an archeologist. Not because I was interested in biology or evolution or anything like that. Just because I liked the idea of stripped down men and women with bandannas and cutoff shorts digging around in a ditch until a dinosaur appeared. That just sounded so cool." He shrugs. "I've never told you that, have I?"

"No," she says. "But I like it. It's nice. It's you but it's not you."

White afternoon light wanders in through the streetside window. Leafless branches scrape the glass in the wind. Natalie sighs—it is unintentional. Neither makes any move to get up. She watches her own toes grab at his suit pants. All at once she is hungry. "Wanna get a pizza?" she says.

"Pizza." He raises his arms above his head, locks his hands, stretches. "Sure."

"Do you even know how to cross-country ski?" she asks.

"Do I know how? Hell, yes, I know how." He gropes the couch until he is standing. He pulls his shoes off, toe to heel, then starts sliding around the carpeting, swinging his arms out in front of him with ridiculous exaggeration, looping around the sofa, pushing his legs out behind him and leaning forward. "You use every muscle," he says. "Not just the legs. You have to build momentum. Check it out." He slides around some more, past the table, his feet coming down heavily and then sliding out behind him as he pushes off. In terms of gracefulness, it's not much. Soon Dewey takes notice. He emerges from the kitchen and instantly is nipping at Michael's shins. "This is good," Michael says, heaving awkwardly past the dormant television, arms swinging: front, back, front, back. Natalie giggles, flexes her toes. "This is good," he says again. "An obstacle." Apparently he is referring to Dewey. "This could happen in the Vermont wilderness. You have to be ready for wild dog attacks." Dewey snaps at his shin, connects. "Ouch! Come on, Nat. I'll show you the correct form. Dewey, no!"

With strange anticipation, she stands. Michael stops when he gets to her, positions her in front of him. Dewey jumps up onto the sofa, to watch. Michael, reaching around her, takes hold of her wrists and says, "Okay, first off, you have to lean forward a little." She can feel his warm breath on her ear. "Get pointed in the right direction. 'Cause you could end up somewhere you don't want to be. Now, okay, let's go. Left foot first. Slide it forward." She does this, then pushes forward with the right. They begin moving around the living room—she can feel him behind her; his chest against her back, her buttocks against his upper thighs. They are moving in unison, building momentum. The backs of his hands are in her palms and their fingers are intertwined. They shuffle past the front door, the kitchen, and back toward the table. As they pass behind the sofa, Dewey leans out and licks at their arms and then, suddenly, the lesson is interrupted by a thunderous crash, massive metal on metal and with significant force, from outside the window. It stops them short; they both jump, a second or so late, then hold still as the echo fades around them. Dewey leaps from the sofa and darts down the hallway to the bedroom.

"Jesus," Michael says. "What the hell was that?" He unravels himself from around her and they go to the window, next to the lit five-and-a-half-foot tree. Directly below, two cars have hit head-on. Both hoods are smashed in like accordions and steam rises from their radiators into the colorless afternoon air. "Whoa," Michael says.

One car is a blue midsize, a Chevy or Pontiac or some such anonymous make, and the other is smaller, a Honda perhaps—it is difficult to tell because Natalie and Michael are looking straight down on them. The Honda is halfway pulled out of a parking spot in front of their building, facing the wrong way of the one-way street. People often do this: they'll see an open spot on the opposite side and already have passed it, or maybe someone pulled out after they've passed. In any case, instead of circling the block and risk losing the spot, people will just swing around and park facing in the wrong direction. Then, when they leave, they have to swing around again. This car, though, this Honda, apparently didn't see the other car coming.

"I'm calling 9-1-1," Natalie says.

"Yeah. Good."

It's also tough to tell if anyone in either car is hurt as their angle is too sharp to see in the cars' windows. However, no one has yet gotten out of either car. Natalie goes to the phone. She picks it up. She's never dialed 9-1-1 before.

"Never mind," Michael says as the line starts ringing. "Here comes an ambulance."

She puts the phone down. "Wow, that was fast." She hurries back to the window.

"Yeah."

They watch as the paramedics jump out of the ambulance and peer into each car. There are four of them. It's hard to read their faces. After a short discussion they attend to the Honda. They open both doors and lean in. Soon another ambulance arrives, lights flashing and spinning demoniacally, along with two City of Pittsburgh patrol cars. Belefonte Avenue—a quiet side street, especially now, the week between Christmas and New Year's—is clogged. Cars occasionally make the turn off of Walnut, see what's going on, stop, and back up again. The paramedics in the second ambulance attend to the Chevy. Every now and then Natalie can see flashes of movement through the windshield of the Honda. It looks as though the driver is the only person in the car and the paramedics are trying to lay him or her down across the seat. She is watching this when a man in a bright red parka steps from the Chevy. He stands there, watching the action taking place inside the Honda. He rolls his neck around on his shoulders; it's as if he's trying out a new head.

"Geez," Natalie says. "How fast do you think they were going? You can't go but twenty on this road, tops."

"I don't know. But I think that other person may be in trouble," Michael says.

A stretcher is pulled from the first ambulance and wheeled, inches off the pavement, across the street to the Honda's open driver side door. People start coming out of their apartments, gathering on the sidewalk, holding coats over their shoulders.

"Do you recognize anyone down there?" Natalie asks.

"No. You?" He puts his arm around her waist.

She reaches across her body and takes his hand. "Huh-uh."

A big flat board is brought out and slid under the driver of the Honda, who is lifted out and transferred to the stretcher. It is a woman—a young woman, twenty maybe, African-American, long wavy-black hair that hangs over the edge of the stretcher, brushing the asphalt. The paramedics gather around, kneeling, discussing. They pull something, some kind of strap, across the girl's forehead, to hold her spine in place, Natalie suspects. Then they raise the stretcher to waist-level and wheel it to the back of the first ambulance.

The man from the Chevy hangs back, watching. Then he walks over to one of the police officers, holding his arms out as if astounded. Never saw her, his lips are saying. Never saw her.

Natalie feels the carpeting beneath her feet. She can feel her breath coming back at her as it hits the cold windowpane. Michael adjusts his fingers on her hip. "Awful," he says. Just that one word.

"Where do you think they'll take her?"

He shrugs. "Shadyside's closest. Maybe West Penn."

"It feels like it should snow now. I don't know why."

"It's because the sky's so low. Makes the air look heavy."

She takes a deep breath—a cleansing breath, as her yoga woman calls them on her video—and she realizes Michael is doing the same. When the ambulances pull away (they make the red-parkaed man climb into the second one) and the tow trucks appear, trying to negotiate the litter of cars and people, Michael and Natalie turn from the window and head over to the sofa. Dewey reappears, cautious, checking things out. On the sofa Natalie leans up against her husband, pulls his arm around her like a shawl. She wants to make him promise such calamity will never befall them, that they will always continue to avoid it. That's what she wants. The words are caught in the back of her throat in fact, but she is afraid of how they might sound. Sometimes words sound different when spoken and right now she prefers to be sure. The gears of a tow truck can be heard, the grinding of hydraulics, lifting one of the broken cars. She says, "Well." Then she says, "How much do you love me?"

His eyebrows scrunch, considering. He sticks his index finger in his mouth and works it around the hole where his incisor once was. Then his eyebrows spring upwards. "Enough," he says, "to call and order my girl a pizza. How about that?"

She was fishing for something she could quantify, a numerical figure. Fifty, or two hundred eighteen thousand. But she doesn't say anything because she can tell he is satisfied, proud of himself even, as he stands and heads for the phone. Natalie leans back into the sofa cushions, swings her feet up. An engine roars outside and in the waning light—a gradual overlap of gray on gray—the red and yellow strobes of a tow truck flash across the ceiling, then disappear. Michael's voice floats in from the kitchen. "Everything, yeah. The works. But no olives. We hate olives." He leans his head out of the kitchen's doorway and looks across the living room at Natalie. If a facial expression is at all capable of conveying a thumbs-up sign, this one does. Natalie smiles. Her husband's head again disappears into the kitchen and she hears him say, "Okay, then. Fifteen minutes. Thanks."

The phone is set down and Michael comes back into the living room, sliding on his overcoat. "Gotta go get it," he says. "They'll never get through here with this mess outside." He pulls off his tie, flicks on the overhead light. "I'll walk. You'll be okay here by yourself for a little while?"

"Absolutely." She is tired; she can feel her chest rise and fall with her steady breathing.

"Okay." Then he says, "Maybe I'll take Dewey." He opens the closet door and takes down the leash. He jingles it. "Wanna come, boy?"

Michael crouches and the dog, from nowhere, comes to him, tail wagging, trying to maneuver his head to allow the collar to slip on more easily, but in effect making it more difficult. "Hold still, boy," Michael says, but the dog keeps juking, his head twitching in quick staccato bursts, crow-like, trying feverishly to gauge the collar's next movement. Michael lunges with the collar, misses, lines it up again. Natalie leans back into the sofa. She lets her hunger move through her and she settles in, watching this exchange, this awkward game of give and take between her husband and her dog, as each struggles to anticipate the other.

CHRISTOPHER TOROCKIO's stories have appeared in *The Antioch Review, Denver Quarterly, The Gettysburg Review, The Iowa Review, Willow Springs,* and many other publications. He holds an M.F.A. from the University of Pittsburgh and a Ph.D. from Western Michigan University, and has received grants and fellowships from the Connecticut Commission on the Arts, the North Carolina Arts Council, and the Vermont Studio Center. A native of Pittsburgh, he now lives in Connecticut with his wife and son and teaches creative writing at Eastern Connecticut State University.

✳ ✳ ✳

DEBRA BAIDA is a photographer, visual literacy advocate, and picture editor based in San Francisco. Her photographs have been published in *The Adirondack Review, divide: journal of literature, arts, and ideas, The Mountain Astrologer, The Noe Valley Voice,* and are featured on Chemystry Set's CD, "Cobblestone Below My Feet." Over the years, Deb has worked with photojournalist Ed Kashi, *The New York Times Magazine, The Industry Standard, Natural History Magazine,* the International Center of Photography, the Labor Archives and Research Center, and the library of Mary Ellen Mark, among others. She is a volunteer with First Exposures, a photographic mentoring program sponsored by SF Camerawork, and a collaborator with Tuber Creations, an independent promoter of creative minds.

Black Lawrence Press

NEW YORK

www.blacklawrencepress.com